Sacrifice

Book Two in the Chronicles of Bren Trilogy

By Dennis Jernigan

Published by
Innovo Publishing, LLC
www.innovopublishing.com
1-888-546-2111

Providing Full-Service Publishing Services for
Christian Authors, Artists & Organizations: Hardbacks, Paperbacks,
eBooks, Audiobooks, Music & Film

**THE CHRONICLES OF BREN: SACRIFICE
BOOK TWO**

Library of Congress Control Number: 2016938112
ISBN: 978-1-61314-328-5

Cover Design & Interior Layout: Innovo Publishing, LLC

Printed in the United States of America
U.S. Printing History
First Edition: May 2016

DEDICATION

As the journey through Bren continues, new keys to life are revealed. This book is dedicated to all those who are willing to seek the keys to the kingdom and to sacrifice—to lay down their own lives in service or reality—for the sake of another. To all those who discover along the way that the keys to the kingdom of Bren may be applied to living their adventure right where they are.

ACKNOWLEDGMENTS

To all those who have journeyed to and through Bren with me already . . . and to the generations to come who will make that journey. True love is found in sacrifice . . . the laying down of life . . . and in losing one's life, life is found. What an amazing journey life can be.

Robert and Peggy Jernigan—my parents—for sacrificing so much of yourselves and your lives for me.

My wife, Melinda, for laying down your life for me . . . for giving me nine amazing children . . . for taking this incredible journey with me.

My children and grandchildren . . . for daring to believe there is more to life than drudgery. For daring to live out your own adventures and for laying down your lives to meet the needs of those around you.

Danny & Joanna and AIAC—for laying down your lives to encourage me.

Captain James Tiberius Kirk, for being my dad in my dreams as a boy and for transporting me to worlds where no man had gone before!

The High King for commissioning the quest I now pursue . . .

Chapter One

A MIGHTY RUSHING WIND

Lee had gone out early that day to rake the hay his father had mowed the day before. As always, he tended to get lost in his own thoughts, daydreaming and daydreaming for hours on end. More often than not, his dreams ventured off into long forgotten memories of a land far, far away. His memories of the land of Bren, for all intents and purposes, were like quickly vanishing wisps of smoke that lingered briefly around his head throughout the day, never quite lighting for long in his mind's eye. Such days spent trying to recall those memories was like trying to speak a well-known word but having a lapse of mental capacity to actually commit the words to speech. He never quite got there, but it wasn't for lack of trying!

The days spent in search of those almost-remembered adventures went by far too quickly for Lee. On one hand, the monotony of going round and round those hay fields was not monotonous at all, but on the other hand, he often came away mentally exhausted from trying to recall what could not be recalled.

Lee was a year older since returning from Bren. Everyone could see the change. No one could understand how such a formerly weak, fearful boy could suddenly be transformed, as if overnight, into a confident, strong-of-character young man. Respected by his peers for standing up to the bullies that day and equally respected by his elders because of his work ethic and strong, manly way he looked everyone in the eye, Lee was growing into his manhood. Growing into it well.

Still, if only people knew the inner turmoil he faced. Even though he had the respect of the other boys, the teasing continued. He just no longer gave the tormentors the satisfaction of a response, other than to shrug his shoulders and walk away. Mostly his turmoil was a cacophony of messages bombarding his brain. His body was changing from that of a boy to a man—and when he had tried to talk with his dad about it, his dad had seemed more embarrassed than Lee, walking awkwardly away from the conversation. Lee had just assumed that this subject was off-limits—which made him feel ungrounded in his identity, even if he did carry himself more confidently on the outside.

Coupling those thoughts with the struggle to remember all he had experienced in Bren—at least he thought the land had been called Bren—left him mentally exhausted more often than not, but even this served him well. He figured that he spent too much time trying to figure things out if it tuckered him out that much. Even as a young man, he attained the wisdom to enjoy the journey and to live his life as an adventure. Trying to figure things out, he rightly asserted to himself, would work out in the proper time. Crazy as it may sound, he felt like he had some special purpose in life—like a kingly calling he told himself. Funny, but that thought seemed right to him.

As his thoughts were once again drifting back to a horse he had once known somewhere in his dreams, his mind was suddenly jolted back into the present. He had been so enthralled in his daydreams that he hadn't even felt the wind come up or sensed the dark clouds that had drifted over the farm. As the first drops of rain began to pour, Lee stopped the tractor and began to turn the handles that would lift the rake teeth high enough above the ground so as to not drag as he high-tailed it home. Disengaging the rake's gears so the teeth would no longer rotate, he jumped back into the tractor seat and at that very moment, lightning struck so close to him that he froze in fear, his skin growing as pale as the light seemed to be growing around him.

Lightning. Bad news for anyone trapped in an open field. He knew what his dad had taught him. "At the first sign of lightning, get off the tractor and get inside." This warning had been indelibly burned into his senses the day he saw that old milk cow get hit by a bolt from the blue. One moment the cow had been peacefully grazing and the next she lay dead where she stood only a second before. And that day there had been no rain and no wind, just one single bolt from the clouds to the ground! But this was different! Lightning was now dancing all around him in the sky and, as if in some crazed choreography, stepping around the field amid deafening claps of thunder. Lee knew this was bad. How could he have been so foolish as to never see it coming?

He had no choice. There was no safety whatsoever in staying with the machinery. Like a magnet to flecks of steel, lightning would be drawn to the rig sitting as the highest point in the field. Lee began to run, heading for the safety of the barn that stood over a quarter of a mile from where he set out. If worse came to worst he could always hop down into the creek that flowed between the hay field and the barn. At least there he would be lower than the surrounding grounds. Just as he was about to slide down the embankment, a bit of wisdom, again from his dad, came to his mind. "If you're in water and there is lightning in the air, get out." To get into the creek meant to stand in shallow water and lightning could strike up or downstream, far from his position, and still find him.

"Flash floods can descend on that creek, Son, quicker than a dog can root out a skunk! Never, ever be in or even near that old creek when the rains begin to pour."

Lee had run out of options. He had to head for the barn.

Across the low water bridge he ran. He could see the barn, but it was still quite some distance from him. Running in a crouch, not so much to keep the blinding rain off himself (he was already soaked to the bones!) but rather to keep as low to the ground as he could to avoid being the lightning rod he felt he was!

Now the wind was howling so loudly he couldn't even hear the rain! What a strange sensation that was! Yet, he could somehow hear his own heart beating wildly in his chest. Adding to the strangeness of his predicament, darkness seemed to enshroud the farm, but there was light surrounding all sides of the storm—like the storm was only over his family's farm!

By now, Lee had lost all sight of the barn. Within seconds he had the feeling he was going in circles and had already covered this ground once before! Passing by the feed trough, he knew he had made it halfway to the barn. Passing the salt block, he knew he should be coming to the barn soon, but, once again, passed the feed trough—and then the salt block—three different times. Fear had now begun to win out over logic, so the boy simply crouched down as low as he could to the ground without losing his footing—just in case he caught a glimpse of the barn and could make another run for it.

He never saw the twister. How could he have seen it? Cloaked amidst the rain like a giant, jagged knife about to strike the ground, the funnel cloud slowly began to snake its way to the ground from almost directly over the boy's head. Lee had seen several twisters in his short lifetime. In all his days of growing up in Tornado Alley, the common knowledge was that the sound of a tornado could be compared to the rumblings of a freight train. Lee heard no train. He heard only the wind but not the sound like one could expect from a whirlwind. The violent wind had somehow become a soothing, comforting wind—a breeze. How could this be happening? Lee felt as if he was in slow motion as his body began to rise within the twister's dangling, gnarled "fingers."

In a weird twist of fate, the boy's fears gave way to a whimsical thought. Each year the local television station showed the old classic movie, *The Wizard of Oz*, and each year, Lee had never gotten past the scene involving the tornado. In fact, he never knew the movie changed to color when the house landed in Oz! Each year, just as the twister came, his folks called for him. "Lee, it's time for church! We need to go! Turn off that TV now and get to the car!" He was now living a scene from an old movie and it brought a tinge of joy to his heart! Why Lee thought of that now seemed both funny and odd to him. Shouldn't he be more afraid?

Finding himself now floating above the ground, the boy began to lose all sense of balance, feeling like he was being lifted and danced around the room by his granddad at Christmas when he was three years old. Oddly, he felt elation rather than fear—peace rather than utter terror.

At one point, Lee looked down to see the faint glimpse of the barn and the house, growing smaller and smaller until they were gone from his sight. The wind seemed to be lifting him higher and higher with every second, but a forward motion, horizontal to the ground, soon replaced the vertical lifting. Moving at a tremendous clip, the boy could now make out the countryside below, whisking by at what seemed to be supersonic speed. Overwhelmed by the pace of his forward motion, Lee began to lose consciousness, passing out yet still able to sense what was going on—like a dream—a wonderful, familiar dream.

He sensed mountains, sensed mighty raging rivers, and felt the rush of wind created by a flock of geese in a flying V formation as they passed just below. With every passing mile he felt a wash of excitement and adventure beginning to course through his veins. Now the pace began to slow. Still in a dream state, Lee could feel the slightest kiss of pine needles as he glided through a pine forest, the branches gently tickling his skin as he brushed against the boughs. The smell of pine and earthy moss now filled the air. Deer and wild boars occasionally darted out from their hiding places as he flew by. Then something drew him to attention in his dream state. There, just ahead on the horizon, he could make out the silhouette of a man, asleep on the ground, lying on his back, a sleeping giant!

Still not able to put words to his dream-thoughts, he just knew he knew this place. He felt it. Felt like a part of him. Felt like destiny. Flying between the trees and through small, meandering valleys between the foothills, he felt himself descending to what would be the chest of the hill that appeared to be a sleeping giant. And there, as if on cue, a large, black stallion, regal in appearance, saddled and waiting, snorted with excitement and anticipation just below him. As if placed there by colossal, unseen hands, the boy settled into the saddle, dazed and confused but thrilled and alive as he had ever been at the same time. . . .

Chapter Two

HOW DID I GET HERE?

Lee the boy was no longer a boy. Sitting there in the saddle, Lee opened his eyes and looked down to see large, muscular, hairy arms extended as he held the reins. Leonolis felt his age. He felt weary and worn, but satisfied. All he could bring his mind to think was, *How did I get here?* As the faintest memories of a boy in a field running from a barrage of lightning strikes slowly trickled away from his thoughts, High King Leonolis gazed out over the Kingdom of Bren, grateful, fulfilled, not quite so hungry for adventure as he had once been, yet unequivocally unafraid to face any foe that dare threaten this beloved land, this people.

As he sat there on the precipice—on the chest of Reuben of Old (The Sleeping Giant)—a flood of memories began to swarm through his thoughts. It seemed so long ago that the very place he now found himself had helped transform a boy into a man—had helped forge a strong and mighty reign of the boy who eventually became the high king of Bren—by an act of supreme sacrifice. The Sleeping Giant had given his very life to secure the freedom of Leonolis—indeed of the entire nation. Silent words of gratitude gave way to sound as the king, moved with grateful emotion, spoke.

"Reuben. Though I never met you before that day in the Cavern of What-Might-Have-Been—and never even had the honor of speaking with you—please know that your sacrifice has not gone without notice."

Since the day the Sleeping Giant had rescued Leonolis from the hand of Lucian, the good people of Bren had celebrated that day as one of their highest holidays. Calling it "The Day of Reckoning" (most of the locals affectionately refer to the day as "Reuben's Day" to this day!), the day was actually celebrated with a week's worth of activities ranging from reenactments of the battles leading up to the day and mock encounters with the dark lord, Lucian, to booths full of the finest foods of the land and offering the sweetest wines of the vineyards of Bren, to grand nightly galas featuring festive games and dancing into the wee morning hours, with the culmination being a grand parade and time of national thanksgiving for the ones responsible for securing freedom for Bren.

Going on, the high king Leonolis said, "As I sit here it is with great emotion that I am brought back to think about that day and all you did to make freedom even possible. Had it not been for you, Bren would be under the rule of the Dark Lord. Had it not been for you, many more lives would have been lost. Had it not been for you, I would not even be here."

As his words trailed off into the air, Leonolis chuckled to himself, thinking, *What am I doing talking to a mound of earth? Had I not seen it with my own eyes I would think I was losing my mind.*

With that, the old black horse on which the king sat suddenly shifted his weight to another hoof as if to make a statement.

"What is it, dear old Arolis?" asked the king.

"Sire," said the horse as full of wisdom as ever, "you had the honor of witnessing great sacrifice first hand. The events of that day, sure enough, have folded into lore and legend, making it difficult to know where one ends and the other begins. But truth is what it is, regardless of whether that truth is seen with one's own eyes or not."

Leonolis sat there silently, feeling no need to comment—because he knew Arolis was right. For many years now the horse had wisely helped the king through the entire course of his reign. From the days since his capture through all the many twists and turns the kingdom had gone through—the horse and his rider had gone through—Arolis had remained faithful in service to the king. He had remained faithful in honesty as well, never desiring to gain rank or privilege by offering what the king wanted to hear, but rather, offering wisdom—regardless of how difficult it was to bear to the king—that would help bring about goodness, justice, and mercy in the realm of Bren. The kingdom had prospered due to the king's open heart to wisdom.

As the two good friends allowed their silence to fade into satisfaction, the breeze began to pick up. Not brisk, yet constant in rhythm as if a song, the wind began to whisper into the king's soul. "There have been others . . ."

"Did you say something, Arolis?" asked the king, startled out of his reverie by the breeze.

"No, sire. I said nothing."

"But it must have been you. You said, 'There have been others,'" replied the king.

"No, sire. I said nothing."

With that, the two again became still. They had lived long enough and had endured enough magic in the realm to know that magic was astir once again, that perhaps the wisdom of Bren was coming forth on the breeze. Patience and trust now ruled the conversation.

After a few moments, the air was stirred again. "There have been others . . ." and then it trailed off into a sing-song fluttering of the leaves in the surrounding trees.

"Others?" asked the king.

"Others," whispered the wind.

"What does this mean?" asked Leonolis.

"The gratitude you feel toward Reuben is a mere drop in the ocean of all it has taken to get you to this place," came the murmuring reply.

"Teach me, O Wind," asked the king in humility.

"It has taken the sacrifice of many to get you to this place of honor you now hold. Many you readily see but many more—the unseen—has it taken to establish your place in the realm," said the Voice.

Taking his time to reply, the wise king said, "To be sure it has taken many to get me here. Easily do I see so much my father, High King Troyolin, sacrificed to make a place for me in the realm. Dreyden had bravely given himself in place of Leonolis as a boy—and lived life as a cripple ever since. Danwyn—faithful friend and bodyguard—gave his very life in the period of battles known as The Terror of Tormentia. Many warriors have fallen along the way. Even my own wife and children have had to give up so much to bring about all the success I now enjoy. These are apparent but my heart longs to know the unseen and to somehow convey to them the gratitude I feel toward them for all they have done."

"So it shall be," spoke the Voice. "So it shall be."

As Arolis shifted his weight again, the ground began to tremble ever so slightly, the breeze became a little more brisk, the birds ceased their constant chirping, and the forest began to grow still around them. Just as Leonolis had begun this new adventure, he began to feel himself lift from the ground and once again begin to fly to yet another place in the realm. As he drifted upward, he felt the brush of pine needles against his face. Gaining both altitude and speed, he saw the Sleeping Giant fade into the landscape as he began to make out the meandering path of the Runland. Following the mighty flow of the river, he soon saw the outlines of Castle Aerie coming into view. Passing lower now, he could see the hustle and bustle of castle life teeming below as he came to light in the courtyard of the massive structure he had known as home since he was a boy. As his feet touched the ground, he wondered what he would find now. Before he could even mutter a question, he heard the answer.

"This way."

Chapter Three

A FATHER'S GIFT

Turning toward the direction the Voice had come, King Leonolis entered the palace's main entrance. From this entrance, a great hallway led to an outer court area where those who hoped to meet with the king would gather. This hall was called the Hall of Defenders and was lined with the sculpted likenesses of every king who had ever ruled over Brenolin. In addition, the statues of great war heroes and statues of those who had brought great invention or innovation to the realm were housed as well. As you may probably already know, Leonolis was directly related to almost every one of these amazing men and women of Bren. It did not take much for him to realize just how much of his success he owed to each of these who had paved the way for him and the prosperity he now enjoyed.

Walking down this great hallway now seemed somehow new and exhilarating, even though he must have walked these very stones a thousand times before. His heart beating with expectant anticipation, the king was somewhat taken aback when he greeted those he passed. No one seemed to return his nods. No one responded when he said, "Greetings, son of Bren," or "Greetings, fair maiden of Bren." It was as if they could not see him or hear him. In that moment, Leonolis knew the Voice had granted him vision into another realm without the fear of being burdened by the throngs who always vied for an audience with the king.

King Leonolis was a good king—one admired and respected by all. Even his detractors could not argue with his great integrity and kindness, his love of justice tempered with great mercy. The Voice was allowing him to observe without any distraction. What High King Leonolis was about to find out was that he was being granted the privilege of seeing and reliving a portion of his life from a brand-new perspective.

As he pondered this new anonymity, he heard hurried footsteps coming from behind. Forgetting he could not be seen or heard, he instinctively shouted, "Maison! Augurian! What brings you here this day? It has been much too long! Why, I thought you were . . ."

Startled back to his mute reality, the king's heart began to fill with gratitude at being in the presence of two of his most beloved mentors once again. It had been twenty years since he had seen Augurian. The oracle—the wise sage—as he had been called, had not been seen for twenty years, having suddenly and simply faded as a mist into the air during Leonolis' coronation. And Maison, the beloved tutor to the boy and advisor to the king, had given his life to advance the reign of the king some fifteen years before during the Blood Moon Uprising. How was this possible, to see these two beloved and long-gone friends now before him? And how utterly frustrating to not be able to embrace or speak with them now!

Following the two men was a throng of people. Dignitaries. Friends. Family members. Leaders from the many realms surrounding Bren. Government officials and simple townsfolk. Leonolis had not witnessed such a diverse gathering of folk since the Chriostathis. The Chriostathis is the ceremonial passing of power from one high king to the next in line of succession. This ceremony usually can also have significance in family lineage—a birthright passed from father to son. This is also the ceremony that takes place prior to the public coronation of the high king. And then it dawned on Leonolis. This was HIS Chriostathis. He was going to get a bird's-eye view of the very moment his father, High King Troyolin, passed the torch of power and blessing to him!

Suddenly, Leonolis was flooded with sweet memories of that happy occasion. He remembered the sweet kiss his mother had given him just as he was called from her side to take his place before the throne of his father. He fondly recalled the pride he felt from each of his siblings as he nervously made his way past them to the place of blessing. How could he forget the knowing glint of pride in Maison's eye as he looked to his mentor for one last "way to go, boy" from the wise old man? And the strong and assuring gaze of his own father as he was about to be anointed into a long and illustrious line of kings and forefathers still sent shivers up and down his spine and flew into his memory as vividly as when he first experienced this moment twenty years before.

Watching from the viewpoint of those in attendance gave Leonolis a brand-new perspective on an event that had been ingrained in his memory O so long ago. He had relived this moment so many times before in many an afternoon's daydreams and reverie but never from this perspective. As he stood there, the room grew silent as the high king, Troyolin, rose to his feet. With great majesty and regal authority, the high king commanded the attention and respect of all without saying so much as one syllable. Leonolis had seen this so many times during his lifetime and remembered longing for that same level of love and respect during the early days of his own reign. Although he now enjoyed such admiration himself, there was still something wonderfully magical about seeing his own father responded to in such a reverent manner. He felt utter pride at the high character his father demonstrated, and adoration for a man of such high status who was regarded far and wide as a man of the people.

As the king rose from the throne, he stepped toward the young Leonolis. The prince knelt to his left knee (as per instructed by royal protocols), and the king approached him. Lifting his right hand above his son's head, the king began to speak.

"By the foresight of the Founders, the Almighty Creator of Bren and of all existence, and by the wisdom of the ages as passed from one generation of those called Brenolin, I hereby give honor to those who have secured our sovereignty through their own sacrifice of blood and declare my own life as not my own, but rather, the life of one given to service of the realm and good people of Bren. All I have been given in gift and talent, honor and blessing, strength and virtue, I now pass on to he who would be high king after me."

At those words, Augurian rose and began to chant in some long-forgotten language of incantation. It felt very regal and formal while, at the same time, feeling mystical and magical and invigorating. High King Leonolis remembered the feeling anew as he had done while the young man Leonolis knelt in silence before his father. This time he saw something he had not seen before. The look in his father's eyes spoke volumes the younger version of Leonolis had not had the privilege of seeing when the Chriostathis had first been performed for him.

There was an absolute look of serenity on the king's face coupled with an equal look of serious concern. High King Leonolis, again, did not have to ask. The Voice simply answered.

"He is utterly proud of you, Leonolis. Proud of the man you are becoming and proud to have you come from his loins. Yet, he is extremely concerned for you—for your safety, for your sanity—as he knows full well the pressures of the calling of king will place upon your life and, indeed, on those you love and hold most dear."

Leonolis knew this all too well now, having served in the calling of high king for twenty years himself now. "You did not see all he sacrificed for you."

Turning again to the ceremony unfolding before his eyes, Leonolis saw his father bend down and whisper in his ear words known only between himself, his father, and the Founders.

"Son, you have seen me live my life openly and honestly before the people. You have known the cost to you and your siblings and your mother all too well. The lack of privacy. The public airing of all our personal shortcomings. The feeling of living one's life in a cage. The never-ending pomp and circumstance of our royal responsibilities. Our very lives on display for all to see at all times. But you have also seen the consequences of one life laid down for another. How our name—your name, the name Brenolin—is one of honor and valor and all we know and call good.

"You will be honored, but give the honor back to those who bestow it. You will be accused, but bless those who would curse you. You will be misquoted and misunderstood, but always declare what is true and righteous, never blaming others for what is your mistake. Take responsibility for what is yours and willingly share the burdens of our people. You are about to be king. You will be high king in the eyes of the people. But I am about to tell you the greatest secret of the realm—the key to my success as high king. Never forget this, my son. Never forget."

His voice now shaking with emotion rarely shared between men, High King Troyolin spoke.

"He who would be king of all must be servant of all. No matter how many accolades or how much flattery comes your way, the high king sees himself as lowest of all, born to give his life in service for all who are called by the name Bren. Indeed, Son, the highest calling of any king would be to give his life for the freedom of those he leads."

Taking his son by the chin, he lifted the young Leonolis' face to meet the gaze of his own. Looking into the eyes of his son, he said, "The things you have learned from me, Son, pass them on to your sons and daughters and instruct them to, in turn, pass them on to their sons and daughters. What we see in wealth and possessions as high king are as mere rags when compared to the riches of character and identity and family we find and possess in the name Brenolin. Be all that your name inspires . . . and rule as one who knows who they are. Never stray to the right nor to the left. Keep your eyes focused, Son, on the end of the race—the day you stand before the Founders and give account for how you wore the name of Brenolin. With that I bless you this day . . . that you may one day stand before the Almighty Founders and give this account:

'O, great Founders, I stand before You as one who wore the name Brenolin and wore it humbly as servant of all. You know my shortcomings and You know my heart. By Thy help and Thine alone do I even stand before You. I have been nothing more and nothing less than all You have poured into me as king of Bren. In freedom I lived. In freedom I die. This day we conquer! This day we overcome the Dark Lord! This day we live or die for the king! May the strength of Bren be mine—this day and evermore.'"

Troyolin rose from his son's gaze and summoned Augurian to continue the ceremony. Standing behind Leonolis, the wise sage took Troyolin's hands and coupled them with his own. As they pressed their hands together down on the head of Leonolis, Augurian began to speak.

"This day, O great Founders, we call upon all that is wise and all that is good. This day we beseech Thee for the rightful transference of power from he who is king to he who will be. Take the gifts of the father and convey them to the son. May the power of the father be multiplied to the son. May the wisdom of the father be greater in the son. May the safety granted to the kingdom of one be granted to that of the next."

As Augurian continued, he once again began to speak in the long-forgotten language of magic, and as he did, the room began to glow and a slight breeze could be felt (even though not one of the hundreds of candles and torches in the room flickered even once at that breeze.) That moment is now regarded reverently and seen in all of Bren as a physical sign of the Founders' very presence and blessing on that day's events! As the glow thickened and permeated the room, it began to concentrate directly over Leonolis and Troyolin after a few moments. As the glow intensified still more, it began to descend on the two men, Troyolin as he stood opposite of Augurian above the boy, and over Leonolis where he knelt.

As the light intensified, it appeared as a ball of intense energy that words have never been able to define. All present saw what few men have ever seen and lived to tell. The energy began to swirl around the head and crown of Troyolin until his face could no longer be seen. It then began to pulsate and, as it did, began to descend upon the head of Leonolis. Soon the prince was no longer visible, being engulfed in the orb of bright energy that now hid he and his father from view. As if the room would explode from sheer inability to contain such a massive power, the entire fortress began to quake. Those on the outside who awaited the coronation felt an earthquake. Those on the inside knew better!

Not knowing whether to fall to their knees in fear or run in panic for their lives, those in that room were frozen in place by the awe that was unfolding before them. There was no doubt that something sacred was now becoming reality. Suddenly the room exploded with a clap of thunder and the room was fully ablaze in a myriad of lightning bolts! Still, no one moved. Miraculously, all felt fear but simultaneously felt safe and secure in whatever this was that was happening!

As suddenly as the glow had appeared, the room went back to its original dim glow of candlelight. Only now, the prince was standing. As if one voice, the entire throng gasped at once when they saw the prince. His once sandy blond hair was now a flowing, graceful mop of brilliant blond white! Somehow magically transferred from the head of Troyolin to the pate of Leonolis, the crown jewels of the realm now gleamed! And although he was merely thirty-one years of age, the prince now wore the demeanor of one wise beyond his years. Thirty-one may seem old to some cultures but was considered young in the land of Bren where the wisdom of the elders was highly esteemed and honored.

And then all gasped together again when one of the ladys-in-waiting whispered rather loudly. "Look at the high king!"

Troyolin no longer seemed the resilient warrior known throughout the realm. Though still stately and handsome as ever, there was now a weariness to his eyes. No longer did he seem as strong and healthy as before. Now he appeared somewhat frail—as if in only a few seconds of time the weight of his reign had finally caught up to him. What they could not possibly know—what Leonolis would soon discover—was that, in the moment the explosion of light occurred, the gifts and talents of Troyolin were passed into his son. The wisdom. The grace. The ability—the powerful gift to lift objects and immobilize things by the power of thought. This transference had depleted the high king of a measure of his life, but he had given it up willingly for his son, for the sake of Bren.

Although the wisdom, grace, and powerful ability had been infused into Leonolis, it would be up to the new high king to discover and nurture those blessings to the fulfillment of their intended purposes. Like a tiny acorn, Leonolis now contained all the qualities and character of the mighty oak he would become. He would simply need to believe his identity and grow into it. From his younger days, Leonolis had been taught that he could possess all the gifts and talents one could hope for and still walk in pride and weakness. He had been wisely instructed that it was up to himself to put on the right attitude—that of humble servant, defender of Bren. As the ceremony came to a conclusion, Maison stood and began to quote the age-old adage passed on from father to son, from mother to daughter, since the founding of Bren:

"As a son or daughter of Bren thinks, so shall they be."

As the crowd prepared to follow the procession to the grand gathering place outside the Castle Aerie's walls—Warrior's Canyon—for the presentation of the newly crowned king, the Voice again spoke.

"There is more."

As a heavy mist began to engulf Leonolis, he felt a slight tinge of sorrow as he passed from the Chriostathis to the royal bedchamber of his father and mother. Lying on his back, a serene smile upon his gaunt, withered face, the good king Troyolin lay dying. Merely five years after the Chriostathis of Leonolis, the time had gone so quickly for the old man—and for the son. He had hoped his father would live forever (as sons do). This was the strongest man he had ever known—the one who had cared for an entire kingdom and had carried the weight of that sacred burden handily on his shoulders—now reduced to the state of weakness and utter dependence upon others. Leonolis had long assumed his father would always be there to guide and advise, but this was not to be. Yet, in a sense, it was to be . . .

He saw himself standing beside the bed, the queen mother, Melania, kneeling next to him. As his mother knowingly caressed the brow of her husband, she shifted her gaze to the eyes of her son. Beckoning him without words to kneel close to his father, the queen reverently gave place to her son. Touching him with one of those "it's going to be all right, Son" brushes of her cheek lightly against his, she moved aside. As the son knelt, his father stirred ever so slightly from his slumber.

"Is that you, dear Leonolis?"

"It is I, Father," said the son.

"Come close, my son," whispered the king, life obviously ebbing from his body.

"Father, I am here."

Taking several labored, deep breaths, the old man began to speak with a weak rasp, audible only to his son.

"Put your hand here," said Troyolin, weakly patting his heart.

As Leonolis tenderly placed his hand on the chest of his father, the king continued softly.

"Son, you have my heart. You have always had my heart. Soon I will join our fathers in eternity."

Leonolis knew his father was right. It was evident to those attending to Troyolin. It was heavy on the heart of Melania. And deep inside his heart-of-Brenolin-hearts, Leonolis knew there was no denying what was happening to his father. But little did he know of the deep, life-long impact his father's dying words were to have on his own life and reign.

Barely audible even to Leonolis now, Troyolin said, "Son, I go now from your side . . . but I will always be with you. Take the memories we made together and cherish them like precious treasure. And if you remember nothing else . . . if I could tell you only one thing, I would say . . ."

The mist once again surrounded the present-day Leonolis. Of course, all he could think of were those haunting words last spoken by his dear father. Not noticing that he was once again being transported to another time in his journey, the high king was overcome with deep, trembling emotion at just how true his father's words had proven to be in his life.

We'll get to the specifics of those words later.

Chapter Four

THE MATTER OF DREYDEN

Leonolis was awakened from his deep reverent remembrance of the words his father had spoken by cries of anguish, sorrow, and pain. He was back in the courtyard of Castle Aerie, yet this time there was no pleasant banter between neighbors and no bantering back and forth between street vendors in their carts and patrons haggling over the price of wares. This time he was transported back to the very day of his Testalamorphia—and all that had transpired with Dreyden. How could he ever forget all he had gone through with his dear friend of friends? Yet, by this time, Leonolis knew he was about to receive an even deeper understanding of just how deep his bond with Dreyden truly was—and just how much of a sacrifice had been made for him by the good man, Dreyden.

Leonolis could see himself racing ahead of Danwyn, the steed Arolis in full-speed-ahead mode. He swelled with pride as he watched the younger version of himself now prance into position on the Field of Testing, and he winced as his name was now called to go head to head in that fateful Test of Will. Heading full-tilt toward one another and leaping into the air, he saw young Leonolis easily knock the sword from the outstretched (and shocked and disbelieving!) hand of Dreyden. Again, he realized the rush of adrenaline as Arolis bolted for Castle Aerie, having caught sight of the Dark Lord, Lucian.

This time, though, the Voice led him to follow after Dreyden as, bewildered and humiliated, he reined his horse toward the very stand of trees where the Dark Lord lay hiding. Instinctively, Leonolis cried out, "No, Dreyden! Stop, friend!"

And just as quickly, the Voice calmly replied, "He cannot hear you. What has been will be still. One can never change one's past. There is great peace in that statement, High King."

Puzzled at the oddness of that statement, Leonolis' mind was racing with thoughts of *Why Dreyden?* and *What if I had gone to his rescue?*

"Why burden your own heart and mind with something that can never be changed, O King?" said the Voice.

"But if I had only been there for Dreyden—stood up for him—his life might have been easier," responded Leonolis.

"Your pride betrays you, dear king," said the Voice.

"My pride?" asked Leonolis.

"You think you know better than the Founders a playing out of these events? You merely cloud your mind with vain imaginations at such notions," said the Voice.

"That was never my intention," replied the king.

"Your intention was trumped by your attitude. To place one's thoughts and ideas and notions and wisdom above that of the Founders is to place one's own self above the Founders—and that is the territory of the Dark Lord. One can never change one's past, and one can never change the path the Founders have chosen. The duty of the king—of any man or woman of the realm—is to embrace the wisdom of the Founders and to allow Him to use even what the Dark Lord has brought to pass as a means of furthering the kingdom of Bren. What you see with mortal eyes must be taken through the filter of the perspective of the Founders. When that is done, death gives way to life. Tears give way to joy. Despair gives way to hope. Pain gives way to peace. Defeat gives way to victory," said the Voice.

"Now you sound like Maison. Countless are the times he led me to that same wisdom. The wisdom of mere men is weak and meaningless if not sifted through the mind of the Founders. Mortal wisdom gives way to the realm of magic when submitted to the wisdom of the Founders." At this statement, the king was again silent as his gaze turned back to the sequence of events now unfolding before him.

The shield of one of the Dark Lord's henchman suddenly and violently unhorsed Dreyden as it met his unsuspecting head. Dazed and writhing in pain, the boy regained enough consciousness just in time to see Merrywell receive the same greeting as he came to the boy's defense. Struggling to get to his feet, the boy received a kick to his jaw and was again knocked cold to the ground. At the Founders' mercy, the boy lay unconscious and unaware of much of what Merrywell was to endure before meeting his end, but this time, Leonolis was not spared.

Each time Merrywell tried to regain his footing, he was mercilessly kicked and beaten. But without so much as one thought for his own safety, the Second of Dreyden kept responding with, "I am defender of the good lad Dreyden. May the strength of Bren be mine today!"

Even though Leonolis wanted to look away, he could not deny the power of the magic and the persuasiveness of the Voice that kept his sight fixed on what transpired before him. "There is strength to help you see this, O King. Trust the Founders. Even in this sorrow and tragedy you now experience, there is a deeper magic at work. Let it do a deeper work in your heart and mind. Where your sorrow meets your inability to do anything about what you are experiencing, the strength of the Founders' magic will be. Take the cup given and drink deeply. It will serve you well in the journey that is to come."

Startled back to the scene unfolding before him, Leonolis heard the words uttered by countless warriors of Bren through the ages.

"This day we conquer! This day we overcome the Dark Lord! This day we live or die for the king!" cried the staggering Merrywell.

Filled with insane rage, Lucian took the weakened yet uncowered Merrywell by the throat and raged profane hatred. "This day you conquer? This day you overcome me? This day you live? You conquer not! You overcome nothing! One thing is for certain! This day you shall die, foolish, mindless swine of Bren!"

Turning toward his small unit of men, Lucian said, "We must make quick work of the matter! The magic of Toralan will last for only a few minutes! Even now the magic is being detected by the seers of Bren! We will be concealed no more once the magic of the White Witch has lifted!"

With that, the men began to torture the Second of Dreyden. Stripping the clothing from Merrywell, they began to mock and ridicule the nearly naked warrior so as to bring as much shame as possible (as was one of the most common tactics of the Dark Lord). Each time he tried to stand, Merrywell was knocked senseless to the ground. After a few minutes of this, the dark forces began to hold him down, one man securing each limb, while a sinister shaman of the dark forces began to make small cuts in the chest and belly of Merrywell.

As he tortured the now-shaking body of Merrywell, the shaman asked a question with each slice of the man's flesh. "Where are the king's forces?"

"I do not know!" moaned Merrywell. "And if I did I would never betray my king!"

"Where is the safe place they have taken the prince?" said the shaman.

"That place is known to none but the king and the prince's Second!" wailed the soldier of Bren.

"Do you wish to see your wife and children alive again?" the shaman taunted wickedly.

"My family? My family gladly lays down their lives in service of High King Troyolin! Say and do what you will, but you will never cause me to turn my gaze . . . or my heart . . . or my destiny from that which the Founder has lain before me," said the defiant Merrywell.

Without rhyme or reason, the torture continued. The questions were no longer in search of information but took a wicked turn. It was as if the shaman, Lucian, and the entire phalanx of dark forces took deep, satisfying pleasure in the suffering of this loyal-to-the-end man of Bren.

"Did you know your wife moaned like a cat as I cut her heart out this morning?"

"Did you know your son cried like a small peasant girl as I cut into his belly?"

"Have you ever heard the sound of life leaving a little girl's body? I did—just this morning—as I strangled the life from the bodies of your daughters," laughed the maniacal shaman.

Though none of those things had actually occurred, the evil in that small wooded glen took great delight in the torment and sorrow it brought to the ever-weakening Merrywell. Still, the brave man met the punishment with deep, unashamed bravery and loyalty to Bren, never once wavering at what he was now undergoing. In his heart-of-Bren-hearts, he saw into the realm of the Founders. What Merrywell saw and heard gave him the strength he needed to endure to the end. And Leonolis saw it—and heard it—too . . .

From his vantage point, Merrywell looked into the canopy of trees above him, now seemingly numb to the pain and mockery taking place, and saw a fiery bank of mist. In that mist, a circle of the heroes of Bren gazed down upon him. Though he had never seen any of these figures, he knew from the stories from of old who each and every person in that circle was.

There was the very first high king for which Bren was named— King Bren—the one who had brought the realm into its existence by help of the Founders. And next to him was Forsten, mighty warrior of legend who had led the armies of Bren against the Pestulents from the eastern lands of Morbium. And right there next to Forsten was Abigail the Deliverer who had fought heroically during the period known as The Great Contemptus, when the realm went through a time of severe winter for seven months on end due to all the women of Bren being frozen by the spell of Contemptia or kidnapped and carried into Hiemsland and forced into slavery. Merrywell had named one of his own daughters after Abigail, so to see her now brought great relief and comfort to his tormented soul.

Leonolis could not believe what he was seeing. At once repulsed at the treatment Merrywell was enduring yet agog at the sight of the gathering of the forefathers and mothers of Bren. He was appalled that he could do nothing to help yet amazed at the power and magical strength Merrywell displayed as he gallantly tried to defend Dreyden—to defend Bren.

The vision continued. Next to Abigail was Gregarian the Great, he who had vanquished the army of Nordegrun even after his sight had been taken from him at the hand of Nequam the Vile. Nequam's army was relentless and spiteful in their desire to rule over the known world. Their strategy was to so terrify the citizens of a certain realm they would maim and cripple rather than put to death, blinding the eyes of the leadership was one of their favorite ploys, but it had not worked on Gregarian who was known for his great wisdom, insight, and unshakable joy.

On and on and on this gathering went. As one face would become apparent another would fade into view. No wonder Merrywell could respond with such valor. He had this great cloud of witnesses cheering him on! And then all these magnificent heroes faded suddenly from view as Merrywell's damaged body was tied face first to a tree, and began to be riddled with arrows. With the first arrow came a burst of utter silence. Disbelief on the part of Leonolis, but simple reverence and honor emanating from the cloud for Merrywell.

And then there was simply a presence, and a Voice. The Voice.

"Merrywell, my beloved son of Bren. Your life is not wasted but will surely endure. You will see your wife and children one day soon, but right now it is time for you to join fellowship with your fathers and mothers in the realm of the Founders where sorrows and troubles are no more. Your adventure is just beginning. Let go, my son, and enter the quest."

And with those words, the body of Merrywell was instantly limp and lifeless, yet Merrywell himself went straight away in the very cloud of witnesses he had glimpsed during the torment. He was smiling and at peace yet still stalwart in his demeanor and determination to see the Dark Lord vanquished and freedom reigning in all of Bren.

Leonolis was now on his face on the ground in the wooded glen as the dark forces lashed Dreyden to a horse's back and made their escape. He had already begun to bow down in honor of the valor displayed by the good man, Merrywell, but when he realized that the Voice he had been led by was the very voice of the Founders, he could do nothing less than fall on his face weeping in utter submission and reverence and in a profound state of gratitude for all Merrywell had done to secure the success he now enjoyed as high king of Bren.

"My son, Leonolis," began the Voice, "let what you have witnessed both cheer your heart and bring great pain. Allow the pain to drive you to always do what is necessary to meet the real needs of those you serve, and allow the sacrifice of this one cause you great joy and pride of having the blood of Bren and the power of the Founders flowing through your veins. And never, ever, ever allow any past failure, present circumstance, or temptation to selfish pride keep you from walking as a son of Bren.

You are no greater than the least of those you serve . . . and I waste nothing. Not even sorrow and pain."

Once again, Leonolis felt himself lifting from the wooded glen and flying high above the Canyons of Callay and to the place nearby called Oaken Fork and to the tree where the body of Dreyden had been tied, completely naked and mutilated beyond recognition. Having been tied face first to the tree just as Merrywell had been, Dreyden had been spared the same fate as his Second. No arrows protruded from the lifeless boy. Leonolis had been told of this moment but had never truly imagined the horror of it so vividly as he now saw it.

The high king Leonolis could hear the troops of Bren approaching and saw the sorrow of Troyolin as he first caught sight of what he assumed was the dead body of Dreyden. Yet as life ebbed back into Dreyden, Leonolis witnessed the amazingly great compassion of his own father as the high king Troyolin cradled the boy's body near his own heart, unashamed tears of gratitude flowing as he caressed the boy, knowing full well the grief Heath, father of Dreyden, would now be spared—knowing full well he may be facing the loss of his own son.

The awe and reverence of that moment was not lost on Leonolis. The highest calling of virtue emanated from the heart and demeanor of his father, Troyolin, causing great encouragement and righteous pride to well up from deep within his own soul.

"Listen," said the Voice.

"Where is Leonolis?" asked Dreyden.

"Don't worry about the prince right now, Son," answered the king. "He will be fine."

"Where is Leonolis?" insisted Dreyden in a whispered yet determined tone.

"Dreyden. Leonolis will be fine. You need to preserve your strength. Your body is in need of rest. We will get you back to Castle Aerie and commence with your healing, Son," said the king firmly.

"Where is Leonolis?" defiantly asked the boy as he faded into unconsciousness.

"He was more concerned with my welfare than his own," said the now-somber Leonolis.

"Yes. That is the heart of a son of Bren, regardless of social status or financial means and regardless of the circumstances of one's life. The success and victory men tend to take credit for are never accomplished alone. What you see as mere random coincidence is actually a well-orchestrated dance between My heart and the hearts of men. All desire to lead, but the greatest leader of all is he who follows the lead of the Founders. Do you not see how I am able to take even the messes you manage to make of your own lives and weave a magical grace and power to transform the ashes you create into great altars of commemoration? For every shrine you build to a great man, there are hundreds that helped achieve their greatness . . . all woven together by Me," said the Voice.

Again, Leonolis was lifted from Oaken Fork to a place he was very familiar with—the royal gardens—and the present-day home of Dreyden and his precious family. As he sat unseen in the corner of the small home Dreyden shared with his family, Leonolis was witness to a very tender time between a man and his wife.

"Dear, sweet Dreyden. Please sit and rest before tending to any more of the gardens. The tomatoes can wait," pleaded Dreyden's wife, Barrelle.

"My love, you know the tomatoes cannot tend to themselves and that this very night my lord and friend, High King Troyolin, is in need of his garden's bounty to host the dignitaries visiting from Brestling. It has been years since such a meeting of these two peoples took place, and I want it to be just right for the king . . . for Bren," responded Dreyden.

"Well, at least take your shoes off and allow me to rub some of the soreness away before you run yourself ragged," said Barrelle.

Wisely, Dreyden responded, "Yes, dear," knowing she would follow him to the royal gardens until he submitted to her request!

Dreyden pulled off his shoes, revealing feet that normally one would associate with an old, old man. Gnarled and rough from the many years of bending to plant and of kicking dirt onto freshly planted seed rows, the feet of Dreyden were even more mangled than Leonolis had remembered. And then it dawned on him. The maiming of his feet had actually taken place at the hand of Lucian.

During the time of his captivity and torture, Dreyden (much like Merrywell) had endured more torture and duress than any man (much less a boy) should ever have to endure. Wanting to leave a message for High King Troyolin and to cause as much pain and fear as possible in the heart of the high king, Lucian had intentionally left Dreyden alive but maimed and crippled.

Leonolis had known about the severing of both of Dreyden's Achilles tendons, but he thought the healing magic of Maison and Augurian had remedied him completely healed. After all, how many times since their boyhood days and after the time of his captivity had Dreyden run and played and wrestled and done mock battle with Leonolis? He had always responded with such great vigor! The present-day feet of Dreyden told a far different story.

"Dreyden. Why do you suppose the Founders have allowed these scars to remain?" queried Barrelle.

"Scars are significant to the Founders. Though I do not know all the reasons why nor do I understand all the reasons why, what I do know is this. These scars are testament to the power and magic of the Founders. Each time I look at them I am reminded that, even though I endured all I endured, it was for the Founders and for the glory of Bren. What greater blessing is there than to be chosen to suffer hardship for the Founders if it means greater freedom for this realm I love so well and hold so dear?"

As the adoring couple sat quietly in one another's presence, so Leonolis sat quietly, soaking in the words and wisdom of his friend of friends.

"You know, darling Barrelle? Every time I feel a twinge of pain from one of these scars, I do not respond in bitterness. You well know how often I have been asked, 'Why are you not bitter toward the Founders for what He put you through?' All I know is that rather than allowing the dark forces to have even one iota of satisfaction at my pain, I would rather respond to the pain from the Founders' point of view. The pain gives me pause to consider the help of the Founders in this present age . . . and it serves to remind me of how precious you and the children are to me, how precious life is to me. I would gladly suffer the same torture and pain if it led to freedom and prosperity for you and the children . . . for Bren. As much as I love my king and as much as I love my friend of friends, they are not the wealthy ones of the realm. I am. All I have to do is to look into your eyes to see how blessed I am. I but have to watch my children laughing and playing to see how fortunate I am. Yes, sweet Barrelle. I would not trade that for anything in the world. I am a wealthy man . . ."

Leonolis wept quietly. There was nothing else to say as he, once again, felt himself lifting from this reality to the next.

Chapter Five

THE BLOOD MOON UPRISING

After his time with Dreyden and Merrywell, Leonolis was silent as he passed from that reality to the next. Even though the Voice said nothing, Leonolis knew that He was there. As they entered the next realm, the mood of the king grew somber as a sense of foreboding seemed to be in the air. As they came to rest upon the southern wall of Castle Aerie near a guard tower, Leonolis remembered.

It was a rainy day in the fifth year of the reign of High King Leonolis. Much had happened in that year. His father, Troyolin, had entered the realm of the Founders through his death. And then, only a few months later, Maison—dear, good and faithful friend, and trusted advisor—had died. Leonolis still carried much guilt and sorrow from all that had taken place surrounding the death of his friend.

It was also the fifth year of the reign of High King Leonolis when they came. From a land far to the south called Scavengia, the Scavacine (as the people of this land were called) were seen throughout the known world at this time as one of the most enlightened peoples on earth. Having no trade connection for generations due to the vastness of the Sea of Aragon that separated them, the existence of the Scavacine had drifted into the stuff of legends.

Though not known for their military expertise or force, the Scavacine (as it would later be revealed) overpowered their foes in other ways. Leonolis' thoughts were suddenly flooded with the memories of that very first encounter. He had been receiving subjects in the throne room, hearing of the needs of the land then making the sometimes tough decisions as to how best to meet those needs. He fondly remembered how Maison had so faithfully stood by his side during such encounters, never forcing his will, but rather, helping guide the king to make the wisest decision possible.

"Water will need to be diverted from the Tower Spring to meet the needs of the small village of Sten," commanded the king.

This decree, in turn, angered the people of the small village of Kenden who had discovered the spring and felt the water was all theirs.

"We are all men and women of Bren. We are first and foremost citizens of the realm, called to carry the burdens of one another when necessary. People of Sten. You will pay a fair market price to the town coffers of Kenden for the water you use," declared the king.

"O, good king Leonolis, son of the good king Troyolin, the people of the village of the realm called DeRochelle have recently reported sightings of Chiroptera surveying their livestock from nearby forests. We fear they are desirous of making our animals their supper. Would the king consider dispatching a small garrison of archers to help protect our livestock, our livelihoods, and even our lives?" asked the representative of DeRochelle.

Knowing he could only spare a small garrison of archers for a brief period, the king wisely turned to Maison (who always stood on his right during these times of public inquiry) for advise.

"Maison. What would you suggest, dear friend?" queried the king.

"Sire, I would suggest a compromise. Use the archers to train others. It is better to teach a man to hunt and feed him for a lifetime than to do the hard work for him and, thereby, teach him to not take responsibility for his own life," said the wise old tutor.

"Good men of DeRochelle, I will send you five of our best archers . . . not to defend you forever, but to train the men and women of your realm in the scientific art of archery. They will spend four weeks training your people in the skills of archery, self-defense, and assisting you in developing a strategy of protection for your people and livestock. I would like periodic reports of your progress once the archers of Bren have departed," said the king. This seemed to satisfy the people of DeRochelle.

Sometimes, as only a king knows too well, needs are not so easily met nor subjects so easily satisfied.

40

"Good king Leonolis, the people of Mendenburg, as you know, are in need of repairs to the roads that were damaged during the recent earthquake in our region. The main pass to Abysstine to our north as well as the southern pass to Treacherin are both completely blocked, forcing us to carry on our trade using the ancient and treacherous mountainous routes. As you well know, sire, these are nothing more than small ledges for much of the way. Already we have lost seven men who have either fallen to their deaths or have been swept away with sudden rockslides. We lost so much in the quake and subsequent tremors that any further loss only adds to an already bitter time of recovery. The sheer amount of loss of lives and livelihoods have taken such a great toll. We desire to be self-sufficient, but have reached our limits and now request as humbly as we know how, assistance from the sovereign of Bren," said the man of Mendenburg.

Again, turning to Maison, Leonolis simply looked into the eyes of the wise old man and could see his wisdom and reply without needing to hear it. Turning to the man from Mendenburg, the king replied, "Dear brother of Bren, we have known of your dire needs since the moment the seers revealed it to us . . . and even as we speak, emissaries have been dispatched to survey the damage and report back to me with recommendations of how best to address your needs. Once we have assessed the need, we will dispatch the manpower and supplies necessary to meet those needs."

"But sire," replied the man, "we are in need of assistance now! If those passageways are not cleared, our people will starve! Surely that is not the heart of the king!"

"Dear brother, we will help. We simply want to make the best use of men and resources. We will send resources of food and other needed supplies back with you and will also send men practiced in the arts of healing to assist your sick and injured. Once our emissaries have reported back to us, we will send the best engineers of the land along with the tools they deem most necessary and efficient for the job, and we will clear those trade routes. In the meantime, remember you and your people are the Brenolinian. The blood of those who overcome runs in your veins. There is no doubt you will rise to the occasion and respond with the heart of Bren," responded the king.

Out of frustration, the man turned angrily from the king and loudly addressed those in the room. "This is the wisdom of the king? We need help now and all he does is send a few parcels of food and bandages and tries to placate us with ancient platitudes! This is the here and now and we need help! Bah!" And with that he stormed out.

Leonolis had already—unbeknownst to the man of Mendenburg— prepared a team of doctors and royal aides trained in the arts of disaster recovery to go to Mendenburg. He wisely dispatched them to attend to the disgruntled citizen.

Yes, all too well, did Leonolis remember such days.

Standing now on the precipice of the castle wall, Leonolis saw the glimmer of lights through the mist coming from the south on the Sea of Aragon. Just as he had heard on that day in the throne room and having the public gathering come to an abrupt end as the bells in the watchtowers began to peal, he watched himself ushered to the gates of Castle Aerie and watched himself ascend the steps, coming to a halt right next to the place next to where he now stood unseen.

"What is it, Captain of the Guard?" asked the king.

"We are not sure, my lord. A series of lights are seen approaching with much haste even though the prevailing winds are from the north. Surely this is some magic that nears our shores. No sail could propel a ship so rapidly with such an opposing wind," said the captain.

"Prepare the Naval Guard!" commanded the king.

And with that, a series of short, coded trumpet blasts alerted the five naval warships anchored in the harbor to go to full battle stations. In addition, the entire Castle Guard assembled below in Warrior's Canyon, archers in the rear, infantry in front of archers, and cavalry to lead the way.

As the king watched himself, his gaze was directed to the sea. "Watch," said the Voice.

Leonolis saw them. The lights were now becoming more discernible through the mist. One. Two. Three. Four lights. Then five. Six. Seven lights were now clearly visible. As if on cue, the skies above began to clear and the light emanating from the vessels was suddenly magnified by the rays of sudden sunshine piercing the dark and rainy clouds. At first, as Leonolis remembered, the lights appeared to be creatures of some sort, but as they neared the docks of the harbor it became apparent that the lights were actually vessels. Boats of pure light! And as if that were not enough, it was clearly visible that these boats had no sails, and no oarsmen. They were powered without aid of oar or sail!

These were boats of crystalline material! Glass boats.

By now, much of the population of Castle Aerie and the surrounding villages had heard of the approaching lights. A huge crowd of onlookers now peered from seemingly every nook and cranny and hiding place and from each and every possible vantage point. As if in one voice, the entire throng gasped in wonder as the revelation of the lights actually being boats of crystal, powered by some deep magic, made its way through the ranks all the way to the farthest reaches of the castle.

As Leonolis watched, he and Maison were escorted down the steps, through the castle gates, and down the road all the way to the harbor. Now he felt himself lifting from his perch on the castle wall and floating above his own head all the way to the docks where the king and his entourage were met by seven brilliant, glowing vessels of light, each displaying large, white flags of surrender and peace from their bows.

As the lead vessel came to a stop next to the dock, a crystalline gangway came to rest on the dock near the king. Almost too brilliant to gaze at for very long, the light began to subside a bit as a tall, stately figure emerged from the light and made its way across the crystal plank.

A tall man walked smoothly and confidently and stood before the king. At least six feet and seven inches tall, the man was dressed from shoulder to foot in a robe of white almost as brilliant as the crystalline vessels. His hair was equally white, long, and flowing, and appeared to be in constant motion—as if the hair itself was full of life! The "watching" Leonolis remembered the awe and wonder he felt when he first met him.

"Good king Leonolis. I bring you greetings from the good and fair people of Scavengia. I am he who is called Scathian, emissary of King Subsidium, lord of the realm of Scavengia. We are come in peace in order to reestablish the ancient unity between our peoples," said Scathian. "We come in peace and desire to bring honor to you and your fair people. Our mission, as it were, is to not only bring about the reestablishment of old relationships but to seek out the wisdom of the world from the various lands and peoples we encounter on our sojourns to do so. In your land, we would be known as masters of the scientific arts. In our land we are known as seekers."

Being the gracious man his father had taught him to be, yet shooting a nuanced glance of wariness toward Maison who nodded ever so slightly in the manner that says, *"I am cautious, too, sire,"* Leonolis replied, "Welcome Scathian, seeker of Scavengia. On behalf of the people of Bren, we welcome you and your fellow sojourners."

Without missing a beat, the now-curious Maison chimed in, "Forgive my boldness, sire, but I must ask, sir Scathian . . . by what magic are your boats propelled? I see no sails nor do I see oars. And by what means do they come to be illuminated? I see no fire nor do I see any other means by which such a light may appear apart from pure magic?"

"Dear lord Scathian, pardon my curious friend. May I introduce to you my childhood tutor who is now trusted friend and advisor to the throne, Lord Maison," Leonolis butted in.

Laughing politely yet with a tinge of impatience, Scathian responded, "It is quite all right, King Leonolis. I understand the little man's curiousity." And turning toward Maison (who was now seething and turning red at being so publicly put down), Scathian said, "In due time, little man. In due time."

As Maison stepped toward the man of Scavengia, Leonolis wisely interceded and stepped between the two, declaring, "In our culture, stature is not determined by physical height but rather by character of heart, Lord Scathian. You have insulted one of the giants of Bren and I would be remiss to not correct your speech, no matter how unintended your insult may have been."

Coughing at the sudden awkwardness he had just caused, Scathian, sputtered to hurriedly interject. "I assure you, my lord, no such insult was intended, and I thank you for bringing the needed clarity. This is obviously a simple difference in culture and communication," said Scathian. Turning toward Maison, he bowed humbly and continued. "Dear lord, a great man of Bren, sir Maison, please forgive my insult. I regret my choice of words."

Being mature and wise (yet still visibly agitated), Maison controlled himself and stretched out his hand toward Scathian who humbly took the hand of the king's advisor. "You are forgiven, sir Scathian."

With that, the king commanded the royal harbormaster to secure the Scavengian vessels. Greeting each of the passengers personally, Leonolis greeted the men of Scavengia warmly and sent servants ahead to prepare the royal guest chambers. That night, the king and his guests met in the royal meeting hall for a feast of the bounty of Bren. Afterwards, the king and his advisors met with the men of Scavengia. It was decided that Maison would act as liaison between Scathian and Leonolis and that Maison would introduce the seekers to the scholars and scientists of Bren and secure any meetings with the various Givers of Wisdom the seekers might inquire of.

The next day, what seemed to be on the forefront of every scientific thinker of Bren was just how the Scavengian boats were powered. Of course, Maison led the barrage of questions himself, speaking on behalf of all of Bren's Givers of Wisdom.

"Lord Scathian, before we delve into the wisdom of Bren, our own curiosity has gotten the better of us. The scholars of Bren, in one voice, request the knowledge of the crystal boats," said the curious Maison as patiently as he could hurriedly express! This seemed odd to Maison—that they all rose spontaneously without one word being spoken—but he gave it no further thought as curiosity once again overruled caution.

Without saying a word, the entire entourage of Scavengians rose and followed Scathian toward the harbor. The scientific minds of Bren rose and followed, whispering and tittering like excited schoolboys about to hear about sex for the first time!

As they approached the lead vessel, Scathian stopped and turned to face the men of Bren. "My wise brethren, this is the vessel *Carina*, the very first vessel formed from the crystal of our land. She has been in service to our people for three hundred years."

The hushed excitement coming from the men of Bren was palpable at these words, inducing an unintelligible barrage of questions from the crowd of scientists.

Standing on a nearby stack of wooden shipping crates, Maison motioned to the men of Bren to calm down. Trying to hide his own glee, the nearly giggling sage held out his hands as he began to speak. "Dear friends, in due time! In due time, all our questions will be answered. Let us control our mirth and allow our friend to speak as he will."

"Thank you, Lord Maison," said Scathian. "This may come as a surprise to you, but your own land contains a deposit of the very crystal these boats are constructed of."

As the entire Brenolinian contingency gasped as one, Scathian laughed and went on.

"You should be excited, my scholarly brethren! You should be, for you see before you vessels composed of pure Phrygian Crystal such as fills your own Crystal Cave!"

Now the crowd was absolutely out of control with excitement. The thoughts of what this would mean to the people of Bren, from the realms of transportation and trade to national security to everyday use by ordinary citizenry, raced through each and every Brenolinian head!

"How is it harvested?" shouted a voice from the crowd.

"How is it formed into a vessel?" cried another.

"How is it propelled?" yelled still another.

"Allow me to explain. I anticipated your curiosity and am prepared to answer every question, my friends. The material is mined as any other mineral and actually, as you already know from the Brenolinian custom of lighting your homes with small Phrygian Crystals, the ore tends to break into small pieces when struck with a hammer and chisel. But we have discovered that it can be broken into various shapes and sizes if we simply use a small, sharpened piece of Phrygian Crystal to draw an outline on a large mass of ore and then, rather than chiseling the material, we use sound waves produced by striking a bell tuned to the tone of D flat next to the outlined area until it literally falls away in one piece into the waiting hands of our miners."

"Incredible!" spoke Maison. "And how do you form the pieces into the shape of a seagoing vessel?"

"Again, we have discovered that if we place two given pieces of ore together then strike a bell tuned to the tone of A flat while simultaneously striking the bell tuned to D flat that the materials fuse together instantaneously," answered Scathian.

"And how is it propelled?" asked the inquisitive Maison.

"This requires much skill and meditation," responded Scathian. "Purely by accident, we made the discovery that pure thought can set the crystal in motion. One cannot simply think the word 'move' and the boat will begin to progress. Very specific thoughts must be incorporated or the vessel becomes so set in place that an army of the strongest horses cannot force it to stir. Only virtuous thought will induce motion, and more specifically, one must clear one's mind completely of any thought other than pure light. To have thoughts of doubt or fear or anger or disappointment or frustration or pain or even discomfort will cause the boat to be cemented, as it were, in place."

Allowing the crowd to take in his words and meditate on their meaning for a few moments, Scathian continued. "For this reason, our vessels are manned by priests of our realm. You would call them eunuchs here, but we refer to them as *devotatis*—the dedicated ones. Their duties as priests of the Scavengian naval and exploratory armada is one of pure mental devotion. May we demonstrate?"

Once again, the entire Scavengian entourage moved as one onto the *Carina*. Scathian motioned the entire Brenolinian throng to join them on the deck. Once there, the pilot walked up the glass-like stairs to the stern castle and seated himself at the helm. The helm was nothing more than a raised pillar that came to chest height of the seated pilot. As deck hands simultaneously released the mooring ropes, the pilot placed his hands, palm down, on the surface of the pillar and appeared to go into an instant state of trance. In the smoothest of motion, the large crystal vessel magically began to move sideways, an impossible movement of conventional sailing vessels, but not for the *Carina*!

In astonishment, the scientific minds of Bren stood in utter silent amazement as the ship then launched into the harbor, heading due south toward the open Sea of Aragon. Even the largest sailed vessels of Bren could not match this unimaginable speed at which they found themselves now propelled. As the initial wonder began to give way to sheer adventure, the men of Bren all made their way to the ships sides and faced into the wind, shouting in glee as they laughed at the incredible power and speed of the vessel, each one wondering how quickly the Crystal Caves could be mined for Brenolinian versions of the *Carina*.

In what would have normally taken several hours in even the swiftest vessel of Bren, they accomplished in a matter of one, sailing from the harbor of Castle Aerie to the Pinnacles of Bren (a rocky outcropping of granite that protruded from the ocean floor in a series of seven spires, the highest reaching to a height of seven hundred feet) that lay forty-five miles seaward from Castle Aerie! Going around the pinnacles, the pilot then turned the *Carina* back toward Bren. Even though a headwind pushed against the bow, the crystal ship did not seem to be slowed in any fashion. As they headed into a sudden thunderstorm, the waves began to grow and the rain began to fall and the lightning began to pierce the darkened midday sky, but the ship did not seem unduly affected or tossed by the waves, able to maintain optimum balance. The men of Bren were rendered speechless as they soon realized that even the rain was not touching them!

"What magic keeps the rain from us?" shouted the dazed Maison.

"See the devotatis stationed around the boat?" answered Scathian. "When faced with rough seas or with sudden rain or snow or weather of any kind, the priests join their minds as one and, using the power of the Phrygian Crystal, producing an oculus or dome in your vernacular, over the entire vessel. You will notice the rain streaming all around us as the power of thought coupled with the power of the crystal produces a protective barrier. This also serves us well against enemy arrows and missiles of the catapult."

Soon the vessel made its way through the storm and into sunny skies. As soon as the rain stopped, the devotatis stepped away from the railings of the *Carina* and made their way to the center of the main deck where they stood motionless for the remainder of the demonstration.

Leonolis had not gone on the trip when it had first occurred all those years ago, so to see it now made all the stories of wonder brought back to him by Maison and others all the more vivid and awe-inspiring, even knowing what he knew about the schemes of the Scavengians now.

Chapter Six

A SUBTLE MAGIC

In the days following, the Scavengians were shown unheard of freedom in researching the libraries and scientific discoveries of Bren. Leonolis remembered how he had been so overwhelmed with the positive feedback from his many trusted advisors—the skeptical Maison included—that he had granted special privileges to the Scavengians, even sending them throughout the land to conduct research. In each village the visitors spent time, a strange thing had begun to occur. Even then, Leonolis had been so seduced by the clever talk and mind games of the Scavengians that he had not noticed the subtle changes to Bren culture and attitude.

Breaking the long silence, the Voice spoke to Leonolis as he observed the events leading to the death of good Maison. "Leonolis, do you remember what you now see?"

Slightly embarrassedly, thinking about how even he had been deceived, he replied a simple, "Yes."

"Once a seed of evil has been planted, it is necessary to get to the root. Otherwise, the weed will sprout and grow another day. The removal of the root is always painful for the good plants as well, having entangled its tentacles with the life-giving roots of the good plants. To rip away the bad, sometimes the good is torn in the process," said the Voice.

"Yes, my lord. This I know now all too well," the king said humbly.

Silence engulfed the king and the Voice as Leonolis was transported to a time he would rather forget. In the months following the arrival of the seekers, Bren culture began to be transformed. As the Crystal Caves were opened to mining of the Phrygian Crystal, industry boomed. It had taken only seven weeks for the first crystal boat to be constructed for the Brenolinian navy. During the construction period, a dozen scholar seers of Bren trained with the devotatis of Scavengia in the arts of meditation, honing their crystal boat piloting skills. Christened the *Primoris*, the vessel was launched to much fanfare and approval. Once word made its way to the surrounding nations, the already highly regarded Brenolinians attained an even loftier esteem throughout the neighboring realms, which only enhanced trade relations and sufficiently affected Bren society to such a degree that the entire citizenry seemed to hang on every word of the Scavengian scholars, especially those of Scathian.

In a whirlwind of images, the Voice silently guided Leonolis into varying scenarios he had not been privy to when they had first occurred. Though he had come to know of all the subtleties with which the Scavengians had turned the hearts of Bren away from the throne, and away from long-held Brenolinian norms and beliefs, he now heard in heartbreaking detail too many to place in these writings. Things like . . .

"Why do the men of Bren not pay more heed to the women of Bren? Why should it always be the men of Bren to lead? In our land, the Scavengian women are given equal standing with our men . . . even more so when it comes to the ways of national security and commerce," said the Scavengian scholar Waymus to the leadership of the town of Bredenton, "while here it appears that men rule over all other citizens, unchallenged. We would never allow such unenlightened thinking to stand in the way of scientific progress."

Even though in the culture of Bren women were seen as equal to men in value, it was a long-standing tradition that each gender operated in roles handed down from the Founders. While men generally went about protecting the land, there were times when the smooth-skinned women of Bren had fought right along side the hairy-chested men of Bren. While women generally did most of the nurturing of children, the men did their part to nurture from a masculine perspective, taking great pains to train their sons and daughters according to the natural abilities each child demonstrated. While the men generally worked the farms and livestock, the women worked in harmony with the men doing the jobs that complemented the work of the men and vice versa. The gender differences were quite celebrated in Bren and seen as complementary of one another and not opposed to one another. But the seekers had brought their enlightened perspective into the mix and, due to the esteem their scientific thought granted them in the eyes of the men and women of Bren, they were able to subtly twist the truth to look like something less than it was.

In the public courtyard of Castle Aerie, the Scavengian scholar Diversus one day gave a discourse on how Scavengian society had been freed of long-held societal oppression by dissolving all marriages in the land. "What is the purpose of marriage but to keep women in bondage and limit freedom? Why so many limitations in such an advanced culture as Bren?"

As he listened anew to that point of view, he was repulsed at how he had allowed such subversive thought to go unchallenged when he had first heard of it. He had wrongfully assumed that the people of Bren would naturally see how much damage to the foundation of Brenolinian culture and life such thought and practice would produce, and he assumed they would reject such notions outright as foolishness. It was as if the "logic" of the Scavengians had been infused with some deep, dark magic. The effect on society had been quick, resulting in more discord among the populace than anyone could ever remember. Marriages were suddenly strained in Bren, a land long known for its strong marital unions.

Next he found himself listening in on a classroom lecture at the local public school for the young men and women of Bren. Since Bren was a mostly agrarian society, the children only went to school one day per week, year round, as had been the practice for generations. This served the nation well, providing a young and energetic workforce for family farms but also served to make for a very high-achieving scholastic system. Since the students had one day per week to learn from the scholars, the education of Bren's young people was among the finest systems in the realm. Young people yearned to learn the history and ways of Bren. They were instructed by the finest among Bren's scholars. And since they only had one day per week to accomplish this learning, the students tended to be very self-motivated and focused on achieving great knowledge for the good of all Bren.

Excellence was expected of all students. Brenolinian school was required from age six until age twelve. After that, each child was welcomed into either manhood or womanhood and expected to become a law-abiding, productive citizen of the realm. In Bren, education was considered a part of living life even after the perfunctory years of schooling had been accomplished. It was well known throughout the land that true wisdom and practical knowledge only enhanced scientific discovery. Much more was accomplished with this system than neighboring kingdoms that required three and four days of instruction per week.

As he listened to the classroom instruction, Leonolis was suddenly lifted from this scene and transported to an area near Council Hill. As the large gathering of young people came into view, Leonolis remembered. The Scavengians had arranged for an all-day gathering of young people as a means of celebrating Bren youth culture and to lecture the young people in the ways of Scavengian philosophy and thought processes. What took place was nothing short of a complete undermining of Bren authority—especially parental authority. Again, the Voice said to the king, "Listen."

Scathian himself ended the gathering with these words.

"O sons and daughters of Bren. What richness you carry in your heritage. How grand is your history. But did you realize there is more to the world than what you see in Bren? What we have demonstrated to you over the past few months during our stay in your land has been, we hope, enlightening. Whether your elders realize it or not, they have kept youth culture in Bren from depths of self-discovery through the vast and lengthy record of Bren history and culture. But are you not tired of this caging in of your ideas and feelings? Are you not desirous to explore the far reaches of your abilities that your own culture all too often, I'm afraid, limits you to what you've seen for generations now? Are you not tired of going over the same old traditions year after year and coming to the same old results year after year?"

As Leonolis watched, his anger rose. How dare this "wise" man so unwisely undermine the ways of Bren. But there was nothing he could do. The damage had been done all those years ago and for some reason, the Voice wanted him to relive this moment.

Going on, Scathian began to stir the minds of the young people further. "In our culture, the ideas and thoughts of young minds are sought out often and given a position of prominence. What is keeping you from this same freedom of thought and expression? What is hindering your own intellectual prominence?"

Growing facetious in tone, Scathian continued. "Could it be the old ways—the traditions? Could it be, dare I say, your parents lording their 'authority' over you, keeping you from exploring what I am sure your Founders truly desire . . . real freedom and real progressive thinking."

By now the young people had been stirred into a frenzy, agreeing loudly now with each statement hurled at them by Scathian. Leonlolis could now see the glint of pride and glee at the clever way his scheme for the minds of the youth of Bren was working. All Leonolis could think of now was how much more valuable the ways and traditions of Bren seemed. How he wished he could have actually been there when this gathering had first taken place in order to counterbalance the words of Scathian. He would have reminded the young people that Bren society indeed had structure and proudly celebrated long-standing traditions— he would have given example after example of just how rich they were and how free they were because of the structure and tradition. Of how that very structure gave the youth of Bren unheard of freedom to create and explore in the safety of those very things Scathian now ridiculed as hindrances!

"What stands in your way?" shouted Scathian.

"Tradition!" replied the throng of teenagers.

"What keeps you from freedom of thought and deed?" shouted Scathian.

"Parents! Rules!" returned the mob.

"Rebellion is good, my young friends. The only thing standing between you and freedom from such grave oppression is no longer your traditions! No longer your parents! No longer the rules and regulations! No, what stands in your way is you! What will you do about it?"

In one voice, the young people shouted over and over again, "We rise! We rule! We break the chains this day! We rise! We rule! We break the chains this day!"

Even as the shouting continued and the young people began to dance around, spinning in frenzied chaos, the Voice led Leonolis to the side of the platform to where Scathian was now standing with several of his assistants. "This way, King."

Leonolis listened as Scathian laughed a scoffing laugh as he spoke to his men. "I told you this would be easy. With the priests casting their mind-magic upon these foolish children it was a simple matter of planting the seeds of doubt and rebellion. Now the headstrong ways of youth will be unfettered by the magic of the Mensian Incantation."

It was that very day that rebellion had broken out among young people all over the realm. Homes were in chaos. Marriages were in shambles. Children in rebellion. Public discourse, once a proud and peaceful tradition, was now anything but peaceful. Friends were at odds with one another over trivial matters. Workers were suddenly doing their work half-heartedly. Commerce began to crumble. Factions began to form demanding their rights from the high king.

Leonolis remembered it all too well as the Voice once again took him to another scenario being played out. In the library of Castle Aerie, a group of Scavengians were holding a secret meeting. Scathian, in hushed tones, addressed the group.

"Are we alone?" asked Scathian.

Nodding in approval, the Scavengian guarding the door bade the man to continue.

"We should be safe to speak here," he went on. "They expect that we are simply conducting research among their historic and scientific volumes. Let me get right to the point. All plans are coming together as expected. Rebellion, whether physical or mental, is already making its way through the ranks of the citizenry. Even now, the Crown is weakened to the point of needing our assistance. Soon, I will call for a meeting with King Leonolis. At that time I will encourage him to allow our help in bringing civility back to the realm and, in the process, lay the groundwork for a peaceful transfer of power. Even if we are not granted full control, it will only be a matter of time before our full help will be required and requested by Leonolis himself."

At those words, the Scavengians began to murmur agreement as a spirit of glee emanated from their very countenances. Perched above the gathering, Leonolis sensed a stirring behind the books on the highest reaches of the wall. Peering behind the volumes, the king saw a figure crouched on hands and knees in the small secret grotto behind the top shelf that he and his siblings had discovered as children. Many were the days spent exploring these secret passageways. It had actually been good Maison who had shown him the vast extent of these corridors as a young man.

As Leonolis took a closer look at the hidden figure, he was taken aback. Crouched like a church mouse in fear of being caught by the cat, was Maison himself! The crafty old tutor had been doing his own research in the room when the group had come in. It had been several moments before he had realized he was not alone due to his concentration on the volume he had been gleaning from—and once he realized that the group was up to no good, he had determined to remain unnoticed in order to hear the evil plans of Scathian and his Scavengian peers.

Again, Scathian began to speak. "The final blow will come when the king makes his annual public proclamation at the Blood Moon Festival on the day after tomorrow. His death will be swift and be seen as an accident—and we will be there to bring about justice and to bring peace to the realm. And, O yes—to take the reins of power from such a foolish ruler."

As soon as the group had scurried from the library, Maison made his way through the small tunnel leading from the library to the main system of hidden passageways in the upper reaches of the castle. As he intently scrambled from one level to the next, Leonolis and the Voice (silent but felt in presence) made their way right along with him. Reaching a small doorway, the wise old man stumbled hurriedly out of the passage and tripped uncharacteristically into the curtains directly behind the throne of the king, so flustered was he.

As Leonolis and the Voice made their way around to face the throne, he saw himself seated there as the royal guards Maison had startled helped the frightened tutor up, bringing him around to face the king. Standing around the throne room was the entire advisory counsel to the king. Leonolis remembered it well, but now saw and heard everything from a new perspective.

"Dear king! My lord, Leonolis! We must act at once!" said Maison between pants to catch his breath.

"Slow down, friend! Slow down!" laughed the king. "What has my wise friend so discombobulated that he now sputters and spits before us? And why are you late to our counsel meeting? We need your input to finalize the Blood Moon Festival festivities!"

"No, my king! No! We must take action at once! Even now, the Scavengians plot your demise and the overthrow of all we call Bren!" said the short, old man.

Stepping from the shadows, Scathian joined the discussion. "How dare you accuse our peaceful delegation of any such thing!"

Turning to the king, Scathian continued. "Sire, some deep, dark disturbing magic is surely at work here . . . or perhaps a bit too much tasting of the festival wine has taken place, but this is pure nonsense," he said with a slight laugh in his voice.

"Maison, say your heart," said the king.

"Even now I have come from a gathering in the royal library in which I overheard Scathian himself discuss plans for your death and our overthrow! Not five minutes ago have I heard such come from his own lips," said Maison, pointing directly at Scathian.

Looking at his friend oddly now, the king rose from the throne and knelt down to face his dear friend. "My good Maison, for the past thirty minutes, Scathian and his entire scholarly entourage have been taking part in this meeting, desirous to learn of the nature of the Blood Moon Festival. (The Blood Moon Festival came about as a commemoration of a major Brenolinian victory over the marauders from Hemagenia—the Hemagens or People of the Blood, as they are known. Leonolis himself was the hero of this victory when he was only eighteen years old!). They were with me five minutes ago. There could have been no such meeting."

"But sire! Some great magic is at work here! You are deceived!" shouted Maison.

Only Maison could have gotten away with such a direct accusation of the king. But it did not deter Leonolis, knowing that he could trust Maison completely. Watching himself interact with Maison now, he could see the subtleties of the Scavengian magic at work. With this new perspective, watching-Leonolis could now see the face of Scathian as he cut his eyes toward his personal wizard, Sauros, whom Leonolis could now see was focusing his eyes intently on the watched-Leonolis. It was obvious that Sauros was using his mind to befog the mind of the king—to befuddle the mind of the entire Brenolinian throng. If only that Leonolis had been able to see that day what he saw now, things might have turned out differently. But that was not to be. Tragic is the only word to describe what transpired from this point.

In that moment, as if on cue, the entire delegation of Bren's wisest men began to call for the silence of Maison.

"How dare you defy the high king!" shouted one.

"Silence, small fool!" screamed another.

"Sire, he is clearly gone mad!" interjected still another.

Maison could hardly believe what was unfolding before him—and, in shame, the watching-Leonolis could not believe he had been so foolish in that moment as to fall for the Scavengian mind games. Yet, he had.

As if years worth of friendship and trust were suddenly shattered, the watched-Leonolis reeled back appalled at the words of his friend.

"Maison, you defy me?" said the king in sorrow.

"Dear Leonolis, I defy the magic that now clouds your mind—the magic that, indeed, clouds all of your minds. The Scavengians have been plotting our overthrow since before they arrived. Everything that has transpired—the trust they have gained, the access they have been afforded, and yes, the chaos that has slowly crept into our very core as people of Bren—has all been part of their dark plan. Sire, bind them at once or face the consequences!" pled the small, wise man.

"Maison, I am brokenhearted and embarrassed at your behavior," replied the king. "You are clearly not in control of your faculties! As I have already pointed out, the entire Scavengian entourage has been with me for the past thirty minutes and could not possibly have met in the library, as you say, 'not five minutes ago'! You have left me no recourse but to secure you to the infirmary for medical attention."

Turning to Scathian, Leonolis said, "Dear friends of Scavengia, please forgive my advisor's outburst. He is evidently under more strain than I had knowledge of. We will see to it that such an affront to you and your people does not occur again."

"King, we are highly offended at such an accusation and would request that this man, Maison, be secured from further interaction from us. Who knows what harm may befall our peaceful delegation should such a man of great wisdom and powerful magic lose his ability to reason clearly," responded Scathian.

"I assure you. He will be dealt with and you have nothing to fear. I will instruct my guardsmen to place him under house arrest and relegate him to his chamber until we are assured all is well," replied Leonolis.

With that, the Scavengians turned and left the throne room, making their way directly back to the library for "further study." The watching-Leonolis walked along behind as the Voice urged him to "follow."

Entering the library, the door was closed after the last Scavengian scholar had entered. Giggles and snickers began to rise from the men as if they had just performed the greatest ruse in history. "Who would have believed it could have been so easy?" asked Scathian. "Sauros, your magical skills are magnificent. Conjuring up our presence in the throne room while actually meeting here was a stroke of sheer and utter genius, my brother! And then to bend the thoughts of the very king and, indeed, his entire phalanx to our way of thinking! Brilliant! Brilliant!"

Speaking now to the Voice, watching-Leonolis asked, "Why did I not see it that day? Why did I not know?"

"You had allowed the seed to be planted and did nothing to pluck it out. Your own selfishness and pride kept you from responding like the king you are. More concerned for being seen as tolerant and open-minded than for what was actually best for your people allowed the seed to take root. The magic used was of minimal power, but the power was in the fact that you bought into the lie from the outset."

Leonolis knew the Voice was right in all he said. After all, he had lived with this reality for many years now.

"Do we need to go on?" asked the king. The Voice was silent. "I do not know if I can face these times again, sir."

They began to move as the Voice broke the silence. "Face again, you must. I waste nothing, Lee. I waste nothing, Leonolis."

Leonolis considered asking why the Voice had misspoken and called him "Lee" but considered that of little importance now. They soon came to rest in the chamber of Maison who was quietly sobbing, distraught and dismayed at the course of events. As Leonolis looked more closely, he sensed an air of deep confusion in his friend.

"Why has my liege turned from me?" cried the miserable Maison. "What deep magic could do such a thing to such a noble man? Have I not myself trained him in the art of recognition—the ability to discern truth from lies, good from evil? Why is this happening, O great Founders? Why would Leonolis even remotely believe I might not be telling the truth?"

As the faithful Maison continued to ponder his predicament out loud, a physician came and attempted to administer a calming agent, but Maison refused the potion, causing the physician to respond in anger.

"Guards, this man, in his belligerence, is hindering me from carrying out the king's orders! Bind him!"

Turning to the physician, Maison pleaded, "My dear Iatros! Why do you bind me? It is I, your friend of friends, Maison—the one who himself has trained you in the arts of apothecary and healing!"

"Quiet, old man! You have contracted some deep sickness or some dark magic. I only attempt to care for you. Do not struggle, sir," said Iatros firmly.

"Do you not see, friend? The same magic that has been wrought upon the mind of the king now besets you! Do not bind me!" cried Maison.

As the guards held him down and bound him to the bed, Iatros forced open his mouth and forced him to drink the potion. Almost instantly Maison went limp. Once the physician and guards were sure he was fully subdued, they unbound the hands and feet of Maison, placed his unmoving body on a stretcher, and proceeded to carry him to a cell that had been prepared for him—in the dungeon!

Chapter Seven

NOTHING WASTED

Watching-Leonolis remembered the day he felt compelled to place his friend in that cell. In that day he had honestly felt that doing so was what was best for Maison and, ultimately, best for the realm. In hindsight, Leonolis knew better. What he was about to learn was that in Bren—by the hand of the Founders—nothing is ever wasted when seen from the proper point of view—even a tragic loss like the death of a dear friend.

As Leonolis and the Voice watched Maison for a few minutes, he lay motionless. And just as Leonolis was about to ask the Voice what they were waiting for, Maison suddenly and miraculously sat upright, seemingly unfazed by the potion that was administered only a few minutes before! Mumbling to himself, Maison said aloud, "Magic of Scavengia holds nothing to the magic of Bren! Fie on them all!" This caused Leonolis to smile to himself, knowing he was now seeing the fully aware, fully himself, Maison. The potion had absolutely no effect on him, having obviously prepared for such a possibility, he had wisely cast a spell to counter the power of the potion!

Standing up now, he sidled ever so quietly to the cell door, taking stock of the guards (there were two) and their positions (one was several yards away at the head of the cellblock while the other was a mere few feet away. As quietly as possible, the small man began to whisper:

O, Founders, hear my feeble plea
And send a power deep
A slumber comes to set me free
O, send these souls to sleep

No sooner had he uttered the word "sleep" than the two guards began to yawn and stretch their arms as if they had just finished a day's long march and now needed a long, long rest. Lying down on the spot where they had been standing, both guards fell into a deep, deep slumber. Again, Maison began to utter another incantation.

By the Founders, see my need
Ageless power increase
Chains and bars and bonds impede
Break this bond, release

And with that, a wisp of smoke came from the lock, wafting out and up from the keyhole, as the door silently swayed open. Cautiously, the little man peered out into the corridor of the dungeon. No other guards seemed to be stirring and there were no other prisoners in this section of the prison since all had been cleared to keep Maison from inspiring thoughts of escape in the minds of others held there (this had come on advisory from the Scavengians). Making his way down the hallway as stealthily as a short, stocky man in full robes can go, Maison approached the main doorway. Repeating the same spell he used to open his cell, he entered the main passageway into the dungeon. Before proceeding, he quietly cast another spell.

Let all now sleep who stand in dark
Who serve the hidden spell
And all awake, the Bren in heart
To serve the Founders well

With that, every prisoner in the dungeon who had fallen under the Scavengian spell now fell asleep in their cells. As Maison passed each cell containing a conscious soul, he summoned them to follow him without saying a word. The look in his eye told the tale—that this was a day of most serious concern for Bren and its people. Like Maison, these men and women now walking from their suddenly opened prison cells had been imprisoned at the request of Scathian due to their vocal opposition to the "progressive thinking" of the Scavengians.

Watching-Leonolis did not say a word to the Voice. He knew the Voice understood his shame and was allowing him to relive it for some reason. As they watched, Maison and his small band of escapees now made their way to the end of the main dungeon corridor, which appeared to be a dead end (unless you have magical powers!). Waving his hand in a left-to-right motion, the wall suddenly revealed a doorway concealed within the stone masonry of the structure. With the slightest touch, little Maison opened the door and beckoned his followers to enter. Once all were passed through, the door magically closed behind them. Of course, Leonolis and the Voice had gone in with them.

A long-forgotten armory, the room was dark and dank, long-abandoned as newer and better accommodations had become available through the years. It now served as the perfect place for Maison to end his silence. Turning to his small entourage, he spoke.

"How many are we?" he asked.

Quickly, the castle blacksmith, Urston, being a man concerned with meticulous detail due to his profession, said, "Seven, my lord. Eight counting you."

"What skills are we?" asked Maison.

"I am a groundsman," remarked Verden.

"And I am a maidservant of the queen," said Corrinne.

"A keeper of the royal bee hives," said Honeyman.

"I am Piscal, fisherman of Arabon."

"Herdstress of the royal flocks of the Callay region," said Ovinnia.

"And I am head quarryman of the Crystal Cave," said Mason.

"What is going on, Lord Maison? Why has good king Leonolis turned his back upon us?" asked Urston with the others in nonverbal agreement.

Without hesitation and with a tinge of anger at the accusation, Maison looked up directly into the eyes of Urston and, pointing his chubby finger at Urston's nose, said, "He has not turned his back on us! Our king would never do such a thing intentionally."

"But this day, just before I myself was cast into the dungeon, our king betrayed you!" chimed in Corrinne. "Though he may have publicly defended you, who do you think gave the ultimate order to have you placed in the dungeon rather than in the royal infirmary? As I protested your treatment, (having been sent to tend to your needs by Queen Abila herself), the king himself commanded I join you in bond since I 'so willfully chose to defend a rebel.' He called you a rebel, good Maison!"

Watching-Leonolis could see the look of dismay and sorrow as it swept the face of trusty Maison. After a few moments, Maison seemed to shake loose from the bonds of this obvious betrayal. "It is obvious. Our king has been bewitched by some subtle magic at the hand of the Scavengians. Regardless of the reason, this was not the response of the heart of Leonolis. He I have known since he was a child. He have I walked through every step of training and every step of his reign. His is not the heart of one who would betray. His heart is for Bren. His heart *is* Bren. This is why we must devise a way to free him—to free Bren."

Watching-Leonolis found himself wiping tears from his bearded cheeks. Although he had been under a spell, the magic of Bren that had normally been a hindrance to any spell had been weakened by the king's acceptance of the Scavengian thought that he himself had allowed to permeate Brenolinian society, allowing the spell a place to light in the heart and mind of the king. In shame he wept, but mostly he wept at the deep faithfulness and devotion now displayed to him by his friend Maison. This only made what the king knew was coming all the more painful this second time.

Taking stock of the skills at his disposal, Maison began to pace back and forth before the now silent group. None had dared speak ill of the king to little Maison after his passionate defense of their king. After a few moments, he spoke.

"With magic I can get us through the castle and outside its confines. Once there, we have no time to waste. Our king's life is to be taken at the hand of the Scavengians as he makes his public appearance at the Blood Moon Festival. We must go at once. I must rely on each of you to do the task I assign without the aid of magic. Let passion and love for our king carry you to see it through. Once we are outside the walls, each of you must make haste."

Turning to Urston, he began. "Urston, we will pass through the royal armory as we make our way from this place. Each of us will carry as many weapons as we can each hold. Once outside, we will put them in a hidden place. You will stand guard over the cache and will place a weapon in the hand of each man sent to you as we gather the men and women of Bren to defend our king and our land.

"Verden, you are keeper of the grounds. As such, you have built and maintained an alliance with the Treesants. Go to them and tell them of our need for assistance. Speak with Lord Sylvan and tell him it is Maison who has need of his service.

"Corrinne, as maidservant of the queen, you have the respect of the women of Bren. Rally them. Go to the nearest villages and to the market places where women gather. Tell them Maison has need of their service to king and country. Their children are in rebellion. You will have their hearts. Encourage them to send representatives to the villages beyond, and likewise once they have done so, encourage them to be at the king's oration at the onset of the Blood Moon Festival. Once there, they can help break the Scavengian spell by their devotion to king and land. Tell them 'a mother's love conquers all.' They will rally behind you.

"Honeyman, summon the beekeepers of the land. Have them bring their wares—vats of the honey of Bren—along with one hive per man. We have need of the sweetness and need of the sting.

"Piscal, summon the nets of Bren. Tell them of our need and that they should station themselves at the vessels of Scavengia. I will send word as to what they are to do once there. The remainder, station them around the upper walls of the Castle Aerie. They will hear from me once they have established their positions."

Lowering herself to be face to face with Maison, Ovinnia awaited her assignment. "Ovinnia, you know the highways and byways apart from the major land routes. The major routes will surely be guarded. Get word to the furthest regions of the land of our need for all the people of Bren to convene at Castle Aerie at the oration of King Leonolis as he begins the Blood Moon Festival.

"Mason, have you worked with the construction of the Primoris?"

"Yes, my lord. I oversaw the mining of the specific stones used in its construct," said the quarryman.

"Can you get to the bells used in the excavation and shaping process?" asked Maison.

"Yes, of course."

"Bring the bells to the harbor by the onset of the Blood Moon Festival."

And with those final instructions, Maison led them through the secret passges behind the castle walls, taking them to the royal armory. Casting a spell of silence over the clanging-metal-laden warriors, they then made their way outside of the castle walls to an area just below Council Hill. Behind an outcropping of boulders and concealed by the undergrowth of wild heather, Maison led the troop to a small cavern embedded in the side of the hill. There, they deposited their loads of arms and each headed quietly to their assigned tasks.

As soon as all had departed, Maison headed back to the castle. As watching-Leonolis and the Voice followed, Maison made his way through nooks and crannies even Leonolis had no knowledge of. From level to level, the magician made his way to the bedchamber of Leonolis and Abila. By this time, it was the eve before the Blood Moon Festival and the royal couple had just settled in for the night. Maison hid himself in the corner as he tried to decide whether to reveal himself to the king and queen. As he pondered his decision, the couple began to talk.

"Dear husband, how long will you keep our dear friend and your trusted advisor, Maison, in contempt?" asked Abila.

In a manner normally out of character for the king, Leonolis addressed his queen curtly. "I will not abide insubordination! You know that I cannot if I am to continue to lead with any authority," responded the king.

"But this has never been your heart. Your father taught you better. And of all the men of Bren, both great and small, there is none more faithful to you than Maison," said the queen.

"And that is exactly why I must address the issue at hand! If even those most trusted feel they can publicly bring affront to my position and I do nothing to counter that affront, then I lose position. I lose power!" said the king almost childishly.

"What has happened, husband? Why do you respond in anger to me? Surely you are not yourself. Surely the Scavengians bring more than their philosophy and science to bear in our land," said Abila.

"How dare you defy me! Is it not enough that my closest advisor rise up against me? And now you rebel! And leave the good name of Scavengian untarnished. They only desire alliance and only desire to bring progress and prosperity to our land," said the very defiant Leonolis.

"But at what cost?" retorted the queen.

"Go to sleep, woman!" demanded the king.

"Or what?" replied Abila. "You'll cast me in with Maison?"

Sitting up in bed, the king glared at the queen. Watching-Leonolis was beside himself with grief at the way he saw himself treating his faithful wife—the mother of his nine children. In all the world, there was none more faithful, none more dedicated, none more loyal and servant-hearted toward Leonolis than Abila. None more loving and willing to die for him. After all, it was she who had laid down her very gift from the Founders to spend her life with Leonolis. That saga is told throughout Bren to this day and is known in legend as The Saga of Leonolis the Dragon Slayer.

"I've seen enough," wept the watching king.

"No. There is much that you have not seen. More to your success and reign than you have known. What you witness now will serve you well in the days to come. What now reaches you from the past will serve to strengthen you for the days ahead. There is a weed that has sprouted in you, son of Bren—and we must get to the root," said the solemn Voice.

Leonolis—the watching-Leonolis—was stunned at the words of the Voice. He had been brought to shame as he watched his treatment of Maison and Abila, but now his perspective had once again changed. His view until now had been of the ways others had brought about his success (and of that, he was still correct), but now his eyes were being opened to the possibility of pride and self-focus—two things his father had always warned him of as he prepared him to be king.

Leonolis was suddenly startled from his self-loathing back to the conversation between the watched-Leonolis and Abila.

"Ever since the Scavengians arrived, something has been changing in you—and it's not a good change, Leonolis," the queen spoke softly.

"Enough, woman! Enough! I do not have time for such frivolous distraction!" And with that, the king stormed out of the bedchamber and slept elsewhere that night, leaving the grieving Abila to tend to her own wounded heart.

"Listen," said the Voice.

Watching-Leonolis lifted his teary eyes to face his wounded queen.

"O Founder. Hear my plea! If You indeed listen as the sayings of old declare, then hear me now! The heart and the mind of the king have become clouded. I fear some strange magic has overtaken him. This is not the man I married. These are not the ways of the king I know. By Your power, break this spell. Even as he sleeps, break this spell. If it Your pleasure, Founder, use me as You will as an instrument of deliverance for my husband. And if it be possible, free good Maison. My husband has need of him—whether he now believes it or not." As the queen continued to address the Founder, Maison stepped out of his magical hiding place.

"O, Queen," Maison spoke softly.

Startled, the queen drew her blankets toward her face in self-defense.

"Do not fear, Abila! It is only I, Maison, at your service."

Leaping from the covers, Abila stooped down on her knees and embraced the wise old man. "Dear friend, I fear for my husband, your friend, Leonolis! Some deep magic has overtaken him! He is surely in need of you. Please forgive his behavior of late!"

"Of this I have no doubt, my queen. Let us waste no time. Even now, I am laying the plans to deliver our king from said spell and require your assistance to complete the tasks at hand," said Maison.

"Whatever you require, Lord Maison. Whatever you require of me, it is done," said Abila.

Maison continued. "Tomorrow evening, as Leonolis opens the Blood Moon Festival with his oration, the women of Bren must be given access to the grand courtyard."

"It is done! I will personally send out a decree in the land that all women are encouraged to be present at this year's festival, as they will receive a royal blessing from me. Leonolis will see this as simply in agreement to my past decrees. What is your plan, Maison?"

"You will see, dear Queen. You will see. I simply need the women to take their authority as women and stand with the men of Bren. Their influence is stronger than any Scavengian magic and will surely work in our favor when the time comes. Trust me. They—and you—will know exactly what to do," assured Maison. "Get rest if you can, dear Queen. Tomorrow we take back the land."

"Dear Maison. Thank you for not . . . for never giving up on my husband or on this fair land. For all the injustice now being heaped upon you, I am indeed sorrowful."

"There, there, my queen. This is of little consequence in the grand scheme of things. With the Founders, nothing is ever wasted . . . if we choose to see beyond that which we see with physical eyes."

"What do you mean, dear friend?" asked the queen.

"With the Founders, all things are transformed by the magic of Bren. Sorrow can become joy. Wounds can become pathways to healing. Tragedy can become laughter. And death be made life. Trust me, madam. Nothing is wasted! Even the foolishness of a spellbound king can become wisdom in the hand and by the magic of the Founders. Let us not gaze upon that which we see. Let us glance at the predicament but gaze upon our hope . . . by seeing every aspect of our life from the Founders' point of view!"

And with that, Maison disappeared from Abila's view. As he made his way through the labyrinth of secret passages, the watching-Leonolis and the Voice followed.

Chapter Eight

THE BLOOD MOON FESTIVAL

B y now, daylight began to push aside the darkness of night. It was the day of the Blood Moon Festival. All day long merry festivities had been planned, from the grand market where everyone brought their wares for sale to the reenactment of the actual Battle of Blood Moon, complete with actors portraying the young King Leonolis leading his armies against the hordes of the Hemagens on that bloodiest of all nights.

Through the course of the day, Maison passed unseen from place to place, securing the help of any he deemed unscathed by the spells of the Scavengians. As he had moved about the castle grounds, it was becoming apparent those he could trust and those he could not. Only a wise old magician could have caught the telltale signs in the eyes and manners of those affected by the Scavengian magic. The eyes seemed to have a faint glint of shadow behind the iris and the normal conversational tone had a slight alteration—a slower delivery, if you will. And the normally boisterous way Brenolinians used their hands to express their words seemed just a bit subdued—slightly slower than what was usual. Of course, the regular populous could scarcely tell the difference—and on a day like today, any difference would be chalked up to the frivolity of the occasion. Everyone acts giddy when celebration is at hand.

As the day progressed, those whom Maison had sent to carry out the various tasks were now making their ways back to Castle Aerie. Since Maison had concealed himself and since they were all supposed to be in prison, none could risk discovery so each had donned a disguise. The spell Maison had worked upon the prison guards was powerful enough to hold for an entire day, but due to the changing of the guards at daybreak, the escape had been discovered. At the urging of Scathian, Leonolis had sent word throughout the castle environs to be alert to Maison and the others with whom he had escaped. The Scavengians were now too near seeing their plan come to fruition to allow a pesky little magician to stand between them and the resources and rule of Bren.

As watching-Leonolis and the Voice observed, Maison stealthily made his way from vendor to vendor and from shop to shop, carefully avoiding discovery through simple spur-of-the-moment spells and by ducking into nooks and crannies when necessary. As noon gave way to afternoon, women began to pour into the castle grounds from all over Bren. It was becoming obvious to Maison that the queen's decree along with the work Ovinnia had done in getting the word out through the highways and byways that the message had been taken to heart.

After making the rounds at as many public vendors as possible, Maison once again made his way to the secret passageways of Castle Aerie. Winding his way through the maze of hidden portals, he came to the place of the military strategy room. Since he could not trust the leadership directly under Leonolis, Maison wisely assumed that he would need to look further down the line of authority to find those not affected by the subtle spells of the Scavengians. As he peered out of an opening behind a large decorative urn, he could hear two voices emanating in hushed yet serious tones from somewhere in the room. Easing into a more hearing-friendly position, Maison listened intently.

"But I am a mere petty corporal and you a private. There is nothing we can do!" spoke the older of the two young men dressed in festive military garb for the evening processional. "If we are found even speaking as we are, we risk military tribunal and are assured of prison time and hard labor."

"We cannot simply sit here and do nothing!" whispered the private forcefully. "We are men of Bren and our king has surely fallen into the spell of these devious visitors. To stand by and do nothing is to simply forfeit our role as men! Death is better than losing our self-respect as men of Bren. Risk and threat of death are certainly worth the possible loss of life as we know it. I say we stand even if none stand with us!"

"You are right. Of course, you are right," spoke the corporal. "Even if no one else sees and chooses to stand with us, even our miniscule opposition may awaken enough of the deluded among our ranks to begin an awakening."

Having heard enough, Maison stepped boldly from his hiding place and confronted the men. "Brave and good men of Bren. We have no time to waste. Even now I have heard all you have said . . ."

Believing they had been discovered by one loyal to the Scavengians, the men unsheathed their swords, quickly placing them on the ground in front of them as they bowed subserviently to Maison as was the customary protocol in such occurrences. As Maison stood silently before them, he waited for the two men to come to their senses.

As the corporal slowly turned his cowered head to look upon the one addressing him, he suddenly jumped to his feet. "Maison! Good, dear Maison! The king—Bren—is in need of your wisdom! I am Corporal Pax and this is Private Gommon. Even this day, we have seen and heard evidence of deceit toward Bren and toward our king at the hand of the conniving Scavengians."

"What have you heard, young man?" asked Maison.

"While guarding over a small group of seekers, we were told to wait at the corner of the hallway as they stepped out of our eyesight and into the next corridor. What they had not counted on was the unique construct of this portion of the castle. The sound of the their whispers echoed quite clearly to the place we were both standing—a good twenty-five feet away! At first, we thought we were surely misunderstanding what was being spoken. But as the conversation progressed, their was no doubt our king—our land—was in danger."

Chiming right in as he joined Pax, Gommon continued. "They spoke of a change of plans since hearing of your escape. They told of this new strategy—how they would use your escape as a trick to fool the people of Bren. They spoke of enlisting the aid of one of the Terrebithians to assume your identity, having found one that supposedly mimics your height, build, and even facial features. The plan is to conceal the Terrebithian cleverly near the place of the king's oration. As the king is about to conclude his speech, this faux Maison will step from the shadows and pierce the king's heart with an arrow crafted of pure Phrygian Crystal. At that time, several of the Scavengians will subdue the fake Maison and hurry him away from the gathering and into their secured custody."

Interrupting, Pax went on. "Yes! Yes! And the seekers will then begin to spread the rumor from their many positions around the castle grounds that you, Maison, had plotted treason against the king and that they had only recently discovered a plot you and those loyal to you have been brewing for years, desiring to overthrow the rule of Leonolis and take the place of power for yourself! And that had it not been for the timely and wise intervention on the part of the Scavengians that even more damage would have been done to the Bren way of life. Their belief is that, coupled with the power of their magical incantations and the undermining of culture they have subtly managed to date, that the consensus of the men and women of Bren would be to concede power, for a few brief days, to Scathian, with the plan to 'help' the sorrowing people of Bren through whatever transition custom required to name the next king. Of course, there is no such plan to relinquish that power, Maison! They scoffed at the stupidity of the people of Bren that they would so easily succumb to the simple treachery they had devised."

"Please believe, good Maison! What we say is true!" exclaimed Gommon.

"Trust me, faithful men of Bren. Before you spoke a word I knew in basis that there indeed was a plan to overthrow the rule of Bren. Why do you suppose I was imprisoned in the first place? Never mind, sons of Bren! This will all be unraveled in the days to come. Now we must put the bravery and wisdom of Bren to the test."

As Maison relayed his plan to the two men, watching-Leonolis listened silently. He knew the Voice, even though hushed, was still present with him. Yet he felt quite alone. Consumed with all that was now being revealed to him he was at once overjoyed at the deep love and devotion toward him as displayed by the forthright Maison, yet he was overcome with regret and shame at "what might have been." As he considered the great loss his contemplation was interrupted by the Voice. "What has been was meant to be, son of Bren."

"No. What has been could have been avoided," defied the king.

"Then you see with blinders on," replied the Voice.

"But you see as well as I what has transpired and even now unfolds before us could have been avoided on so many levels," said Leonolis.

"But what you do not see is that all that has occurred has been ordained before the foundation of Bren itself. We saw this day before it even happened. All you have seen and experienced is according to plan. Even though you might have altered the circumstances, the end result would have been the same," said the Voice.

"But how can that be? And how can that even be good? If you saw this you could have made a way to avoid it," replied Leonolis.

"Son, the reason we are taking this journey is to help you see the bigger picture. What you see as a bad thing we see as a means to display the power of Bren—the power of the Founders. All we ask is that you step out of your limited vision and into the broader vision of eternity. In that place—from that point of view—you will see that pain, as seen from our perspective, leads the Bren heart to seek the way of Bren. Valor. Justice. Mercy. From that perspective, you will see even death is but a mere passage to a greater and deeper reality. All that occurs, whether understood by you or not, is ultimately used for your good and the furtherance of the kingdom. You can learn to trust that sight, Son. Watch and learn."

As the Voice again grew silent, watching-Leonolis was drawn back to the conversation between Maison, Pax, and Gommon.

"Faithful warriors of Bren, go now and find those among your ranks. Tell them of what is about to transpire. Fear not. Whether you live or die, you are men of Bren. One way or the other, we will meet again—either in this life or in the realm of the Founders.

As Maison turned to head back into the secret corridor, the soldiers declared, "This day we conquer! This day we overcome the Dark Lord! This day we live or die for the king!"

Maison responded, "May the strength of Bren be yours today." And he was gone.

By now it was evening and nearing the hour when Leonolis would deliver the festival oration. As the Voice led watching-Leonolis to a vantage point above the main castle courtyard, they came to rest on a spire just a few feet above the dais from which the king would deliver his speech. As the throngs from the day's festivities began to file into the courtyard area, excitement filled the air. Yet there was a definite unrest among the citizenry as the seekers stationed themselves at seemingly random locations throughout the castle grounds. What appeared to be randomness was actually very strategic placement. Scathian had taken great pains to ensure that his magicians were in positions that would afford a joining of their powers over the crowd—like a fisherman's net cast over an unsuspecting school of fish.

Soon the air became filled with the royal fanfare that signaled the entrance of the king and his entourage. Watching-Leonolis actually marveled at the aura of pomp and circumstance, of majesty and royalty that emanated as respect from the good people of Bren and that flowed down through the ages from the realm of the Founders. For a few brief moments, he forgot about all that was about to unfold and reveled in the fact that, indeed, he was a son of Bren—a son of a king—a king in his own right. Even had he not held the power of the throne, he still felt this was the heart of every man, woman, and child of Bren. They were a people of destiny. A people of vision. He was proud to be counted as one—king or not.

As watched-Leonolis made his way to the dais, he came to rest at the center near the front most banister that separated him from the crowd. The royal dais was some twenty-five feet above the courtyard below. On either side were spires of the castle—the shorter spires (one of which served as the observation point for watching-Leonolis and the Voice) that rose fifty feet high and served as watchtowers. From the courtyard below and looking up one had a clear view of the magnitude and massiveness of Castle Aerie. From the lower spires the castle seemed to explode above and carry the eye to the corresponding five tiers of spires that rose in ever-increasing heights until the highest spire of the castle—the Eagle's Roost as it is called—where the king and queen often went for times of quiet repose and meditation. In all, Castle Aerie had twenty-eight spires. From a distance, the castle was even more awe-inspiring.

The courtyard itself could accommodate a crowd of ten thousand. From there, a throng typical of the Blood Moon Festival would spill out through the castle gates and down in Warrior's Canyon, all the way to the harbor. This day was no different. It seemed as if people were everywhere. Along with the mass of people packed into the castle grounds and spilling out into the canyon were people lining every possible place along the castle walls, hoping to get a glimpse of the king and hear even a snippet of his royal decree.

As watched-Leonolis stood gazing out upon the throngs, he began to raise his hands in greeting to the people. As he did so, the already boisterous crowd raised the level to deafening as they began to cheer the presence of their beloved king. Soon, the air began to fill with the chant, "Great is the king! Hail to the king! Great is the king! Hail to the king!" This was quite customary behavior for the people of Bren, passed on from generation to generation. Though to the foreigner it may have seemed a silly custom, what could not be seen was the hearts and minds of the people—who truly loved and respected their king. Leonolis had become a good king, and was about to become a great king, whether he realized it or not.

As the king began to lower his arms, the people grew quiet, as was the protocol. By the time his hands had come to rest by his side, the crowd—all the way through the gates, through Warrior's Canyon, all the way to the harbor, had grown very, very still. Such great awe and respect for their king. Then the king began to speak.

"Hear, O good people of the great land of Bren! This day we gather to remember and to celebrate. We remember those who delivered us from the hand and the schemes of the marauding Hemagens. We remember those who laid down their lives for the very freedom we now celebrate this day. We remember . . ."

As the king continued to make his opening remarks, watching-Leonolis observed what he had not seen that day when he first experienced what was about to take place. Stationed incrementally around the outside of the castle walls were the hives of bees from around the land of Bren. No one had taken much notice of such a thing since such wares were commonly displayed and sold on such occasions. Moving quietly through the crowds, the beekeepers carried discreetly hidden honey pots, brimming with the sweet nectar of the bees. As per their instructions from Maison, they made their way to each of the Scavengians as they were able. Once directly behind them, the beekeepers craftily brushed the lower portion of the Scavengian's robe with a slight dab of honey. The king continued to speak.

"People of Bren, this day we give thanks for our abundance! This day we give thanks to those who bravely fought and laid down their lives to secure victory over our foes!"

As watching-Leonolis glanced around the throng, his eyes were drawn to netting being raised over various entryways around the courtyard. The fishermen, at Piscal's bidding, were going about their assignments covertly. If anyone inquired as to what they were doing, the fishermen, per instruction, replied that they were merely adding to the festivities by drawing attention to the fishing industry of the land. The nets, in effect, were being lifted in celebration of the bounty of the sea. And the king's speech went on.

"By the Founders, we have been granted freedom! By the Founders, we have been given much to be thankful for! By the Founders, we are a prosperous land! By the Founders, we have been granted a deep respect for hard work—and as we look around at the abundance of the bounty of the land displayed in our shoppes this day, we have obvious evidence of the Founders' hand! As a result of all we have been given by the Founders, much is required! With great freedom and bounty comes great responsibility!"

Watching-Leonolis' attention once again strayed from the oration to the workings of Maison in their midst. Among the trees and shrubbery scattered in the castle grounds as well as the groupings of trees and brush surrounding Castle Aerie, the leaves were astir with subtle movement that only meant one thing. Verden had reached the Treesants—and they were, even now, among them, awaiting the word of Maison. The king's words drew Leonolis back to the oration, but this time, watching-Leonolis saw movement in the spire immediately opposite his perch. A small, cloaked figure, reminiscent of Maison, took a position directly to the side of the king as his speech was drawing to its climactic conclusion.

"And now, people of Bren, let us begin the festival! Let us enjoy the bounty of the land! Let us remember why we celebrate! Let us rejoice with one another and remind one another of all we have been given. Let us laugh! Let us sing! Let us give thanks! I declare these festivities commenced!"

The crowd began to roar and the musicians began to play. A scream went out from somewhere in the crowd that sent quieting chills through the crowd closest to the dais.

"There he is! The traitor Maison!" shouted Scathian from the dais, slightly behind the king. "Seize him!"

As the throng turned toward the spire where the cloaked figure stood, he pulled out a long bow and strung an arrow of pure Phrygian Crystal. Pulling back on the string as far as his arms would allow, "Maison" released the arrow toward the heart of the king! As if in slow motion, the entire crowd inhaled a collective gasp as the arrow coursed its way toward the chest of Leonolis. In the same instant, the Scavengians strategically stationed around the castle grounds, simultaneously threw back their cloaks and waited for the moment, their scheme unfolding as planned.

The arrow, though flying with seeming speed of light, shone with evil brilliance as it sped toward the king. Without much notice, a small, dwarfish figure leapt from the shadows among the curtains directly behind the king. Making his way toward the king—who seemed to be frozen in place at the disbelief at this utter betrayal at the hand of his most trusted friend—the figure bounded upward, soaring between the king and the missile.

The arrow found its mark, striking the real Maison squarely in the center of his chest. Crumpling to the ground in a heap, Maison lay motionless as the crowd began to fall into confusion and disarray. As if awakened from a deep slumber, Leonolis looked down on his friend in horror as he instinctively crouched down and cradled the wounded Maison in his arms. Picking up the lifeless head of his friend, the king began to cry out for help.

"Send for the royal physician! Someone help us!" Turning toward Scathian, Leonolis cried, "What have you done?" and just as quickly, turning toward the royal guards, "Seize the Scavengians at once!"

Before the king had even finished uttering those words, Scathian lifted his hands—which was a sign to his magicians—and they, in turn lifted their hands toward the chaotic throng of people. A weird silence began to take over as the multitude began to grow still where they stood. The Scavengians had come too far to allow this minor disturbance to deter them. By magic they would subdue the people and by magic they would subdue the king, forcing their will upon the people of Bren. By now, the subtle mind games had already made the people susceptible to the magic they were now be subjected to. This would be a mere annoyance in the grand scheme of things.

As the magic of Scavengia began to take hold, the body of Maison began to stir ever so slightly, causing Leonolis to return his attention to his friend. Somehow, the connection of the hearts of these two lifelong friends had caused a small realm of freedom for the king and his advisor. Opening his eyes slightly, Maison looked into the eyes of Leonolis.

"My dear friend! What have I done?" wept the king.

"This is not the time for sorrow, my son," said the frail Maison. "Now is the time for the magic of Bren to shine and pierce just as this arrow shines and pierces my body. Lift me up, King, so that I might face the people."

Obeying the words of his friend, Leonolis gently lifted the body of Maison so that he could face the people of Bren. Gasping for breath and fighting to maintain his consciousness, the little man feebly lifted his hands up, palms facing the crowd—and he began to speak softly yet with measured authority.

> *"O, Founders great!*
> *From Thy deep well*
> *Break this curse!*
> *Release this spell!*
> *O, Founders great!*
> *O, Founders wise!*
> *Let blind now see*
> *With open eyes!"*

At once, the entire throng was released from the magic of the Scavengians. As the Scavengians realized their power had been broken, Scathian began to scream a high-pitched, blood-curdling scream—like a wild animal summoning its starving pack to a fresh kill. All at once, hundreds of men throughout the multitude began to throw off their cloaks revealing white-haired, white-robed Scavengians. During the many months of their stay in the land, the Scavengians had slowly and steadily been bringing in reinforcements using many different routes. Some had stowed away on sailing vessels, making their way into hiding by cover of night. Some had come from the lands in the west, clandestinely traversing the river Runland and hiding in the western forests. Still others had been smuggled in via caravans from the northern realms by way of Abysstine while many more had come through the eastern reaches by way of similar guise, pretending to be traders so as to conceal their true identities and purposes.

Armed with swords and bows and arrows crafted of Phrygian Crystal, the cunning seekers had placed themselves in position to subdue even the armed forces of the land of Bren. It seemed, even though the mental spell had been broken, the people were still at the mercy of the Scavengians . . . or so it seemed.

With one last breath, Maison lifted his head and spoke in the most amazing and pure tone these three words: "It is time!"

As his words parted from his lips, they seemed to waft through the air like the sweetness of honeysuckle on a crisp, spring morning in Bren. The sound carried to each and every ear of each and every man, woman, and child of Bren gathered for the festival. The words drifted like a fragrance over the walls, touching the ears of all who stood there. They made their way through the gates of Castle Aerie and throughout those gathered in Warrior's Canyon, making their way all the way down to the harbor. And as those words made their way to the last of those men and women of Bren, a marvelous cascade of activity began to commence.

On the outside of the castle, beekeepers knocked over the waiting hives, sending the bees scurrying. By preordained spell, Maison had ordered the bees to seek out the honey of the land when they heard the words, "It is time." Like a million bolts of lightning, the bees made their way to the men of Scavengia marked with the daubs of honey. As the Scavengians were swarmed with bees, their swatting motions only spurred the bees into anger, sending the seekers running. This had the further affect of breaking any further magical spells the Scavengian magicians may have tried to cast since the magicians worked to put as much distance between themselves and the bees as possible!

As the crowds began to come to their senses, the others in Maison's plan went to work. Since the Scavengian magic had been planted upon the subtle suggestion of Scavengian philosophy, there was still quite a hold on many of the people, causing even further confusion—especially among the men. This is when the women went into action. While there was still much confusion surrounding the attempt on the king's life (most had assumed that Maison was the perpetrator), the men automatically went into defender mode, assuming the Scavengians were somehow in control of the situation. With few words, the women stepped between their sons, their husbands, and their brothers and snapped them out of their confusion. The power of a woman's influence is great, wielding more power than the brute strength of men when all is said and done . . . and this day was no different. The women played a soothing role in refocusing the attention of the masculine population of Bren that fateful day from the deceit of the seekers to the reality of the ways of Bren.

As the Scavengian forces began to realize their predicament, they all began to brandish their weapons, frantically striking out at the defenseless Brenolinians. At least, what they assumed were defenseless Brenolinians. According to the plans set in motion by wise old Maison, Urston had been able to smuggle the arsenal of weapons through the castle gates and into the hands of the men of Bren who had not fallen under the spell of Scathian's magic. Holding the Scavangian swordsmen at bay was one thing, but upon the realization that Scathian had wisely placed his best archers at strategic points around the upper reaches of the castle put the men of Bren at a very distinct disadvantage—until Mason went to work!

When Mason had realized what was going on, and having placed one of the mining bells with a trusted stonecutter who awaited instructions at the harbor, he took the bell (one tuned to D flat) and emerged from one of the central, higher spires of Castle Aerie. Once the Scavengians had wielded their crystal weapons, he had emerged from hiding. As soon as the archers slotted their arrows, Mason lifted the bell and with one resolute strike of a hammer, rung the bell. The tones of the bell began to resonate with brilliant clarity throughout the castle grounds and well into Warrior's Canyon. Because it was tuned to D flat, and because the Scavengian weapons were constructed of Phrygian Crystal, the weapons began to fall into pieces as their crystalline nature began to vibrate with the specific tuning of the bell. What with the bees stinging, the people of Bren awakening, their weapons falling to pieces in their very hands, and the men of Bren suddenly brandishing weapons of their own, the Scavengians began to take flight!

Running as best they could from the men of Bren, they each began to make a beeline (very ironic since bees were in hot pursuit!) toward the main gates of entry into Castle Aerie. The people of Bren, now becoming magically (chalk it up to the forward-thinking Maison!) aware of what was truly going on, began to part and allow the Scavengians access to the gates, knowing full well what awaited them! No sooner had the seekers come near the gates than the fishermen began to drop their nets, sufficiently subduing them in their tracks! While those in the castle confines were subdued and taken into custody, Scathian had somehow managed to evade capture and was now nearing the dock where all those Scavengians outside the castle grounds had now made their way. Converging on *Carina*, the lead boat from their small armada, this desperate band of evildoers was attempting to make hasty their escape.

As the docks became crowded with fleeing Scavengians, the armed men of Bren closed in on them from all sides except the harbor. As Scathian ordered the moorings released from the *Carina*, he and the fifty or so seekers who had managed to board pushed away from the pier while they watched nets from the fishermen of Bren drop down from the many booms and cargo cranes high above them and subdue most of their remaining brothers on the dock. From his vantage point, Scathian could see the decimated ranks of Scavengian men fleeing in all directions from Warrior's Canyon, some running for the eastern regions while others attempted to swim the Runland to the west.

Watching-Leonolis was captivated at all that was unfolding in vivid detail before him. He remembered feeling completely consumed with Maison that day and had only been told of the bravery and heroism of the people of Bren after the fact. To see it from every conceivable angle now caused great righteous pride to well up in his soul, not the arrogant kind of pride that says look at me, but rather the grateful pride of one who recognizes all he has been given and all he has become is due to the giving of others—whether they be the Founders or his royal subjects. What had taken several days to unfold before, Leonolis was now watching in a mere matter of minutes—or so it seemed. As we will find out, the magic of Bren is quite impossible to understand with the human mind, but the great joy of that reality is the very journey of discovery that such magic beckons the human heart to undertake.

As Scathian made his getaway, a stonecutter named Gemnus stepped from the shadows, having been waiting per instruction, and held high the other mining bell tuned to D flat. Watching in horror, the facial expression of Scathian turned from sneer to sheer terror as the hammer rose high above the head of Gemnus and fell with resounding power upon the bell. As the sound waves coursed through the air, those close enough to witness said the water itself began to vibrate. As the tone of the bell filled the air, it seemed to move with the pace of honey on a warm day (at least that's what it seemed to watching-Leonolis!). As the first sound reached the *Carina*, the vessel began to reverberate from stem to stern. Shaking violently like a dog shaking itself after a swim in the Runland, the movement caused the would-be escapees to all lose their footing.

Grasping for the side rail, Scathian managed to pull himself to his feet. Now looking pitifully like a child in need of rescue from a bad dream, the Scavengian ring leader pled to Gemnus, "Please stop! Please cease! We surrender! Do not strike the bell again or all will be lost!"

Paying no heed to the plight of Scathian, Gemnus again raised his hand as high as he could reach and with the honor of Bren in mind, brought the hammer down with such resolute force that the bell itself cracked slightly, causing a raspy tone to be released from the mining bell. As the sound of that oddly beautiful rasp connected with the crystal of the boat, the vessel began to shake even more erratically. After only a few seconds, it was apparent to all watching that they should probably step back as far as possible—even those hundreds of feet away from the vessel.

It was obvious that the *Carina* would not be able to withstand this final volley of sound. Whether due to some unseen magic or the simple intensity of the vibrations, the ship began to rise above the water and hover. As it did so, the outline of the shaking vessel began to grow unrecognizable. No longer was the image of a boat visible, but the entire vessel and its passengers were now consumed in a ball of light. As the light grew to the level of being unbearable to gaze upon for very long, the vision of the boat came sharply back into view. Hovering and still above the water, the boat seemed to be intact, yet an uneasiness filled the air as a rumble began to fill the air—like the rumblings of the first tremors of an oncoming earthquake. Soon the rumble grew to such a degree that everyone began to cover their ears—and just as it reached the most deafening pitch, the entire vessel shattered into bits like grains of sand!

What took place next, no one could have seen coming—at least not by the common citizens of Bren. As the bits of crystal shimmered from the air and floated into the sea like flakes of snow on a winter's morning, the very flesh of the Scavengians began to shake every bit as violently as the *Carina* had shaken. They began to glow, and then all was still. And then the rumble—that dreadful rumble—began to fill the air again. Like shards of glass the size of grains of salt, the bodies of the Scavengians shattered in midair just as their vessel had done. Since that day, it was discovered that, by deep Scavengian magic, the very bodies of the people of Scavengia had been tied to the Phrygian Crystal they used to build their seagoing vessels. So deeply ingrained was the magic that the people of Scavengia could no longer survive without it—unless some great magician broke the original spell.

When the tone had been struck and the *Carina* had begun to shake, all those Scavengians on the shore—even those who had been running for their lives—stopped and turned to watch all that had unfolded. Since they had not been actually touching the boat in that moment, their lives had been spared—but they knew their race would cease to exist without further exploitation of Phrygian Crystal. Although the people of Bren were ecstatic at their deliverance from the Scavengian hold, they were— as the good people of Bren are—sympathetic to the plight of the people of Scavengia, making what happened next even more amazing than what they had just witnessed.

Chapter Nine

THE HEART OF MAISON

His heart about to explode from all he had just seen, watching Leonolis again turned his attention back to the wounded Maison and the amazing level of grace he was about to see as his former self interacted with the wise little dying man.

Still holding his friend's body near his chest, the king knelt to the ground as Maison's spell was cast. As the ensuing battle and subsequent victory transpired, the king stayed focused on his friend. Waves of revelation at the way he had been duped by the Scavengians clouded the king's rueful mind—and somehow Maison knew—and responded.

"Dear King . . . all . . . is . . . for . . . a . . . purpose," whispered Maison, struggling for each breath between words.

"Hush, my friend. Please save your strength. I know all is for a purpose, but that does not forgive my need to take responsibility for all that has transpired—and for all that I could have done to end this months ago," spoke the sorrowful king.

"Nonsense, my son. It has occurred just as it was ordained. Though you could have reacted and acted differently, the end results would have still been the same," continued Maison. "Just because you are responsible does not mean you could have changed one iota of reality surrounding the outcome."

"Then why did it have to happen at all—if it was, as you say, ordained so? Could not the Founders have concocted another way without the resulting loss of life and damage to the kingdom?" asked the king.

"What is of most importance is the picture . . . not the frame," coughed the little man. "You are so focused on the framework surrounding the vista that you are missing the beauty of the art being painted right before your very eyes."

Maison closed his eyes and breathed in a long breath of air.

Choking slightly, Maison went on. "You see through a layer of self now that clouds your ability to see the grand vista of all that is afoot in the kingdom. The events of today—if you will allow them to, Son—will serve to point you to the bigger picture, the greater reality of all that surrounds you."

At that moment, watching-Leonolis sensed a movement at his side. The Voice, an unseen entity to this point in the journey, suddenly took form. Similar in height to Leonolis, the Voice wore a robe similar to that of the king, replete with the royal colors of the house of Bren—blue and grey. Over this robe was draped a cape of deep purple velvet, emblazoned with the coat of arms of the house of Bren. As watching-Leonolis observed, the Voice moved from his side to a kneeling position next to Maison. Crouching down next to the watched-Leonolis, the Voice placed his right hand on the chest of the little man. Turning toward the watching-Leonolis, the face of the Voice was indiscernible. More than features, there emanated a light from eyes that communicated the expanse of eternity. Rather than a mouth with lips there was an awareness of words spoken from before time that reassured Maison—and all who witnessed this moment that day—that all was well. Instead of a smile, a light "smiled" radiantly from the face of the Voice that communicated the lack of need for any unnecessary words to be spoken. All those in the courtyard that day witnessed this in silence, the Voice having revealed himself to those with eyes to see.

After a few minutes of the Voice touching the breast of Maison, he spoke. "My dear friend, Maison, it is time."

Able to open his eyes for brief periods, they appeared mere slits where once captivating sight emanated as Maison looked into the eyes of the Voice. "Indeed, my Lord, it is time."

Unable to keep quiet, watched-Leonolis held Maison closer to himself, almost pulling the wee man's body from the touch of the Voice. "What do you mean 'it is time'?" asked the king. "Time for what?"

Even then in the day it had first occurred, watching-Leonolis knew what was meant. And he knew it now. Maison was dying, and it was time to bid him farewell.

In tears, watched-Leonolis began to sob these words: "My teacher from childhood, my tutor in the art of royalty, my most trusted advisor to this day—my friend of friends—would it be that there is a way, a bit of magic left, that might alter what I fear is happening?"

Maison smiled as he gazed through narrow slots for eyes and a tear began to trickle down his cheek. The Voice remained silent and simply gazed at watched-Leonolis.

"Can we not turn back time and allow me to make the right decisions, to utter the right command, to keep you with me—with us—a little longer?" wept the king

In a very faint whisper, Maison spoke. "My son, you see through the lens of time, and the realm of Bren transcends time. You see through the glass of loss and all you see is death, when the realm of Bren transcends even death. May the journey I now take lead you to a greater understanding of the width, depth, height, and breadth of what it truly means to be a son of Bren."

And opening his eyes fully, he looked one last time into the eyes of his king, and said, "It is time." And Maison was gone.

"Leonolis (both of them) was consumed in grief—almost inconsolable—until the Voice reached out and touched his shoulder and uttered these words. "It is done, son of Bren. It is done. There will be time for mourning, but right now your subjects need to see what a kingdom perspective looks like—and that can only come when they are shown the way to see as a king sees. Show them, son of Bren. Show them now."

As the body of Maison went limp in his arms, only King Leonolis saw what happened next. Rising from the body of Maison, the spirit of Maison rose and took the hand of the Voice. Together they walked out of the courtyard and into the northern horizon. In the mind of watching-Leonolis, he had watched them for nearly an hour before rising from the body of Maison. In Bren time, only a few seconds had passed.

As he stood, the king's physician and attendants took the tutor's body and gently carried him away for proper care and to make preparations for the royal burial that would ensue, as was the custom of Bren. Watching as they carried his friend away, the king finally turned toward the crowd as they stood in silent grief at all that had just taken place before their eyes. Speaking with solemnity yet with great authority, Leonolis began.

"For these past few months, we have undergone a deception as a people. For that, I take full responsibility. As a nation, we have endured many things, many wars, many acts of aggression, many acts of treason, and many natural disasters, but never have we endured such a national deception. We have too easily fallen for the schemes of these, come to find out, not-so-well-intentioned men of Scavengia. I am sure details will bring even more light in the coming days the true depth of how far we have so unknowingly fallen. But we are Bren! We are resilient! And as your king, I publicly kneel before you and seek your forgiveness for having led you into this now-revealed darkness."

Leonolis knelt to the ground and looked out into as many eyes as he could come in contact with. After a few moments of his piercing gaze, the humbled king went on. "Will you forgive me?"

No one moved. Never before had they witnessed one of their leaders in such a seemingly weak position—and intentionally and willfully so! They were stunned.

After a few more moments, Leonolis said again in a louder voice, "Will you forgive me?"

Still, stunned silence. Being there was no protocol for such a display, the people simply did not know what was proper.

After a few more minutes of silence, the king finally stood and yelled with all his might. "WILL YOU FORGIVE ME?"

And in the moment his passion went out for all to see, the crowd roared as one, "We forgive the king!" As that first response died down, another rose. "We forgive the king!" And as if in an endless echo, the cry went out from the castle walls, through Warrior's Canyon, and all the way down to the dock where they still stood in shocked amazement at the disintegration of the *Carina*! "We forgive the king! We forgive the king! We forgive the king! We forgive the king!"

Even as the public statement of forgiveness grew into a distant chant and those in the castle grounds grew again silent, Leonolis had caught a glimpse of the eternal realm of Bren. What he had assumed would be seen as a communication of weakness in a human sense had actually increased his power. It was not the words that had done the deed, but rather his attitude and perspective that had proven so powerful. With one act of submission he had transcended human understanding and seen a small opening in eternity that was to lead him for the rest of his days. As he pondered these things in his heart, he was brought back to reality by the necessity of the tasks at hand.

Attending to the body of Maison was first and foremost in his mind even though he knew that, had Maison been advising him in such matters, he would be tending to the restoration of order in Bren and dealing justice to the Scavengian perpetrators. The truth was—especially with hindsight—was that he knew it was futility to try and pretend Maison would even want to come back from the realm of the Founders, even if that was the deepest desire of King Leonolis. He also knew that Maison would have told him to use his grief to soothe the grieving hearts of his subjects. As the king led in grief, so would national grief be observed. Leonolis would grieve well.

In the next few moments, Leonolis was led by the Voice to the state funeral of Maison. Held the very next day after his death, the Ceremony of Homegoing, as it was called, was held in the courtyard of Castle Aerie so as many as possible could pay their respects to the wise little man. The lines of grieving people had begun forming the night of Maison's death and had stretched for miles. Not everyone who had desired to do so was able to see the body, such was the outpouring of love and respect for Maison. Literally ten thousand people more had hoped to bid him farewell. The crowd spilled from the main courtyard and out into the areas surrounding the castle. Spreading all the way down through Warrior's Canyon and into the harbor area, the people gathered to pay their respects.

As the time came, Leonolis watched again that which he had already lived once—and felt the same weight of sorrow he had felt then. As the ceremony progressed, dignitaries from near and far expressed many flattering words and sentiments. In death, the little man seemed larger than life as each accolade poured out on his behalf seemed to be greater than the last. Leonolis knew, had Maison been in attendance, he would have grown impatient and disgusted at all the compliments, honor, and praise. Leonolis had known it well as he spoke.

"Good men and women of Bren. We have, indeed, lost a national treasure. But more than that, we have lost a good man. A good friend. A faithful servant of Bren. We have lost a part of ourselves at such loss. But be of good cheer. Think of all we have gained for having had our life and history graced by such a man as this. So many of our scientific advances and medical wonders—so much of our progress—can be directly traced back to the heart and mind of Maison. Words cannot begin to express what each of us must feel when faced with the loss of one who has meant so much to all of us. But rest assured, we will reap the benefits of his life for generations to come."

Pausing to maintain his composure, Leonolis continued. "I will not lie to you. I will miss this man . . . this one whom I have known since I was a young boy. Maison taught me so much more than the books he required me to read were able to convey. What I learned from watching him was how to be a better man . . . how to be a faithful friend . . . how to place another's needs above my own . . . how to truly live. Even in death I saw him display these very traits in ways words never could. By laying down his life he has brought our nation—in one selfless act—from the very brink of destruction."

Tears streaming down his cheeks—and tears flowing freely throughout the throng of people—Leonolis concluded. "Let us not grieve what we have lost. Let us reflect on what we have gained in knowing this man, Maison. He was not merely friend of friends to me . . . but he was friend of friends to an entire nation—an entire people. He loved you, Bren! Let us celebrate this life by living as he did—willing to lay down our own lives to preserve the heart of Bren."

Turning his gaze now to the body of his friend, the king said, "Good-bye, dear friend. I will see you soon enough." Raising his hand in signal, the royal guard bore the body of the little giant of a man toward the castle gate, followed reverently by the king and his entourage. As they passed through the crowd, knees bowed as the bier approached and then stood in respect once it had passed by. All the way through Warrior's Canyon and down to the dock, the processional proceeded in silence. Once they had reached the end of the dock, the group stopped.

As if handling the most precious and fragile cargo, those tending to the body tenderly placed the corpse in a coffin composed of Phrygian

Crystal that craftsmen had worked through the night to prepare. As the lid was placed over the body, King Leonolis placed his hand near the place where Maison's heart was and breathed one last silent farewell to his friend. Placing the casket on a small wooden dinghy, the boat and body were sent out into the southern currents as predetermined by Maison long ago in anticipation of this day. His body would find its final resting place wherever the Founders saw fit.

As the throng watched in silence, the boat seemed to be moving forward of its own accord, almost as if Maison's own will was guiding it from beyond. At least that's what Leonolis remembered thinking. And then the most unthinkable thing happened. The boat began to slow—and seemed to be taking on water! The funeral boat was sinking! Immediately, the king dispatched the royal Naval Guards to tend to the boat, but their efforts were futile. The boat was sinking so quickly they had not had time to reach it. As evening fell, the grief of the masses was sent into the deep places of their hearts just as Maison's body sunk to the deepest place in the royal harbor. As if one collective sigh breathed, everyone's thoughts were those of devastation.

As the darkness grew and the sorrow intensified, the crowd began to murmur. King Leonolis sent his royal divers to survey what would be required to retrieve the casket and the body of Maison. With their ability to go to a depth of about seventy feet in one breath, the depth at which the casket came to rest was about 150 feet of water. There was literally nothing that could be done aside from magic—and the body of the greatest magician of the land lay at the bottom of the harbor!

When Leonolis realized that nothing could be done, he began to make his way back to Castle Aerie to address the crowd and try to help them come to terms with this deeper plunging of the knife of grief into their national heart. Halfway up the road through Warrior's Canyon, a cry began to grow from behind the king.

"Look! Look! Something's happening!" came the shouts as people pointed to the center of the harbor.

The darkness of night had now fully engulfed the land, but that darkness was now suddenly pierced by a shaft of light coming, seemingly, from the depths of the harbor—from the place where Maison's body had come to rest! Like a mighty sword piercing the night, the beam emanated into the heavens for ten thousand feet, giving a soft glow to the faces of all who stared in amazement at what was occurring.

As the king realized what was happening, he continued to make his way through the crowd and up into a place on the castle wall where he could be heard. In as loud a voice as he could muster, his previously downcast and grief-weary heart was lifted to one of jubilation and laughter.

"Do you see?" shouted the king. "Do you see what is happening? This day we are not piling grief upon grief at the sudden turn of events! To the contrary! We are all—every one of us—bearing witness to the work of the Founders and the magic of the realm! It has been said from days of old that the magic of a pure heart would one day light the way of Bren when that heart has been pierced with the Founders' truth! What we thought through the ages was that this was merely a picture of the heart of Bren, but what is now unfolding is a physical manifestation of a spiritual truth. Just as Maison's heart was pure for Bren and was pierced by the truth of the Founders, in life he was a spiritual light for the realm. But what we are beholding—as unbelievable as it is—is the very physical heart of Maison being used as a beacon for all of Bren! Let us not forget this night! Never forget what we have all seen. Tell your children! Tell your grandchildren and all to come of the mighty works of the Founders on our behalf!"

The crowd, respectfully quiet as the king spoke, erupted in passionate shouts and laughter as the reality of this national blessing was now unfolding before their very eyes! Through the entire night the crowds celebrated, turning a most somber occasion into an absolute celebration of victory. Those who had not been able to attend the Ceremony of Homegoing made their way through the night to join the festivities. As the night faded into dawn, the light from the harbor began to subside, becoming a soft glow from the depths that was still faintly visible whenever a cloud would pass over during the day. What everyone had assumed would be a one-time event—the piercing light from beneath the waters—actually occurred the next night . . . and the next . . . and the next! From that day forward, the harbor of Bren had no need of a lighthouse to guide lost souls from the Sea of Arabon into the safety of its borders.

In the following years, King Leonolis declared the Feast of Maison would be celebrated during the Festival of the Blood Moon. Some say that the light that pierces the harbor sky each night actually grows brighter and whiter during the feast celebration. Perhaps that is only Bren imagination—or perhaps it is an ongoing magic. Whatever the case, the light still serves to remind the people of Bren of their national identity.

After those first days of celebration subsided and people went back to their homes, families, and work, King Leonolis dealt with the remaining Scavengians. Since Scathian had met his just reward when the ship shattered, Leonolis and his advisors put in place a very just arrangement with the people of Scavengia. Those who remained in custody would serve seven years in prison for their misdeeds, including the Terribithian who had conspired to impersonate Maison. The nation of Scavengia would be required to pay restitution for all they had instigated. And, as is often the case in Brenolinian justice, mercy was extended to the nation of Scavengia. Realizing their need for Phrygian Crystal to survive, King Leonolis granted them the right to buy a certain amount of the precious crystal each year, paying full price—with the stipulation that the Scavengian scholars and magicians work together to find a solution to their dependency on the Phrygian Crystal.

Leonolis watched as his former self went through all these events again. "Why have you led me to see what I had already experienced? Was it to punish me? Was it to remind me of how much I do not know? Was it so I could avoid the same mistakes in the future?" he asked the Voice.

"There was no need to punish you, Son. You punished yourself enough—and even that we did not ordain. It was your choice. There was no need to remind you of that which you do not know. Living life well has a way of unveiling that which you need to know just when you need to know it. Without the mistakes of life how would you know the joy of forgiveness? No, my son. You have been allowed to see from our perspective in order to afford you the best vantage point from which to see that true freedom and true life always comes with a price. The freedom of Bren has been secured by those who gave their lives to win that freedom. The life you now enjoy was worked for by others who have served you along the way. Indeed, there is much you do not know—but more already planted within your royal heart that is simply waiting to be called forth," said the Voice.

"Yes, my own father, my own mother, and my loyal advisors and teachers have all played a role in getting me to where I am. Without their great sacrifice I would be nothing," responded the king.

In a somber tone, the Voice said, "This you speak, you speak well enough, but there is more. There are many more who have paved the way for you—and for the future of all of Bren. Even your wife and those nine children borne to you of her womb have given you freedom and have been life to you. Come, now. Abila and the dragon will not wait."

Chapter Ten

WHEN THE DRAGONS CAME

Flying through the air once again, watching-Leonolis and the Voice launched into a journey that began when Leonolis was still a young prince of fourteen. As he flew, the words of the Voice had already taken him to a time when he had first seen her—really seen her. Sure enough, here they were, alighting just outside the entrance to the Crystal Cave. He could see himself emerging from the cavern with his buddies, all soaking wet. He could still remember those "boy" thoughts of pretend battles, of adventures yet to be undertaken, and of glories yet to be revealed—of manhood to come. Leonolis remembered, wondering what it would be like to be a man—and how he would know when that day had arrived. What he now witnessed brought all those thoughts quickly to his remembrance. He now watched as the group of adolescent boys collapsed to the ground in laughter at some long-forgotten joke that's funny only to boys, while simultaneously he noticed a group of giggling girls a few yards away, snickering as softly as possible as they peeked out from behind the bushes that served as their hiding place.

Without saying a word, the Voice nodded toward the girls, beckoning Leonolis to watch and to listen. And then he saw her. Abila. He had never seen nor heard what he was about to see and hear. Had not even imagined it. He observed as one of the girls broke into an old Brenolinian rhyme teenaged girls are prone to.

"Abila! Abila! Pretty and shy!
Look at her blush when her beau she does spy!
Swaying and swooning, unable to stand
Whenever she spies Leonolis, her man!"

"O, stop! They'll hear you!" whispered Abila as softly yet as adamantly as possible so as to not alert the boys to their presence.

"You know it's true!" said her friend Lolly.

Cheeks turning bright red, she batted her eyes coyly at her friend as she admitted, "Yes! Yes! It is true! Isn't he handsome? Isn't he dashing? Isn't he brave to have helped save the kingdom from the dark lord, Lucian?" Fanning herself as she pretended to faint at the mere mention of his many wonderful attributes, she said, "He has my heart—and he doesn't even know it!"

Watching-Leonolis was taken aback at this revelation. He had not known she felt this way—and had spent months wooing her before she ever noticed him! It had all been part of her clever, girlish charms. And, he laughed to himself now, it had worked! As the girls burst into laughter, his attention went once again to the group of boys. At the sound of the feminine mirth, the boys had all stood to their feet and were now running toward the not-so-well-hidden girls.

"Who is there?" shouted young Leonolis.

Only giggles could be heard from behind the bushes.

"Come out at once or we're coming in after you," he cried.

More giggles.

"I'll give you until the count of three and then you'll be sorry you ever dared spy on us!"

"Or what?" defied Abila, trying to deepen her voice to sound like a boy.

"Or we'll strip you bare and send you home crying like girls!" replied the prince.

Abila replied in her lowered voice and shushed the other girls as their giggles now became snorts, "You may want to think again about that, boy! We are not like other boys who simply give way to the prince's demands. Had I not been overruled by my companions we would have had your clothes taken from the place you laid them in the cave. Had we no mercy, it would be you who was stripped bare and sent home crying like girls!"

"That's it!" shouted the now angry prince. "I'm coming in!"

As the prince prepared to teach a lesson on knowing one's place to these defiant boys who had dared to challenge his more mature status, out stepped a dainty foot, draped in bright purple cloth festooned with floral patterns, which was the customary dress—for girls!

Upon the realization that girls had pushed him to the edge of anger, his anger melted into embarrassment, and quickly back to anger as he thought about how to handle himself in a manly manner in front of his friends. As his cohorts felt his rage, they fell into giggles and snickers as they watched their leader go through such a range of emotions at the sight of a girl. And then her face, momentarily obscured by the branches of the shrubs from which she emerged, appeared—and Leonolis melted into a puddle of mumbled words, which only added to the awkwardness he now felt at the sight of Abila.

"O! It's you . . . um . . . er . . . I would have . . . uh . . . I never would have . . . you!" was all the prince could utter. Of course his buddies began to nudge him and push him toward her, which only served to embarrass the red-faced boy all the more.

"I am so sorry, Abila! Had I known it was you I . . . I . . ."

"You would have what?" asked Abila before he could finish his thought.

"Kissed her!" came a reply from one of his friends behind him. This, of course, led the girls with Abila to begin to giggle and titter amongst themselves, and of course, this then encouraged the boys to do the same, leaving Leonolis and Abila painfully yet wonderfully face-to-face in every boy's nightmare and every girl's dream!

For several weeks now, Leonolis had been consumed with thoughts of Abila. Her beauty was rare. Her face—her beautiful face—captivated his dreams. The way she batted her eyes whenever he walked by sent shivers up and down his spine. The way she said his name left him speechless and usually unable to return conversation with her due to his entire body becoming flushed and leaving him weak-kneed! He had never felt such things and did not understand what was happening. His masculine body had been awakened to something his father, King Troyolin, had told him would one day come. It had taken him several weeks to come to terms with what he was now feeling—and he thought he had a handle on it—until this moment!

In a show of wisdom, grace, and maturity beyond her years, Abila quickly diffused the situation. Her wise mother had taught her to recognize and respond to moments of fragile male egos (having a father and three brothers to deal with in her own family). Reaching her hand out, she gently laid her hand on the outstretched hand of the defensive prince and said, "I am sorry, good Leonolis. You were right to defend yourself and the honor of your friends—and perhaps I could have responded to you without disguising my voice. Please forgive me, sire."

Instantly, the heart of the prince was rescued from the abyss of embarrassment and mockery at the hand of his friends by one deft turn of words by a gracious thirteen-year-old girl. "No, it is I who should have responded with grace, milady. My friends and I apologize for causing you any fear or trepidation."

"Nonsense, milord. We are grateful to have been spared your terrible wrath," said the now-teasing girl with a hint of giggle. Turning to her friends who stared at her in amazement at the way she had handled the confrontation, "Ladies, we must be off."

As the girls prepared to make their way back to Castle Aerie, Leonolis spoke. "This is not a good time for young ladies to be alone. Did you not hear the royal decree that this is the Annum Serpentia?"

Turning suddenly serious, Abila asked, "The Year of the Dragon? Are you sure?"

"Quite sure. My father, er, King Troyolin decreed it so just this morning. By omens sent forth from the Founders, Augurian and Maison have determined that today is the first day of Ovumula—the first of the hatchlings. I would rather you and your friends not venture out again until the hunt has taken place. We will escort you to the safety of the castle."

At the heroic gesture of Leonolis and the other boys, the girls all swooned a little at this sudden turn of chivalry. Together the boys and girls walked happily—and perhaps a bit romantically—all the way back to the safety of Castle Aerie.

Long ago—during the time of the Founders—evil was introduced into the realm by dark magic. You have already met one of the consequences of that evil in Lucian. One scourge released by the darkness was the curse of the dragon, Obscurum Nyoka. This dragon had been formed from the very essence of darkness itself and, therefore, was cloaked from sight in the dark of night except during the time of the full moon. Of course, the dragon was fully visible in the light of day—but, as dragons do, she did most of her hunting at night. Every twenty-five years she was released to lay three eggs. Once her three eggs were laid, she was drawn back into the darkness of the otherworld after a three-month period. Once back in the realm of darkness, she could not emerge for another twenty-five years. By the power of good magic, the dragon had been remedied impotent to bring death or destruction upon Bren in a direct manner. Obscurum Nyoka's only way to bring her evil upon the people of Bren was through her offspring. If those offspring reached maturity—after a period of three months—they were free to wreak havoc upon the land. When the curse was cast, it was also prophesied that the curse would be broken only on the Day of Recrolution—the day the Founders returned and brought final absolution and peace to Bren.

The Venere' Serpentia Trium—the hunt for the three dragons—had not been held in the lifetime of Leonolis and Abila until now. Until now it had only been the stuff of legend—bedtime stories told of the exploits of the heroes of Bren, stories that caused little boys to dream of gallant quests in the name of Bren and caused little girls to dream of being swept off their feet by one of these knights in shining armor!

As watching-Leonolis pondered these long-ago thoughts, he was brought back into reality by the Voice. Rising through the air, they were now far above the group of teenagers, moving among the crags and crannies surrounding the Crystal Cave. Never out of sight of the young people, the Voice and the king seemed to be following them as if they were stalking them. One moment they were peering out over a rocky outcropping and the next they were darting for cover as if the teens might see them. Leonolis knew better. "What is it? What do you want me to see?"

The Voice spoke and Leonolis felt a breath come from the direction of the Voice. It was as if the Voice was clearing the air of smoke, so strong was the pressure of the breeze He created. Like a fog-draped tree suddenly revealed by an early morning breeze, the shape of a massive beast unfolded before the king. The image took his breath away as he realized the invisible Obscurum Nyoka was now crouched above the children below as if waiting to pounce.

"Watch," said the Voice.

As Leonolis watched (he could not take his eyes off of the terrible yet magnificent beast), this serpent with legs continued to stalk the children—all the way to the eastern gate of Castle Aerie! Held at bay by the good magic of Augurian, watching-Leonolis had not seen the dragon for twelve years—since the eighth year of his reign—and had certainly never seen what was unfolding before him now. "Look," said the Voice. Leonolis' gaze was drawn to a lone, robed figure pacing slowly along the upper wall of the castle. Peering into the areas surrounding the castle, the magician seemed to "know" something—seemed to sense that evil was in the midst. As his eyes pierced the darkening sky, Leonolis heard his friend Augurian speak forth an incantation.

"Wicked wings and rancid breath,
On venom's poison arrows thou doest fly;
As far as east is from the west,
Let evil's vile beast come no more nigh.

Of one now three, the evil grows
And seeks the flesh of men.
Invisible yet present like cold that brings the snows
Until the three meet sword and shield of Bren."

With that, the wizard continued pacing along the upper walls, stopping at each cardinal point to repeat the incantation. As Augurian moved along the wall, Obscurum followed stealthily, unseen yet "seen" by the wizard. With each casting of the spell, the great beast seemed to grow more and more agitated—as if it was being doused with a healthy dose of full moonlight, revealing its every move. By the time Augurian began reciting the spell for the fourth time, the dragon had heard quite enough. Like an acrid dart that pierced the falling night, the smelly beast shot past the Voice and watching-Leonolis, giving the king an undesired whiff of rotting dragon breath. At first this caused the king to begin to panic. You see, Obscurum Nyoka was not a fire-breathing dragon. Her power—her weapon—was something other. Like a blast from a hot furnace, her breath was hot enough yet did not flame. Her breath was her weapon. As the breath filled the air around her victim, the vision of the one under attack would begin to grow fuzzy and blurred, causing great confusion and fear. Once the mist was fully breathed in, it rendered the one who inhaled it into a paralytic state, unable to run and unable to fend off the leviathan. Unable to move, the victim was easily subdued.

As the dragon flew, watching-Leonolis and the Voice followed. In past occurrences of Annum Serpentia, the dragon's lair had been confined to the northern craggy peaks of the dark northern Mountains of Endoria due to the power of Bren's good magic. This year had been different. During this Year of the Dragon, Obscurum Nyoka had made her hiding place right under the noses of the royal huntsmen. At the first decree of Annum Serpentia, the royal hunting party, consisting of three separate units of twenty-five men each—one unit assigned to each dragon offspring—had been dispatched to the far northern reaches of Endoria to begin the quest to rid the land of the serpentine pestilence.

"Why was the dragon's realm widened?" asked watching-Leonolis.

"I'll show you," replied the Voice.

Once again, the Voice exhaled a mighty breath and opened a gap in time. From their present location, the two could now see a lofty peak high above the city of Abysstine. Standing on top of that peak was a lone, darkly robed figure. As their vision came into focus, they could now see a beautiful woman with long, raven-black hair whipping about in the wind behind her.

"Who do we now look upon?" asked Leonolis.

"The one they call Tormentia," came the reply.

Watching-Leonolis need know no more. Just as her son, Lucian, had been a vessel of evil, his mother lived on as the embodiment of that same evil. As she spoke, the reason for Obscurum's new freedom became apparent.

"On gossamer wings let darkness fly!
What cannot be let be!
Tear down the ancient barriers high!
What once was bound now free!

By the power of Endor's darkest night
From the abyss of Overhwelm
Unleash sweet Discord's cutting fright
To roam the southern realm!"

As the night air above Abysstine was pierced with lightning and the clap of thunder resounded through the valleys, Obscurum Nyoka emerged from a slit in the mountain's side and darted toward the southern sky as Tormentia laughed scornfully. As suddenly as the opening had appeared, it closed, bringing Leonolis back into the flight at hand.

The Voice and watching-Leonolis had been following Obscurum as she wafted through the sky away from Castle Aerie. In that dreadful day so long ago now, all had wondered why they had not discovered the place of the Ovulum—the birth nest. Watching-Leonolis now knew. Speeding away from the castle in a northerly direction, she had played her role well. Making sure to dive toward various farm houses and villages on her way northward in order to be seen and reported as heading north, none had seen her swoop down through the Canyons of Callay and make her way stealthily back to the low-lying peaks of the Crystal Cave region. She had made her nest a mere five miles away from Castle Aerie in a long-abandoned cave not too far from the place where young Leonolis and his companions had swum that day!

The spell of Tormentia had freed Obscurum Nyoka from her normal boundaries. The resulting inability to find her nest nearly cost young Leonolis—and Abila—their lives.

Chapter Eleven

A GIFT REALIZED

Abila was a beautiful girl, mature beyond her thirteen years. Weeks ago she had finally caught the eye of the prince, Leonolis. Her mother had warned her that Brenolinian boys took longer to mature, but she had not been prepared for the lack of response the seemingly unaware boy would be of her romantic interests. From the young prince's perspective, he had not come to understand his manly feelings for her for quite some time. Up until a few weeks before their swimming-hole encounter, he had seen her as merely a girl—someone to tease. But once his masculine urges kicked into gear, he had certainly noticed her in a whole new light—and felt she was out of his league! This only added to her intrigue, causing her to intensify her efforts to be noticed. This, in turn, caused him to be even more confounded at her flirtatious ways.

As watching-Leonolis and the Voice observed Abila, the king felt that he was to say nothing. Enraptured by the innocent beauty of the girl who would one day grow into the woman who would be his wife—the queen—he was enthralled at seeing his precious wife in ways her childhood stories could never have conveyed adequately. What he saw only made her that much more dear to his heart.

After the walk back to the castle that day, he had felt accepted by Abila. And he felt a deep desire to protect her and to keep her safe. She found this chivalry very flattering but unnecessary, feeling she could protect herself. Little did either know what lay in store for them in the coming days—how Abila would need his protection . . . and how Leonolis would be tested.

Though young Leonolis did not know it at the time, Abila was also of a royal lineage, her father and mother both being of the ancient Brenolinian tribe of mountain kings—some of the earliest settlers of the land. As in the royal line from which Leonolis came, Abila's heritage also included special and magical gifts from the Founders. Though she had not come to fully understand the potential or power of her giftings, she would learn to walk in them soon enough. Her first inclination at the gift of healing came when her younger brother, Mattias, had fallen and scraped his knee. She had only been nine years of age at the time but had been assigned the task of caring for three-year-old Mattias while her mother tended to the lessons of her two other brothers, Tobias and Lenden.

Running to catch a grasshopper, Mattias had tripped over his own feet and badly scraped his knee. Blood flowed freely from the grisly wound, covering his shin and ankle as it flowed out. As her brother cried out in pain, Abila ran to his side. Her mother, having heard the commotion, ran from the house just in time to see Abila reach out in compassion toward her sibling and touch his knee, and then pass out, crumpled to the ground. The very moment this happened, Mattias instantly ceased his wailing and looked on as his mother knelt down and cradled Abila's head in her lap.

"Abila! Abila!" cried her mother as she frantically stroked the girl's face. Abila lay pale and motionless. "Abila!" But the girl remained pale and still. "Tobias! Fetch me a cloth and a pail of cool water! At once, boy!"

Obeying his mother, Tobias brought a pail of water drawn from the nearby well. Placing it near his mother, he ran to find a cloth. Lenden had heard the commotion and had already fetched the cloth. Dipping it into the cool water, Abila's mother wiped the face of her daughter, hoping to bring relief and bring her back to consciousness. After a few moments, the color began to flood back into Abila's cheeks, and her eyelids began to flutter ever so slightly. Soon she gasped for a breath of air and sat upright in her mother's arms.

"Mother, what are you doing?" cried the confused girl.

"You reached down to comfort your brother and fainted dead way to the ground! I have been trying to rouse you for several moments! I . . . I thought you . . . I thought the worst, dear sweet Abila! What happened?" asked her mother.

"As I touched Mattias, a sensation of heat went through my body . . . out of my body . . . into Mattias. It was as if the very power of life passed from me . . . and into him," said Abila. Turning to Mattias who sat gazing at his sister as if in a daze, Abila asked, "Mattias, are you all right?"

Mattias continued to stare at the girl as if he had heard nothing. "Mattias! Are you all right?" asked Abila more insistently. Still nothing but a stare.

Reaching out to Mattias, his mother said, "Mattias, my darling, you are quite the mess. Come here, Son, and let me wipe the blood from your knee and tend to your wound." Still the boy stood in stunned silence, just looking intently at his sister.

As Abila's mother wiped the blood from the wounded knee of her son, she dropped the cloth and stepped back in amazement and bewilderment and began to stare at Abila in much the same awe as Mattias. Rising from where she now sat, Abila rose to her knees and turned to her little brother. "Let me see that knee, Mattie."

She would not have believed it had she not seen it with her own eyes. In the place where her mother had wiped away the blood from his knee—the place where just minutes before a deep gash had torn into her brother's flesh—there was not so much as a faint scar or blemish. The knee had been completely healed the very instant Abila had touched it. After consulting with Maison and Augurian later that day, it was determined that Abila had been granted the gift of healing from the Founders. Her gift was more than healing—it was the gift of compassion and mercy that actually performed the healing work. In the coming days she would discover that as she felt compassion and reached out to those who were sick or wounded that somehow the power of her mercy and compassion would flow out of her touch and into the body of the afflicted one. She was warned that the transference of power would result in a draining of her own life-strength—that her own life lay in the balance between healing for those she touched and complete ebbing away of her life force. Their stern warning: that she would need to walk in great wisdom and discernment as to when and how to apply her unique gift.

Yet this gift was only one of several the young Abila was to discover. Soon after the knee incident with Mattias, she found herself again face-to-face with something about herself she had never seen before. On this occasion, Abila, her mother, and three younger brothers had gone into Castle Aerie to do the week's shopping for provision. As little boys often do, they ran circles around their mother. Abila tried her best to help her mother rein them in, but as they entered the market area just on the outside, where they spilled out of the castle grounds, the throngs of people going about their business were quite stifling at times. On more than one occasion, Abila's mother lost sight of one or other of the boys and had to take them by the hand (and sometimes by the ear!) to keep them close to her side.

In this great hustle and bustle, the wagon lanes that ran through the narrow streets of the castle grounds and out the gate were constantly in motion. Small wagons filled with carrots and potatoes. Medium-sized wagons filled with melons and pumpkins. Large wagons filled with straw and grains. Lots of wheel barrows pushed by farmers toting their wares to market. Onions. Tomatoes. Corn. Beans. All manner of produce and wares. Among these many wagons came small herds of livestock. Sheep. Goats. Donkeys. Oxen. Swine. Ducks. Geese. Chickens. The constant coming and going of so many exciting things captured the attention of the boys and only made them that much more difficult to control. Then it happened.

As Abila walked with Tobias holding her right hand and Lenden holding her left, her mother corralled little Mattias by his collar. All seemed under control—at least as under control as three small, very active boys in the midst of noisy chaos might be—until Mattias set everything in motion.

As a small herd of pigs consisting of a sow and eight curious babies passed by, Mattias could not resist the temptation. The curly little tail of the piglet closest to the boy was simply too tempting. Reaching out he easily grabbed the tail and pulled, sending the little pig into a squealing frenzy, which, in turn, caused the seven pig siblings to respond in like manner. This, of course, caused mama pig to go into full protective mode. She wheeled around and focused directly on Mattias.

Amidst the sudden cacophony of oinks and squeals, Tobias and Lenden released the hands of their sister and headed straight for the commotion. As Tobias ran toward his little brother, a horse and wagon loaded down with melons careened out of control. Spooked by the mother pig frantically trying to protect her babies, the horse headed straight for Tobias. Simultaneously, Lenden ran into a nearby crowd of onlookers and out of Abila's watchful sight. Panicked by the horror of her three little brothers now each in harm's way but with no way to rescue all three, she froze in place. She had never felt such dread and fear before—and at the same time, never felt so much peace! Peace?

As if time had stopped, Abila's mind saw the unfolding events as if they were moving in slow motion. She saw her mother's face, frozen in horror, yet in the slightest of movement heading to put herself between Mattias and the mad sow. Turning toward Tobias, she saw the pounding hooves of the horse as they bore down on her still-unaware-of-the-danger brother being run down from behind. As if able to see all three at once, she saw Mattias fall beneath the feet of the crowd as people tried to avoid the raging swine and out-of-control melon cart. Feeling as if there was no time to respond to all three situations, she—from somewhere deep inside—suddenly felt she had more than enough time.

Stepping between her mother and the sow, Abila socked the beast on her nose. Moving now to Tobias, she calmly pulled him from beneath the horse's hooves and took the horse by the reins. Going from the now-stilled horse and cart, she reached down to Mattias and pulled him from under the feet that were trampling his little body. Then everything shot back into real time.

Like lightning that strikes in an instant, everything began to rush back into Abila's mind. Just as quickly, the mother pig stopped in her tracks—as if she had just seen a ghost. The horse and cart screeched to a sudden halt as if reined in by some unseen magic. The crowd that had been so boisterous in the confusion suddenly grew quiet—as if they had all seen an unexpected feat of magic that took their breath away. They all stared at Abila, mouths agape, not able to fully fathom what they had just experienced.

The girl could not quite understand what had just happened either. Some said they had witnessed magic. Some thought they had seen some forest spirit moving like the wind among them. Still others insisted that Maison or Augurian had foreseen the moment and had intervened magically from afar. That moment is still talked about in the Kingdom of Bren to this day.

DENNIS JERNIGAN

Abila and her mother looked at each other. Her mother looked at her daughter with awe and wonder. Abila's look was one of utter bewilderment and disbelief at what she had just experienced. Rushing to embrace her daughter, the two wept with relief that the boys had been protected—and wept with joy, and a bit of confusion, as yet another facet of Abila's gift was being revealed by the Founders. In the days to come—in fact in the moments to come—that gift would prove to be vital to the future of the entire realm.

As the crowd began to disperse and the market began to return to its normal hustle and bustle, Abila and her mother once again corralled the now compliant boys. This sudden compliance was due more to the awe they felt toward their big sister than the danger they had just been rescued from. Gathering her brood, Abila's mother headed for the Throne Room to request an audience with Augurian. Before they could get through the throngs, the air had grown suddenly windy—at least directly above Abila and her family. As the air stirred ever more violently, an acrid odor began to permeate the atmosphere and a shadow began to descend upon the courtyard marketplace on this sunny, cloudless day.

Turning toward the sky, the people began to scream and scatter in every direction as Obscurum Nyoka descended upon them. The beast was massive, the wind generated by her flapping bat-like wings causing awnings to be swept skyward and dust to further darken the surroundings. All panicked but not all ran. Many were so paralyzed by fear that they could not move, Abila being one of them. As her mother ran with Mattias, Tobias, and Lenden in tow, she had assumed her daughter had followed. She had not.

With the usual din of the marketplace a steady low rumble of noise, young Leonolis at once perked up when the usual was replaced with loud terror-filled screams. Running from the stable where he had been brushing Arolis, the boy fell back in horror at the sight of Obscurum Nyoka coming to alight in the courtyard. Picking himself up from the ground, he knew he must alert his father. Just as he turned toward the castle entrance and the Throne Room where his father held daily court, his eye caught a glimpse of something—someone—familiar. Abila! Standing frozen in place literally beneath the outstretched claws of the beast she stood. *Why does she not run?* thought the boy.

110

Without hesitation—without thinking about how foolish this was—Leonolis ran toward his friend. Drawing his sword, he put himself in front of the girl and directly in sight of the dragon. As the creature extended its left foot toward the two teenagers, Leonolis sliced through the air with all his strength, opening a slice in one of its gnarled talons. This, of course, only angered the beast, sending it briefly upward and out of reach of the boy and his sword. Realizing the brief respite, Leonolis took Abila's hand and pulled her toward the stable from which he had just emerged. The sky-demon quickly countered, fluttering down to the earth between the pair and the stable.

Wielding his sword above his head, Leonolis instinctively began to thought-speak to Obscurum Nyoka. *Be gone, vile vermin! Be gone!*

At this the dragon ceased its fluttering and sputtering and settled back into an evil laugh heard only by the boy. *It speaks!* she said as she laughed sneeringly. *By the Realm of Darkness, it speaks!*

I am nothing of the Realm of Darkness! I am son of the Realm of Bren, protector and prince of the realm. By the Founders I banish you from this place! yelled the bold son of Troyolin.

Ah, yes. Son of the realm. I thought I smelled the hint of royal blood coursing through those measly little veins. By the Founders? Hah! It is the very Founders who enable my existence. You have no more power than what I give you, little fool, seethed the beast.

Suddenly finding her breath again, the girl—already frazzled by the previous events surrounding her brothers—was now very aware of her predicament. "Leonolis, what will we do?" she cried, holding tightly to the sleeve of his left arm.

"Just stay behind me, dear Abila!" whispered the prince.

Dear? she thought. *He called me dear Abila!* Infatuation often becomes love in the most interesting places and under the oddest of circumstances. She would never view the prince as anything less than her hero—her knight in shining armor—from that day forward.

"Abila. When I say 'run' you run with all your might toward the castle well in the center of the courtyard. I will distract the beast while you slip down into the well. She will not be able to reach you there. Do you understand?" asked the prince.

"The well? Are you sure, Leonolis? I so fear close spaces—and who knows what lurks in the waters there?" responded the girl.

"Abila, we have no other option at this point. Once the dragon has left us, someone will pull you from the well. As for creatures that may or may not lurk in the well . . . could any be worse than what we now face?" asked the boy.

Looking up at the dragon's menacing gaze, she whispered into the prince's ear, "I will run!"

As the boy lifted his sword, he spoke to the dragon again. *You may call me "fool" but I am no fool. By the Founders I am a son of Bren. A son of Bren I was born. A son of Bren I will gladly die defending Bren's honor.*

No sooner had he spoken those words than the boy yelled to Abila, "Run!" Running with all his might toward the dragon, the girl darted toward the well. The boldness of the boy so confounded the beast that enough time was given for the girl to make her way to the well. Slipping down into the well, she stood on one of the cross beams that supported the bucket mechanism so as to see what would become of Leonolis. If the dragon were to head her way, she would easily and quickly step and drop into the water below.

Running like a crazed man protecting his beloved land and new love, Leonolis never made it to the dragon to inflict his blow. Instead, the beast began to laugh as she brushed the boy back with the flick of a wing. *Ha! Ha! Ha! See how the prince does fly! Foolish boy! You thought it was the girl I desired? It is you I have come for.*

Picking himself up from the ground, Leonolis once again lunged for the heart of the dragon. This time, Obscurum Nyoka simply reared back her head as if inhaling deeply and then leaned toward the boy, exhaling a hot, greenish mist. Had he realized what was taking place, the boy might have been able to withstand the poison (having the ability to hold his breath for quite some time due to his many hours spent swimming through the Crystal Cave), but he had instinctively inhaled deeply as the heat of the dragon's breath sent his body into shock. Just as his sword was within inches of the dragon's heart, the weapon fell from his hand. As the paralyzing poison began to course through him, the boy's body began to stiffen. Falling to the ground, Leonolis was now helpless to defend himself.

By now, the high king Troyolin had been alerted to the dragon's presence and had dispatched the Royal Guards to the courtyard. The watchmen who had been assigned for special "dragon watch" duty had been completely caught off guard at the monster's sudden appearance— as if it had materialized above the castle by magic. Watching-Leonolis, enthralled at seeing from his new vantage point what he had experienced personally those many years ago, was drawn back to that rocky crag above Abysstine and, once again, to an incantation performed by Tormentia.

"O, mighty creature, clothed in darkness
By daylight is revealed
Be now covered by the darkness still
Through noontime's rays concealed."

And, once again as quick as lightning, watching-Leonolis was transported instantly back to Castle Aerie and the helpless watched-Leonolis where he now lay beneath the dragon. Tormentia had cast a spell rendering the dragon invisible as noontime approached. The spell was simply a momentary spell meant to lend the element of surprise to Obscurum Nyoka. Since before the foundations of time and the evil had been released in the land, the dragon knew it could not be vanquished until the end of time—being given limited freedom for three months every twenty-five years. Yet, she also knew her powers were limited: namely, that she could be held at bay by force and good magic; that she could consume no human flesh (that was reserved for her offspring), yet free to feed upon the herds and flocks of the land as she was able, along with any wildlife she could manage.

Even young Leonolis knew that after the three offspring had hatched that they were free to feed upon human flesh—and that they could, more importantly, be given even more intense power from the Dark Realm should they be able to consume the flesh and blood of royalty. It had always been understood by Leonolis and his family that during the period of the Ovulus—the three-month period beginning with the hatching of the three eggs and ending with their maturation into full-fledged bat-winged, poison-spewing monsters—that he and his family must be protected at all costs. That is why it was of vital importance that the nest be found and the hatchlings destroyed before the end of that period.

Now the great flying fiend had the young prince right where she wanted him. As the dragon waited for the poison to have its full affect on the boy, an amazing series of events began to unfold that can only now be told. Even though watching-Leonolis had lived the events in his youth, it was not until the future that he was able to fully understand and appreciate all that had been sacrificed to assure his continued reign as high king of Bren.

Chapter Twelve

ABILA AND THE DRAGON

High King Troyolin watched helplessly as the great dragon's poison took hold of his son. As the royal archers began to pelt the beast with a barrage of arrows, the royal trebuchets were set in place. The two giant catapults soon began raining down a bombardment of boulders and massive balls of compacted straw, soaked in oil and set aflame. The dragon hardly flinched at the boulders and flaming straw and seemed to not even notice the hundreds of arrows glancing off her scaly body. Troyolin could waste no more time. From his position on the wall above the courtyard he began to focus all the strength of his gift toward the dragon.

At first, he was able to freeze the beast in place by the focus of his thoughts. His goal was to allow his royal guards enough time to secure the dragon with chains and rope, but as soon as she realized what was happening, Obscurum Nyoka began to intensify her fury. It was evident at first in her eyes, glaring at the High King with such hatred that it seemed they would burst from their sockets. As if her anger somehow increased her power, the monster began to shake violently—like a royal hunting dog emerging from the water and shaking herself of water—the great dragon began to shake free of the king's grip. Exploding with rage, she leapt from the courtyard straight into the air, the downdraft of her mighty wings sending a gust of wind so forceful it knocked the king and all in the courtyard onto their backsides.

As quickly as she had risen from the courtyard she fell back to earth, landing on her razor-clawed feet with a mighty thud, causing the entire castle and ground for miles around to shake as if from an earthquake. Cocking her head backward in defiance of the king's power, she let out the most blood-curdling scream any in the kingdom had ever heard. Sounding like a wounded animal in the throes of death yet coupled with the sound of pure evil madness, the resulting shriek rang in the ears of all those who heard it that day like the stench of a decaying body that one wishes they had never smelled. That sound lingered in the ears and in the air for what seemed like a dreadfully too-long time—and then all fell silent.

All the people began to right themselves and stand to their feet as the beast simply sat there in the courtyard, head cocked to the side as an animal does when searching the air for a scent—or a sound. Then all those in the castle environs that day became deathly still at what they heard next. From somewhere not too far off came a small, shrill echo of what they had just heard. All assumed it was an echo until the echo continued to resound again and again. Soon the echoes grew into a chorus of screeches and squeals, which seemed to be echoing from three different directions all at once. It seemed to be growing closer and closer. Still the great dragon, Obscurum Nyoka, sat there in the courtyard, her head no longer cocked. Now she seemed to sit there smugly, confidently—arrogantly—as if waiting with a "you foolish humans" attitude.

It had been assumed that the Ovulus had begun only a few days before, but the scholars and seers had all been deceived by a great delusional spell cast by—you guessed it—Tormentia.

> "In days gone by the light has dawned
> Before the deed was done
> Bringing light to darkest night
> And death to all but one
>
> I summon now the furies of night
> The great beasts rise again
> Let early come by dark of night
> Of three score days and ten."

The hatchlings had emerged from their shells some ninety days before! This meant they were now mature and able to wreak their evil havoc upon the good people of Bren. Since the Venere' Serpentia Trium (the hunt for the three dragons) had commenced only a few days ago, the three new dragons had simply kept hidden away in the lair near Crystal Cave, knowing the hunting parties had all been dispatched to three different areas of the northern reaches of the kingdom. In all times past, the she-dragon had laid each egg in a different place so as to give a higher probability of at least one of the offspring going undiscovered, but they had always been found in time—until today.

The first to come into grisly focus was the female, Mendax, swooping up from the south. Mendax the Liar, as she would soon be known, had the ability to spew her poisonous exhalations and induce such strong delusions in her victims that they were rendered incapable of believing the truth for several hours, making them pliable to the will of her mother, Obscurum Nyoka.

From the northeast, flying in just above the treetops, came Decipere' the Deceiver, whose gaseous emissions rendered her victims into seeing her as a being of light and goodness rather than one of darkness and evil. Her spell, like that of her sister, could last for several hours—long enough to do much damage to the kingdom.

Appearing at the same time from the northwest, diving toward the castle, came Abutor—the sole male of the three—whose putrid exhales rendered his victims blind for many hours at a time. His venomous emanations seemed particularly more evil than those of his siblings simply because those reduced to blindness were still very aware of the terror they could no longer see. At least with the spells of Mendax and Decipere' the victims were basically unaware of their altered states until many hours later.

At the sight of her brood, Obscurum Nyoka once again became very agitated and began to bounce up and down as she flapped her leathery wings while the people in the courtyard all bolted for cover, leaving only High King Troyolin and his faithful guards to attempt a rescue of the now fully paralyzed Leonolis.

Abutor was the first to reach the courtyard. As he flew directly into the onslaught of arrows, he breathed a reddish misty breath into the phalanx of soldiers. Before the king had time to yell, "Hold your breath, men!" the guards had succumbed to Abutor's potion. Left completely unable to see, the men began to drop their bows and take up their swords, blindly flailing into the air whenever they sensed the nearness of the beast. With great horror, King Troyolin watched as the ravenous beast took a fallen soldier and began to devour his body as he lit in the courtyard near Leonolis.

By now, Augurian and Maison had arrived on the scene and had begun to fill the air with incantations of light, attempting to build a barrier between Castle Aerie and the two incoming dragon siblings. With cracks of electricity, they sent bolts of lightning toward the monsters from the tips of their outstretched wands. This seemed to slow the beasts somewhat, sending them scurrying helter-skelter through the air to try and avoid the fiery blasts.

While the two seers kept the flying dragons at bay, Troyolin once again stretched forth his hand toward the great Nyoka who still towered over his stricken son. This time, rather than respond in fury and rage, the monster simply stared quietly—knowingly—at the king, content to allow herself to be subdued by his magic. As Abutor devoured the last of his "meal," he began to slither toward the prince. Instantly, Troyolin stopped him in his tracks just a few feet from the boy. Unable to move, the boy was still able to "hear" Obscurum Nyoka and respond as well. She spoke to Abutor while the boy listened.

Is it done, my son? asked Nyoka.

Snickering like a precocious child, the male dragon said, *Yes, Mother. It is done. They will be arriving in mere moments.*

Who will be arriving, wretched beast? demanded the frozen prince.

Why, the "good" people of Bren, dear prince. They are coming to my aid, calmly replied the dragon.

My people would never come to your aid! shouted the boy.

Indeed, they will, replied Nyoka. *Indeed, they will.*

While the wands of Augurian and Maison continued to fill the air and while the two dragons in the courtyard were immobilized by the high king, a great murmuring sound began to emerge from somewhere outside the castle grounds. Although young Leonolis could not turn his head toward the sound, he could certainly hear it—the rippling sound of a gathering throng of people rushing in from around the walls of Castle Aerie. Within a few minutes, the courtyard was bustling once again with hundreds and hundreds of people. Even as Troyolin continued to hold Abutor and Nyoka in his magical grip and even as Maison and Augurian kept Mendax and Decipere' at bay, the crowd continued to swell inside the castle grounds—as if the people were completely unafraid of the odiferous beasts before them.

By now, even Prince Leonolis could see people gathering around him. Encouraged by the sheer bravery of his fellow countrymen, he shouted, "Bind them, good people of Bren! Bind the beasts!" As the people continued to crowd in around him, his heart was even further compelled to urge them on. "Take the chains! Take the ropes! Fetter their feet! Bind them to the ground!" But the people stared blindly at him—as if they were actually rather appalled at the words he was uttering. Then the crowd began to murmur.

"Why should we bind the ones who have been sent to free us from the unjust rule of Troyolin?" asked one tall, burly man.

"How dare you 'command' us to put chains on such a lovely creature of hope and light?" pled a woman from somewhere nearby.

"It is you we would bind, rebellious prince of Bren! It is you and your kind that have led us to the state of bondage that now runs rampant through Bren!" cried a man Leonolis recognized as a mayor of a nearby village.

In shock, Prince Leonolis cried out, "Have you all gone mad? Do you not see the dragons that besiege our beloved land—daring to defile the sacred ground of Castle Aerie and defile all we call good? What is wrong with you?"

Unable to move yet still able to speak to the mind of the boy, Obscurum Nyoka began to snicker at the boy's words. *Dear prince of Bren, do you not see? Their minds have been swayed by the work of my daughters. While you and your ilk have been hunting for my brood in the faraway places, we have remained hidden under your very noses. Even today, my daughters have flown throughout the southern regions of Bren, releasing their venomous fumes on many towns and villages. Entire cities are even now working their way here to do our bidding.*

How can that be? What have you done to them? These are good people. What have they ever done to deserve your poison? thought the prince.

Good people? Good people? What is your version of good but a skewed perspective of what we in the darkness call good? What you call evil, we call good. Your vantage point is the only difference in the matter of the spirit of the realm. All we have done is open their minds to the possibility of another point of view. What you call poison we call magic that opens the mind to endless possibilities. Mendax has moved their minds to see what we see—and they have responded accordingly. Decipere' has moved their minds to see beyond what you call hideous and see a greater beauty. You call it evil. We call it a truer way of thinking. What is right and what is wrong? You have one way of looking at it. We have quite another, responded the she-monster.

Do you not see the deception of your ways? Do you not see the selfish focus of your way of thinking? asked the prince.

Selfish! You dare call me selfish? Look around, O, servant of the people! You say you are not selfish but you have devised a self-centered scheme allowing you and your family to rule for generations. How is that not selfish? You allow no other point of view to fashion the culture. You say you have the blessing of the Founders yet what are the Founders but a means of holding a nation captive? Your fathers concocted quite the story. Brilliant, I must say! To hold the foolish hearts and minds of your people in such bondage for millennia was so very simple. So very, very brilliant. All we have done is to open their minds to realize the error of their ways. Our poison only aids the release of what is already in their hearts and minds. We have merely empowered them to be free! said the dragon.

Prince Leonolis lay silently watching the crowd press in closer and closer to him. Even though the great Obscurum Nyoka was powerless to move any closer to him, her breath continued to bathe his body in its toxic fumes, rendering him perilously close to losing consciousness. It seemed he would pass out—in some ways that sounded much better than what he faced in reality right now. As his eyes began to flutter, he began to dream—or at least that's what he remembered.

There was Abila, staring down into his eyes from directly above as if she were hovering like a fairy. Beautiful and radiant, Abila touched him and he began to feel life and clarity come back to his mind and body. The longer he felt the pressure of her hand on his shoulder the more he came to his senses. This was no dream! Abila was touching him and nothing had changed—except that everything seemed to be moving in a very slow manner. As his eyes darted to various faces in the crowd and back and forth between the two dragons towering above them in the courtyard, he felt that everything else was moving at the pace of warm molasses on a cold morning breakfast plate.

Abila had remained in the well, standing on the bucket mechanism, the entire time. When the incoming throng of people had blocked her view of the prince, she had determined that she must come to his aid, rather, something deep within her—like the good magic of the Founders from before the foundations of Bren—compelled her to act. Even though she was still reeling from her own very recent revelation of the depth of her gifts, she went into a state of relying on the teachings of the Founders and reacted. Before she could even fathom what was happening fully, she was at the prince's side, touching him. Giving him life. Sending healing power coursing through his poison-soaked body—all this happening faster than the speed of light it seemed!

"Abila! What . . . ? How . . . ? How is this possible?" implored the prince.

"Even I do not understand why I am able to do this, Leonolis! We have no time to ponder this right now! There will be time for musing and understanding later! Let us fly at once!" cried Abila.

With that, they were off toward the nearest entrance to the castle—the entrance leading to the Throne Room. Just as they neared the portal, Leonolis looked up to see his motionless father, hands lifted toward the dreadful beasts, and loosed his grip from the hand of the girl. Instantly, the entire panorama shot back into real time. Abila was gone and Leonolis was left standing directly beneath Abutor. A small group of men near him recognized the prince and began moving toward him as one yelled, "There he is! Seize him!"

Leonolis looked frantically for a way of escape and could see none between him and those who would subdue him. Just as the hands of the men were upon him, time once again stood still. Taking him by the hand and pulling the prince toward the castle entrance, Abila cried, "Hold on to my hand, Leonolis! It is the only way!" Within less than a second they were safely hidden in the Throne Room in the secret chamber directly behind the throne of the king.

"What is going on, Leonolis?" asked Abila.

"The dragons have obviously come to maturity and completely caught the royal hunting parties off guard. We must come to the aid of my father—to the aid of Bren," replied the prince.

"But what can we do? We are not adults as they are? I am but a girl!" she answered.

"But a girl? Surely you jest, Abila! Do you not remember what you just did? You rescued me from the grip of the dragon—from right under her nose! But a girl?" said the prince with as much sarcasm as he could muster!

"You know what I mean, Leonolis. It could not have been me who did this, but rather the power endowed on me by the Founders for such a time as this," she retorted.

"Indeed, for such a time as this! They endowed YOU and no one else, silly girl! We have no time to argue the point. All I know is that you must walk in the power given to YOU—for such a time as this," said Leonolis.

"I will try," said the humble girl. "What can we do?"

"Let us come to the aid of my father—come to the aid of Maison and Augurian. If nothing else, let us go to their side and seek their wise counsel," said the boy.

With that, they were off. Hand in hand, they headed up the stairway to the point where he had last seen his father, arriving in a flash. Standing directly in front of the king, Leonolis shouted, "Father, we have come to assist you! What would you have us do?"

Nothing.

"Father, it is I, your son! Father, why do you not answer?" pled the boy.

Still nothing.

"I think I know what to do," replied Abila.

Reaching her hand toward the king while still grasping the hand of the prince, she touched his shoulder. He immediately became animated, momentarily dropping his hands from the work they were doing in holding the dragons at bay. Catching himself, he again put his hands back in position, still focusing on the work at hand yet speechless at the sight of Abila and Leonolis. After a few seconds of wonder, his awe gave way to speech.

"Abila! Leonolis! How can this be?" asked the frantic king.

"Father, there is not time. Suffice it to say, Abila has a gift from the Founders for such a time as this!" said Leonolis.

"Quickly, children! Go now to the place on the castle wall to Augurian. Seek his counsel!" said the king. And the children were off.

Coming almost instantly to the side of Augurian, Abila touched his arm. Rather than respond in surprise, Augurian said, "Ah, there you are! Finally! I've been expecting you!"

"Expecting us?" asked the prince.

"Yes! Even this morning as I rose I felt a stirring in the realm of magic alerting me to the awakening of one of the most treasured gifts of the realm bestowed by the Founders. So, Abila is the one. I would never have suspected. So like the Founders to confound the wise with the simple!" he said as he chuckled to himself.

"You are the one we have been expecting for generations. I only imagined it could happen in my lifetime—and here before me stands the dream! You are the one in prophecy called Senare Tempus Peragro—the healer who travels through time! You are granted the power to bring healing by a mere touch. You are granted the power to travel with ease between the dimension of time and the dimension where time is no more. You are here for such a time as this!" declared the seer.

"What would you have us do, good Augurian?" asked the prince.

"Time is of the essence to all but you, Abila. You must trust your gift. You must trust me also. The people of Bren are under strong delusion. If we can hold the beasts for a few more hours, the poison will wear off, but we do not have a few hours. The magic of the dragons is powerful, indeed, and only made more so by the dark magic of Tormentia. Go at once to the northern realm and bring back the three hunting parties."

"But how will I find them? How will I ever bring them back in time?" asked the bewildered girl.

"Trust your gift, child. The Founders have bestowed the gift on the one able to wield it with honor and grace. With the gift comes the Voice of the Founder himself. Listen with your heart. Believe with your mind. Walk where you are led," said the calm Augurian with a twinkle of delight in his eye that seemed so out of place under the circumstances.

"But—" began Abila.

"There is no time for 'but' even for a girl to whom time means nothing! Off! Leonolis, go with her."

"Do not let go of my hand, Abila. I trust your gift—and I trust you! I can guide you to the northern realms," encouraged the prince.

Like lightning, the teens were off. Down the castle wall and out the gate, the two ran with all their might up the eastern road, around Forbidden Swamp, past the Sleeping Giant, past Oaken Fork and directly into the Great Forest. Like pure energy—pure light—the pace of their feet did not match the incredible distance they were able to cover in a few seconds. It seemed to Leonolis that they were skimming across the earth like a perfectly cast stone skims across a still body of water, making it from one side to the other! In fact, they came to Menden Lake and actually skimmed right across the surface of the water in one simple bounding leap! Coming to a stop just to the east of the castle spires of Abysstine, they encountered the first of the three hunting parties.

Taking the party commander, Reginald the Bold, by the hand, the commander tried to jerk his grip loose from Leonolis, but the boy held firm.

"Reginald, we have no time for explanation. Some great magic has released the three dragons earlier than we had foreseen. Even now they besiege Castle Aerie. Trust me, my lord! We will explain later. I will release you. Do as I command. Instruct your men to join hands with one another. Tell them they are about to experience great magic. By the order of High King Troyolin, they are not to let go until released to engage the four dragons at Castle Aerie." As the boy released Reginald's hand, the commander gave the order and the mighty men of Bren took one another by the hand. As the last man joined hands, Leonolis once again took the hand of Reginald and cried out, "To the Mountains of Endoria!"

Chapter Thirteen

THE DRAGON BATTLE

In a flash, the long line of men, many on horseback, flew through the air occasionally glancing the ground, looking so bewildered yet like little boys taking their first bareback ride at full speed—sheer elation and giddy amazement! Ecstatic joy and utter shock! Over high peaks and across impassable crevices, the long train of men and horses streamed. Only once did they have to circle back and pick up the last man in the line who let go just above a gently flowing creek. The water had cushioned his landing. As he was taken by the hand once again, he was none the worse for his spill. Just thoroughly drenched!

Nearing the furthest reaches of the northern lands of Bren, they came upon the next hunting party, led by Stephon (also known by his men as "The Doctor" because of his propensity for effectively and quickly binding wounds on the field of battle). Leonolis again took the commander by the hand (the prince and Abila felt it would be better to be startled by someone they knew than by a teenage girl. It was also considered inappropriate for a young woman to touch an adult male and vice versa).

Again, the response was one of shock and being rendered utterly speechless. Soon the unlikely train had grown by twenty-five more men and their horses as Leonolis shouted the command, "To the eastern Forest of Endoria!" To the men it seemed they were flying rather than running across the earth. The horses seemed to be less frantic than Leonolis had expected, which was a great testament to the training regimens of the horsemen of Bren—that the horses would be so obedient even under such unusual circumstances. Flying over mountain peaks, through forest glades, through a couple of village market centers completely unnoticed, the entourage raced. Across streams and lakes and over unsuspecting herds of deer and flocks of sheep, they tore through the air untouched by the bonds of time. Unable to find even a trace of the last hunting party in the Forest of Endoria, Leonolis began to grow bewildered. Abila noticed.

"Leonolis, what is wrong?" she asked.

"My father had dispatched the third group to the Forest of Endoria, yet they are nowhere to be found. Something is wrong!" replied the prince.

"Wait," said Abila as she brought the entire group to a sudden stop.

"What is is, Abila?" asked the boy.

"A stirring," was her reply.

"A stirring? Up ahead? Friend or foe? What do you see?" asked the prince.

"A stirring in the air—like magic. I cannot 'see' anything with my eyes, yet I 'see' something in my mind. Dancing. Yes, dancing," she said as her voice trailed off in obvious amazement at what she was seeing.

"Dancing?" queried the prince.

"Yes, dancing," was all she could say.

"People dancing? A party? A festival? What do you see, Abila?" he asked again.

"Not people. A place," she said.

"Of course! The Founder is speaking to you of a place! It has to be Dancing Meadow! To Dancing Meadow!" shouted the prince. And they were off! In a mere breath of time the group came to the place called Dancing Meadow, just to the southeast near the very southern border of the Forest of Endoria. Sure enough, there was the third group of dragon slayers!

Taking the commander by the hand in what was becoming very routine for Leonolis now, the prince said, "Ventus, it is I, prince Leonolis! We have no time. I come by decree of High King Troyolin. Castle Aerie is under dragon siege. I will explain on the way there. Instruct your men to take one another by the hand and to trust the Founders' magic."

Within moments, the entire band of two teens and seventy-five dragon slayers were on their way back to Castle Aerie. The journey to locate and bring back the dragon hunters had seemed like many minutes to Leonolis but had actually taken less than ten seconds in real time! In fact, Augurian, Maison, and Troyolin were positioned almost exactly where they had been on the castle walls when Abila and Leonolis had left! Stopping just outside of the castle gate, Leonolis began to explain the situation to the men.

"Mighty men of Bren! Hear me and hear me well," began the boy. "The dragon Obscurum Nyoka is even now being held at bay by the gifting of my father, High King Troyolin. One of her offspring—a male—is under his grasp as well in the courtyard. He can only hold them for a few more minutes at best. Two other offspring—both she-dragons—are being held in check by Augurian and Maison. Let us stay connected while we bind the feet and snout of the male. Once bound, Reginald and his men will release their hold of Abila and commence to dispatch the dragon. Separate his head from his body with all haste! Be careful to not breathe his offensive fumes, as this is his means of subduing us!"

Without hesitation, the line of men made their way to Abutor by way of the castle smith shoppe where they quickly gathered chains and rope. While silent and paralyzed in time, they made quick use of their timeless state. Making sure to stay connected by touch, the men were able to bind the feet of the beast with chains. Another group, climbing on one another's backs, hastily made their way to the snout that was tied shut with rope. As soon as the deed was done and the men were clear, Leonolis gave the command, "Release!" and Reginald and his men were suddenly relegated to real time.

Instantly, the dragon Abutor's rage became frenzied as he began to panic and strain against the chain and rope. Unable to spew his poisonous gas, he began to flap his massive wings violently. Lifting from the ground, the dragon quickly began to make his way skyward and away from the castle. Just as he was about to clear the castle wall, the great beast was jerked back to earth by the chain the men had wisely tethered to a stake that had been driven into the ground. Flapping wildly, the monster began knocking the crowd all about the castle courtyard. Oblivious to the danger due to the effects of the poison, those who were not killed instantly, got right back up and headed—injured and otherwise—right back into the fray.

"The wings!" shouted Leonolis. "The wings!"

Realizing they had not taken into account the dragon's ability to wield death and destruction with its wings, Leonolis and Abila again touched Reginald, saying, "We must bind the wings, Reginald!"

Quickly the mighty Reginald went back down the line of men still connected to Abila and made his way to the now motionless wings of Abutor. Climbing on the shoulders of the men, Reginald threw more chains around the wings of the beast. Leaping down from the back of the dragon, he then commanded the men to pull the loop of chains as tight as possible. The wings began to close against the dragon's back until they were flush against the scaly skin of the beast. Reginald then released his touch from the group and went back into real time just as Abutor, in his panic, fell to his side from the imbalance caused by the new fetters. Without another moment's hesitation, Reginald drew his sword from its sheath, walked over to the writhing neck of the monster, and lifted the weapon as high above his head as possible. With all the force he could muster, Reginald brought the sword down against the flesh of the beast.

The body of Abutor shuddered and then fell suddenly motionless in death, the head rolling a few yards through the courtyard and coming to rest directly beneath the massive chest of his very confused and angry mother. This, of course, sent Nyoka into such a frenzy that she was able to break free from the magical hold of King Troyolin. The breaking of magic was so powerful that it sent a shockwave back to the king, knocking him from his feet and backward into the wall. Hitting his head as he fell, the king was rendered unconscious by the force of the blow. Nyoka glanced in horror at the head of her son and, looking up to the one she blamed for his demise, began to bear down on the motionless body of the king.

Instantly, Abila and Leonolis and the fifty remaining dragon slayers were at the feet of Nyoka, now frozen in place (albeit unknowingly to her!). Stephon motioned his men to begin the chaining process. One group worked on tethering her feet to the ground while another group bound her snout. Once these areas were restrained, they went to work on binding of her wings, having learned their lesson with the flailing wings of Abutor! When the bindings were checked and double-checked, Stephon released his hold on Abila and Leonolis and reverted back to real time.

Obscurum Nyoka, due to the magic from long ago, could not be killed until the end of time. Once her offspring were dispatched she could only be sent back into the dark realm for another twenty-five years. As she strained against her fetters, Nyoka writhed and wriggled, trying, in vain, to free herself. While helpless on the ground, there was nothing she could do to protect her young—but she could speak to them by thought.

Mendax, to the High Place! Summon our queen! Have her summon the darkness! Fly at once, child! screamed the beast in thought.

Without vacillation, the dragon Mendax darted toward the north—and out of the reach of the magic of Augurian and Maison. Flying like a maniac through the air, the rapid pace was so intense that it created a piercing whistling sound that echoed through the land for miles, causing houses to quiver and shake and horses to throw their riders. In mere minutes, Mendax reached the highest pinnacle overlooking Abysstine. Hovering just in front of a dark opening in the southern face of the peak, Mendax let out a horrific wail. As she cried out to the mountainside, the opening became flooded with blinding light. Piercing even the sunny sky, the brightness of the light shone out from the entrance of the cave giving the appearance of a spear jutting out for miles into the blueness.

"What word have you for me?" asked Tormentia.

"Mother, the worthy Obscurum Nyoka has been subdued and my brother, the mighty Abutor, has been sent back to the darkness! I have been sent with haste by Nyoka with the words 'summon the darkness'," answered Mendax.

"With haste, fly back to her aide, my dear! By the time you are there, darkness will have fallen over the entirety of Bren!" responded the witch.

As Mendax turned and headed back toward Castle Aerie, Tormentia turned her attentions to dark magic. Lifting her hands toward the south, palms facing outward, she began her incantation.

"O, power of darkness
Great black abyss
O, force of blackest night
Send forth thy harshness

With a kiss
Remove them from the light . . .

On ebony's wings
Perform thy task
Of stealth and moonless night
Obscure the things
That man doest fear
The beasts from in his sight."

As her words echoed into the sunlight, a groaning as of thunder began to fill the air. As if the sun itself was moaning under some great pressure, its light began to dim, growing darker and darker with each second until the entire star was blacked out by a complete and utter eclipse unlike the world had ever seen. Within minutes of the spell, the entire land was consumed in the darkest night. So much was the sunlight obscured that not one bit of light was able to penetrate the darkness. The spell had worked—now the dragons would no longer be visible to the eyes of men!

As she headed back to her mother's side, Mendax was no longer visible, being obscured by the darkness Tormentia had brought on the land. The only thing betraying her presence was the whistling scream her rapid flight once again produced. As she neared Castle Aerie, she slowed her pace so as to squelch the shriek her wings had produced. Coming to light on a turret above the castle grounds, Mendax could see that Augurian and Maison had ceased from their defenses, having lost sight of Decipere'. Decipere' was merely resting on another turret just a few feet above her sister. Of course, they could see one another and they could see the people cowering in fear below them, but no one could see them. They would allow the silence to induce even more fear. Once the fear of the king's men was at a sufficient level, they would begin their dark work.

Still writhing against her bonds, Nyoka lay on her side in the courtyard below. Sensing the nearness of her remaining brood, she struggled to raise her head. Spying her two girls perched above her, she cried out to them in the power of thought.

Mendax and Decipere', I am subdued. They cannot slay me but they can limit my reach. Use the darkness and free me. Use your venom and bring weakness to the Royal Guard. Even now I sense the high king has been dealt a serious blow. I no longer sense his power. Seek him out. Lay him waste. Devour his flesh and gain new strength. Be wary of the two seers on the wall. Their power is still formidable. They cannot hinder what they cannot find. Use the people you have already infected. They are in the prime of their delusion. Be not afraid yet beware the prince, Leonolis. He walks in some strange magic beyond what I am able to discern. He lurks somewhere nearby. It is he who has dispatched Abutor. I have sensed it though I have not seen it with my eyes. The prince is responsible. Avenge your brother. Capture the boy—and bring him to me, said Nyoka.

As the great mother dragon lifted her head to survey the surroundings, the two sisters gently glided from their perches to the courtyard below. Though darkness blinded the humans, those under the spell of their poison could still see the three dragons. Hundreds in number now, those under the power of the beasts were now rallying around the dragons, prepared to do their bidding. Leading the way to Nyoka, Mendax coaxed the hypnotized throng toward her mother. Surrounding the shackled monster, several began to pull at the rope used to bind her snout while others worked on loosing the chains from her feet and wings. Soon, the terrible Nyoka would be free.

Unable to see but drawn to the noise in the courtyard, Augurian and Maison began to make their way to the wall overlooking the great dragon. Fearing they might harm the deluded people, they withheld the lightning bursts of energy they had used to hinder the dragons in the daylight. Feeling their way quickly along the wall, the two magicians crouched as they worked their way closer to the commotion. As they came to a stop just above where the sound was emanating, Augurian quietly cast a spell.

> *"Through evil's blackness*
> *Pierce this night*
> *On every torch*
> *Let there be light!"*

Instantly, every torch in the courtyard and every lamp in the castle burst forth with flaming brightness! Suddenly, the scene below took

131

shape. As the dragons were once again exposed to the light, the two sisters began hissing frantically and began whipping their heads from side to side, much as a snake does when feeling threatened by a mongoose. Responding more from fear than from strategy, Mendax darted into the sky and was once again consumed and hidden in her ebony cloak. Decipere' began pacing hysterically around her mother, protecting her from the unseen foe she knew hoped for her demise. Spewing her noxious gases in hope of subduing that which she feared, she only dimmed the senses of the people who were still working on freeing her mother from the bonds that held her wings and feet, rendering them too weak to be of any use. Still, they had managed to free her beak and feet.

Standing now, though unable to fly, Nyoka headed toward the last place she had seen the king standing. Once she reached the wall of the castle entrance, she hopped and tried to flap her wings, but of course, they were completely bound to her back by chains. Normally one small hop and a flap of her leathery flying limbs and she would have been atop the wall, one neck's length away from her prey. In futility, she lunged against the wall, trying to grasp and climb with her feet, using her chin as a means of grasping the masonry. Luckily for Troyolin, she was unable to make any headway.

Meanwhile, Decipere' slinked her way to the wall directly underneath Augurian and Maison, sensing their presence. Stealthily, she scaled the wall using the claws protruding from the joints of her wings. Holding her head just beneath the level of the wall's rim, she held her breath as she waited for the strike. Trying not to stir, the two seers knelt just a few feet from where she now lurked. Holding their breath, the men knew that one small misstep—one tiny gasp—would betray their positions. The dragon slowly inched her head upward and extended her snout. With a short burst of breath, she expelled a blast of noxious gas that instantly engulfed the men. Augurian did not flinch. Maison was another matter.

He was quite adept at holding his breath. Having already held his breath for almost one minute, Maison had attempted to catch a quick fill of his burning lungs at the precise moment the dragon had snorted. Even though he had not breathed in any of the fumes, his tongue had caught a slight tinge of the taste of the dragon's breath, causing him to spit and sputter ever so slightly, but it had been enough to belie his position!

The dragon lifted her serpentine neck like a giant cobra preparing to strike. Now fully honed in on the one who had made the sound, she hissed a horrific hiss and drew back as far as she could. As fast as lightning she lunged at Maison. From her position in the courtyard Obscurum Nyoka saw the attack and knew her child's fangs had found their mark. As she watched, her daughter's neck began to jerk violently back and forth much as a crocodile does when overcoming a hapless gazelle. Great was her pride and great was her sense of victory at the sight. Great was her horror at what she witnessed next.

As suddenly as Decipere' had lunged at Maison and had seemingly made her kill, her neck jerked violently away from the wall—minus her head! Extending high above the wall for all to see, the headless dragon's body went magnificently limp as the life drained from her body and she crashed to the courtyard below.

Just as she fell to the ground, dozens of heads mysteriously appeared at the wall. Peering down at the slain beast was Ventus (bloodied sword raised in victory), Abila, Leonolis, and the men of Ventus' hunting party! Seeing what was about to transpire, Leonolis had led them to the wall where Ventus positioned himself by standing on the rim of the wall just above the head of the waiting dragon. When he felt ready, he turned to Abila and said, "Now!" Releasing her hold on his ankle, Abila had let go of Ventus just as Decipere' had lunged for Maison. She never saw the sword or the swordsman. As sword met dragon flesh, it sliced cleanly and quickly through her neck with little sound. All that was heard was the sound made as her head fell with a mighty thud right on top of poor Maison, who was none the worse for wear and tear and a coating of dragon saliva and blood.

In that instant, for a few brief victorious seconds, Augurian, Maison, Leonolis, Abila, and the hunting party had forgotten about the matter of the remaining she-dragon, Mendax. It had only taken a few seconds for the last living offspring of Obscurum Nyoka to descend to the courtyard and free her mother.

Chapter Fourteen

THE LAST DRAGON

Descending in complete silence, Mendax came to light behind Nyoka as Augurian and Maison were still being distracted by the demise of Decipere' and the ensuing chaos it had caused. Using her acidic saliva, she quickly dripped her spittle on the chains that bound her mother. Putrid smoke began to rise from the iron as the acid ate through the chain. Before Maison or Augurian could turn their attention to Mendax and Nyoka, the mother and daughter were free! Bounding into the darkness, they rose above the fray and began to take stock of their situation.

At this point, watching-Leonolis, who had been spellbound at the point of view he had just witnessed of all he had lived through so many years before, was stirred into awareness by the Voice. "Let us listen," was all He said. Lifting from their previous perch, the watchers ascended into the darkness above Castle Aerie and came to hover some five hundred feet above the highest turret of the fortress. As watching-Leonolis tried to adjust his eyes, the air filled with a rancid odor he remembered all too well. Dragon's breath.

Turning toward the direction of the horrendous bursts of air, he heard them before he saw them. Obscurum Nyoka and Mendax were devising their next move.

"Daughter, you have done well. Let us beware of the two seers below. Great is their magic. That magic has grown even more powerful in light of the loss of your brother and sister. We are at a disadvantage so we must make the best use of our resources. By stealth we will avenge. By the magic in our breath we will overwhelm. And, by all means, we must consume royal flesh if we are to increase our strength against their wizardry," spoke Nyoka in a very matter-of-fact way.

"What is your bidding, Mother?" asked Mendax.

"The high king, Troyolin, is even now still reeling from the last blow we were able to inflict. The prince, Leonolis, continues to boggle my mind, as he is somehow able to disappear and reappear at will. It is by his hand your siblings have been slain. It is my desire to consume his flesh. Let us use his father's predicament to lure him from his place of hiding," responded Nyoka.

"How shall we proceed?" asked the daughter.

"I will descend upon the high king, pinning his feeble neck to the ground beneath my talons. As the boy realizes what is about to take place, he will surely come to the assistance of his father. In that moment I will strike them both dead and have my feast. Your task is to keep the wizards engaged and occupied with trying to subdue you. By your stealth, stay as near to the darkness as possible, swooping in and out of their visibility, let your flight be so erratic that they have no idea when or where you might appear next. By confusion their downfall will come. Be wise, my dear. Do not alight as your brother and sister did. That was their downfall and too late was I in this discovery to be of any help to them," warned the beast.

"But, dear mother, they will slay you should you alight!" said the agitated Mendax.

"No, by decree of the Founders, I cannot be slain—only bound. Trust me, my child, we will have our vengeance if you stay airborne and allow me to flush out the boy. Prepare to fly, Daughter! Once I begin my descent, you must wreak havoc upon the seers. Now we fly!" shouted Nyoka as the two fell toward earth like crazed, blood-thirsty bats.

Following Obscurum Nyoka, the Voice and watching-Leonolis descended to a tower just above where the king still lay semi-conscious from the concussion he had received and lit there as the events began to unfold.

The king had been lying there for only a short period but long enough for the dragons to set their plans in motion. Nyoka fell to the tower floor where the king was laying with such force that it seemed—at least for a couple of seconds—that the floor would give way. Such was the sound of her landing that it startled Maison, Augurian, Leonolis, Abila, and all those with them back into the battle at hand, having been distracted by the victory over Decipere'.

Leonolis was the first to respond. "Father!"

Even amidst his shout, Leonolis caught the eye of the great monster that now loomed over his father's body. She glared at the boy with such intensity that the boy could not even blink, having been somewhat mesmerized at the strange connection he now experienced with the dragon.

Shouting his thought, he addressed the beast.

Devil-monster! Release my father at once or I will have no choice but to use the power of the Founders to send you to the nether-world with your children! yelled the boy.

O, dear prince. Have you already forgotten the teachings of your own scholars? Slay me, you cannot! Indeed, you cannot even send me back into the abyss of darkness unless and until all my children have been slain. Even as you speak, there is still one who lurks above, said the dragon with much glee in her voice.

Even now she makes her way through darkness. What will she do? Where will she appear? She will not be so foolish as her brother and sister as to place one of her precious talons anywhere near the earth. As for your use of the power of the Founders, should you suddenly disappear, you will not have time to keep me from piercing your father's heart. As you can see, he has no idea that he will soon walk with your precious Founders in the afterlife. Should you make even one motion—should you lift so much as one of your princely fingers—I will thrust my talon, my dagger, right through his still-beating heart.

Leonolis stood frozen in place now, not daring to move one bone of his body. Abila had no idea of the conversation taking place between Leonolis and Nyoka. All she knew was that they needed to do something—and now!

"Leonolis, take my hand!" shouted the girl as she moved toward the prince.

"No, Abila! No! Should I move even one inch the beast will pierce my father's heart! Even your gift cannot save him now!" warned Leonolis. And without taking thought for his own safety—without even considering that he might once again utilize the gifting of Abila to suspend time—he spoke to the dragon.

What will you have me do? Spare my father and I will do whatever you ask, pleaded the boy.

137

Shaking her head in an up and down motion, she said in a snicker, *There's a good boy. Tell all your friends to step away from you. Instruct them to clear the wall for a hundred feet in any direction. Command the seers—your magicians—to conceal themselves within the confines of the stairwell leading to the courtyard. Once they have complied, my daughter will descend and carry you to me. When you are by my side, I will release your father. That is it. Do as I say and your father will be spared. You have my word.*

"What is she saying to you?" asked Augurian.

"She says that should I make a move of any kind to attempt to use the gift of Abila she will instantly pierce father's heart. I told her to spare him and I would do whatever she asks. She is willing to spare his life in trade for mine," said the boy in as much calm as he could muster considering the circumstances. Abila, though mortified at the thought of his predicament, was equally awed at the prince's poise and willingness to sacrifice himself. She knew she loved him in that moment.

"You must not comply," said Augurian sternly.

"She will kill my father!" responded the boy.

"Your father would have it so, Leonolis. He would sooner sacrifice himself for your sake—for the sake of the kingdom—than to live and lose both," replied Augurian.

"This is true, Son. This is truth," chimed in his trusted friend, Maison.

"No. There is no other way," said Leonlis.

Without warning, Mendax buzzed by, just above the heads of those on the wall with the prince. So close did she come that all were swayed by the wind her wings produced—all were bathed in her poison before they realized what was taking place. Luckily, the sudden appearance of the dragon had caused all but a few to hold their breath in fear, thus protecting them from her venom. It had also been quickly dispersed and weakened by the velocity of the wind her leathery sails had induced, causing the poison to be ineffective. Even Augurian and Maison had not had time to respond.

As Mendax darted in and out of visibility, Leonolis remained frozen in place, lest he cause harm to come to his father. Abila, out of respect for Leonolis (and a bit out of her own fear) also stood motionless.

Speaking into the chaos, Nyoka addressed the boy again. "What will it be, boy? Shall I pierce your father? What would you have me do? I am losing patience. Instruct your magicians that should they turn their wands toward me, the king is dead. Have them do as I say. Now!"

Turning his head slightly toward the seers, Leonolis spoke. "Dear friends. We have no choice. We must do as she says if my father is to be saved."

"You always have a choice, dear prince," said the fatherly Maison to the boy. "Your father is king. It is his will—you know it to be so in your heart—that he lay down his life for the realm. That is your choice. Either obey the way of the realm or risk losing it all, Son. That is your choice. Do what is right. Do the will of your father and save the kingdom. Do anything else and you risk losing everything."

"You are right, dear Maison. Those are my choices—but you forget one thing. I am the son of my father. His blood courses through—rages through—my heart as well. It is my choice to make, and make it I have. This is what we will do."

Speaking loudly enough for all on the wall to hear, he instructed them as Nyoka had told him to. As soon as he finished, both Augurian and Maison began to slowly make their way to the stairwell. Something in their heart of hearts told them it was the will of the Founders to do so—besides, they knew the stubbornness of Leonolis well enough to know there was no use arguing the point any further! Seeing the wizards go down into the dark of the wells caused Ventus and his unit to back toward the opposite stairwell and begin their descent. Soon, all that was left on the wall was Leonolis and Abila. Turning his head slightly toward the girl, he gently nodded. As he did so, Abila could not help but notice a little gleam in his eye. Without using a word, she felt he was saying, "Go ahead. You know what to do." And she reluctantly slipped down into the stairwell following Ventus and his men.

As she withdrew from sight, a fluttering sound began faintly from directly above the prince. As Mendax dropped cautiously from the darkness above, Leonolis remained as still as possible while fixing his eyes directly upon Nyoka, who, in turn, did not break her gaze back at the boy. The dragon roughly took the boy's shoulders in the strong grip of her talons and jerked him skyward. He was no longer afraid, but rather, silently determined. Flying from the wall to the tower floor where Nyoka had the king pinned, she was careful to not actually alight on the floor herself, carefully following her mother's instructions. As she hovered above her mother, Nyoka spoke.

"Place him here," she said as she pointed with her snout to a spot near the boy's father. Dropping five or so feet from above his father's head, Leonolis was careful not to land on the king. No sooner had he landed than he began pummeling the dragon's scaly snout with his fists, demanding, "Let him go! Let him go now!"

Laughing snidely, Nyoka brushed the boy aside, causing him to lose his balance and land on his backside. Releasing her grip on Troyolin, she immediately pinned the prince to the ground with one arm as she simultaneously held his father in the talons of her other. He looked lifeless to the boy, yet he could see his father writhe a little from the pain of her grip on his midsection. At least he was breathing. Lifting them both from the ground, she said to the boy, "Say good-bye to your father, boy. His reign is done." Laughing, she tossed Troyolin over the side of the tower wall saying, "Here, daughter! Feast and be empowered!"

As Troylin's body flew through the air and disappeared below the turret wall, Leonolis saw a dark streak follow his father's body down. He knew it was Mendax—there was nothing he could do to help his father anymore.

Leonolis tried to reach for his father, but the dragon's grip was vise-like, causing him to struggle for breath. Still he cried out, "Father! No!" Turning toward the dragon's face, he shouted, "You said you would spare him! You lied!"

"And you were foolish enough to believe me! Ha! You know as well as I do that one does what one must to preserve one's life. You would have done the same had you been in my position, incredulous little fool!" she mocked.

"Your father's reign is ended. Yours is about to end as well. With your flesh I will gain power that not even the magic of the Founders can contain. No more shall I and my kind be bound to brief interludes of freedom! We will be released to rule the light just as we rule the darkness in the realm beyond! The realm beyond is, this day, joined with the realm of here and now!"

"You will never rule the light! You will never rule this realm! Darkness has no real power over light and you KNOW it!" shouted the boy.

"Then what shall we call me ruling over you in this moment? A slight inconvenience! Ha! Ha! Ha! How foolish!" she laughed.

Through angry tears, Leonolis shouted, "My father will be avenged! You shall pay for his blood with your own! This day you will die! You will pay!"

Tightening her grip on the boy (Leonolis thought he would be crushed), she stopped and stared intently into the boy's wet eyes. "Yes, vengeance. Let us speak of vengeance. It is you and you alone I hold responsible for the death of my son and daughter. You, the good and fair prince of Bren, by your own hand have rained down terror upon me—forcing me to watch in horror the heinous slaying of my children this day. For that, you will suffer."

As she placed the boy on his back on the floor of the turret, she ripped away his shirt revealing his bare, smooth skin. Keeping him pinned down by the shoulders with her left fore claw and subduing his legs with her left hind claw, Nyoka slowly raised the razor-sharp index finger of her right claw and began to slide it ever so gently across the boy's chest. At first, she went only deep enough to produce a scratch so fine and precise that one would have sworn a cat had clawed the prince. Leonolis writhed in pain but refused to make one whimper. This only seemed to enrage the hatred and bitterness of the monster.

"Cry out for Papa, boy. See if he can hear you. Oh, wait. What's that? Papa's dead? What is that I hear below? Could it be his bones being crushed as my daughter makes a feast of his flesh?" Nyoka said without mercy. "It matters not whether you make a sound or not, O prince. Once I have tasted your flesh my power will be magnified and multiplied. Once my daughter has consumed the flesh of your father, we will be invincible!" she said with a snide laugh.

Once again the monster placed her finely honed talon on the boy's chest. Beginning at his left shoulder and moving diagonally down to his right torso, she began to make a very fine incision, effectively and cleanly laying the boy's flesh open perfectly. So exact was her cut that not much blood yet poured from the wound. Just as she had done with the left shoulder, she moved next to the right, slicing slowly from the upper right shoulder all the way down to the left side of the boy's torso, leaving a gaping wound in the shape of an X.

Now the boy could no longer hide his pain and began to cry out in agony—such agony that all who heard in the courtyard that day said they had never heard such groanings before. Heartwrenching is the only word that truly describes the sound Leonolis made in the midst of such gruesome agony. Augurian heard it. Maison heard it. Ventus and his men heard it. And Abila heard it. All stood in shock, frozen in place, as the dragon performed her deed.

Taking her time, enjoying the agony she was inflicting on the prince, she never even took thought at the fact that Mendax had not made one sound as she had flown down to take her prize in the courtyard below. She had, indeed, heard bones crunching—but that sound was not coming from what she imagined. Releasing her grip on the now unconscious prince, she slipped her head over the wall to get a glimpse of her daughter having her way with the high king.

As her eyes adjusted to the light below, she saw that Mendax was lying directly over the body of the king, his feet jutting out from under her neck. "Daughter! This is a time for diligence! Be alert! Take no rest now! There will be time for that later!"

Mendax did not move.

"Mendax! Arise at once!"

Still nothing.

Leaving the boy's bleeding body, she hopped down from the turret to the courtyard below. Lying in an awkward position, her daughter's eyes were open but she was not responding.

"Mendax! Daughter! What are you doing?" shouted the now fearful she-dragon.

With her paw, Nyoka nudged her daughter's shoulder, trying to rouse her—only to watch in horror as her head began to roll away from the neck!

"What has happened?" shouted the dragon.

From somewhere above her, Nyoka heard a voice saying, "She has been slain—slain without ever tasting one drop of royal blood. High King Troyolin has been spared. His reign has not ended! It is your reign that ends this day!" shouted Maison from the wall of the turret where she had left Prince Leonolis!

"What magic has wrought this? This cannot be!" seethed the dragon.

With one bound she leapt to the wall above, landing where Maison had been standing but had vanished! The fury of the dragon's rage became so palpable in that moment that all who witnessed what transpired that day felt her anger in the form of intense heat emanating from the dragon's great breast. Hopping down from her perch, she landed near Leonolis. Lifting her paw to strike the deathblow, she was suddenly brought to a halt in mid-stomp! To her horror, High King Troyolin was standing directly below her—paralyzing her in place by the grip of his power. All she could do was watch and breath—in fear.

What Obscurum Nyoka had not seen—could not have seen—was this: once Leonolis had been transported by Mendax to his father's side, Abila had gone to work—and so had Augurian and Maison. As the king's body was tossed over the side of the turret wall, Maison and Augurian (having concealed themselves in the courtyard by good magic) cushioned the king's fall, laying his wounded body gently down on the smooth-stoned courtyard.

As this was taking place, Abila had transcended time once again, taking Ventus and his men with her to the courtyard where they met the two seers. The timing (which is quite humorous since they were actually avoiding time) of Abila and Ventus and his men could not have been more precise, more perfect. No sooner had she arrived at the king's side than she brushed the king's body with her hand. Having only a slight concussion, her touch had been enough to heal the king instantly! Little did she know (but was about to find out), but deep healing requires much more concentration—meaning that she could either heal or she could transcend time but could not do both simultaneously with any effectiveness.

Releasing the hold she had with the hand of Ventus, the dragon slayer had once again appeared at the exact moment the dragon's great head had gone in for the kill. This time, he had not been able to fully separate the dragon from her head. It had actually been the mother's nudge to rouse her that had finished that job!

Once Nyoka had bounded back up to the turret, Abila had once again gone beyond time and allowed the men of Ventus to help Troyolin up from under the dragon's neck, make their way to the side of Leonolis, and release time once again. That is where things began to come into focus.

As all the events came back into real time, Troyolin held Nyoka in place while Abila went to the side of his son. Kneeling beside Leonolis, she took him by his hand, gripping it tightly, the now gently crying girl began to focus on healing the body of her friend. Intently, she blocked out all other noises and poured her life and its power into the tattered body of Leonolis. Soon, his eyes began to flutter, as eyes do when one wakes from a long sleep. Even as he began to regain consciousness, the wounds on his torso began to miraculously close. Then the lightning came.

Lightning? Lightning! From somewhere high above and just to the north of Castle Aerie, a bolt of lightning came crashing down striking very near the feet of Troyolin, causing him to loose his hold on Nyoka. This freed her enough to plant one of her feet squarely down upon the right foot and ankle of the boy, causing him to cry out in pain! Just as quickly, the king's focus was renewed and he again immobilized the great monster—just as another bolt of lightning struck from above!

Before that bolt could find its mark, Augurian had responded with a flash of power emanating from the end of his outstretched wand. Reaching the point where the first bolt of lightning had come from, the sky exploded, revealing the source. Tormentia!

Again, she sent a streak toward the king, and again the king lost his grip, allowing the beast to bring further crushing force down upon the leg of his son before he could regain his hold. Shouting to Abila he said, "Daughter of Bren! Cease time and continue your healing work!"

Without saying a word, she shifted her focus to that of stopping time—but as she did so, the life again began to ebb out of the body of Leonolis. She had no choice. She released time and went back to concentrating on healing. This continued for several minutes. Lightning bolts were exchanged between the king's seers and Tormentia. Troyolin would falter whenever one of Tormentia's bolts found its mark. Leonolis would respond with agonized moans. Abila would cease time and try to heal—and once again, life would flow from Leonolis. She knew what she must do.

Running to Augurian and touching him, she caused time to stand still as she cried out, "O, Augurian! I cannot both heal Leonolis and stop time. If I bring time to a standstill, the healing ceases. If I heal, I cannot stop time! Either way it appears I can only do one or the other. Please help me!"

With calmness and wisdom he simply said, "We will do our part. Search your heart, Abila. You will know what to do. Trust the gift and trust the Giver. Now go." Releasing Augurian, she was instantly back with Leonolis. Touching him, she let go of time and gave all she had to infuse his wounds with healing power.

As she did so, Augurian looked to Maison and said, "Summon the power of all that is good and use the power to keep Tormentia at bay. I will cast her away."

Maison knew what that meant—he began to blast the air so violently with bolt upon bolt of lightning that people as far as fifty miles away thought some great thunderstorm was taking place over Castle Aerie! This gave Augurian his chance.

Sheathing his wand, he raised both hands to the sky in Tormentia's direction and began to chant.

> *"O, gossamer wind from near and far*
> *O, mighty breeze of dawn*
> *Break forth through night with light of day*
> *And now reveal the dawn.*
>
> *Beyond the sphere! Beyond the stars!*
> *To the universe's depth*
> *Bear forth the power of Founders' strength*
> *And breathe Your mighty breath!"*

Suddenly, a breeze began to pick up. This breeze was not ordinary. It could be heard but it could not be felt! As it blew, everyone knew a mighty wind was blowing, but the normal evidence of wind was nonexistent! Then, something marvelous began to take place. As if borne on the power of this magical wind, the darkness began to peel away from the sky—light began to flood in like waves upon the ocean. It was spectacular to witness but very difficult to fathom or explain. This "wind" was literally blowing the darkness back from whence it had come—the power of the light began to overwhelm even Tormentia. Though she was pale-skinned and clothed in white herself, the dinginess of her evil state gave away her position in the bright sky, allowing Maison to hone in like a mighty laser. With one last, mighty blast of his wand, he sent her reeling out of control back to the northern abyss from which she had risen.

While all this was taking place, Troyolin had begun to lose his grip once again. After all, he had only a few minutes before risen from an unconscious state. Abila's healing had not yet run its course on Leonolis, such was the depth of the wounds he had received from the claw of Obscurum Nyoka. Once more, Leonolis' eyes began to flutter and once more he began to come to. Even though his leg was being crushed by the weight of the mighty dragon, the power of Abila's gift was bringing him back. Soon he was fully aware of what was happening, and he gazed with wonder at the girl he had not so long ago tried to rescue. It was she who was now rescuing him. In that moment he knew he loved her.

She never saw his gaze. She only intensified her power in that moment. She never saw the dragon begin to pull free of the high king's grip. She never saw all that had transpired between the wizards and Tormentia. She never saw any of it, because she had so fused her mind with her dual gifts that she had not even realized what she had done at all. Time stood still. Healing flowed into Leonolis' body. So much power issued forth from her touch that, once the beast had begun to fall, the power of her combined gifts became one mighty resounding bolt of sheer energy such as the world had not seen that it had sent the creature reeling skyward. Once Obscurum Nyoka felt the purity of this power she fled as quickly as she could back to the dark abyss she had come from, not to be seen for another twenty-five years!

Abila collapsed, completely unconscious and oblivious to all that she had brought forth by her own hands that day. Leonolis held her in his arms, amazed and humbled by such a display of sacrifice. It reminded him so much of a Sleeping Giant he once knew that had saved the kingdom. She had saved the kingdom and she did not even know it!

Cradling her in his arms, Leonolis called out to Augurian. "Good Augurian! She has collapsed! I cannot rouse her! Please help her! Please help her! She is not breathing! She has no pulse of heart!"

As the seer knelt down beside the girl, he could feel no heartbeat. Yet he did not sense her life was gone. He grew deathly still, meditating as it were, while holding fast to her hand. After a few moments he spoke.

"She is not dead. She will not die. But she will sleep. It is the sleep of one who has seen the Founders and lived to speak of it. It will take days—weeks perhaps—before she will regain what she has lost. She has given her life without dying—and that takes much from the human soul. Maison, let us remove her to the royal guest chambers and prepare her for the Recuperatio Somnium—the sleep of recovery." Nodding in agreement, the two instructed Ventus and his men to take great care in carrying her with utmost tenderness to the royal guest chambers for the Recuperatio Somnium.

Watching-Leonolis stood with the Voice, tears streaming down his face. "I never knew. I mean—I knew—but now to have seen the sheer and complete sacrifice she made for me has rendered me utterly grateful beyond my ability to express. What I saw that day was a mere glimpse into the reality of all she gave up—for me."

It would take three complete months for Abila to fully recover. Little did Leonolis know of the true extent of her sacrifice until the next generations began to appear.

"She has given so much more than this, Leonolis," responded the Voice. "Let us go. We have a royal wedding to attend and the birth of the nine kings and queens . . ."

Chapter Fifteen

SONS AND DAUGHTERS

As the Voice trailed off in silence, the turret on which they had perched was suddenly transformed before watching-Leonolis. They still stood watching but the dragon bodies littering the courtyard disappeared and the grounds of Castle Aerie were suddenly festooned for a grand occasion, white drapery adorning every wall and purple flowers adorning seemingly every nook and cranny. Crowds of laughing people flowed into the castle grounds and a huge gathering of people from all over Bren was amassing in Warrior's Canyon.

"Do you remember?" asked the Voice.

"How could I ever forget my wedding day?" replied watching-Leonolis.

The courtship had been long by some standards and short by others. At the age of fourteen, Leonolis knew that he loved the girl. Desiring to honor and protect the purity of Abila, Leonolis made the Votum Sanctimonia of Bren—a vow of purity taken by the men of Bren. By taking this vow, Leonolis was declaring to the world that true manly honor comes from preserving purity rather than defiling it. By taking this vow, he was saying to the women of Bren, "I honor your purity above my own life. I will save myself for the honor of my wife and her alone." By making such a commitment, Leonolis had said to the women of Bren, "You are safe with me." Of course, not every man would take the vow and not every man would keep the vow, but in the mind of Leonolis it was a vow he was willing to sacrifice for.

"What were you feeling when you took the vow, Leonolis?" asked the Voice.

"I remember thinking about my father—and his father—and how the purity of our royal line has been held together by a common thread of honor and tethered to an anchor of hope by a willingness of my lineage to lay down its life for another. My thoughts were drawn to my mother and to her mother—to generations of the women of our line who honored their men by giving them their lives. Such is the nature of sacrifice. The wisdom of the world would have me think I must take what is mine and that the world revolves around me. I know that is not truth. All my thoughts were consumed with so much more than thoughts of romance or even of meeting my needs before their time," responded the king.

As he watched the proceedings for a few minutes, his thoughts began to be refreshed concerning the vow. He continued to speak. "I remember feeling overwhelmed with a bigger and broader picture of the expanse of my own history and identity—that nothing is without reason, that nothing is wasted in the kingdom if it is met with the perspective of the Founders. In that moment of realization—that I was part of something bigger than myself—it became easy to take the vow. My heart was actually full of joy."

As he pondered his feelings from so long ago, watching-Leonolis was drawn to a fluttering beneath him. Like a blur of light, the whiteness glided from somewhere beyond the upper reaches of Castle Aerie and came to alight on the canopy above the wedding grounds.

"Ollieman!" shouted the king.

Of course, the wizened old owl-friend could not hear him now. The king was delighted nonetheless. He watched and listened as his old friend engaged his younger self.

"Leonolis! Leonolis! Prince of all the land! This day of days when hearts are joined brings joy throughout the land!" rhymed the bird.

"Dear friend, Ollie! I've been waiting for you. It is time!" responded the prince.

At that moment, the royal trumpeters began the wedding processional—a fanfare of pomp and regality heard only at royal weddings of Bren. At the first strains of the music, many of the women wiped away nostalgic tears as they remembered the last time they heard that sound—at the wedding of Leonolis' mother and father! It is worth noting—though they would all deny it—more than a few men were spied wiping away a tear or two of their own. This was such a glorious day in the history of the land because it served to inspire and remind the people of the coming generation of the glory of a life lived in honor and destiny of purpose. The marriage of the prince was a reminder to all the young men and women of the land that the true meaning of love—the ultimate act of love—is the laying down of one's life for another.

As the fanfare progressed, the castle doors swung open wide revealing the bride. Such was her glow—such was her beauty—that the entire crowd gasped as one. As if appearing from nowhere, the visage of the most radiant feminine beauty suddenly emerged from the darkness of the doorway. So striking was her appearance that many thought they were viewing a statue of porcelain. Once she moved from the doorway, it was apparent that this was, indeed, no statue!

Watching-Leonolis sat stunned just as he had been stunned by the beauty of his fair bride, Abila, on their wedding day so long ago. "She's amazing," was all he could say.

Her alabaster skin seemed to shine against the light of day as it peered into the courtyard. Like a cascade of auburn sunshine, her long hair fell down the back of her long, white gown, seeming to become one with the very rays of sunlight that danced upon even her slightest movement. Trailing behind her was the train of her dress—twenty feet in length—being tended by three young ladies-in-waiting. Even though her father walked with her (as is the tradition of Bren), no one noticed him, so fair and majestic was the splendor that was Abila.

Everyone cooed and sighed and whispered and gawked as the soon-to-be-princess of the realm made her way toward the wedding canopy. Adorned with massive amounts of white linen, the many bolts of cloth flowed down from high above the wedding altar giving the appearance of soft, white clouds on a sunny day. All along the pathway to the altar, white and purple flowers of all kinds, shapes, and sizes lined the way. Shoulder to shoulder the people stood, each trying to catch a glimpse of the girl. As she passed by, the crowd ebbed and flowed with her every movement as eyes followed her movement and shoulders turned to follow suit.

Then their eyes met. Leonolis—the normally staid and boisterous prince—was rendered speechless and befuddled and weak-kneed, enraptured with his fair maiden. Her gaze was so fixed upon him that it was obvious that her heart belonged to no one but Leonolis. He was in love with this girl and she was in love with him. Then they were face-to-face.

Abila's father took his daughter by the face and planted a kiss upon the forehead of his little girl whose appearance was anything but that of a little girl. As little girls have a way of doing, she had grown into a mature and honored woman of the realm. Taking her right hand, he placed the hand of his daughter into the right hand of Leonolis. Bowing to Abila's father, Leonolis looked up to his woman and whispered, "I love you." She simply nodded and said, "And I, you." They then turned to face King Troyolin.

The king began the ceremony. As is the custom in Bren, the wedding ceremonies of the princes and princesses of the realm are conducted by the high king as a symbol of the line of succession as well as to convey to the people of the realm the sacredness and seriousness of the marriage bond.

"As is the custom of our land, it is my duty as father of the groom to perform the rites of marriage for my sons and daughters," began Troyolin.

Turning to Abila, he said, "Daughter of the realm, is it your desire to unite yourself with this son of the realm?"

"Yes, sire. It is my willful desire and I enter into this realm-within-the-realm called matrimony with steadfast assurance that this is the will of the Founders."

Turning to Leonolis, he continued, "Son of the realm, is it also your desire to unite yourself with this daughter of the realm?"

"Yes, sire. It is with all my heart and it is my willful desire to enter into this realm-within-the-realm called matrimony with steadfast assurance that this is the will of the Founders."

Addressing the entire crowd gathered there, Troyolin spoke. "This day do you, the fair people of the realm of Bren, bear witness to this sacred rite of union? Do you promise to help guard this union and, as a people, help hold them accountable to the vows they are about to make?"

As one voice, the entire throng responded with a resounding, "By the wisdom and might of the Founders, we will!" This response was so beautiful in the way it transpired, beginning in the courtyard and carrying out in waves to the throng that had spilled out into the grounds surrounding the castle and all the way down through Warrior's Canyon. Echoing and echoing for quite sometime, it was as if a national commitment was being sealed by some great magic that held the kingdom together. As the oath died down, the king again spoke.

"Leonolis, son of Bren, make your vows to your bride and to the people of Bren. Make your vows to the Founders. Say what you mean or say nothing at all."

Responding, the prince said firmly, "By the Founders of old and by the blood that flows in my veins, with all my heart and with all my strength I say what I mean and I mean what I say."

Continuing, the prince made his declaration. "I, Leonolis, call you, Abila, to be my bride. Just as I have been pursued by the spirit of the Founders, I have pursued you. A man who finds a wife finds a good thing—I have found a very good thing. Had I nothing of earthly value, I would still be the richest man on this earth. I have known wealth and good fortune. I have known sorrow and pain. Knowing the depths of joy and the depths of agony has made me a better man, owning my life completely and finding fulfillment in my purpose and destiny. Always, in spite of that fulfillment, there has been an empty place. I have tried to fill that emptiness with pleasure and have found myself empty still. I have tried to fill that emptiness with manly pursuits, protecting the people and serving the realm, and have found myself incomplete. Diving headlong into my work, finding great accomplishment on the battlefield, experiencing grand adventure and conquest, and receiving the camaraderie of my fellow warriors—as grand and noble as they are—none of these things has brought fulfillment to that still empty place in me. Only you, Abila, has been able to fill that empty place."

Pausing to wipe a tear from the eye of his soon-to-be-wife, Leonolis continued. "Even though I have known you for years now, I realize you, my woman, are a great mystery to this man." The crowd began to snicker at this, only adding to the sweet national sentimentality permeating the realm in this moment.

"I promise to spend the rest of my life exploring the mystery of who Abila is. I promise to love you in action when words will not suffice. I promise to be your protector and provider. I promise to value your life and your honor above my own. I promise to love you for who you are and learn to allow your strengths to cover my weaknesses. My pledge is to lead you by serving you, to be a place where your heart finds safety through the storms of life. My life is now yours and yours is mine. I give you all of me and pledge my life and love to you whether you ever fulfill your promises to me. I make no contract with you this day. I swear a covenant between you and me, promising my faithfulness whether or not you are faithful to me, pledging to lay down my life for you whether you lay down your life for me or not. You are my treasure and I plan to spend my life exploring the mystery of who you are. I am your man and you are my woman. By the wisdom of the Founders I declare this vow before this multitude of Bren, before my father and mother, before my siblings and friends. I am yours and no other's!"

As Leonolis grew silent, King Troyolin turned to Abila and said, "Abila, daughter of Bren, make your vows to your groom and to the people of Bren. Make your vows to the Founders. Say what you mean or say nothing at all."

Abila replied, "By the Founders of old and by the blood that flows in my veins, with all my heart and with all my strength I say what I mean and I mean what I say."

Looking intently into the eyes of her Leonolis, Abila began.

"My sweet Leonolis, you are my covering. You are my warmth through the cold times of life. You complete me. You have filled an empty longing in my heart as well. I will go where you go. I will serve where you serve. I will bear your children and bear your burdens with you. I forsake all others and take my place at your side. Through hard times, I will be your comfort. Through storms, I will bear them with you. In conflict, I will stand resolutely by your side. When discouragement comes, I will cheer your heart. When confusion comes, I will help you find wisdom. When you are confronted with difficult choices, I will trust your leadership. What is weak in me will find strength in you. What is weak in you will find strength in me. My hope is not in you but in the strength and life we build together."

Abila paused before continuing. Looking fiercely into the eyes of her soon-to-be-husband, she continued as Leonolis gently took both her hands into his own.

"I promise to spend the rest of my life extolling the wonder of who my Leonolis is. I promise to love you in action when words will not suffice. I promise to be your comfort and encourager. I promise to value your life and honor you with my words and actions. I promise to love you for who you are and learn to allow your strengths to cover my weaknesses. My pledge is to follow you by serving you, to be a place where your heart finds warmth and shelter through the storms of life. My life is now yours and yours is mine. I give you all of me and pledge my life and love to you whether you ever fulfill your promises to me. I make no contract with you this day. I swear a covenant between you and me, promising my faithfulness whether or not you are faithful to me, pledging to lay down my life for you whether you lay down your life for me or not. You are my knight-of-knights and I plan to spend my life extolling the wonder of who you are. I am your woman and you are my man. By the wisdom of the Founders I declare this vow before this multitude of Bren, before my father and mother, before my siblings and friends. I am yours and no other's!"

Placing his hands on the head of the prince and his bride, Troyolin spoke. "By the authority of the Founders, we will hold you to your vows this day. You have made an oath before the Founders and before this realm. Should either of you waiver in your vows the people of the realm stand as protectors with you in this adventure called marriage. Your faithfulness is our faithfulness. Your success is our success. Your union represents our union. Do not bear it lightly and do not regard it with lack of esteem, but rather declare with your life the worth of your union and let your life together stand as a beacon to all the reverence of what we seal this day. I bless you with long life and health, with good friends and with victory, with many children and grand memories, with victory and with abundance. I bless you—man and woman—husband and wife. Seal now your oath with the sacred kiss of union!"

As Troyolin lifted his hands in blessing over the couple, Leonolis swept Abila into his arms and planted his lips on hers in what is said to have been the longest most passionate public embrace of any royal couple in the history of Bren! The crowd went wild with applause and cheers of good fortune and blessing. As is tradition, the royal newlyweds made their way from the ceremonial area up to the castle wall above the

main gate. As they made their way to the front of the wall overlooking
Warrior's Canyon, the throngs outside the castle grounds filled the air
with resounding fanfare and the roar of national approval. This was,
indeed, a day to remember.

Watching-Leonolis was startled from his most pleasant reverie by
a gentle breeze that suddenly arose—and by the dark clouds that had
so quickly appeared that happy day so long ago. Then he remembered.
Because of all that had transpired during his life as high king, Leonolis
had not given much thought to the devilry of Tormentia, even though
what he was about to witness again (this time from a brand-new
perspective) had caused him many sleepless nights through the years.
Age had brought wisdom and wisdom had brought subsequent maturity,
but now he was about to see what he had not seen before.

As bright as the day had been when the wedding had taken
place, the sky grew suddenly bleak and dark and dismal. The sudden
wind threatened to bring down the grand decorations and adornments
throughout the castle grounds. Like a bad dream that invades a peaceful
sleep, Tormentia appeared slightly above and in front of the couple.
Hovering in midair, her voice boomed and resounded like thunder for
the entire throng to hear. She began to laugh.

"Ha! Ha! Ha! What a precious little couple these royal misfits!"
she mocked. "Why was I not invited? Why no representatives of the
others?"

Stepping in front of his bride, Leonolis shouted, "What others
do you speak of, witch? Why do you dare to interrupt these sacred
proceedings?"

"The others? The others? Of course you would say it thus! The
outcasts of the land! Those you dare not associate with! Those you
would sooner tread underfoot than give a place at the royal table! The
werewolves! The Chiroptera! The Terrebithians! The dwellers of the
underworld! The wretched, the poor, the dwellers in darkness! They are
citizens of the realm as surely as you are prince of the realm! What is
their place? Why do you despise the children of the other worlds? Why
do your despise the children of the rest of your kingdom?" she seethed.

"We despise no one!" declared the prince. "We cannot have
relation with the children of darkness—with those who refuse to dwell

in the light. We have not refused them. It is they who have refused us! You, witch, are the Mother of Darkness and you have no place in this celebration! Be gone! Back to the realm of darkness with you!"

Laughing so deeply that she appeared to be on the verge of falling from the sky, she caught herself and began to inch toward the prince and Abila.

"Witch? You call me witch? Ha! Ha! Ha! You call me Mother of Darkness! I say finally you have said something truthful! What you call darkness we call light! It is you who has been deceived, little prince! You will rue the day you dared to defy my truth!"

Lifting her wand and aiming it toward the couple, Tormentia began to chant.

> *"Mother to mother*
> *Light to dark*
> *Let darkness's fall bring forth a spark*
> *The womb of she*
> *Where royals birth*
> *Be filled with night devoid of mirth*
> *The royal line*
> *Both she and he*
> *Must walk in sorrow's misery*
> *The kings and queens*
> *From this womb born*
> *Will see despair, destined to mourn."*

As she cast the spell, Leonolis continuing to stand between Abila and the witch, defying her with all his will as he shouted, "No spell of darkness has place in the light! Your words are merely that! Words! Meaningless words!"

As he turned to embrace and shield Abila, the royal archers drew their bows and prepared to dispatch Tormentia. As they released their arrows, the witch vanished and the arrows arced and began to fall to the earth, screaming toward the helpless people below.

Before the people had even realized what was happening, Augurian appeared from above Leonolis and Abila on the gate turret directly above them. Waving his wand toward the careening arrows, he began to make circles in the air in the direction of the missiles. Just as it seemed dozens of people would be on the receiving end of the darts meant for Tormentia, they each exploded into a thousand embers of sparkling light. As the stunned people watched, the sparks began to rise from above their amazed gaze. Ascending higher and higher until the embers of each arrow began to gather into one cloud of pulsating light, the cloud, responding now to the outstretched wand of Augurian, hovered a few feet above the heads of Leonolis and Abila. As the individual sparks coalesced with one another, the cloud became a mist of purest light and began to descend upon the couple, enveloping them so completely that they could no longer be discerned. Intensifying, the light began to pulsate as Augurian cast his spell.

> *"As sorrow and suffering are both assured*
> *The royal line will stand, endure*
> *What was meant for evil, once understood*
> *Will not be wasted, but used for good."*

What watching-Leonolis now witnessed he had somehow missed on that day enveloped in the light so long ago. Now he could see something else that had taken place in that cloud of brightness that he had not been allowed to see before. Even though Augurian was casting the spell from above them, he had also been in the midst of the cloud with them! As he heard what he had not heard before, the heart of watching-Leonolis was humbled.

Augurian had been there, taking Abila by the hand—time had stood still. As Augurian whispered gently into Abila's ear, watching-Leonolis heard and suddenly understood the true depth of his wife's love for him. "Dear Abila," began Augurian, "your curse will be your blessing. Yes, your children will suffer and will know sorrow, but who in this life does not? It is by your willingness to lay down your life that your children will be born into blessing. With each child, a portion of your gift will be granted unto them to help them put down the spell of Tormentia. There will come a day when you will no longer be able to stop time. Your life will be full and enriched beyond what you can now see. This is still your choice. I wait your word."

Without so much as one moment's hesitation, Abila looked into the eyes of Augurian and very strongly affirmed, "I gladly give up my gift for my children, for my husband's line, for the sake of Bren."

Watching-Leonolis found himself in tears as the cloud disappeared and the darkness lifted from the royal newlyweds. The festive mood was instantly restored and the nation was even more blessed in its identity than if the witch had never appeared and had never cast her spell. It was as if the words of Augurian were already holding true—that what had been intended for evil upon the land was already producing an abundance of national good!

Then he began to fly from above the festivities and be carried toward the inner recesses of the royal chamber of Castle Aerie. He remembered those soft whimpers of the baby's cry from so long ago. And then he saw his newborn son . . .

Chapter Sixteen

THE BIRTH OF KINGS
AND QUEENS

As the wedding grounds faded from view, watching-Leonolis could hear the sound of a baby crying. Nearing the bedchambers he and Abila had shared for so many years now, the king and the Voice came to rest in a corner above the bed where Abila had obviously just given birth. He saw himself hovering over his firstborn son. He listened as he and Abila talked.

"He is magnificent!" said the king.

"Like his father," gently encouraged Abila.

"No, he is magnificent! He will be better than I! He will do greater things than I! The Founders have indeed blessed him!" exclaimed Leonolis.

"The joy of a father's pride allows you to see this," laughed the queen.

"No! No! I mean it! See the way he even now opens his eyes and follows mine? It is as if he is already aware of his place and calling!" said Leonolis almost shouting.

Curious now, Maison walked from behind the king to observe for himself. Intently watching the infant, the wise old man rubbed his chin for a few moments, the whole while gazing directly into the baby boy's eyes.

Then Maison took a deep breath—a brief gasp—and said reverently, "Magnificent, indeed. The gift is deep in this one."

"What do you see?" asked Abila.

"This one shows the signs of the seer. He will be able to see glimpses into the future—both near and far. He also bears the signs of his grandfather, Troyolin. See how the corner of his blanket raises slightly even though the child is not moving? This is strong evidence that he will be able to immobilize an object and lift it by his mental power. This is the mark of a king. He will one day be high king."

As they marveled at the newborn boy, Abila asked Leonolis, "What shall we call him?"

"My heart is so full of love! I could never have imagined the feeling I now feel for my son; this causes me to be overwhelmed by what my own father must have felt toward me! It is strange, but a good strange, but I feel so loved in this moment, Abila!"

"I feel it, too, my love. Let us call him Carus—beloved one. Every time we say his name we will be blessing him with our love," suggested the queen.

"And every time he hears his name he will be reminded of our love! Yes! Carus it is!" replied the king.

At this, the Voice spoke into the silence of watching-Leonolis. "What do you remember of this day?"

"I remember the ecstasy of joy and the massiveness of the weight of the love I felt. I recall simultaneously feeling the great burden of raising my son in the ways of right thinking, the responsibility of protecting him, and of preparing him for manhood—preparing him for life," replied the king.

"What else?" asked the Voice.

Puzzled at the Voice's question, the king thought what he had just shared was the most important memory, yet something stirred within him to remind him of a deeper reality he experienced on that day so long ago.

"Abila," said the king.

"Yes, Abila," echoed the Voice.

"She sacrificed so much for our son—for each of our children. She bore them in her own body. She nurtured them for nine months in ways I never could. Literally she gave her life in so many ways to give them life. The labor of Carus was difficult. For a few brief moments the midwives did not know if she would survive, such was her loss of blood. Yet, she was so excited and full of love for Carus that she—even after nearly losing her life—told me after seeing Carus' little face that she was ready to begin working on a little sister for him! Amazing!" said watching-Leonolis.

"And what else?" asked the persistent Voice.

"Her gift," replied the king. "Her gift." And he paused to ponder the depth of this realization.

"Though I did not know it at the time, with the birth of each child she lost a portion of her own gift. By the birth of our ninth child, she was virtually devoid of the original gifts she had been given. Her ability to suspend time had been exhausted. Her ability to heal with her touch was all but gone. She gave up everything—sacrificed completely—her own life for the sake of mine and for our children," said the king reverently.

"Yes, she did. But what does your heart of hearts tell you about the gifts lost—about the reality of Abila's power?" asked the Voice.

"I do not know what you speak of?" responded watching-Leonolis.

"What you saw was the way of the Founders lived out in true sarcifical manner. She willingly laid down her power to endow the power upon her children. But what did she gain in return?" queried the Voice. "Think about all you know of Abila now after all these many years."

"I would say her loss of power has made her even more powerful— even formidable," chuckled the king. "Such is her respect within the realm that she merely mention a need or make a suggestion and those around her, from greatest to least, move mountains to carry out her wishes. I would say she is more powerful than any in the realm," laughed watching-Leonolis.

Going on, he said, "And as her gift to touch and heal began to wane, she became even more creative. Her deep sensitivity to the wounds of others has caused much healing in the hearts and lives of the citizens of the realm. Her many public declarations that 'True healing must come from the inside out' has revolutionized the way we practice medicine— and truly revolutionized the way we deal with sorrow and emotional wounds on a national level." Pausing for a moment, he went on. "Her sacrifice has brought health and life and vibrancy and joy to the entire land. By what she has lost, an entire people has known gain beyond earthly riches. She has affected Bren for generations to come!"

"You have discerned well," said the Voice. "And now about your sons and daughters. They, too, have sacrificed for you in ways that have never occurred to you."

"Go on—please," said the humbled king.

"As high king, it was not often you were able to spend as much time with your children as you would have liked. You did a commendable job balancing the demands of royal protocol with the needs of your children, but they—as children do—always long for more time with their father. This is just the way it is. Abila taught them to respect and honor you even in your sometimes-long absences due to your official duties. But each of your children, in their own ways, made sacrifices for you. Per your desire that they be a part of public culture and life, they had to endure occasional teasing and jealousy, but rising to the reality of who and whose they are, they always responded with grace and humility, often at great personal expense of their own feelings. And then there came the time for each of them to grow up and move into their own places of leadership in the realm—always, always—did they honor you and the calling of your royal lineage," explained the Voice. "Would you like to see a glimpse of their lives and adventures?"

"Are you serious? Of course I would!" exclaimed the king. "But would that be wise? What if I see harm come to them or worse? I do not know that I could bear such a thing."

"Loss and sorrow are each a part of life. It will always be there, but rest assured, High King, that you have taught your children well. They will learn from their mistakes, just as you have learned from yours. They will be made stronger by their woundings, just as you have been by yours. After all, there were many times when you wondered if you would ever make it—yet here you are," responded the Voice.

Almost in a whisper, watching-Leonolis said, "Show me."

What transpired next could best be described as what one would experience if a kaleidoscope somehow combined with a whirlwind! Whisked from the bedchamber, watching-Leonolis found himself flying about the realm seeing everything in a blur yet seeing everything in minute detail, able to somehow experience a lifetime's worth of memories yet experience those memories in a mere few seconds of actual time.

He saw Carus, a young man and serving as emissary king of Bren in the years before he took the throne as high king, replacing Leonolis himself. Having taken a wife, Chrissadan, from the southern kingdom of Solus Sidus that lies across the Sea of Arabon to the south, Carus had made his mark even as a young man, even before he was married and placed as emissary king. When the evil hordes from the land of Mendicant to the east were sent to plunder the land of Bren, it had been young Carus who had led the war party through enemy lines to put an end to the Mendicant leader, Lord Mordant. Those feats—a part of Brenolinian lore and legend now—are recorded in the *Chronicles of Bren: The Mordant Wars.*

No sooner had he witnessed a brief glimpse of the feats of Carus than he was transported to the birth of his second-born, a daughter Abila and he named Annavan. She had been given this name because of her graceful appearance. Loving to dance as a little girl, she would often be found far outside the grounds and walls of Castle Aerie playing and dancing through meadows and through the woods and by the streams. More often than not, she would be accompanied by animals—not just those of the domesticated kind. Watching-Leonolis remembered vividly the first time he himself caught a glimpse of what he had heard about his little girl. He had gone to look for her and, much to his dismay, saw her frolicking with a pack of wolves and chasing a mother bear and her cubs! As he rushed to "rescue" Annavan, the animals had scattered and Annavan had yelled at her father, taking him by such surprise that he almost fell off his horse.

"Father! Put your sword away! Do not harm my friends!" she had shouted in the tone only an angry daughter of the king can get away with when addressing the high king!

Annavan had her father's gift. She could communicate with animals!

Later in life, she, too, would take a husband from Solus Sidus. His name was Topherkan and he served as royal assistant to High King Leonolis for many years. Because of her ability to communicate with the animal kingdom, Annavan would serve as queen of Fauna for many years even while Leonolis was on the throne. It would be Annavan who would rally the animals of the realm when the Dreadlin Conflicts arose during her teen years. The Dreadlins are a race of creatures that live below the surface of the realm but are known for their subversive ways. For many years they had manipulated the animal realm to such a degree that it became very unsafe for a human to venture into the northern woods lest they be set upon by wild beasts—not just lions and wolves and bears but by all wild beasts. Though it is not the time nor place to share this, let it serve as a reminder that even the most humble of creatures, when deceived, can deliver the most heinous of injuries to the human body. From timid rabbits to flying squirrels, from meek and mild-mannered deer to the shyest wild turkey, the Dreadlins had brought much evil to the land. Annavan had saved the day. Her adventures are chronicled in *The Chronicles of Bren: The Dreadlin Conflicts.*

As if having just witnessed the entire life of Annavan yet feeling like it had only been a few seconds, watching-Leonolis once again found himself flying through the countryside of Bren. Before he knew it, he saw the densely wooded campsite he and Abila had chosen to stop in for the night. On their way from Abysstine where they had just come from a royal feast in honor of the northern citizenry, they had stopped to set up camp for the night. Eight months with child, they had not anticipated the events that were about to take place. During the night, Abila had gone into sudden labor. Not expecting to have need of the royal midwives so soon, she had only her lady-in-waiting to attend her. As only can happen in lands such as Bren, the Fairy king, Kelsin, had sent his own emissaries to watch over the royal entourage as they passed through his realm. Noticing the turmoil being caused by the unexpected labor, he dispatched his fairy midwives to attend to the queen.

Born in a hail of fairy dust and sparkling light, Haventura entered the realm, being so named due to her already-apparent adventurous nature! When she was only one year old, her gifts began to emerge. On Haventura's first birthday, Abila had come into her bedchamber to dress her for the day only to find her levitating above her bed! As time went on it would be discovered that Haventura would transport herself mentally to different places and dimensions, which would serve her well in her own adventures. In her adult life, Haventura would marry King Ashland of Subdefero, the kingdom far across the Sea of Arabon to the opposite side of the world. Serving as queen of Subdefero, Haventura would help conquer the Desert Queen, Saxum, and her army of fantastical creatures like the kangoalas, fierce hopping bears that love to drop from trees onto unsuspecting victims below and shred them with their fangs and claws. She also defeated the horrible brumbycroc, a type of horse with the head and tail of a crocodile! The adventures of Queen Haventura and King Ashland are told in *The Chronicles of Bren: Adventures Down Under.*

No sooner had he seen the life of Haventura than the Voice took him to the birth of Gloriana. Given the name Gloriana for two reasons (a third and more important would reveal itself later!), the third daughter of Leonolis and Abila was born after a long, dark winter, one in which the sun had not shone much. On the morning she was born, the sun burst through the clouds for the first time after many weeks. It was glorious! Then everyone gasped when she was laid in her mother's arms. Like a princess from a fairy tale, the infant girl was adorned with the most radiant strawberry red hair! Glorious! There was no other name but Gloriana! Did she ever live up to that name!

It was not until she had become married to King Shaunovan of Cardinalis, a land to the north of Abysstine, that the true gifts of Gloriana began to become very apparent. Being a northern land, Cardinalis was often consumed in darkness. Blustery and given to storms, Cardinalis was a wonderful land but could be treacherous at times. It was during the epic Tenebraen Wars that Gloriana began to shine, literally. It was during this series of conflicts with the evil lord Tenebrae that it was discovered that Gloriana could bring forth light with a mere thought, but she could also still even the most violent wind for a brief period of time. Of course, the saga of Queen Gloriana and King Shaunovan is told in *The Chronicles of Bren: Light in the Darkness.*

Like a whirlwind, the scene before watching-Leonolis changed so suddenly that it left his head swimming. The next thing he saw took his breath away. He saw his son Exaviance—the second son but fifth-born child—running through the woods near the river Runland on one of the royal family outings. Only about two years of age, Exaviance already had a maturity beyond his years and a gleam in his eyes that told the world that he was all child and all boy but that he also had a sense that he was more aware of adult things than anyone might imagine. As the boy ran laughing from his older siblings, he came precariously close to the edge of a sheer cliff at the river's edge. He had seen his older brother, Carus, take the plunge the day before with his father. He imagined himself able to do the same!

Watching-Leonolis responded the same way he had on that day. As he watched he could see his son's trajectory and could see the determination on his face. The boy was going to jump! Leaping to his feet and running from his place beneath a mighty sycamore tree, King Leonolis shouted to Carus and the girls, "Stop him!" And yelling at Exaviance he screamed, "Exaviance, stop right now!"

Before his siblings could reach him, Exaviance had leapt into the air and dropped horrifically toward the deep, clear waters below. Leonolis ran toward the cliff and, without hesitation, dived into the air toward the river below. Expecting to see the disturbance where the boy had entered the water he was stunned and overjoyed to see what he had not expected. Obedient to his father's words, the boy had stopped—in midair!

That was the beginning of the discovery of the gifts of Exaviance. It was determined that Exaviance possessed the deepest of magic of the realm—able to alter time, able to walk between dimensions, able to conjure spells and cause objects to disappear or materialize as needed for the good of the realm. It would be Exaviance—even as a young boy— who would be used to conquer so much of the Dark Realm through the advent of his days in Bren. His adventures are recorded in the book *The Chronicles of Bren: The Brooding Deep.*

The next thing he knew, watching-Leonolis was in the royal bedchambers again, this time during the birth of his sixth child, daughter Galensia. The labor had begun normally enough but had progressed rather slowly. After several hours it had become apparent that something was not quite right. As Abila strained to bring forth the child, she had begun to lose a lot of blood. As the midwives used their wisdom and skills, the child was quickly brought forth, but the injury to Abila was quite severe. As the midwives worked frantically to minister to Abila, it was obvious she was losing consciousness. Abila would recall later how she felt her life ebbing from her in those moments.

"Give me my child," she whispered weakly to those attending her.

"My lady, you are much too weak. We will tend to the child. You must rest," said one of the midwives.

"Now! Give—me—my—child," she said haltingly but firmly.

Nodding to the midwife who had looked to him for direction, High King Leonolis directed the child to be laid in her mother's arms. No sooner had the infant girl touched her mother's outstretched arms than life—rosy red life—began to pour back into the pale skin of Abila. Abila knew what had happened. Her ability to heal had been transferred to her daughter—just as Maison had said it would.

Galensia became known as the Healer Queen—even during her teen years. Due to her ability to wisely determine a course of action when facing conflict, she had risen quickly during the Terrebithian Conflicts and was instrumental, through various acts of valor, in bringing an end to those terrible wars. Her story can be found in *The Chronicles of Bren: The Terrebithian Conflicts*.

Emotionally exhausted from all he was seeing, watching-Leonolis considered asking the Voice for a period of rest. Just as he was about to make his request, he felt an unseen hand touch him on the shoulder. Instantly he was filled with new strength and a sense of adventure all over again, spurring him to keep moving in this vision—or whatever it was!

Now he could suddenly hear rain. Not just a gentle soothing rain, but a deluge—a downpour! Every time it rained he could not help but think of his seventh-born child, daughter Aquarain. Her birth had been an easy birth with much celebration going on throughout Castle Aerie even during the labor. Having gone through a drought of several months, everything had changed the instant she was born. As the birth took place, the early morning skies became cloudy, covering the starlight. With the first strains of the little girl's first cries, the rain had begun to fall!

Going on for three days after the birth of Aquarain, the streams of the land began to overflow. The wells became full again. Ponds and lakes precariously low were now suddenly and thankfully running over their banks! The land had been blessed with rain, thus she was called "Aquarain"! As was expected, the little girl had quite the knack for finding water. Those in the kingdom who were in the business of digging wells for new farms often came to the king and queen to request the service of Aquarain in seeking out the right place to dig. On many occasions Abila accompanied her little girl to farms near and far so she could discern where the men should dig! She was always right on the money!

It would become obvious in her teen years why Aquarain was granted this most special gift. During the Siccus Rebellion her gift matured to the point of her even being able to cause it to rain over certain regions for brief periods of time! The dreaded Pravitas Arenus—sand monsters of Siccus—need moisture to survive, but crave obtaining that moisture from consuming the water found in living things rather than simply drinking water from a well. It was Aquarain who led the armies of Bren to defeat the Pravitas Arenus and brought stability to the land during the Siccus Rebellion. Her adventures are found in *The Chronicles of Bren: The Siccus Rebellion.*

Before he knew the scene had changed, watching-Leonolis found himself at one of the highest turret windows of Castle Aerie. Once again, just as he had done those many years before, he instinctively reached out to his three-year-old son, Arucus, who stood perched on the ledge hundreds of feet above the castle courtyard! Eighth-born and twin brother of Faveo, Arucus had always loved high places. When his father would playfully throw him into the air and catch him, Arucus always screamed with delight, "Higher, Papa! Higher!" Abila even recalled how the unborn Arucus would move around restlessly in the womb whenever she would look north to the Mountains of Endor or whenever she would gaze down on Warrior's Canyon from the walls of Castle Aerie.

Watching-Leonolis reached for the boy but knew he could not touch him now—but still he wanted to—even though he already knew the outcome. As he watched his younger self reach for the boy in futility, the boy dove from the ledge to the horror of the king! As the king watched the boy drop helplessly toward certain death, he had collapsed to the floor, unable to fathom the death of his baby boy.

Now sobbing in a heap below the windowsill, the king kept saying to himself, "Arucus! Arucus! Not my baby boy! Why, Founders? Why? Not my Arucus! Arucus!"

Then the weeping king was startled to silence. He heard a sweet little-boy giggle from the windowsill. "Surely I am delusional! Surely I dream! Now I lose my mind. Why do you toy with me, O, Founders?"

"Papa! I fly-ded!" said a voice that sounded like the innocent little Arucus. "Did you see me? I fly-ded!"

Daring to look up at what his mind could not begin to conceive, he saw his precious little boy standing proudly on the ledge above him! It had been generations since this particular gift had been visited on the realm, and Arucus had been thus obviously granted this gift! It would be Arucus who would prove to be instrumental in years to come in the defeat of Obscurum Nyoka and her slithering brood as they once again raised their ugly heads against the realm. His feats are told in *The Chronicles of Bren: The Dragon Wars.*

Once again, the scene morphed instantly to another. Now he found himself watching his younger self seated on the throne, receiving visitors from the realm, many in search of royal wisdom or to bring attention to a need in the kingdom. As he often did, the twin brother of Arucus, Faveo (ninth-born child), came to get a hug from his father before heading off to playtime with his siblings. Just as his father brought the three-year-old up to for a quick sit on his father's lap, the next person waiting to be received by the king posed a question.

"Sire, I am Lonicus, farmer from the region east of the Canyons of Callay. And this," pointing to an angry man standing to his right, "is Mallinica, fellow farmer of the region."

"Why are you here, good men of Bren? How may I serve you this day?" asked Leonolis.

Speaking up and slightly shoving Lonicus aside, Mallinica said, "Let us get to the point and stop wasting the time of the king. This very week my wife has given birth to a son, but this very week the wife of Lonicus has stolen him, saying the boy was her son! This is a lie!"

"My lord, long have we awaited the birth of this, our only son. Ten years have we been married yet only now are we granted a child—a precious son—and the wife of Mallinica has stolen him claiming him as her own. We would that you bring wisdom and justice to this most grievous situation. My wife is still weak from having given birth and cannot be here. This woman," pointing to the wife of Mallinica, "would have you believe she carried this child to birth," lamented Lonicus.

In a half-joking manner, Leonolis asked the boy still sitting on his lap, "What shall we do, Faveo? What is the course of wisdom in this case?" Putting the boy down and pushing him toward his mother's outstretched hands, Faveo turned toward his now-very-serious father and said, "Cut the baby in half and give one half to each man," and then scampered into the arms of his mother who quickly carried the boy from the throne room.

Weighing the gravity of the situation in his thoughts, King Leonolis could not help but be intrigued by his son's response. "From the mouth of an infant has come wisdom this day. Let is be so. Bring the baby here. We will settle this dispute fairly. Sword, please!"

Mallinica turning with a smirk and sneer toward Lonicus, grabbed the baby from his wife's arms and hurried toward the king saying, "Here! Let it be so!"

With no hesitation, Lonicus fell to his knees and begged the king with these words, "Spare the boy! Give him to Mallinicus! I would rather live with him alive and in someone else's care than to live without him in death!"

Standing and holding the boy toward Lonicus, King Leonolis decreed, "This child is your child, good Lonicus. The love of the true father has shown itself apparent in these proceedings. Only the true father could love like that. Take your son and go to your wife."

Turning toward Mallinica and his wife, King Leonolis decreed, "For your lack of honesty and for your heinous act of malice and envy and evil toward the good family of Lonicus, I sentence both you and your wife to one year in the royal prison, or one year of serving in the royal capacity of working with the boys and girls of the realm under my direct supervision as we prepare the next boys for the Testalmorphia and the girls for the Estrogenia. It is your choice."

Of course the couple chose to serve the king by training the young men and women for their respective rites of passage into manhood and womanhood. The story of the wisdom of Faveo was spread throughout the kingdom.

As Faveo grew, his wisdom followed suit. As his wisdom grew, another gift began to appear. Being a musical boy, he soon discovered that he could change the atmosphere of the room he was in by the use of melody—whether played on a flute or sung. So strong did this gift become that he was able to utilize the gift of melody in battle, able to bring confusion and chaos to the enemy forces by the turn of a melodic phrase! The legend of Faveo is remembered in *The Chronicles of Bren: The Melos Aido Uprising* recounting his adventures during the onslaught of the forces of the Silencio Brotherhood against Bren.

Without so much as the blink of an eye, watching-Leonolis found himself in the Crystal Cave, but this time he knew why he was there. Calling out to the Voice he said, "No. Not now. I—am—not—ready."

Chapter Seventeen

WHAT LEONOLIS SAW

Watching-Leonolis somehow knew what he was about to see. That "knowing" sense was actually a part of his gift from the Founders, but it did not always feel like a gift at all, especially when this sensitivity led to foreboding feelings that something bad was about to take place. Watching-Leonolis remembered how he had felt even as a young boy. He felt he knew where he was being transported before he actually saw with his eyes. He watched and followed his little-boy self now as the boy-Leonolis made his way to his father's throne room.

Coming from behind the throne in one of the secret passageways his father had shown him—the same one his father had used when he was a little boy—the little prince pretended to sneak up on his father from behind so as to scare him as little boys love to do to their fathers. Of course, Troyolin had known the boy was coming and even expected him to do this, because the boy did this every time he came to visit his father! Troyolin played right along, pretending to not notice the scuffling, shuffling little feet sneaking up behind the throne.

Little Leonolis slowly crawled underneath the throne on which Troyolin sat and then, reaching stealthily from directly behind the exposed boots of his father, the boy grabbed his father's feet and pulled with all his little-boy might. At that moment, the king pretended to not be able to get away from his attacker's grip and frantically began calling to his Royal Guards (who, of course, were in on the trickery from the start), "Help me! Guards, even now I am besieged by some unknown beast—some mighty man of stealth and valor! Help me at once!"

As the guards ran toward the throne, little Leonolis loosed his grip and sprang from beneath his father's seat and jumped to his feet. Standing akimbo, the boy proudly laughed, "I got you Papa! I got you good!"

"Yes, I'm afraid you did, Son!" replied the king.

Leonolis quickly melted into his father's expectant arms and became a wiggly, laughing ball of giggles as his father tickled the boy with parental glee.

"Papa! Stop! Papa! Stop!" laughed the boy hysterically. He and his father both knew he actually meant "don't stop"!

"I will punish my attacker with endless laughter!" bellowed the king to his son. "Never again will I be caught off guard by such a formidable foe!" He knew they would repeat this same scene tomorrow! After a few more seconds, the king stopped the tickling and stood his son in front of him.

"Son, today I have an important task for you," said the king very solemnly.

"What is it, Father?" said the now-serious boy.

Leaning close to his son's ear so as to not be heard by the others in the room as well as to convey the reverence of the secret bond between a man and his son, Troyolin instructed the boy.

"Son, I want you to meet me in the Crystal Cave in half an hour. Take the secret path I showed you last week. Once there, wait for me. I will come to you for a lesson only those in our royal line have the honor and privilege of knowing. Tell no one where you are going. This is our secret."

Whispering to his father, his voice filled with little-boy-longing-to-be-a-man pride, Leonolis said, "Yes, Father. I will meet you there. Our secret is safe with me," and off he scampered, sheepishly filled with joy and pride at being entrusted to take this solo journey to a secret rendezvous with his father for reasons known and shared only by the two of them.

Watching-Leonolis relived those steps as he silently followed his little-boy self through the secret doorway behind the throne, traveling along passageways he had walked and stole through countless times throughout his life. As the little boy came into the main cavern of Crystal Cave, he uncovered one of the Phrygian Crystals and illuminated the dark room. Obediently, he took a seat on a stone near the water's edge and waited for his father. Even though it would be three more years before he would be allowed to traverse the underwater labyrinth of the

Crystal Cave, he just knew today he would be allowed to swim in the deep, dark waters of the first pool!

Watching-Leonolis knew what was coming—had relived the next few moments over and over again, many times during the course of his life, always asking himself "what if?"

"Sacrifice comes in many forms," said the Voice.

"How can you call my poor choices sacrificial? I acted in pure selfishness and it nearly brought ruin to Bren in the process," responded watching-Leonolis.

"You have lived this too many times from your own perspective, but the greater reality—the true reality—is to see from the vantage point of the Founders. Quiet your soul, son of Bren. Quiet your soul and observe a bigger picture than what you have seen to date," calmly stated the Voice.

As watching-Leonolis steadied himself to see what he knew was coming, a calm reassurance came over his mind. He did not know how the perspective of the Founders would play out. He just knew from experience that he could trust the Founders. In that same moment, an image began to appear on the surface of the pool. Though in the cavern he could now see what was taking place back in the throne room. He had always wondered what actually took place that day to keep his father from their appointed time. Now he would see in full.

In little-boy time, his father should have been there many minutes ago, but in reality, the reason Troyolin had not shown up on time that day was due to kingdom business. Just as the king was about to excuse himself from the throne room and head for the rendezvous with his son, the court herald had brought news of a strange visitor entering the throne room for an audience with the king.

"He will have to wait until I return," spoke the king.

"I think you will want to see him, sire," explained the herald, "as he brings news of a possible plot against the realm."

At this, the king sat back down and motioned for the stranger to enter. In the back of his mind he had planned to hear the initial news the visitor was bringing, send him for an audience with his royal advisors, then meet his son. What the king heard and saw made history of those plans very quickly.

Shuffling slowly toward the throne came a tall, hooded figure, clothed in a long, flowing robe, walking with a staff much taller than himself. His face was not visible yet a wave of awe went through the room as all—due to his demeanor and the staff—assumed this was some great wizard from some unknown realm. As the stranger neared the steps below the throne, the herald spoke.

"Greetings in the name of the Founders. Greetings in the name of Bren. Good King Troyolin, I present to you Praemonitus, seer from the realm of Acerbia."

Watching-Leonolis was taken aback by this news. "Acerbia? The Place of Gloom? The place between the darkness and the light?"

The Voice said not a word in response. Watching-Leonolis took the silence as confirmation.

King Troyolin began to speak. "I have never met an envoy from Acerbia and have only heard stories passed down through the generations of Bren that such a place even actually exists. Why do you now choose to reveal yourself?"

Pulling back the hood, the visitor's appearance caused all those in the room to gasp. While all had assumed the being to be human, what they saw was something quite different. As the hood dropped behind his head, two long ears popped up to attention. Long, grey hair flowed like a mane behind his head—his face was like that of a donkey! Though his snout was not quite as elongated as that of a donkey, the features themselves were somehow those of a common ass yet weirdly mixed with those of a human! His hands were human in appearance, though the fingers were long and bony. As the creature pulled back his robe to retrieve a pouch concealed within, his feet could be seen to be those of a hoofed beast!

Speaking with the slightest hint of a donkey's bray at the end of each phrase, the creature Praemonitus spoke. "I bring you tidings from the realm of Acerbia but bear news of impending gloom-hee-yah."

Some in the room snickered at the sound of the visitor's voice, but it only took one stern look around the room by the king to still this rude response.

"What news? What gloom do you speak of?" asked Troyolin.

"Let me show you-ee-yah," continued Praemonitus as he pulled a crystal orb from his pouch. "May I approach the throne, sire?"

Nodding to the two guards standing beside the beast, Troyolin bade the creature to approach.

As Praemonitus neared the king, he held the clear globe out in front of him. "Watch, sire," said the creature.

As the king and those near enough to see watched, the globe began to become milky in appearance. Soon the milkiness gave way to flames. In the midst of the flames it appeared that people were running from the flames in all directions. First, the king could see the city of Abysstine, its buildings and environs being consumed by fire and its people running from within the walls. From there, the scene changed to the fields and farm homes of an area between Castle Aerie and the Canyons of Callay. Again, homes were aflame and people could be seen running for their lives in all directions. Next, to the horror of the king, Castle Aerie itself was ablaze, every tower crumbling in heaps of burning embers to the castle courts below, people running and screaming, people leaping from the walls and turrets to try and get away from the fire.

"What is this? What does this mean?" demanded the king.

Stepping back and tucking the orb back into its pouch, Praemonitus explained, "I only see what you have seen, sire. But according to stirrings among the realm between the dark and the light, some dark magic makes its way to your realm from deep within the recesses of the Mountains of Endor, but there is more-ee-yah."

"What do you mean, 'more'?" asked the king.

"The gloom will come through the most innocent of means. I have seen this in the mists of Endor when a vision came to me last week-ee-yah. We Acerbians are the keepers of the realm between dark and light and, as such, are called to warn when that gulf is breached by evil. Evil, even now, has entered the realm of Bren and is seeking to use an innocent from your citizenry as a means of fulfilling its purpose-ee-yah."

"An 'innocent'?" asked the king. "What do you mean an 'innocent'?"

"A child," responded Praemonitus.

Turning to Augurian and Maison who had joined the king as the creature had approached the throne, Troyolin asked, "What say you, wise seers of Bren?"

Augurian, without hesitation, said, "Sire, the stirrings of magic bear witness to what this one says. Even this morning as I was in meditation, a small wren beckoned me to the shadows near the Place of Seeing. Once there, I saw a similar vision but waited for confirmation before burdening you with it, sire."

"I, too, have seen a similar vision during the past night. In my dreams I saw a small being bearing a small flicker that eventually became an unstoppable inferno throughout the land. The Acerbian seer bears truth, sire," affirmed Maison.

"Is there anything else, good Praemonitus?" inquired the king.

"There is that of most importance, sire. Innocence will be sacrificed for the sake of the kingdom but that innocence must be restored for true freedom and safety to be realized-ee-yah," continued Praemonitus. "I have received permission from my realm to stay and seek out the magic necessary to stop this inferno before it even begins. Though we dwell between the dark and the light, we bear witness to the power of the light and find our safety and sanity there-ee-yah. Yes, we are bearers of gloom, but we are equipped and destined to do so for the sake of the world we inhabit. Some are called to the light. We are called to bridge the dark and the light and lead many from the realm of darkness. Should harm come to the realm of light, we all suffer. I am here to serve, sire-ee-yah."

"Maison and Augurian, accompany Praemonitus to the Place of Seeing at once. Seek out the seers and conjurers of the land and beseech the Founders for wisdom in searching out this child who would bring darkness into the realm," commanded the king.

"Justinian, gather my counselors at once and meet me in the counsel room," said Troyolin.

Suddenly, the image emanating from the pool vanished and watching-Leonolis was, once again, transfixed on his little-boy self. As the pool grew still and the boy sat quietly, a small flicker could be seen flitting through the water from somewhere deep within the Crystal Cave. Brilliant red in appearance, the light was the size of a small apple, yet its radiance completely filled the dark room and glimmered as it moved, leaving a trail of miniscule sparks to fade into darkness behind.

The watched-Leonolis had caught sight of it right away. At first he imagined it to be some shiny fish or water creature, but as it neared the surface, he could see flittering wings. Bursting from the depths, the flying "thing" began to fly and flit around the room, causing the boy to gaze in wonder at such a display of light. As the boy watched, the creature suddenly came to a hovering stance just above and in front of his face. He could see it now! A fairy girl! A brilliant red fairy girl!

Reaching out to touch the tiny creature (as all boys would do!), his finger was repelled by a tiny, bright, red lightning bolt!

"Ouch!" exclaimed the startled boy. "Why did you do that?"

"I am not to be touched without permission!" scolded the little fairy in a tiny, sweet voice.

"I only wanted to pet you!" replied the boy innocently.

"I am not some common house pet in need of petting!" said the girl.

"Who are you?" asked Leonolis.

"Who are you?" insisted the fairy.

Stepping back from the creature, Leonolis declared as bravely as he could, "I am Prince Leonolis, son of the high king, Troyolin. Now, tell me who you are."

"Silly boy-creature. I am Rubranna, the red fairy. I carry the Fire of Bren in my heart. It is my task to keep the fire burning. I rule over campfires and cooking fires and clearing fires and lightning. I ensure that even the fires of love burn strong in the land. You do not know of me?"

"I have never heard of you," responded the boy. "How do I know you are a good fairy? My father says that not all fairies are good."

"Are all humans good, boy?" came the fairy's retort.

"Well, er, I guess not," replied the boy.

"Just because you have never heard of me does not mean I am not good. Perhaps your father thinks you too small and immature to know of my power and me at this time. Perhaps his reasons are good for not telling you of me yet. Do you trust your father, boy?" asked Rubranna.

"Of course," said the boy defiantly. "I trust my father in all ways!"

"Then perhaps you should trust him to tell you of me when he feels you are ready. Until then, I am fine if you keep our meeting a secret between you and me," said the fairy.

"I do not keep secrets from my father," said the boy. "That would mean I do not trust him."

"Ah, the precious innocence of a foolish child!" laughed the red fairy. "I understand the wisdom of your father in not sharing with you about my existence. When you are older you will be better equipped to be able to bear the sheer weight of importance your father places upon my kind and me. Sometimes it is better that magicians not be seen. Mystery begets wonder. Wonder begets awe. Awe begets power and power is key to the kingdom. When you are older your father will entrust you with more and more power. In the meantime, I suggest you not tell him I have revealed myself to you. In this way, your father will have no reason to distrust you," said Rubranna.

"My father has no reason to distrust me," the boy retorted.

"Ah, but doesn't he? How will he know you didn't conjure me up yourself? Why should he not believe you are up to some mischief? Why would he not question why such a mischievous boy given to pranks would not be able to conjure up one such as I?" she asked.

This line of questioning began to confuse little Leonolis. His mind suddenly felt clouded and he felt unsure of himself. Perhaps Rubranna was right. After all, she was the powerful red fairy and he was but a foolish little boy with no reason to have contact with such a powerful magical being.

Speaking now to the Voice, watching-Leonolis asked, "How could I have been so foolish? How stupid of me to follow her devious line of reason!"

"Your innocence was still intact, Leonolis. You responded as any eight-year-old boy should. You responded in loyalty and obedience to your father in light of your own experience to that point. You did nothing but honor your father and the people of Bren," said the Voice.

"But if I was so innocent, why was this allowed to happen?" asked Leonolis incredulously.

"Sometimes the need to be right gives way to the path love is paving to freedom," responded the Voice. "Have you learned nothing in what I have been showing you? You have been seeing life from the wrong perspective, son of Bren. See with the eyes of the Founders and you will find freedom from your guilt and freedom from the shame that haunts you. Open your eyes."

Watching-Leonolis felt scolded—yet he knew the Voice spoke wisdom and truth. Even though he did not fully understand why all he was about to experience was being allowed, he trusted that one day he would. He told himself that, even if he never fully understood, he was confident that the Founders would waste nothing in his life if seen from Their point of view.

Just then, watching-Leonolis was startled from his silent musings by the surface of the pool coming to a roiling boil of commotion. He watched his little-boy-self reeling backward at the sight and remembered the dread and fear that he had felt when he had experienced it so long ago and how he wished someone had been there to stand between him and the "things," as he now wanted to do for his small self.

Chapter Eighteen

THE TROGLODYTES

Little Leonolis fell backward to the ground as the creatures emerged from the deep darkness of the pool. In the fiery light produced by the red fairy, the "things" appeared to be ablaze, their scaly, wet skin shimmering in the red glow. Three short creatures waddled from the water on webbed feet and headed directly toward the boy. Little Leonolis, his face full of dread and his mind paralyzed by fear, simply stared up at them.

These were Troglodytes, cave-dwelling creatures from the deepest recesses of earth. This particular race of Troglodytes were actually from the oldest line in the Troglodyte race, able to breath under water through small gills on each cheek and able to breathe through their skin when not under water. The skin of the creatures, though scaly, was quite smooth and the palest green in color. Each looked very similar physically but had very different faces. While appearing fish-like and lizard-like, at the same time there was also something very "human" about them.

This humanness became even more pronounced as they began to touch the boy. Touching the boy's head, the first creature began to take on the appearance of the boy's face. The second creature touched the boy's hand and began to take on the characteristics of his hands. The third Troglodyte touched the feet of the boy and his feet became less webbed and more human. Watching-Leonolis reached out to little Leonolis but quickly realized there was nothing he could do. It was like reliving a horror but from two different points of view at the same time. Double horror is not something that is easily explained. Watching-Leonolis remembered and wanted to protect his little self while little Leonolis—little eight-year-old Leonolis—endured the hideous touch of the Troglodytes.

The hideous thing about being touched by the creatures was that innocent, little Leonolis took on some of their characteristics. He suddenly felt an urge to plunge into the deep, dark waters. His emotions began to run toward hatred and self-loathing. Worst of all, his mind began to think horrible thoughts about himself—and about others. As the creatures continued to touch the boy, Leonolis could not stop thinking about how terrible a son he was to his father, while at the same time, despising his father for his arrogance and lack of concern for his son. This caused little Leonolis so much confusion that he felt—if little boys can feel such a thing (and I think they can)—he was somehow not deserving of his place in life, of his place in the royal line, of his place as even a little boy! As the boy continued to be caressed by the creatures his thoughts even went so far as to consider he had no future—that there was no hope for him to ever be a man!

Suddenly, Rubranna spoke to the Troglodytes. "Tactus! Tangere'! Palpan! Enough! He is but a boy. He will be driven mad if we give him too much too soon!"

Immediately the three Troglodytes released the boy and almost instantly the boy could think clearly. As he burst into tears, Leonolis shouted at Rubranna, "Leave me alone! You are not a good fairy!"

Getting up and running toward the secret passageway from which he had entered the chamber, Leonolis knew he had to get to his father. Just as he was about to make it through the portal, he was jolted backward by a small red lightning bolt from the outstretched finger of Rubranna who had flown to the entrance to cut off his way of escape. Leonolis was again knocked backward, landing on his behind.

"Where do you think you're going?" scolded the red fairy.

"I'm going to tell my father! He will take care of you and these 'things'!" said the boy between frightened sobs.

"So you think your father is perfect and all powerful and loves you like no other?" mocked the fairy.

"My father loves me and even now comes to meet with me! You will be sorry!" replied little Leonolis.

"Was he not to meet you over half an hour ago? Yet he is still not here. Perhaps that should tell you something, boy!" screamed the red fairy.

Hovering next to the boy's ear as he cowered away from her on the cavern floor, Rubranna set her spell in motion by simply twisting the truth,

"Your father, obviously, does not care for you as much as you might like to think. Look at the truth, boy. HE IS NOT HERE! Would you like to know where he is? He has forgotten about sending you here. Even now he is spending time with your little brothers because he truly loves them more. Even now he plays with them because he actually likes being with them. He simply tolerates your pitiful presence because he has to for the sake of appearance. Right now he is boasting about the hunting skills of your brother Paulus to his grand counsel. After that he will be extolling the virtues of your brother, Robrance, to the counsel of royal arts. And then he will take your youngest brother, Samal, with him all around the castle grounds, bragging about how great a son he is to any who will listen. You know this is true! You have seen it yourself, boy!" said Rubranna.

"No! My father loves each of us equally! You are lying!" cried Leonolis.

Motioning for the Troglodytes toward the boy, the red fairy said, "Help him see."

As the creatures touched the now fear-paralyzed boy, his mind was taken over by their thoughts. He could no longer tell what was coming from his own mind and what was being forced upon him by theirs. Just as clearly as he had known no doubt concerning his father's love for him just a few seconds before, now it was clear just how much Troyolin despised Leonolis—of how much more proud his father was of his siblings than of himself.

"The seeds are planted," said Rubranna to the Troglodytes. "He has had enough for today. He is ours now. Release him."

As the creatures let go of the boy, he sat there dazed and confused, his mind now full of doubt and fear, not fear of the creatures or the fairy, but the fear that he could no longer measure up or be deserving enough of his father's love. He now had an overwhelming desire to please his father at all costs—to prove himself worthy of his father's love. Though he had not realized it at the time, his mind had now been taken over by the lies of the red fairy and once her seeds had been planted the boy was under her delusional spell.

"Get up, boy. Your father may one day be able to love you. That is all up to you now. I can help speed the process. Do as I say and all will be well and you will be able to one day earn your father's love and affection," encouraged the fairy.

"What must I do?" asked the now defeated little boy.

"Meet with me here—daily. I will instruct you each day concerning the winning over of your father. There are also things you will need to do to prove yourself to him. I, along with Tactus, Tangere', and Palpan will guide you through the necessary steps. You are different than other little boys, Leonolis. You are different than your brothers. You are just one of those special boys who will need a little extra help in getting to true manhood. I know you feel guilty for not measuring up to your father's standards or to the standards of Brenolinian manhood. I know you feel ashamed for being so different. That is simply normal for you, but do not fear. I will be here to help you," soothed the evil little fairy.

"Here is where we must begin. Meet with me here each day after your morning lessons. I will give you tasks that will be sure to endear you to your father. Today's task? Your father will question you and ask you if you trust him. This is simply his way of testing you. He does not expect you to trust him without proving your trust. You must answer 'yes' even if you feel 'no.' This is what a real man of Bren would do. Remember, this is a test your father is giving you in the moment. To pass the test, answer as you believe would please him. To prove yourself, perform some task to show how much you trust him. Life is about doing things to please others. In addition, simply promise me two things. You must promise to meet with me each day and you must promise to tell no one of these meetings; otherwise, your father will be very ashamed that you were not man enough to go through the necessary steps to assure his affections. Will you promise, boy?" asked Rubranna.

Leonolis stood before her in silence, trying to wade his way through the deep confusion of his thoughts. Sending a bolt of tiny red lightning, she struck the boy's ear and shouted, "Do you promise!"

Cowering in submission, the boy grabbed his ear and shouted back, "I promise!"

"There's a good boy! You made the right choice, Leonolis. Now my friends—your new friends—and I must leave you. Your father will soon be here. Remember your promise. We'll be watching. We will see you tomorrow," she said as she flitted into the water and was soon gone.

As the red light vanished, the room was once again lit only by the faint glow of the Phrygian Crystals. Watching the three Troglodytes wade back into the water and disappear into the deep darkness, Leonolis wiped the tears from his eyes and went back and sat obediently on the stone facing the water while he waited for his father.

Within a few moments Leonolis heard the familiar pace and cadence of his father's footsteps. As the king entered the room, Leonolis did not run to him as he normally did. This time he sat—partly out of mental exhaustion and partly out of fear—and waited for his father to approach him.

"Are you all right, Son?" asked the perplexed king.

"I'm fine. Perhaps a bit tired, Father," said the boy, his voice still shaky from his encounter with Rubranna.

"What did you do? Run all the way here?" asked the king as he chuckled to himself.

"No, Father. I have just been here waiting," responded the tired little boy.

"About that, Son. I am so sorry I was not here when I said I would be. Some urgent matter presented itself and I had to attend to it right away. Still, I should have sent someone to let you know. Son, will you forgive me for being late?" asked the repentant king.

"Of course, Papa. I forgive you," replied Leonolis.

Stooping down, the king embraced his son and said, "Thank you, Son. Now, on to the reason I asked you to meet me here. Stand up and come with me."

Taking his son by the hand, he led Leonolis to the water's edge. The closer they came to the water the more Leonolis resisted.

"There is nothing to fear, Son. There is nothing in these waters but a few albino minnows. They will not harm you," assured the king. "Come, let's take off our boots and stockings and wade in a bit. If you like, we may even have swimming lesson today."

Shaking his head back and forth, the boy whimpered, "No, Papa."

"Where is the boy who just yesterday urged me for a lesson on how to swim to the first indention of air?" joked the king as he playfully slapped his boy's back.

"I just don't feel like it, Father," said the boy.

"There really is nothing to fear, Son. I will be with you every step of the way. Come on. Off with the boots!" said the king with a chuckle.

Ripping his hand away from the grip of his father, Leonolis ran into the secret passageway, tears streaming down his face in shame, his mind full of fear that if his father ever found out what his son was truly like he would surely reject him. Of course, this was all complete poppycock. Leonolis was under the spell of Rubranna and did not even realize it. How could he? He was but a boy with no experience in the ways of magic, whether of the Light or of the Dark.

Running after his son, the bewildered king caught up to the boy halfway to the castle. Taking him by the shoulder, he spun his son around and embraced him, picking him up and holding him tightly.

"Son, whatever it is, let us deal with it now. I know you are afraid, but there is no shame in admitting fear. A healthy dose of fear keeps one's mind sharp and helps one stay alive in battle. What battle are you facing in your mind, Son? Tell me. You can trust me. Do you trust me, Son?" asked the king.

As instantly as the boy had melted into his father's arms, the memory of the words of Rubranna came back to haunt him, causing him to stiffen against his father embrace. *He will ask you if you trust him. This is a test,* rang her words in every corner of his mind. *Answer yes and then perform some task to prove your trust.*

"Yes, I trust you, Father. Put me down and I will show you!" replied the boy.

No sooner had the king put his son back on the ground than the boy began to rip off his boots and stockings. He then ripped off his shirt and trousers and headed back toward the Crystal Cave leaving his confused father standing there!

Laughing out loud, the king chased his son crying out, "Where are you going, Son? Why the hurry?"

As the king entered the chamber of the Crystal Cave, he came in just in time to see the feet of his son as they disappeared beneath the waters! Knowing his son had absolutely no knowledge of the twists and turns of the maze that the tunnels can be, he ripped off his own boots and stockings and dived into the waters in pursuit of the naked boy!

Before the little boy could reach the first pocket of air, he ran out of breath. In a panic, he began beating the water frantically trying to make his way to the surface. Completely disoriented, the boy could no longer discern up from down. In utter fear, he roiled the water like a spinning top. It was quite easy for his father to follow the churning wake the boy left, reaching his son just as he bumped his head on the cavern wall. The king quickly swam with his unconscious son back to the chamber where this "adventure" had begun.

Laying his son's still body on its back, the king firmly compressed the boy's chest, which, in turn, forced the water in the boy's lungs to be expelled with force. As the gurgling boy came to, the king instinctively embraced his boy and held him close, saying, "Don't ever do that again, Son! Do you hear me? Never, ever do such a thing again."

Of course, the boy was reduced to unimaginable shame because, in his mind, he had utterly let his father down, unable to prove his worthiness. Crying and completely and utterly confused at the day's events, Leonolis simply said, "I tried, Papa. I tried."

"Tried what, Son? Tried to kill yourself? What on earth ever possessed you to do such a thing?" asked the king.

"I was simply doing what you wanted me to do! Did I not prove my trust, Father? Did I not pass your test?" asked the boy.

"Prove your trust? Pass the test? Where did such thinking come from?" implored the king.

Just as Leonolis was about to spill out everything that had transpired that day between he and Rubranna and the Troglodytes, little Leonolis saw a faint glimmer of red—the merest faint sparkle—from a crevice in the cavern ceiling above. He remembered the words of the red fairy and changed his mind.

"I just want you to know that I trust you and that I can perform any task you give me! Forgive me for my fear, Father! Forgive me!" replied the very confused and fearful little prince.

"Son, there is no shame in admitting fear! If you trust me you will realize that I do not require you to prove anything to me. Do not believe such rot! I love you just because of who you are, Son!" replied the now-shaking king. "I could have lost you today, boy! Never, ever—NEVER, EVER—pull such a stunt again! Do—you—hear—me?"

Once again, melting into his father's arms, the boy replied, "Yes, Papa. I hear you."

That night, the king cancelled all his meetings to be with his family—to be with Leonolis. Everyone noticed. Something was different about the prince. Something was terribly wrong.

"Perhaps it is but a phase he is going through, Troyolin," urged Abila. "After all, he is growing up. What eight-year-old boy isn't always trying to prove himself to his father?"

"You are probably right, my love. Still, let us keep an eye on him. Whatever it is, he will still need our guidance and encouragement through this 'phase'," responded the king.

The next morning, Leonolis woke with a sense of dread. He obediently performed his chores and quickly completed his morning lessons. On his way for his appointed meeting with Rubranna, his mother's voice caught him off guard.

"Leonolis, I need you to take this note to your father for me before you head out to play with your friends," said Abila.

"Yes, Mother. Right away," responded Leonolis.

Now fearing he would be late, the boy ran as fast as he could to the Throne Room. Bursting into an important session between his father and a dignitary from another nation, Leonolis rudely exclaimed, "Father, here is a note from Mother!"

Handing the note to a nearby guard, the boy began to run from the room, hoping his father would be too consumed with the meeting to say anything that might delay him. He was wrong.

"Leonolis! How dare you be so rude! Have you forgotten the royal protocol of this court? Come here at once!" demanded the irked king.

Sheepishly stepping up to his father's throne, the boy was taken aback at his father's not-so-subtle-nor-gentle response. "You will seek the forgiveness of our visitor for interrupting his moment at court. You will go straight to your room and wait for me there!"

Turning to the dignitary, the boy quickly said, "I was very rude to interrupt you, sir. Will you please forgive me?"

Nodding to the boy, the man replied with a grin (knowing that sometimes boys will act this way when they are in a hurry to play), "Of course, I do, Son!"

Turning back to his father, the boy waited for what his father would lay out for punishment. "You have lost your play privileges for the day, young man! You will not go to your friends! You will not dilly-dally around the castle! You will go straight to your room and wait for me there!" demanded the angry king.

Hesitating as to whether to beg his father to change his mind, the boy did not move.

His father assumed this as even more insolent attitude and behavior so he yelled, "Go! Now!"

Leonolis was off like lightning toward his bedchamber, but rather than go straight there, his fear of the red fairy seemed more fearful than facing the anger of his father, so he ducked behind one of the statues in the hallway and into a well-concealed hidden passageway. Soon he was standing in the main chamber of Crystal Cave.

Standing alone in the darkness for but a few brief seconds, the boy was startled by the sudden appearance of Rubranna and the Troglodytes from seemingly out of nowhere!

"Where have you been, boy?" demanded the angry little fairy as she sent a bolt of red lightning hurtling toward his nose.

As the lightning found its mark, the boy doubled over in pain as he rubbed his burning nose between his hands.

"You are late, boy!" replied the red fairy.

"I had to run an errand for my mother! Then, because I was trying to hurry, I incurred the wrath of my father, who, should he find me not in my room as he demanded, will soon banish me from my playtime—our meeting time—altogether!" pled the boy.

"Enough!" cried the little red fiend. "We have work to do. Your lesson for today is quite simple, even for a stupid boy like you."

Leonolis looked up from his shame toward the fairy. No one—except for his siblings (and he knew they did not mean it)—had ever called him stupid. Yet, that is exactly how he felt in this moment. Not wanting to appear even more stupid, he responded to the fairy with, "I am ready. What is the lesson?"

Obviously pleased with the boy's reply, she responded with a hint of pleasure toward the boy in her voice, " Well! Well! Perhaps you are not so stupid after all! Let us get to it."

As she motioned for the Troglodytes to position themselves around the boy, she flitted just above him. As she began to speak, the creatures once again began to touch the boy.

"Your family—even your kingdom—has need of your help, boy. Tactus will fill you with the necessary responses to those who would question your new outlook on life. Tangere' will fill you with the necessary ability to transform yourself into what others think of you—how to play the games that people play in order to appear pleasing to one another. Palpan will fill you with the necessary ability to choose just the right people to bring forth our plans. Above all, we must protect Bren. All we do in these moments is for the good of Bren," lied the fairy to the boy.

Watching-Leonolis knew it from experience but it still pained him to see his smaller more innocent self go through these moments again. He knew he had been deceived. He knew he had learned to lie well in the process of that deception. He had learned to lie convincingly to others—even his father. He had learned to lie to himself.

"In the days and lessons to come, you will become more like us. Wise and powerful. Keep these truths to yourself lest others become jealous of you and come between you and the good you bring to the land. In our touch and in our magic, you will come to know the greater way. It is in this knowledge that your shame and guilt will be forever banished from your existence," replied the fairy.

As the "lesson" wore on, Leonolis seemed to lose sight of his true identity as prince of the realm and began to take on a greater sense of self-sufficiency, even coming to believe that he actually had more wisdom and discernment than his own parents! Looking down at his hands as the creatures finally released their slimy grips, he noticed his own hands and feet—at least for a few moments—had taken on the appearance of the features of the Troglodytes, and they, in turn, looked a lot like him!

"Now you must go, boy," commanded the red fairy. "Take the punishment your father puts upon you. Own it. This is who you are. The shame and guilt will soon pass. They will make you stronger in the long run as you become more and more who you truly are in the realm."

Turning to go, the boy looked at the Troglodytes. Somewhere deep inside he felt pity for them. Somewhere deep inside, he knew he would never be like them. Before he could take one more step, Rubranna called for his attention.

"There is one more thing, boy," she said,

"What is it?" asked the boy.

"I will visit you in your room tonight. Once there, I will introduce you to a new friend," replied the fairy.

"But you will be seen," responded the boy. "How will you get in without the magic of Bren making our seers aware of your presence?"

"By you allowing me into your mind I have been granted access beyond the boundaries of Bren's magic. This is a good thing. This is us working with the magic of Bren," she lied once again.

"Go now. We will see you tonight," said Rubranna.

Chapter Nineteen

A NIGHT VISITOR

Watching-Leonolis and the Voice were instantly transported back to the bedchamber Leonolis had used as a boy. Already there was little Leonolis, trying to sleep, restlessly unable to find any solace in the comfort of his snug, warm bed. Secretly he had hoped that if he could just fall asleep then perhaps he could avoid the red fairy, yet he also tried not to think any thoughts at all just in case Rubranna was there already reading his mind!

"I remember this torment all too well," watching-Leonolis said to the Voice.

"But there have been hidden treasures you have not yet seen. What is not seen cannot be utilized. You have been granted quite the bounty, yet you still do not see," responded the Voice.

"What treasures?" asked the king.

"In time. In time. Among this treasure you will also find the keys to the kingdom, one key reigning above them all. With this single key, your lineage will capture the heart of Bren for the good of all. With this key, you will defeat any foe. With this key, you will endure any hardship. With this key you will find the key to the very existence of this fair land," continued the Voice. "And with this key, you will find joy that transcends any evil darkness that would harm you."

Suddenly, watching-Leonolis noticed a stirring in the room—a brief flicker of brilliant red light—as Rubranna suddenly appeared. As she flitted around the room she went from door to window searching to make sure no one else was there. Flying under the bed and through the wardrobe, she seemed quite paranoid. This disturbed the boy.

"What do you search for?" he asked the red fairy.

"Quiet, boy!" as she sent a bolt of tiny red lightning to sting his nose. "Do you wish to expose the task we are about? Do you hope to weaken our ability to help the good land of Bren? Do you not know there are spies about us who seek to thwart our plans?"

"Spies? Why would anyone spy on us?" asked the boy innocently, his response causing another bolt to strike his forehead.

"Why do you keep doing that?" he said to Rubranna as he winced in pain.

"You must know your place, boy! I am only trying to help you! Can you not see that?" came her retort. "Secrecy is of the utmost importance, and for that secrecy to be maintained I must be able to trust you, boy. Can I trust you to keep our secret? Can I trust you to keep your voice down? My little darts are nothing more than training lessons in these matters of highest importance. If you hope to be a man like your father, I suggest you toughen up a bit and learn to endure the pain," she said. "Can I trust you?"

Not wanting to be called stupid again and not wanting to be stung again, the boy responded, "Of course you can trust me."

"Good," she went on. "Now let us get to the business at hand. There is someone here I would like you to meet."

With the wave of her tiny right hand, a magical wand appeared. As she waved the wand in a circular motion, a tiny cloud of bright crystals began to form. After a few seconds, the cloud began to take shape.

"What is that?" whispered the boy.

"Shh!" replied the fairy as she glared at the boy. "Do not interrupt the spell!"

As little Leonolis watched, the cloud suddenly disappeared with a tiny burst of light, leaving a small wiggling worm in its place on the lap of the boy. It appeared to be a regular inchworm and Leonolis was about to swat it off of his bed when the wiggling stopped and the worm "stood" up! Of course, the worm had no feet so it wasn't really standing, but it was definitely able to erect itself and face the boy. Leonolis suddenly gasped in shock as the worm looked at him with the facial features that looked just like himself! Leonolis felt he was looking into some tiny mirror and saw his own face in that of the worm!

"What is this?" asked the bewildered boy.

"Why, this is your new friend, Ideman," replied the fairy. "He will bring your next lesson."

"Yes! Yes!" chirped the tiny creature in a whiny little voice. "I am here to guide you, boy! Are we ready?" he asked as he turned his attention to Rubranna.

"Yes, we are ready, aren't we, boy?" she asked.

"Ready for what?" came his reply.

"Do you trust me, boy?" she glared with the same expression she seemed to have on her face each time she sent out her dreaded stinging charges.

Wincing as he closed his eyes expecting a shock, the shock never came. Opening his eyes, the boy looked up at the hovering red being and nodded his head as he wearily said, "Yes, of course I trust you."

"Lie down, then," she said as Leonolis laid his head down on his pillow.

"Turn your head to the left. Your ear needs to be a bit closer to the blanket," she demanded.

"Ideman, you may proceed," she said to the worm as it began to inch its way to the helpless boy.

Turning her attention to Leonolis, she instructed him. "Lie perfectly still. You do not want to crush your good new friend. He is going to crawl into your ear. You will feel nothing but a slight discomfort, but the joy and pleasure you will receive in return will far outweigh any discomfort."

"I do not want him crawling into my ear!" said the boy in fear.

"Hush and do as I say or find a bolt to your head, boy! Trust me!" she yelled in her raspy little voice.

Shaking in fear, the boy felt helpless. He feared that if he cried out to his father that the fairy might cause him even greater harm. So he obeyed.

Watching-Leonolis cringed as he watched the worm slither to the side of the boy's head, remembering all-too-well exactly what he had gone through in that moment long ago. To watch himself go through it from this new perspective was even more painful than he recalled when he had experienced it as a boy!

Slowly, Ideman made his way to the lobe of the boy's left ear. Leonolis felt creepy and dirty as the worm slithered into his ear, but was weirdly calmed as the worm began to speak.

"There, there, young boy. This won't hurt a bit. This fear will subside the quicker you simply give into my presence. I am not here to harm you. Quite the contrary. I am here but to help you and to bring you great pleasure. You will never be alone again, boy, because I will be right here with you," said the mousy little voice.

As Ideman made his way to the end of the boy's ear canal, he began to burrow into the flesh. This is when the real discomfort began. Even watching-Leonolis now winced in agony, as did the boy on the bed. Just as little Leonolis reached the point of crying out in pain, the discomfort vanished! Instead of feeling fear and pain, the boy now experienced complete assurance and the deepest sense of joy he had felt since he was last embraced by his father!

A calm assurance began to run through the boy's body—like a warm bath on a cold winter's night—the feeling seemed to go from the top of his head all the way down to the tips of his toes. He had never recalled feeling so good.

After a few minutes of allowing the boy to acclimate to his presence, Ideman began to whisper to Leonolis. "I will show you who you truly are. When you are tempted to think 'wrong' thoughts, I will be right here to guide you to the truth. Trust me. Trust us."

And then the worm began to sing. What Leonolis could not have known was that he was being sung a spell.

Do not worry—Do not fear
In your need I am right here
Simply change your point of view
I am here with you
Sometimes darkness is really light
Sometimes daylight really night
Sometimes lies are really truth
You are living proof
Go to sleep now
Rest your mind
Wake refreshed and you will find
Higher planes of thought and peace
Do not trust all you see

When you wake I'm but a dream
You will not remember me . . .

As Ideman sang, the boy was slowly lulled to sleep. During the night, Ideman whispered and sang to the boy. What the boy did not know was that whenever his mind would begin to dream of good things—like playing with his brothers, or being tucked into bed by his mother, or like wrestling with his father—Ideman would step into the dream and divert the boy's attention to other places. During that first night, little Leonolis' world was turned upside down and he had not even realized it. Rather than being able to focus on the good things, all his attention and energy became focused on the negative things in his life. The sad truth was that what Ideman led him to believe was negative was not even reality. The trick of the work was simple. Get the boy to focus so much on himself that he is unable to recognize the needs of anyone else around him. The plan of Rubranna was ingeniously very uncomplicated. She would take love away from the boy and cause him to be motivated by performance and power rather than by the simple "repugnant-to-her" power of love.

Little Leonolis woke early—earlier than normal, at least, to his mind—due to the odd nature of his dreams. In actuality, the boy had slept longer than usual. As he stretched and yawned and stirred to come fully alert, he had the most vague recollection of a worm, but try as he might, he could not remember why. Perhaps, he thought to himself, he had spied an inchworm while playing in the woods the day before. He did remember the red fairy. Peeking out from under his covers, he looked around the room. Not seeing any red glittering light, he stepped quietly out of his bed and dropped silently to the floor.

Not seeing Rubranna, the boy hurried to dress himself. With great excitement he threw on his shirt and leggings and socks and boots. All he could think of was how today was the day he and his brothers were going to get to go on a ride with their father—all the way around Castle Aerie! Of course his younger brothers (seven-year-old Paulus, six-year-old Bobbin, and two-year-old Novus) would be relegated to riding in the royal coach driven by one of the royal drivers while Troyolin led the way on his own horse—and Leonolis followed on his! He was only eight years old, and he was getting to ride by himself all the way around Castle

Aerie—with his father—for everyone to see! What joy filled his heart as he ran out of his room and down the corridor toward the royal stables.

Thinking to himself, *I will be there early and show my little brothers how much like Father I am,* Leonolis burst out into the castle courtyard and made a mad dash for the stable doors. Running faster than he had ever recalled running before (that's what joy of anticipation does to the heart of a boy who can't wait to be with his father!), he realized he was about to run past the stall of his new horse, Arolis. Sliding past the door, Leonolis fell to his backside and just as quickly hopped to his feet. Slinging the door open, he stepped into the stall and greeted his horse out loud (this was before he knew of his gift of speaking with those in the animal realm), "Good, good Arolis! I am here! Let us ride!"

Perhaps his eyes had not adjusted to the dim lighting in the stable. Perhaps the horse was lying down in the far corner. The boy began to panic and grow frantic as he ran around the stall. There was no horse to be found. Arolis was gone! Darting out of the stall and back up to the stable entry, he quickly found the stable master, Equiness.

"Equiness! Equiness! Arolis is gone! Arolis is not in his stall!" shouted the boy in frustration.

"I know, young prince. I know. He was taken from the stall over an hour ago and prepared for your royal ride with your father and brothers. Even now he is tethered near the castle wall near the entry gate," replied Equiness.

Turning toward the entry gate, the boy ran out of the stable, but not before Equiness caught him by the shoulder and said, "Master Leonolis, I have instructions from your father."

"What instructions?" said the frantic boy.

"You have missed the ride, Son. Your father has instructed me to keep you here until his return. You are to clean and muck the stall of Arolis," replied the stable master.

Lurching away from the strong hand of Equiness, Leonolis ran toward the castle gate—just in time to see his father astride Arolis! He was riding his horse and he could hear his brothers shouting with glee to their father as he rode side by side with the wagon right out of the castle gate. Running with all his might, the boy began to cry out for his father.

"Papa! Papa! Don't leave me! I am here! Papa! Papa! Papa!" he cried as he ran toward the gate. He reached the entryway just in time to see the entourage go below the rise that leads down to Warrior's Canyon. Weeping uncontrollably now, the boy began to run after his father and brothers, but he was stopped short by the firm grip of Equiness who had been given orders to keep Leonolis in the stable and put him to work.

"Why did he leave me, Equiness? Why would my papa leave me?" sobbed the boy.

"That is between you and your father," wisely stated Equiness as he led the boy back to the stable.

Leonolis was in shock now. Never would he have dreamed that his father would ever abandon him—yet he did. At least that's what Leonolis began to think. Having forgotten about the worm, Ideman, Leonolis began to think horrible thoughts that only the day before would have seemed impossible to his little eight-year-old mind. In reality, it was the worm whispering lies into the mind of the boy.

"It is obvious he loves your brothers more than you. I wonder what it is about them that would cause them to be more lovable to your father," murmured the worm. *Paulus is better at hunting than me,* thought the boy after listening to the worm. *And Bobbin is much smarter than me. And Novus is just a baby—yet father loves him more than me. There is something about me that my father does not like.*

It may seem incredible to believe, but that was how simple the plan and scheme of Rubranna was. She knew that if she could come between the boy and his father. If she could get him to see himself as less than he was, she could easily rule the Kingdom of Bren one day—from inside the boy's head via Ideman!

Leonolis decided that day that he would prove his worth to his father by outshining his own brothers and anyone else who got in his way. If Paulus could hunt a bird, Leonolis would hunt for a lion. If Bobbin mastered the skill of math, Leonolis would amaze the scholars of the land with his mastery of logic. If Novus would do lovable "baby" tricks for his parents, Leonolis would out-trick him with his antics. Thus began a long slide into the abyss of the mind for the boy Leonolis.

By the time his father and brothers returned from the ride, Leonolis had cleaned the stall like never before and had proceeded to muck ten more stalls! Expecting a joyful and proud response from his father, Leonolis was taken aback by the words of the king.

"Son, I am disappointed in you," said the king gently yet firmly to the boy. "I expect my sons to be respectful of my commands and responsible for carrying out those commands in immediate fashion and order."

Leonolis interrupted his father, "But, Papa—"

But before he could continue, his father spoke. "Silence, boy. Your disobedience and lack of respect and utter lack of responsibility have cost you what I had intended to be a day of joyous pleasure for you today, Son."

Just then, one of the stable hands was lifting Novus out of the wagon when he giggled in innocent delight and said, "Lee-lee not ride! Lee-lee not ride! Lee-lee silly!"

Something foreign and frightful suddenly rose up in Leonolis. Fueled by sudden jealousy, the bewildered prince lunged at his younger brother, but was stopped in mid-lunge as his father stepped between him and his younger brother.

"Leonolis! What has come over you, Son?" shouted the king at the boy. "This is not who you are! It is not an infant's fault you missed the ride, nor is it the fault of your brothers or anyone else! We waited for you for nearly one hour, Son. I did not send for you because you are old enough to ready yourself for the day, boy! This is no one's doing but your own. Have you mucked the stall of Arolis?"

Nodding his head in shame, the boy said, "Yes, Papa. I even—"

But before he could explain all the extra work he had done to make his father proud of him, the king broke in. "Finish your chores then go ask your mother if there are any tasks she has for you today. There will be no punishment for you aside from that which you have visited upon yourself in missing the ride." And with those words, his father's stern glare etched forever in his mind, Leonolis stopped crying and gave into the rage internally as his father walked back toward the castle.

Seething still in deep anger and jealousy toward his brothers, the worm continued to whisper lies to the boy. The giggling of his brothers— not even directed his way—as they skipped out of the stable and across the courtyard only intensified his rage. Ideman whispered, "You'll show him! You'll show them all!"

And what happened next is still talked about throughout the kingdom to this day!

Chapter Twenty

THE LION HUNTER

Leonolis felt humiliated by the response of his father and by the giggling of his brothers. Blinded by the lies of Ideman, the boy had perceived a reality that was not even true! King Troyolin was proud and accepting of his son regardless of his occasional disobedience. His brothers were simply being happy, laughing boys (who happened to adore and look up to their older brother!). Unable to see reality any longer, the boy began to grow dependent upon the red fairy for guidance, stealing away for clandestine meetings with her in the Crystal Cave. The once-honest boy had soon grown accustomed to stretching the truth—lying to his parents. When asked why he was late for dinner, he would respond with "I was swimming in the Crystal Cave with my friends" or "I forgot my knife and had to go back to the Crystal Cave." His parents just assumed he was going through a phase—testing his independence—and that he would grow into maturity soon enough.

Growing more and more sullen with each passing day, the boy began to crave the approval of his father. It was the subtle lies of Ideman that kept little Leonolis from the truth. He had had his father's approval all along—without performing for it! So intense was the magic of the worm and the red fairy that Leonolis had forgotten about the worm's existence. When the voice of the worm would speak, Leonolis simply assumed these were his own thoughts.

After several weeks of daily meetings with Rubranna, the red fairy, little Leonolis had grown so used to her place in his life that he no longer gave thought to trying to escape her hold on him. He somehow felt she understood him and how he felt. She was always so quick to affirm his feelings of self-pity over the way his father treated him. She was always so comforting in the way she affirmed his feelings of jealousy toward his brothers at the way they seemed to flaunt being their father's favorite sons. She completely understood why the boy could possibly be so angry at the injustice of it all. Thanks to Ideman, her words were always backed up with the whispers in his own mind that said, *What she says is true.*

Watching-Leonolis spoke to the Voice. "How could I have been so blind? It is so obvious what was taking place? Why did my father not see? Why did my mother not sense what was taking place? How could Maison and Augurian both have missed this?"

Allowing the watching-Leonolis to think about what he had just said, the Voice responded after several minutes. "Wrong thinking blinds one to the lies of things like self-pity, jealousy, and rage. Believing such lies leads one to only be able to see themselves from their own point of view. Though you have gone through much since those days and have experienced much healing from the mental and emotional wounds you suffered at the hands of Ideman and Rubranna, you need to see from this point of view if you are to rule the Kingdom of Bren with justice and mercy—and love. Your parents are not responsible for your choices—no matter how young you were. Maison and Augurian are not responsible for your choices. There is only one with the power to choose for you . . . and that one is you."

"But I was but a boy!" exclaimed the exasperated king. "I had no choice in the matter concerning the worm!"

"This is true, but this truth does not negate the wisdom of the Founders. There has been great purpose in allowing you to go through the events of your youth. Do you think the Chiroptera and the swine rats were coincidence? Did you assume that the sacrifice of so many to get you to this place were afterthoughts? Do you dare rage against the dragons that were sent during your youth—sent by the Founders themselves? There has been purpose in what you have called chance. There has been destiny in all you see as coincidence. Nothing is wasted in the kingdom if seen from the Founders' point of view!"

Watching-Leonolis was stunned at this revelation. He really had had no choice. Even this lack of choice was by design for a greater purpose and a grander design. He was about to watch it unfold before his very eyes from a whole new point of view. Stunned at the depth of this thought, watching-Leonolis slumped down onto a nearby stone as he watched his little boy self head toward the domain of the lion.

Still wrenched of all emotion at this revelation, watching-Leonolis and the Voice began to rise into the air and follow the boy as he sneaked out of the castle that night so long ago. Watching-Leonolis, though numb in emotion, began to feel a surge of adrenaline as he watched himself begin his ill-advised quest to hunt down the lion. The king remembered why he had set out as a boy to defeat the lion. It had all begun the day he overheard his father in a meeting of his royal advisers.

Watching-Leonolis began to have a flashback to the moment his father's words pierced his heart. Gathered in the council chambers of Castle Aerie, King Troyolin and his advisors met to discuss urgent business. Little Leonolis had been listening from the secret passageway he had only recently been shown by his father, as his father had shown him when Troyolin had been a boy. It had all begun with a stirring among the men in the castle that day. Urgent word had come from an outlying region of Bren that something terrible had taken place in the kingdom.

Upon hearing of this news, Rubranna had instructed the boy to "attend" the meeting from his secret hiding place. She had told the boy that the men would look down upon him should he try to offer his help, but that she considered him wise beyond his years. In addition, she told him that many would one day recognize his greatness by this stealth mission she was sending him on, and that, though they may not understand now, the wise men of the realm would one day revere the boy as a hero for his faithfulness to be willing to stand alone against all odds. Watching-Leonolis cringed at how foolish he had been to have ever believed such obvious lies.

"Sire," said Justinian with great urgency in his voice, "we have just received word that a lion has begun ravaging the villages of the northern realm. By way of courier, Ragaman, overlord of Treacherin, has sent this parchment."

As Justinian handed the document to Troyolin, the crowd of wise men began to murmur amongst themselves. After a brief moment, the king began to read aloud.

To High King Troyolin, Protector of the Realm,

Your highness, there is no time to relay the complete story of what has transpired in our

region over the past few weeks. Suffice it to say
that we are even now under siege and at the mercy
of a most vile beast. Since a fortnight ago, we
have lost seven people in our village alone.
Succumbing to the fangs and claws of a ravenous
lion, the unsuspecting victims were pounced upon
by the cat. The carnage the beast leaves in its
wake is far too grisly to even describe to your
royal highness. While we sent out a hunting party
as soon as the first body was discovered, the
lion operates with a cunning we have never seen
before. When we set a trap, he attacks somewhere
else. When we leave poison bait, he avoids it.
When we send out our best huntsmen, he seems to
know and spring at a distant location. It is as
if he knows our thoughts and is able to be one
step ahead of our best-laid plans. As I write we
have heard nothing from our hunting party in over
two days. I fear the worst. We are at a loss. We
beg you as humble citizens of the realm, please
assist us in ridding the land of this beast.

In Humble Service to King and Realm,

Ragaman, OverLord of Treacherin

Addressing his council, Troyolin simply asked, "What say you, wise men of Bren?"

Without hesitation, Justinian began to address the king. "Sire, it is obvious this brute is no ordinary lion. While lions, by nature are both sly and cunning, the lions of Bren are not known to be man-eaters. From the details mentioned by Ragaman, my belief is that some strange magic drives the beast. May I humbly suggest that we send two small contingencies of huntsmen accompanied by Maison and Augurian. With each regiment having a royal magician to discern the magic involved, the beast will be much more easily subdued."

"Sire, I concur that this would be the most wise plan of action," the usually silent Augurian chimed in. "There is, indeed, a stirring in the realm of magic within our borders. Both Maison and myself have sensed this stirring even among the shadows of Castle Aerie. Something—

210

someone—is up to no good, sire. Let us consult the spirit of the Founders and be on our way. The sooner the better."

Nodding toward Augurian and then to Maison, Troyolin said, "Let it be so. Justinian, appoint the eldest of the hunstmen to recruit fourteen men to each regiment of hunters from the royal hunting ranks. I sense this is not a time for youth but a time for maturity. Send your most seasoned and wily trackers and those most skilled with the bow and spear. Advise each to walk in the ways of council as discerned by the magic of Augurian and Maison."

"Yes, sire!" said Justinian as he trotted from the room.

In that moment, watching-Leonolis could hear the worm speaking to the boy. "No time for youth? What does he mean this is no time for youth?" whispered Ideman contemptuously. "You must show him just how capable and wise you are in your youth! If you ever wanted a chance to prove your worth to your father, that time is now! Go, boy! Steal away on Arolis and head for Treacherin!"

The boy scurried quietly to the Crystal Cave where he had only recently tethered Arolis after a morning ride. Rubranna had conveniently told the boy to leave the horse there and to sneak into the hidden chamber from beneath Castle Aerie. Even as the boy mounted the steed, he had thought to himself what a wonderful coincidence it had been that he had left Arolis there.

As he kicked the stallion and said, "Let's go, Arolis!" the boy had not been able to hear the mighty horse ask, *Where are we going, Prince?* since his gift had remained hidden for another day. If only he could have heard, much of the history of Bren might be different to this day. But one cannot live in the land of "what-might-have-been" and have a very joyful existence.

Riding through the afternoon sunshine, the hair of the stallion's mane trailing back into his face, the boy Leonolis felt somehow free and invincible. Only when he passed a farm where three yellow-and- white cats lay lounging on the porch in the afternoon sun did he consider what he would do once he found the lion. Reaching down to his left he felt the shaft of his small bow and felt the quiver and the three arrows stowed there. Then taking the reins in his left hand, he felt for the small sword he had placed in the scabbard on the right side of the saddle.

Sensing the boy's sudden fear at the revelation of what he was about to undertake, the worm whispered, "Your father will be so proud! He will finally love you after you put down the beast! You will show him! You will show them all."

Still, the boy felt fearful, having never truly engaged in battle with anyone other than his little brothers and closest friends his own age and that with a flimsy wooden sword!

"Hush those thoughts!" murmured the worm. "You are the son of the king! It is in you to be the hunter, to be the warrior, to be the deliverer, to be the one who vanquishes the lion from the realm!"

In those moments of believing the lies of Ideman, the boy gave place to pride and arrogance not befitting a little boy, or anyone else for that matter. At the thought of receiving accolades and affirmation and love and acceptance by his father and, indeed, the entire realm, Leonolis spurred the horse into a frenzied pace. Having a head start on the royal hunting parties dispatched by King Troyolin, he was now several miles ahead of them. As he rode on and on, the time was of no consequence to him, so blinded by the lies of the worm the boy was. Passing by farm after farm and through village after village, those who saw him recognized the prince and wondered why he was out alone and where he could possibly be going at such a frantic pace. Did he not know he was nearing the region of Treacherin and the hunting grounds of the lion?

By now, the royal hunting parties were making their way to Treacherin, never knowing—until it was too late—that Leonolis was ahead of them, intent on confronting the lion. Stopping at a stream just before entering the forest region of Treacherin, the hunting parties stopped to give their mounts a rest and a drink of fresh water. As Justinian dismounted, he noticed a frail old woman attended to by a teenaged boy approaching him with looks of concern.

As she neared Justinian, the royal counselor asked her, "Madam, do you not know that a dangerous lion lurks about these woods? You and your son should not be out here unarmed."

"He is my grandson, good man. Are you sent of the king?" she asked.

"Yes, milady, I am sent to flush out and put down the fiend who ravages these environs," replied Justinian.

"My grandson has something to tell you. Tell him, boy!" said the grandmother sternly.

"Yes'm," said the boy shyly. "Even this day have I seen the prince, Leonolis, riding into yon woods, sword drawn and bow at his side. When I called for him to beware the lion he ignored me and continued on his way. Even now, at the urging of my grandmother, have I determined that good king Troyolin should know of the whereabouts of his son and of the grave danger he has placed himself in."

"By the love of the Founders, what is the boy thinking?" said the now-fearful Justinian out loud. "Where did you see him? How long since he passed this way?"

"Passing through the square of Treacherin not fifteen minutes ago," replied the young man.

Calling out to his personal aide, Justinian cried, "Gregor, come at once!"

"Yes, milord," responded Gregor.

"Ride with great haste back to Castle Aerie. Give this word to High King Troyolin. Even now, Leonolis is in the region of Treacherin—alone and on horseback. Come at once!"

As Gregor leapt to the back of his steed, Justinian swatted the beast on the rump and declared, "May the blessing and speed of the Founders be yours! Fly, Gregor! Fly!"

Gregor tore through the afternoon air back toward Castle Aerie while Justinian alerted the men to what he had just learned. Cutting short their rest stop, the two parties agreed to split as originally planned but to proceed with utmost speed in the hopes of cutting off the boy before untold horrors befell him at the hand of the lion.

Watching-Leonolis and the Voice were still with the boy as he sped through the square of Treacherin and on through the town. The boy never once stopped to think about how he would ever find the beast. "Something" inside—Ideman, of course—told him the exact direction to go. With each twist and turn through the forest, down every embankment and through several streams, the boy went frantically on. Then something told him to stop.

Riding headstrong through the heavy woods, the boy brought Arolis to a halt when he came to a very narrow place in the streamed he had been following. On either side rose jagged columns of stone, each concealing potential hiding places for a lion ready to pounce on some unsuspecting victim below. Before he even had time to think, the boy heard the splash of pebbles that had been sent from an unseen ledge above. Turning rapidly to see what caused the rocks to fall, he caught a glimpse of the lion's tail as it darted back from the ledge and into the cover of a crevice.

Arolis had caught the scent of the lion almost in the same instance that the pebbles had disturbed the brook below. He was now prancing on edge, every sense keenly tuned in to the surroundings. Sniffing the air with a snort, the horse reared so as to alert the boy to the impending danger. With every hair on his body standing at attention, the great stallion whirled around to head back in the direction from which they had just come and to safety.

Leonolis was now intensely aware of his utter fear and frailty concerning the situation at hand. As the horse reared upon his hind legs and whirled around to flee toward safety, the boy crouched as close to the horse's neck as possible, grasping the flying mane with all his little-boy might. Just as the horse prepared to hit the ground running, he stepped out of the shadows in front of them.

"Whoa!" said the man's voice firmly as he took the dropping reins of Arolis and began to calm the horse. "What is the hurry, good boy?"

"Sir! There is danger here! A lion lurks above! We must run!" said the boy, now hysterical with fear.

"Lion? There is no lion now. We must have frightened him," said the man with more calm than Leonolis thought he should respond.

"We frightened him?" asked the boy.

"Yes. We did! Even now I caught a glimpse of his tail heading away from us in the deep brush beyond the rock walls," said the man. "Why are you here alone in these woods, boy, when a dangerous beast herein lurks?"

"I have come to slay him!" boasted the still shaking boy.

"Slay him? With what, may I ask?" asked the stranger.

"I have a sword and I have a bow and arrows," replied Leonolis, "and I know how to use them!"

"I am sure you do! That lion knew what was best for him so he ran from your very presence," said the man in a half-mocking tone.

"And who are you, sir? Why are you here?" asked Leonolis.

"Me? I live in these woods. This is my home. I was merely out for a walk, gathering berries and wild onions to go with my evening meal. It is late. Should you not be heading home or seeking shelter for the night?" asked the man.

Not having been aware of the time until that moment, the boy suddenly grew panic-stricken. He had never found himself in such a dire set of circumstances. His father had always made sure they were safe for the night should they be caught away from home for any reason, be it hunting trip or family outing.

"I fear I have no place to go," responded the boy.

"Then it is settled! You will come with me and I will give you food and shelter for the night," he said.

"Who are you, sir? What is your name?" asked the boy.

"I am Dolus, keeper of the woods of Treacherin. I hunt game for a living and sell pelts to local merchants who, in turn, make garments for the good people of Bren. You will come with me," Dolus insisted.

"My father would not approve of me spending the night with a stranger," countered the boy.

"Your father is wise, but he underestimates you, boy! Let us decide to not be strangers and that problem will be eliminated!" he again insisted.

Of course, Ideman could not pass up the chance to use the words of Dolus to further confuse and confound the boy. "You made it all the way here without your father's help. You may be a boy, but you are wise and strong beyond your years. Make friends with this good stranger and be strangers no more!"

Leonolis thought about if for a few seconds and then proudly replied, "I would be honored to make your acquaintance, good Dolus. No more will we be strangers." With that, the new "friends" set off in the direction the lion had supposedly just gone. This caused Arolis to balk. As the horse came to a stubborn stop, Leonolis gave him a gentle kick, urging him to keep moving. Obstinate and unwilling to budge due to the danger he sensed, Arolis began to be come irritated with the boy's now belligerent prodding.

"What is wrong, Arolis! What a stupid beast you are!" said the angry little boy. Taking a strap from the saddle, Leonolis began to slap the horse's behind with it. Still Arolis would not budge. "Arolis! Let us go!" he again demanded. Mustering all the strength his little boy arms could, the boy struck the side of Arolis' face, causing him to wince in great pain. Still, the brave horse would not budge.

"Here, boy. Come down. Obviously the horse fears the scent of the lion. Let us walk from here. It is not far at all," coaxed Dolus as the boy slipped down from the back of Arolis.

Taking the boy by the hand, the two began to walk beside the stream and between the rock columns that towered above them. Snorting with rage and fear, the great horse Arolis tried to warn the unknowing boy. Sending Leonolis ahead, Dolus turned around and stared at the horse. Something in the gaze of the man reminded Arolis of a great beast eyeing his prey, ready to pounce. Then the horse froze in place as Dolus lifted his hand and pointed a finger at the horse. As the finger unfurled, it began to change in appearance. No longer was the finger a slender appendage of a man, but the entire hand had become the paw of a fearsome beast. The finger had become an extended claw, long and sharp and menacing.

Arolis whinnied for the boy but Leonolis was too blinded by the worm to even understand the reason for the horse's fearful screams and snorts. Arolis had no other options. He turned and bolted, his only hope to somehow alert the king to the danger his son now faced.

As Arolis ran, Dolus once again assumed his human form and followed the trusting little boy into the darkness.

Chapter Twenty-One

THE LION'S ROAR

Arolis tore through the growing darkness with lightning speed, leaping streams, dodging low-hanging branches when possible, tearing through thorny brambles, and hoping beyond hope to run across someone who might be able to help. Having run for what seemed like miles, the trusty stallion was nearing the place of exhaustion, having already spent most of the afternoon on the long trek to Treacherin. Still, he could not risk stopping for even a quick breath or hasty sip from one of the many brooks he encountered along the way. Leonolis was in danger. His safety was all that mattered to the steed.

Darkness had now completely fallen around the horse yet he never slowed his gait. Bounding and leaping, sweating and snorting, he made his way through to the outlying farms of the village of Treacherin. From several windows he could see the faint flicker of a candle or the warm glow of a fire being stoked at a hearth. He could smell the wonderful aromas emanating from the evening meals being prepared in each Brenolinian home he passed by. Would any of these good people be able to help? Would they even stop to consider a horse might be trying to communicate a need for assistance to the heir to the throne?

Watching-Leonolis, of course, was able to follow along with the presence of the Voice always near enough to sense but never to be seen. What he saw now he had never quite realized before—the incredible sacrifice of his beloved mount. As Arolis came into the city square of Treacherin, the watching king was able to see his friend and recoiled in horror at what he saw.

Foam and saliva dripped from the mouth of Arolis and his entire body was wet. The horse seemed to be laboring deeply for each and every breath, and it appeared to watching-Leonolis that the horse might collapse at any moment. Then he saw the blood! Dripping from all four of the horse's mighty limbs from shoulder to hoof—from haunch to hoof—were rips in the horse's flesh, caused by the many brambles he ran through and by the coarse underbrush the animal had been forced to run through. The chest of Arolis began to fade from foamy white to foamy pinkish red as the blood from the horse's wounded breast began to mingle with the sweat and foam.

The king was now silent as tears streamed down his agonized face. "I never knew. I never knew. How faithful is my friend. How much he gave for me . . . without one thought for his own safety. This was all my fault! How foolish I was!"

"You can only take responsibility for what you were responsible for, Leonolis," comforted the Voice. "What you are seeing is the true meaning of love played out before your very eyes. The greatest act of love is not the physical relations between a man and his wife. The greatest act of love is the laying down of life. Arolis is but one in a long line of those who have done just that for you."

As watching-Leonolis wiped the tears from his face, he noticed Arolis sliding to the most amazing stop right in the middle of the town square. Sliding for what appeared to be about thirty feet, the horse came face-to-face with a startled white horse, and on top of that horse, a startled Augurian!

"Whoa! Whoa, good Arolis!" said the calm yet firm voice of the seer. "Where is your boy?"

Arolis began to wheeze and cough and even stumbled back several feet, but righted himself just before he fell completely to the ground. The poor exhausted beast was frantic in his whinnies and neighs, which were indiscernible to all but Augurian.

Speak your thoughts to me, good Arolis, spoke Augurian in thought.

Lord Augurian, the lion—the man called Dolus—has the boy! thought the horse to the seer.

Is it a man or is it a lion? responded Augurian.

They are one and the same! said Arolis.

This is what I feared and what I have sensed in the magical realm. You have only confirmed what I have sensed. Can you lead us there, Arolis?

Of course, I can! said the stallion as he reeled around to head right back into the darkness.

Wait! Wait, dear friend! cried Augurian. *We must send word to the other hunting party. Give me a general direction to send them to once they have been found.*

North of Treacherin by way of the seventh stream one passes after leaving the last house of the city. Tell them to follow that stream for at least five more miles. They will come to a narrowing in the streambed framed with tall stone columns on either side. The lion, last I saw him and the boy, were passing through those columns and into the night.

Aurgurian relayed the instructions to one of the huntsmen and sent him on his way, giving Arolis a few moments to breathe and to gulp down a much-needed drink from the public water fountain in the town square. Then they were off in the direction Arolis had just come from, yet this time at not such a frenzied pace. Leading a regiment of mounted hunters through the dark of night was not such an easy task. Augurian also urged a quieter approach once they came near the place where the boy had last been seen so as to not spoil the element of surprise they hoped to maintain.

When they arrived at the stream, the group followed Arolis as he veered from the well-kept road and into the path he had just traversed in the streambed. Just as the last horseman was leaving the road, the faint sound of hoof beats caught the ear of Augurian.

"Hold!" he shout-whispered to those in front of him. "Listen!"

The entire regiment stopped and grew silent as they strained to hear. Unable to discern whether they were friend or foe, they instinctively knew to remain silent until the intentions of whoever these riders were could be ascertained. Closer and closer came the sound of many horses thundering down the road behind them. And then the air grew silent. Only the occasional snort of a horse in the darkness could be heard from the road. Whoever this was, they were now trying to conceal themselves.

After a few moments, the slow and steady hoof beat of one horse could be heard approaching the stream. With each second, the men already in the streambed put hand to sword, preparing to defend themselves. The horse stopped. So palpable was the tension in the air that Augurian felt he could hear the heartbeats of both men and their mounts piercing the night air.

There came a faint whisper. So silent was the night that this whisper of a question thundered through the air like lightning, causing each heart to stop for a brief second.

"Who goes there?" was all the voice said.

Nothing. No one responded.

"Who goes there?" said the voice again. "I know you are there. I sense your presence."

"Maison? Is that you?" asked Augurian.

"Yes! It is I!" replied the wise old Maison, "and I have brought the other regiment with me. Let us waste not more time! Lead on, Augurian! Lead on!"

For the next two grueling miles, the group trudged through the night, walking in almost total silence. The huntsmen of Bren are known for their stealth. Their horses are so well trained as to be almost cat-like in their ability to avoid even the stirring of dry leaves or scattered twigs on the ground. Of course, the magic of Augurian and Maison did not hurt the cause either, having cast a spell of silence on the forest they now traveled.

Soon, they found themselves at the place of the stone columns where Arolis had last seen the boy and Dolus. Quickening his pace, the great horse Arolis began to head straight between the columns, his only focus now on retrieving the young prince.

Whoa, there Arolis! said Augurian. *Let us strategize before we rush into the situation. If what you say is true, this is no ordinary lion but is a metamorph—a creature able to change his very appearance, moving freely between the animal world and the human. We can trust no one and must consider that he might assume the identity of the prince. If he was born a human with the gift it is one thing. If born a lion with the gift, then we have quite another problem on our hands.*

How so? replied the horse in thought.

When born a metamorph in the human realm, the instinct to kill is but for self-defense. In the case of the metamorph being born into the lion realm, the instinct to kill is for his very survival. He must kill in order to live.

Then what must we do? asked Arolis.

We must think like a lion but utilize every sense and every bit of magic we can muster, responded the short, wise seer.

Turning to Augurian, Maison asked, "Do you concur, good Augurian?"

"Of course I concur. Even now I sense that the boy is still alive but in grave danger. Whatever we do, we must do with haste and deep wisdom."

Addressing Justinian and the two regiments of huntsmen, Augurian spoke forth his plan. "Men of Bren, this is no simple lion we face, but rather a monster. He is of two worlds—two worlds that cannot coexist peacefully. The beast within him rages against the human forms he often takes, despise that form so much, he does. Good Justinian, send one regiment to the hillside above this stream and proceed northward. Send the other to the hillside on the opposite bank and proceed northward, both groups staying out of sight of the stream but close enough to follow its path. My sense is that we will run into the beast and trouble soon enough. Arolis, you will lead the way for Maison and myself. Use your equine hearing, your equine sight, your equine sense of smell, and above all, your equine ability to sense fear to help us root out the beast. One more thing," said Augurian.

Everyone already on edge from the sheer tension of the situation, became even more intent as the seer began to speak an incantation:

"From Founders of old to present day
Bring from the darkness light
Open the eyes that good might see
Concealed from evil's sight
Come blur the sense of evil's eye
From sky to 'neath the ground
Let none be heard though haste be made
Not even one step's sound."

As the last words of the incantation were spoken, a wave of power went through the group of huntsmen. Instantly they could see their surroundings as if it were daylight and simultaneously all sound ceased, though hoofs were shuffling and steeds were snorting!

Seeing the wonder that now engulfed the hearts of the men, Augurian said, "Good men of Bren, you may speak freely now. No one other than those in our group will hear you. As long as you stay within sight of me the spell covers you. It should last for at least an hour. Arolis, you may lead the way."

With that, the groups split up and made their way to either embankment above the stream while Arolis, Augurian, and Maison stayed with the stream itself. Making sure to keep within sight of the seer, each group walked freely and quickly, able to see through the darkness, avoiding previously unseen obstacles. They were also able to give direction and receive direction as the entourage continued through the forest.

The men and the horses were all quite alert and quite energized by the spell of Augurian and were able to make great headway in a short amount of time. After several minutes of this, the silence of the forest was pierced by the most blood-curdling scream any had ever heard—like that of a young child in terror. That scream was followed by the roar of a great beast—the lion. At the sound of the roar, all three groups headed for the sound without even looking at one another. They instinctively knew this was the one they were searching for and wasted no time as their careful walking gait gave way to full-on gallops!

After a few hundred yards, they came upon a small farmhouse. The roof of the cottage was beginning to be consumed with flames and a small girl was huddled over the body of a man, bleeding profusely from his chest and abdomen.

"Papa! Please don't leave me! Papa! Papa!" cried the little girl.

Sliding to a stop just before the body, Augurian slid from the horse's back and immediately went to the man's side. Without saying a word, he was joined by Maison and together they began to administer a spell over the barely breathing man.

"By Founders strength and Founders wisdom
Make growing wounds ungrow
Where evil's stricken bear Your light
And end the reddened flow
Close up the wound and bind the flesh
Bring rest and cleansing deep
What was intended for the worst
Reverse with life to keep."

222

Stepping back from the body for a moment, both Augurian and Maison drew from the small pouches tethered to their waists a mixture of herbs and dried plants. Maison placed his concoction just below the man's nostrils while Augurian sprinkled his over the gaping wounds in the man's abdomen. Within seconds, a small column of smoke began to rise from the man's wounds as he began to take in deep breaths where only seconds before he had been gasping for each small breath. To the wonder and amazement of all who were witness to this that day, the man's wounds began to close and his eyes began to open. Still in shock over what he had just lived through, the man was unable to speak. Looking toward the two seers with gratitude, he collapsed back to the ground, tears now streaming down his cheeks as he locked eyes with his daughter.

"What happened, child? Who did this?" asked the seer Augurian.

"A lion . . . er . . . a . . . man . . . something," whimpered the confused girl.

"What do you mean 'something'?" asked Augurian.

Looking toward her father, the girl looked into his eyes for assurance. The weakened man nodded to his girl and then looked at the seer and nodded again. Having been reassured that her papa was all right, she turned to Augurian and spoke.

"A man came to our door. I had seen him earlier in the twilight hour picking berries with a young boy—down near the stream yonder," she said while pointing to the north.

"I was alone so I would not open the door to him since Papa was still not home from his trip into Treacherin for supplies. I simply asked 'Who are you and what do you want?' just as my papa had taught me. He replied 'I am Dolus. I am in need of a local huntsman. There is talk of a lion in these woods and I fear I am ill-equipped to protect myself.' I told him I could not allow him into our home but that Papa was a huntsman by trade. He then told me he understood my fear and would simply wait near the stream for my father's return."

"Was the boy not with him when he approached your door?" asked Maison.

"I never heard him speak nor did I see him when I peered through the curtains to make sure the man kept his word. Papa had given me a crossbow and taught me well in the art of defending myself, so I was quite ready for him should he dare to enter our home without invitation."

"What happened then?" he asked.

"I heard Papa whistling as he came up the stream bed as he always did. This was our signal that it was him and that it was safe to open the door. Peeking out the window before I dared to open the door, I could still see the man sitting on a stump near the water's edge. Because I could now see Papa, I went ahead and opened the door. I saw Papa reaching for his sword, but . . . where the man had been . . . a lion now sat! I screamed just as Papa saw me! He yelled, 'Get back in the house, Tarason! Now!' So I ran back inside and bolted the door shut. I crouched in the corner near the hearth in fear. Then all grew silent. I then waited for Papa's command to open the door . . . but he never came. The next thing I knew, the man had broken the door down and began sniffing the air like a wild beast in search of prey! He must have sensed where I was because he suddenly turned and headed straight for my hiding place. When I saw there was no other way, I stood and let my arrow fly. It struck him in the left shoulder and he howled like an animal, stumbling into the hearth. His cloak caught on fire, and he knocked the loose coals to the floor, causing our home to catch fire. Then something must have frightened him . . . . like he sensed something coming his way. He ran from the house and I ran to Papa . . . and then you appeared."

"It is the metamorph," said Augurian solemnly. "And he is wounded. We must waste no more time."

"Brave Tarason, you have done well for Bren this day," said Augurian. Then turning to face her father, he said, "May the strength of Bren be yours today!"

"Men, this day we conquer! This day we overcome the Dark Lord! This day we live or die for the king!" shouted the seer as the entire hunting party bounded back northward following Arolis who had picked up the scent of the beast.

The entire time this scene was unfolding, watching-Leonolis was overcome with gratitude on so many different levels. He was, of course, taken aback by the devotion of his dear horse, Arolis, but no less stunned by the sacrifice made by each member of the hunting party—willing to lay down their very lives—for him! Not only that but, in a sense, even the girl and her father had sacrificed for him and for the kingdom. He was beginning to understand what the Voice was trying to communicate through the adventures at hand. Even though the scene unfolding before his eyes was anything but one of peace, he still enjoyed a sense of reverie as he pondered such thoughts. Suddenly he was startled back into the reality of the moment.

Arolis, followed directly by Augurian and Maison, suddenly slid to a sudden stop. Simultaneously, the entire group on either side of the leaders swooped in, one regiment closing in on each side, nearly piled into one another. Had it not been for the magic of Augurian and the lifting of darkness to the eyes of the men and their mounts, this could have been a tragic moment. Watching-Leonolis saw it once the dust cleared a bit—the tail of a lion as it disappeared into the recesses of a dark cave opening.

Augurian and Maison slid from the backs of their horses as did Justinian. The two seers held their hands out in front of them, palms facing the cave in preparation to cast a spell, while Justinian drew his sword and prepared to enter.

"Wait!" said the seers simultaneously. "Let us discern what it is we face before we proceed," continued Augurian.

Speaking loudly and directly into the cave opening, Augurian said, "Are you the one they call Dolus? We know you are in there! You have no place to run! Show yourself!"

Nothing.

Again the seer spoke, "Dolus, you are surrounded! We will not withhold our fury but for a few more moments. Do not make us do something you will regret! Come forth at once!"

Just as the seers prepared to cast a spell of lightning, there came a stirring near the cave's entrance, like the sound of small pebbles falling down a creek bank. A small voice came from the cavernous darkness.

"Good Augurian. It is I, Leonolis. Please put down your hands. My friend has been wounded and is in need of a healer," said the prince, still out of eyesight.

"Leonolis! Is that you?" shouted Justinian. "Come out at once! We have come to help you!"

"Help me?" replied the boy. "Did you not hear? It is my friend, Dolus, who has need of help!"

"The one you call Dolus is neither a friend nor a human, Son! He means you harm! Run to us at once!" pled Justinian.

"I will not leave him . . . he means me no harm. Why do you not understand, good soldier of Bren?" asked the boy.

"Good solider of Bren? You call me 'good soldier,' Leonolis?" said the now-confused captain. "What is my name, Son?"

Silence.

"Leonolis? Who am I?" he asked again.

Still more silence.

"You cannot be the real Leonolis if you do not recognize your father's friend of friends!" said the now-angry Justinian.

"But is is me!" replied Leonolis.

"Then show yourself, boy!" said the captain sternly.

After a few more seconds, the pebbles began to stir again as the boy shuffled through the darkness to cave's entrance. Not knowing a spell of light had been cast over the entourage, the boy did not realize he could be seen.

"You are not Leonolis!" shouted Justinian.

"But I am Leonolis, fool!" shouted the boy right back.

"Leonolis would never address his father's captain in such a manner, and why is it that the arrow from the crossbow of a little girl now protrudes from your left shoulder? You are Dolus!" cried Justinian. "Seize him!" he yelled to the huntsmen.

In an instant, the boy transformed himself into the form of a lion. Without hesitation, the beast leapt through the air and swiped across the upraised shield of Justinian, knocking it from his grip. Just as he was about to deliver a death blow to the man's head, lightning shot from the hands of the two seers, causing the lion to reel around in pain and dart back into the cave.

"Inside!" cried Justinian. The entire group began to dismount and head into the cave entrance without one thought for their own safety. As they bounded through the cave, they had to enter single file, but the further in they came, the wider the cave became until it opened up into a magnificent cavern, full of light and splendor. In the far end of the chamber was a raised platform, completely covered in gold plating. Upon this platform sat a magnificent throne, adorned with all manner of priceless jewels. Rubies. Garnets. Opals. Jade. Amethyst. Hanging from the very center of the cavernous ceiling was a stupendous chandelier, silver-plated, with diamonds hanging in a countless array of glorious sparkle.

Not taking the time to ponder what sort of room this might be, the group continued across the cavern floor, smooth as polished marble, adorned with statues of lions and lionesses, some of bronze, some of granite, some of marble, and some of pure gold! As they neared the grand expanse of the enthroned platform, there appeared three new cave passageways! The floor, being clean and smooth, left no dust to disturb. This, in turn, left no tracks for the men to follow! What to do?

"Arolis! Send for Arolis!" shouted Maison. "His sense of smell is needed!"

Before the captain could even relay the order to the men to bring the horse, Arolis was sliding across the floor to them!

He is my boy! There is no way this lion will have him if I have anything to do with it! thought the horse to the seers.

Ears perked up, the great steed went to the first passageway and sniffed a long, loud sniff. Shaking his head and snorting, he moved to the next and went through the same routine. Again, he shook his head and snorted. As he came to the third passage, he simply entered with a gallop as he called back to the others, *This way!* Of course, the men only heard a frantic whinny while the seers heard his words!

Running with the spell of Augurian still intact, the horse and the men were able to see their way through the cave clearly. Within a few minutes, the horse caught sight of the lion's tail as it whipped around a corner. *I see him! The lion is within our grasp!*

Arolis picked up his pace (if that is even possible!) and quickly caught sight of the lion, but something was not right. Something was on the lion's back, or someone!

With the lion but a few yards ahead of him, Arolis was quickly closing in on the beast. Just as the great horse was about to pounce on the back of the brute, he stopped in his tracks. That something or someone was Leonolis!

Coming to a great chasm in the cavern floor, the lion could go no further. Turning to face the horse and gathering huntsmen, he began to speak.

"The boy knows what you are up to! He has seen through the many lies of the realm of Bren!" Tell them, boy!" snarled the lion.

"It is true! It has been revealed to me that things are upside down and thoughts are backward! My father cares not for me, much less for the Kingdom of Bren. He loves my brothers more than me—he loves his power more than he loves his people!" shouted the boy.

"What magic are you under, boy?" replied Maison.

"I am under no magic! I am under truth!" replied the boy.

"A boy does not speak the way you speak! A boy does not alter his ways as you have done apart from deep magic! You have been seduced, Leonolis! But we can help! Just do as I say!" pled the boy's wise old tutor.

"I am tired of being enslaved to the old ways of Bren! I am tired of no one believing in me! I must do what I must do! Trust me; it is for the good of Bren that I do what I now do!" shouted the boy back at Maison.

With that, the boy crouched down behind the lion's mane, holding on tightly as the beast whirled around and jumped out above the abyss. Flying across the chasm, the lion and the boy disappeared into the darkness as they came to light on the other side of the tunnel. The seers, Arolis, Justinian, and the men sat there bewildered, unable to make such a daring leap across such a wide expanse.

Chapter Twenty-Two

THE SERPENTINE STEPS

Watching-Leonolis and the Voice hovered quietly above the men in the tunnel, able to hear every word uttered by the group. As the lion escaped into the depths of the tunnel, Justinian and the seers discussed the matter at hand.

"Did you see the look of defiance on the boy's face? Did you not hear the rebellion in his voice—the bitterness with which he spoke?" asked Justinian. "Surely he is under some dark magical spell?"

"Indeed, he is being led by dark magic of that I am sure," spoke Augurian confidently. "But reality is thus: Leonolis is young and immature and probably has no idea of the magical influence he is now under."

"Yes, but let us not forget. Royal blood flows through his veins. He is the son of the high king. At some point, true identity will rule over the lies he now assumes to be truth," interjected Maison.

"True, Maison. 'Tis true. Let us prepare for the worst but believe for the best," added Augurian.

"Then how do we proceed?" asked Justinian.

At that moment, watching-Leonolis spoke to the Voice. "They never once stopped believing in me—regardless of my attitude, regardless of my actions. I never knew. Simply amazing."

"How does that make you feel? What does that do to your heart and soul?" asked the Voice.

"It makes me feel loved. It causes my heart and my soul to feel . . . well . . . invincible!" replied the king.

"That is what truth and true love do. They leave the heart and soul feeling rooted on an unshakable foundation. This is true strength in spite of one's circumstances," responded the Voice. Again, the hidden watchers turned their attention back to the men below them.

"We proceed in two ways," said Augurian. "Maison, create a bridge across the chasm. Justinian, divide the men into two parties again. You and Maison lead the first across the bridge and continue pursuit of the lion. I will take the other regiment and return to the upper world and head north. I will consult the Founders and ask for discernment as to where the tunnel resurfaces. I suspect he seeks a way out of this maze. My deeper suspicion is that the lion is not working alone. Metamorphs are not gifted in the ways of magic other than their ability to change forms. Something or someone else is wielding the magic over the boy. Let us go at once."

Augurian then headed back toward the cave entrance with his group while Maison erected a magical bridge over the chasm. Casting his hands out in front of himself, the seer simply said,

"Chasm be gone.
Unseen hand.
O'er the abyss.
Magic's span!"

The men, along with Arolis, stood there.

There is nothing spanning the chasm, thought Arolis to Maison.

O my! Of course! It is there, good Arolis. This bridge must be crossed by trusting hearts. When trust is there, the way will be seen!

Turning to the men, Maison said, "Good men of Bren! The bridge will be seen when trust fills your heart. Do you trust me? Do you trust the heart of King Troyolin? Do you trust the Founders? Then your eyes will see."

Arolis, stepped out first. As his hoof clopped out over the nothingness, the sound was that of hoof meeting stone. Arolis could easily see the span! As the horse walked across the bridge, he turned back and gave a look of confidence to the men as a way of saying to them "It's all right, friends! Follow me!"

The entire regiment began to move forward. After the last man had made his way across, Maison walked across. With each step, the bridge disappeared behind him, leaving nothing but a dark abyss below.

Suddenly, watching-Leonolis and the Voice were no longer with Maison and his regiment. They were now flying through the tunnels just above the tail of the lion. Little Leonolis was still clinging tightly to the lion's mane as he bounded down, down, down, ever deeper into the tunnel. One would have thought there should have been total darkness in the cavern system so far beneath the surface of the earth, but the tunnel seemed to be filled with a deep red glow, emanating from somewhere just ahead of the lion.

Soon, the eyes of watching-Leonolis adjusted to the light and were able to clearly see the source of the red glow. Rubranna. Before he could speak his thoughts to the Voice, the red fairy and the lion came to a sudden stop. Slipping from the back of Dolus, little Leonolis asked, "Why do we stop? By the magic of both Augurian and Maison, surely those who pursue us will not be far behind!" said the boy in panic.

"Ha! Do not trust their magic, boy! Remember, they want to bring you harm and desire to relegate you to mediocre status in the realm! You have just entered the season of manhood and are on the verge of true authority simply by standing up to the ridiculous rules and traditions of Bren! And besides, we have a little magic of our own," replied Rubranna.

"I can run no more as the lion," replied Dolus as he morphed into the form of a man. "My shoulder has been pierced, and I have lost the strength to support that limb. We must do something or I fear the boy is correct."

"Are you serious, Dolus?" asked the red fairy incredulously. "I thought you were stronger than that! You disappoint me!"

Pointing her tiny red wand at the arrow still protruding from the man's shoulder, she sent forth a bolt of lightning, simultaneously filling the tunnel with light and burning the arrow instantly away as the wound closed and the flesh bore not even the faintest scar.

While the lightning filled the room, little Leonolis could now see they had come, once again, into a large cavern, revealing a huge underground lake.

"We have nowhere to run?" exclaimed the boy. "There is no way out and they will be upon us soon! What will we do?"

"You will never learn, boy! Watch!" responded Rubranna.

Pointing to the water, the lake began to stir directly in front of the trio. The stirring soon became a bubbling upheaval and this upheaval gave way to the appearance of three slimy, web-footed creatures Leonolis had met before.

"Welcome, dear Troglodytes! Take us through the waters!" commanded the red fairy.

"Through the waters?" exclaimed the boy.

"How else do you expect us to avoid capture, boy?" came her retort.

"But we cannot breathe under water! We will die!" he exclaimed.

"Trust me!" was all she said.

Flitting down and lighting upon the shoulder of the first Troglodyte, the red fairy took the hand of the creature and the pair quickly submerged, leaving an eerie, faint red glow for the others to follow. The second creature took Leonolis by the hand and began dragging him beneath the surface. Choking as the water filled his lungs, the boy suddenly became overwhelmed with a sense of peace, like it was going to be all right to simply give up to the urge to get to the surface and simply submit to the water.

Expecting to wake and find himself in the realm of the Founders, the boy's heart began to fill with wonder as he opened his eyes and looked ahead to see the red fairy and her Troglodyte just ahead of them. The boy was amazed as he suddenly had the ability to see clearly underwater—no differently than he could on dry land! It dawned on him, he could also breathe freely just as he could on dry land! Turning around to look behind him, he could see the third Troglodyte and Dolus, still in the form of a man, swimming after them.

The magic of the Troglodytes was their ability to not only assume the characteristics of those they came in contact with but also to grant their ability to survive underwater to those they joined with. As soon as Leonolis had been taken by the hand of the Troglodyte this process had begun. What the boy had not realized was that he was not breathing through his nostrils or even his mouth, but through the tiny gills that had suddenly developed on either side of his neck!

Of course, watching-Leonolis had a bit of trepadation as he and the Voice also plunged beneath the surface of the lake. Leonolis suddenly recalled the panic he had first felt as his head went beneath the still water's surface. He knew this was silly and soon recovered his composure. The Voice simply said, "Here we go."

For several minutes, the Troglodytes swam with their partners through many twists and turns of this submerged tunnel system. At one point, Leonolis feared he might panic as the tunnel became almost too narrow to pass through. Yet as they came to the narrow place, the Troglodytes shifted their form to comply with the slight amount of space this particular passageway afforded them. They became weirdly thin! As the panic rose in the boy, he soon found himself easily passing through the narrows, as his own body contorted and conformed to the smallness of the passage! His own hands appeared to be thin as his mother's pancakes! It was then he discovered that he could laugh under water—and hear too!

"We are almost there!" said the red fairy without so much as one gurgle. "Wait here while I check ahead that our way is clear."

Upon her words, the Troglodytes guiding Leonolis and Dolus hovered perfectly in the water about ten feet below the surface. As the red fairy and her companion cleared the water above them, it became suddenly dark again, the red glow of the fairy's light now gone from them. By this time, little Leonolis had grown accustomed to his new abilities and did not even consider the darkness. Soon enough, the red glow appeared again as the red fairy stuck her head beneath the water's surface and simply said, "Come!"

With a few swift kicks of their webbed feet, the Troglodytes had both Leonolis and Dolus to the surface and to shore. Once again they found themselves in an expansive cavern, filled, of course, with the red glow emanating from Rubranna. Yet Leonolis noticed a faint light coming from the far end of the cave. Before he could even open his mouth to tell Rubranna about the light he saw, the red fairy began barking orders.

"Dolus, take your lion form and come with me. Boy, you stay here with the Trogs. Trogs, keep eyes on the water and on the boy," said Rubranna as she flitted toward the faint white light with the lion Dolus bounding after her.

Meanwhile, watching-Leonolis and the Voice were suddenly back at the lake watching Maison prepare his small troop for the next phase of their adventure. Having gained much confidence from the men when they walked across the magical bridge, it took little convincing for him to persuade them to step into the water. As each man lowered his head beneath the surface of the lake, they were immediately surrounded by a bubble of air! Rather than rising to the surface as bubbles normally do, these magic bubbles continued to surround the men, keeping them perfectly dry and with a full supply of air to breathe! It did not take long for each man to discover that he could will the bubble to move in any direction he chose to go!

The most humorous thing of all (if we may inject a bit of humor into the telling of such a serious tale) was the moment the great stallion Arolis took to the water. The men could not help but snicker as the horse soon found himself upside down inside his bubble of air! After several somersaults and a few angry whinnies, the horse finally righted himself and realized he had been trying too hard! Soon, the merry band of bubble warriors were on their way, Maison leading the way, wand lighting the way ahead. Following the same path the red fairy and her minions had taken, they went through many twists and turns and found themselves amazed at the wonder of the depths of the underground lake.

Then they came to the narrow passageway. Maison did not miss a beat. He simply stuck his wand out through the surface of his bubble and blasted a lightning blast of power toward the narrows, blowing a hole wide enough even a horse would easily fit through (which was quite fortunate since a horse had to fit through!).

Upon hearing the faint explosion of rock from deep within the lake behind them, the Troglodytes immediately took the boy and headed in the direction the red fairy and lion had gone just a few moments before. As they made their way to the light, the boy began to realize they were moving steadily upward again. Nearing the light, his eyes began to squint as Leonolis realized they were nearing the surface—an exit from the cave! In the same moment, he began to hear the sound of moving water, like the sound a waterfall makes as it heads over the precipice.

Now almost blinded by the brilliance of the sunlight, it took several minutes for the boy to recognize his surroundings. When he could finally open his eyes fully he almost jumped up and down for joy! There several hundred feet below them was the river Runland! There was no mistaking it! He had been on many excursions with his father along the higher banks of the mighty flow. The sound of the waters was not that of a waterfall, but rather the incredibly loud sound of the Banshee Rapids, so named for the sound of the wind and crashing waters combined. This particular stretch of river ran through a narrow channel, forcing the water to crash mightily against the many fallen boulders that littered the riverbed. Again, due to the narrowing of the river canyon walls, the wind was also forced through causing the velocity to increase and the wailing sound. At times, the combined sound of crashing waves and wailing winds reminded one of the wail of the Banshee. Thus the name. Though spectacular in appearance, the beauty of the Banshee Rapids veiled a grave danger. No one had ever traversed the entire rapid and lived to tell about it! Little Leonolis was quite taken with this close-up view of the majestic rapid.

That reverie proved to be short as the tiny, rasping voice of Rubranna broke through even the tremendous sounds filling the canyon. "What are you doing here? I told you to watch the water and watch the boy back at the cavern lake's edge!"

Speaking in a lizard-like hiss, the voice of the Troglodyte sounded as slimy as the creature looked. It occurred to the boy, oddly at such a moment, that he had never heard the creatures speak. Up until now he had only conversed with them through thought. He had just assumed this was how they spoke. It would not occur to him for many years to come that this was one of the ways he had been gifted to speak!

"We heard (*hissssss*) a booming crash (*hisssss*) coming from the lake behind and beneath us (*hissss*). We assumed this was what you were commanding us to watch for (*hissss*). Was this not your command?" hissed the Troglodyte.

"A booming crash? Magic! We were followed! Dolus, take the boy upon your back. Trogs, back to the cavern and to the lake. Keep those who follow busy so as to allow our escape! Down the road we fly!" commanded the red fairy.

Climbing on the back of the lion, Leonolis once again gripped the lion's mane as he watched the Troglodytes trudge quickly back into the darkness of the cavern. The trio bounded down the "road" as Rubranna called it. In actuality, it was nothing more than a two-foot wide ledge along the steep rocks of the river wall! Leonolis dared to look down once as the lion bounced along after the fairy. One look was enough to make him bury his head deep in the lion's mane and to begin to pray to the Founders for sure footing for his lion friend!

The Trogs made it back to water's edge just as Maison and the men were beginning to surface. Without being seen, the trio of Trogs slipped beneath the surface and went to work. Maison, leading the way, made it to shore. As his feet finally touched the rocky lake floor his bubble burst, sending a hiss into the darkness and a blast of fresh cool air into his nostrils.

Just as Justinian was about to set his foot down upon the shore, he suddenly found himself being pulled back into the deep waters of the lake, no longer able to will his bubble where he intended to go. Without the aid of Maison's light, he had been unable to see the slimy web the Troglodyte had cast around his bubble. With great strength for such a small creature, the Trog had been able to pull the captain to the very bottom of the lake and tether the bubble to the lake floor! Covered in complete darkness, Justinian began to panic and cry out for Maison's help. But the seer could not hear him.

One by one, the Trogs spun a web around each bubble. From a gland just behind the elbow, each Troglodyte could cast a strand of slime that became stronger than rope when it came in contact with water. Adept at casting their web in such a manner as to weave a net in a matter of seconds, the three Trogs had been able to tether each of the men and their bubbles to the very bottom of the underground lake!

It did not take Maison very long to understand that something evil was taking place beneath the waters. Just as he was about to plunge in, the top of the bubble containing Arolis came to the surface, just as the Trog's web flew over the horse's bubble! Dragging Arolis quickly downward had required the joined forces of all three Trogs, so great was the will of the great horse against them!

The Trogs never saw what hit them. Like liquid lightning, shafts of brilliant light pierced the creatures simultaneously, rendering each unconscious and loosing the horse's bubble from their grip. As Arolis rose to the surface, Maison, wand leading the way, darted to the lake floor. One by one, he severed the slimy webs that tethered each bubble, sending the entire regiment safely to the surface. Waiting now at the shore, Arolis greeted each man as the bubbles burst. Once Maison was on shore, Arolis shouted, *Light ahead! This way!* And they were off!

Reaching the source of the light, it took the men and the horse a few seconds to gauge their whereabouts. Quickly discerning they were at the Banshee Rapids, Arolis told Maison his thoughts and just as quickly picked up the lion's scent.

I have found the way, thought Arolis to Maison. *I have detected the odor of the boy and the odor of the lion—and something else.*

Something else? queried the seer.

Yes! A similar smell I smelled once in the realm of Kelsin, thought the horse.

Of course! He is being led by a fairy! exclaimed the seer.

But the fairies I have smelled before have a deep floral sweetness about their smell—a flowery aroma. This is different. There is a tinge of sweetness yet the stench of something bitter. Fairy—but not! thought Arolis.

"This is the work of a dark fairy, no doubt working at the behest of Tormentia herself!" said Maison. "We must pursue!" Off they went, Maison now on the back of the steed with the men following as quickly as their Brenolinian legs could carry them!

Watching-Leonolis and the Voice had somehow been able to take in all of the action, as if they were with the fleeing lion, fairy, and boy, yet also with Maison, Arolis, and the men of Justinian's group. Watching the saga unfold before him, watching-Leonolis was staggered at the depth of love, bravery, and devotion his men and horse now portrayed before him. Had it not been for the excitement of seeing his own life unfold before him from so many different perspectives he would have been reduced to emotional uncontrollable tears!

Suddenly, he could see the red glow of the fairy below and could see Arolis and Maison now closing the gap from behind as they continued on their northern route along the ledge. Suddenly, movement from the cliffs above caught his eye. Turning upward, watching-Leonolis saw the other regiment being led by Augurian. He remembered the stories of this day he had lived so long ago, but now he was about to see with his own eyes what had taken place that day!

It was obvious to all that Rubranna and the lion were trying to get to the darkness of the Abysstine Forest and the spell of blindness Tormentia had placed on the region. That blindness was actually a spell that served to dull the senses of any human that entered. Sight would become blurred. Hearing would become dulled. Touch would be without feeling. There would be nothing but the foul stench of a thousand dreaded fire skunks of Bren (so named for the rancid smell that made one's nose feel as if it were on fire!). Worst of all? A lack of mental acuity that caused any thought to be overcome with paranoia! In other words, every good thought would be replaced with a skewed perspective. Once there, the fairy knew it would take an army to find her. Maison knew this as well.

The last hurdle the trio of runners had before the safety of the forest engulfed them were the Serpentine Steps. The Serpentine Steps were actually once a bridge that spanned the river Runland as it ran between the region of Endoria and the Abysstine Forest. The river served as the boundary between the dark forest and the southern route to Bren. All that remained of the bridge were the massive columns of stone that once held the span in place. Having been destroyed by an earthquake generations before, the bridge had never been rebuilt. The only way to cross the Serpentine Steps was to have the ability to jump the twenty feet between each column—something a lion can easily do and a fairy can simply sail over.

From above, Augurian could see where they were headed and with his great wisdom had already discerned that this was the work of a dark fairy, having seen the faint red glimmer flying directly in front of the lion's head. There would not be enough time to traverse the mountain trail leading down to the ledge from above. If there was to be any hope of cutting the trio off from the Serpentine Steps, the seer would have to find a new route to the ledge. Watching-Leonolis had heard of the great daring of Augurian and his men that day but seeing it play out before him was, well, quite spectacular!

Chapter Twenty-Three

THE ABYSSTINE FOREST

Drawing near the edge of the cliff above the southern approach to the Serpentine Steps, Augurian knew they would never be able to traverse the switchback trail leading down to the steps in time to keep the runners from entering the Abysstine Forest. Yet he did not seem to be slowing his speed. The concern of the men following him grew rapidly more tense as they sensed the seer was not going to stop but seemed to be rather intent on flying out from the cliff's edge and into thin air—a drop to certain death.

Augurian had no intention of meeting his doom that day. He already had a plan in mind. Turning his head around, he shouted to the men in such a supernatural volume that his voice seemed to thunder and echo throughout the canyon. Watching-Leonolis remembered that sound from so long ago, and just as it had done that day, it sent shivers of pride and encouragement through his entire body, building to such a crescendo of power that all good men and horses who heard it were filled with a feeling of invincibility, and all who were not good were filled with a sense of dread and dismay!

"Do you trust me, valiant warriors of Bren? Will you trust the word of the Founders? Will you dare to follow me for the sake of freedom?" he shouted.

To a man, each soldier shouted, "May the strength of Bren be mine today!" and every horse whinnied their agreement. Amazingly, all those following Maison and Arolis and Justinian from the ledge below echoed the sentiments of their compatriots hundreds of feet above, shouting, "May the strength of Bren be mine today!"

In that moment of complete agreement and utter trust, Augurian decreed with a voice like a thousand waterfalls, "This day we conquer! This day we overcome the Dark Lord! This day we live or die for the king!" He plummeted over the side of the precipice! As watching-Leonolis gazed upon the faces of each man as they approached the cliff, he was stunned at the lack of fear he saw. Having not had the privilege of seeing from the vantage point he now enjoyed, he was moved to both pride and tears and an overwhelming sense of worth and value from these dear men of Bren—knowing that they willingly plunged down that cliff that day—for him.

What watching-Leonolis had not expected was to actually experience the plunge with the men. As the last man and horse flew over the edge, watching-Leonolis and the Voice went with them! Seeing the feat of daring from this place gave the king a whole new appreciation for the valor and bravery of his men! By some stroke of magic, Augurian had created a pathway straight down the face of the cliff, like a mighty slide from the top directly to the ledge hundreds of feet below. The horses and their riders simply slid down the pathway. You should have seen their faces. Not only was there never once a hint of fear, now the watching-Leonolis could suddenly see them from below and could see the boyish glee on each man's face and could feel the exhilaration of both man and beast as they slid onto the ledge in a perfect formation just ahead of the lion, fairy, and boy.

Just as the last man slid into place on the ledge, Rubranna, Dolus, and the boy came to a sliding stop just a few feet from the glare of Augurian. Almost as quickly, Maison and his crew arrived to seal off any hope of escape for the runners from behind. Staring intently into the eyes of the red fairy, Augurian's gaze never wavered once. Defiantly, Rubranna glared right back at the seer, little sparks of lightning shooting out a few inches from her face. To say she was defiant and angry would have been an understatement. She seethed a thousand year's worth of evil toward the timeless goodness emanating from Augurian.

Finally, she spoke. "Let us pass, foolish mortal!"

"Or what?" firmly replied Augurian.

"Or you will see and feel the wrath and fury of a hundred storms unleashed on you and your men!" she said as she raised a tiny hand to lash out.

"Do what you will, Red Demon. Evil cannot prevail over the goodness of the Founders," he said with calm assurance.

Without hesitation, she sent a large lightning bolt toward Augurian who calmly deflected it by the palm of his hand, sending it directly back at the fairy and knocking her from the air and into the ground.

Dazed, she quickly flitted back into the air and lashed out with an even bigger bolt of lightning, which Augurian once again deflected back to her. Slower to get back up this time, the fairy was obviously shaken physically, but it was her countenance that betrayed her sudden loss of confidence and exposed her very real fear.

In that moment, the lion lunged at Augurian with such ferocity that Leonolis had fallen from his back. The boy would have been crushed by the lion's body as Augurian sent him flying back to the ground had the boy's quick reflexes not caused him to move toward the cliff at the last second.

Unconscious for a few seconds, the beast lay precariously close to the edge. Had it not been for the mercy of Augurian, he would have dropped into the rapids—certain death—below. As Rubranna and Dolus were adequately subdued in their stupors, Augurian turned his attention to the boy.

"Leonolis, step away from the red demon and go to Maison," he commanded the boy.

"Why do you call her Red Demon? She is a fairy, and she only desires what is best for me," defied the boy.

"She may appear a fairy to you, but make no mistakes, Son of Troyolin, she is a demon born of the darkness from long ago. She is one of the minions of Tormentia. Her only goal is deception. Her magic has seemed to work on you. Now, do as I say and step away from the demon. Take your place with Maison while I deal with these who would bring destruction and calamity upon Bren," said Augurian.

Just as the boy reluctantly sidled toward his tutor, a thick cloud of dark mist began to darken the sunlight. So sudden was the darkness that even Augurian turned momentarily from his focus and looked behind him to see the source of the darkness. Wafting from the other side of the canyon and emanating from the Abysstine Forest, a thick, dark cloud moved quickly across the Serpentine Steps and began to surround the entire regiment. The horses began to grow nervous and skittish as when they could sense a danger in their surroundings like the presence of a wild beast. They began to paw the ground and snort.

Then they saw her. With a brilliant display of light directly to the right of Augurian, a beautiful woman, clothed in white, with long raven-black hair hovered above the Runland—in midair!

"Tormentia!" said both Maison and Augurian simultaneously.

"My fellow sorcerers, why do you torment my good servants?" asked the witch.

"Your servants defy the laws of Bren and have subdued the son of the king!" said Maison.

"The boy? Subdued? I think not," said Tormentia as she turned to face Leonolis. "Boy, have you been taken against your will or do you do the bidding of the kingdom?"

Filled with pride and sudden confidence, little Leonolis said, "I am not taken against my will. I chose to go with the red fairy and Dolus. They have shown me things I have not seen before. They can see dangers you cannot see, Maison! They have a task for me that is meant to save the kingdom," replied the rebellious boy.

"And have you asked your father about this? Have you sought his wisdom in the matter?" said Maison.

"My father does not care about me! He cares only for himself and loves only my brothers! Why should I care about what he thinks of me? I know what he thinks of me!" shouted the boy, angry, bitter tears now streaming down his face.

"Let us be sure, boy, that what you speak is born of the darkness! Your father was set as king of Bren by the decree of the Founders from generations of old! The wisdom of the ages has been handed down to him by and through the hands of time. It is the immature heart and mind that resort to jealousy and bitterness, Son! You are but a boy! And rest assured, to a man—to a man throughout the kingdom—there is no doubt, absolutely none, about the place you hold in your father's heart and eyes! He lives and breathes for you! He talks incessantly among his peers about you! He lays down his life for you! Don't be so foolish as to abandon the highest place of honor and replace it with pride and fear and vain imaginations planted in your mind by the foolish lies of the red demon! She cares for nothing but the demise of your father and the fall of the kingdom. Why do you think Tormentia is here?" said Maison.

Leonolis began to be flooded with thoughts of his father's love. Like a frozen layer of ice on a pond that begins to thaw under the spring sunshine, all could see the boy begin to melt at the wise words of his tutor. Without waiting for the boy to respond, Maison continued.

"Do you not see? Why have you been chosen for this supposed 'task' by this red demon? She knows—Tormentia knows—that if she can get to you, she can get to the heart of your father. If she is able to hold your father by holding you, she can hold sway in the kingdom! Defy her, boy! Defy her now!" shouted Maison.

The boy began to sob as he ran toward Maison. Quickly dismounting, the seer knelt down and embraced the boy as he sobbed, "Forgive me! Forgive me, Maison! Please forgive me!"

"Not so quickly!" shouted Tormentia. "I have not come this far to concede defeat!"

With the twirl of the wand in her right hand, the cloud began to swirl about the entire group, causing the darkness to completely envelope them. As the cloud swirled, the sound of a mighty whirlwind began to fill the canyon. Thunderclaps began to boom and echo and bolts of lightning darted all around the river canyon. Suddenly, the cloud began to lift and move swiftly back across the Serpentine Steps and into the Abysstine Forest.

Once the air cleared and sunshine returned to the ledge, a sense of dread overwhelmed them all. Rubranna had vanished. The lion had vanished. Leonolis was gone! Dread overcame the men. Justinian tried to coax his horse around so as to direct the men, somehow across the Serpentine Steps. His efforts were futile. Even Augurian and Maison seemed to be unusually perplexed as to the next step of action. As the group settled into a dread-filled silence, the air was once again pierced with sound. This time, rather than thunder and lightning and whirlwind, the faint, shrill blast of a trumpet filled the air.

"The fanfare of the king!" shouted one of the men. "There!" shouted another as he pointed toward the rim of the canyon hundreds of feet above them. "The king approaches!"

With an entire battle group of his own, numbering one hundred men and their horses, the king made his way down the long switchback that led to the Serpentine Steps. While the king and his men made their way downward, Augurian, Justinian, and Maison were able to make their way to the place where the trail would eventually lead the king. At this point, the ledge widened into a broad expanse large enough to allow the men and their horses to stand at attention seven abreast as they waited for the king and his men to descend.

Before he had even made it all the way down, Troyolin was calling ahead to Justinian, "Where are they? Where is my son?"

Wisely waiting for the king to get to him, Justinian spoke solemnly to the king as he came to a halt facing his friend of friends. Shaking his head, Justinian simply said, "Tormentia has taken him into the Abysstine Forest."

Turning to Augurian and Maison, the king asked, "Is there another way to cross or must we devise a way to cross the Serpentine Steps?"

"There is a natural crossing further east, my king, but, alas, it is a two-hour ride from here. We would lose valuable time, sire, should we attempt that route," said Maison.

With one gaze from their king, the seers knew what they must do. From the backs of their horses, the seers turned toward the Serpentine Steps and cast this spell:

> *"O Founders, from beyond the mist*
> *Fly o'er this chasm from ridge to ridge*
> *By power of light from days of old*
> *Bear those who cross—restore this bridge."*

Right before the eyes of all who were witness to that day, a bridge of stone began to grow from the broken remnants of the old bridge. Growing from column to column, the span took on the serpentine shape of the former bridge, revealing in full detail why the name was given to the Serpentine Steps. Before the final gap between support column and the far shore had materialized, the king and his men set out in full gallop across the expanse.

Riding beside the king, Augurian shouted out, "Sire, the bridge will last but 'til dusk. When the last ray of the sun leaves the southern shore the span will disappear."

"The task at hand we must do quickly then!" responded the king.

"And, sire, there is one more thing," Augurian went on.

"Yes?" shouted the king as he continued to gallop along.

"The matter of the spell of the Abysstine Forest—the spell of blindness Tormentia has placed upon this dark region," warned Augurian.

"Call the men to order once we have crossed the span, Justinian!" commanded the king.

Once the king and those leading the charge placed their feet on the opposite side of the chasm, Justinian ordered the full stop. "Men, the king would have a word before we continue!"

"Good men of Bren. What we now face is something I have never had to ask any of you to face before this day. Tormentia, long ago, filled this region of the forest with a spell of blindness. What does that mean? Your senses will be attacked, blurred, dulled. Your eyes will deceive you. Your hearing will be filled with voices uttered by no one. What you touch will betray you. Your sense of trust will be questioned. Your thoughts will be twisted to such a degree that what you see as right side up is actually upside down. What you perceive as dark could actually be light. Do not trust your senses!" encouraged the king. "You will be tempted to the point of paranoia!"

"Then what do we trust, sire? How will we know that what we see is real or not?" asked Justinian.

"If I may, sire," interjected the wise old Maison. "Lay aside your thoughts of fear. Lay aside your emotions. Lay aside anything but your heart of hearts. When a thought presents itself, simply remind yourself 'I am a man of Bren.' There is deep magic in that very simple statement, because it is formed from the very foundation of the kingdom and is the purest truth of all. When darkness is faced with such light it must give way. In that moment, sight will be restored. Hearing will become sharp. Touch will not betray you. Thoughts will become clear.

"And one more thing. You may encounter visions of fairies or angelic beings. Do not trust them though they speak with uncanny knowledge of your most hidden thoughts. These are demons and dark fairies, surely sent by Tormentia to cause confusion and division among us. Do not be swayed," said Maison.

Speaking again, the king continued, "Men, trust the Founders. Ride, stand, and fight on the foundation of who you are in your heart of hearts! Trust the foundation. It will surely uphold you! Now we ride!" They were off and within moments of riding upward through the forest, the torments began.

Following the trail, it was easy to see the footprints of the lion in the damp dusty path, yet Justinian immediately began to doubt what he was seeing. "Sire, I have lost sight of the tracks." Coming to a sudden stop in midtrail, Justinian continued. "All I can see are the tracks of a horse ascending up the trail before us!"

"Justinian! Get a hold of yourself! The tracks are those of a lion!" shouted the king.

"Now you are calling me a liar?" asked Justinian incredulously.

"Justinian! Are you a man of Bren or a man of no kingdom?" asked Troyolin.

With that simple question, the spell was broken from Justinian's thoughts and he snapped out of it as if awakened from a dream. "My Lord! Forgive me! I do not know why I responded with such insubordination! Forgive me!" begged Justinian.

"Shake it off, brother! The lie is exposed! Be the man of Bren you were born to be!" encouraged the king.

Once again, Justinian focused on the paw prints leading up the trail before him. Charging into the darkness of the forest, the minds of the men who followed the king were put to the test, yet following the king's example, having witnessed the king's interchange with Justinian, each man quickly put off the darkness with the light of the Founders. It was, indeed, a glorious thing to witness—the heart of men embracing their deepest identity and releasing powers from of old to dispel the darkness!

Of course, it did not take long for the senses of the men and their steeds to be challenged. Coming upon a stream that bordered the road, the tracks of the lion veered from the path and along the trail that followed the stream as it left the trail and made its way from somewhere high in the mountainous region of Abysstine. At one point the trail crossed to the other side of the stream. The horses leading the charge slid to a sudden stop, refusing with loud snorts to ford the shallow waters.

"The stream has grown too wide and too deep to cross!" shouted one of the men.

"Fie!" replied Justinian. "It is a mere ten inches deep and only seven feet wide!"

"But the horses are not swayed by the spells, are they?" responded the soldier.

"Of course not!" said Augurian. "They respond according to the attitude of their riders! They sense fear in you! Are you men of Bren or not?" Once again, the hearts of the men responded from deep within the core of their true identities as men of Bren and the spell was broken. Sensing the freedom in their riders, the horses all bolted across the stream in rapid succession and continued the pursuit of the runaways!

Several times during the course of the chase the men had to stop and remind themselves of who they were, but the spell was always broken by the truth. As they bounded through thickets and traversed rocky debris from the upward trajectory of the chase, all could sense they were closing on the demon and the lion. The tracks seemed fresher and the scent of the lion even more pronounced upon the nostrils of the steeds. The higher they climbed, the slower the pace grew, but the passion of the men never lessened one iota!

Nearing a rocky outcropping, the stream came to an end in the place beneath these rocks where the stream trickled from somewhere deep in the mountain. As King Troyolin dismounted, the entire battle group came to a halt. Since the ground had grown more and ever-increasingly rocky, the tracks of the lion became more and more difficult to discern. Bending down, Troyolin asked, "Maison, what do the Founders tell your senses?"

Struggling to climb up from the saddle of his horse, the short, round seer stood up as tall as he could from the top of his mount's saddle. Lifting his hands high above his head, it appeared the little wizard was going into some sort of trance. With horses snorting and men murmuring, the king glared at his men, knowing their restlessness indicated more deception. "Quiet, men of Bren! Let us give way to the Founders in this moment." As the king's words echoed through the mountainside, the spell was once again broken and the horses settled down as their riders did!

After a few minutes, Maison lowered his hands and sat down in the saddle with a thud. "Sire, they have continued into the high places."

"But the trail seems to end here at this rocky place! There is nowhere else to go but back down from here," responded the king. "We are now above the tree line, Maison. Surely they have taken cover in the darkness of the forest below."

"My king, my senses have discerned what the Founders have foretold. 'The son of the king will always have a target on his back. Where evil abounds, the power of the Founders will be greater.' Do not believe every strategy you would use will be the logic of evil. Step outside of the logic of all that is good and think—just for a moment—as one who walks outside the bounds of honor and good. It is there you will find the scent of darkness and be able to follow with the light," said Maison.

As if on cue, a blue mist began to materialize before the face of the king. With light emanating from within the mist, a most beautiful angelic girl appeared, wings flitting behind her as she hovered just above and in front of the king.

"Good king Troyolin," she began. "I am Mercurial, messenger of Tormentia. I bring news of your son."

"What is this news?" asked the king.

"You search in futility for that which you cannot have," she replied.

"That is your news? That which I cannot have!" shouted the king.

"There, there! If you will calm down I will be able to give you the entire message. Interrupt me and I cannot," she said without any emotion.

Seething in anger at her unemotional response, the king caught glimpse of Maison shaking his head back and forth as if to say, "Just listen, sire."

As the king contemplated how he would respond, he simply said to himself in thought, *I am a man of Bren,* and the anger lifted from him.

"Go on, Mercurial. Please continue," he said softly and with as much patience as he could muster.

"You search in futility for what you cannot have, as I said before. But the good and merciful Tormentia will allow you to see your son from time to time. All that is required of you is that you banish Maison, Augurian, and the other seers of Bren to remain solely in the southern realms of Bren—their jurisdiction from the southern border of the river Runland as it separates lower Bren from Abysstine and its environs. Tormentia and her seers will remain free to oversee the higher realms and environs of all the lands north of the river Runland in the region of Abysstine and all lands to the north."

"I will do no such thing!" shouted the king indignantly.

"Then you will never see your son again," replied Mercurial in the most eerily calm manner.

Upon the words of the king, Mercurial began to disappear into the blue mist, but just as she was about to vanish, Maison shouted, "Wait! Mercurial! Wait!"

Just as she seemed about to vanish, the angelic being returned from the mist and again hovered in silence above the wizard. "What would you have me do, little wizard?" she asked.

"I would ask that you wait. After I have consulted with my king we will have a word for you to deliver to your queen," replied Maison.

Dropping down from his mount, the seer motioned for the king, Augurian, and Justinian to gather around him. In the smallest of whisper, he addressed the king. "Sire, tell her what she desires to hear. Banish us to beyond the river Runland to the southern regions. We will go as far as the Serpentine Steps to give the appearance of compliance. Once there, Augurian and I will cast a spell of invisibility and rejoin you in the search. I think it is important that we call her hand in the matter, and use the gifts of the Founders for the good of the kingdom."

Turning to Augurian, the king simply asked, "And what say you?"

"It is wisdom from which good Maison speaks. Let us proceed and feign compliance and watch what unfolds. We will rejoin you but remain hidden until the proper time," replied Augurian. "All you need remember is who and Whose you are, sire. It is in the power of the Founders that you and the men will find solace and protection. We will return with the wind. You will know our presence in the subtle wind. May the strength of Bren be yours today, sire."

"What shall I tell my queen?" asked Mercurial as the king and men turned from their secret conference.

"Tell her the seers are banished . . . and that I would see my son," responded the king.

"You have chosen wisely, good king Troyolin. Be gone, foul seers. To the south with you," said the unshakable Mercurial.

Mounting their horses and heading back down the mountain toward the Serpentine Steps, Maison and Augurian left. As they disappeared into the tree line below, Mercurial addressed the king.

"Look upon the rocky outcropping," she said matter-of-factly.

As the king and his men watched, the rocks from which the stream emanated began to fade away, revealing a cavernous ravine leading higher up into the heart of the mountain.

"This way," said Mercurial as she flitted above the stream and headed into the ravine.

Without any hesitation and without having to say a word to his men, the king followed the angelic being. As the last horse and man crossed into the ravine, the rocky outcropping once again concealed the stream and the trail of the king and his men. What they had just entered no man should ever dare to enter—on purpose.

Chapter Twenty-Four

THE SEETHING TORMENTORS

Watching-Leonolis and the Voice followed near King Troyolin and Justinian as they made there way ever higher into the mountain through the ravine. The stream they followed was a mere ribbon of clear, cold water now, barely a foot wide and six inches deep. Even at this altitude there was green life sprouting from the sparse soil abutting the stream. Now the air had grown much colder and one could easily see the small puffs of breath of both horse and man as the warm exhalations met the colder air.

All were silent as they trudged upward, following the radiantly glowing Mercurial. It seemed to all that day that the lightness that surrounded her—the blue light—grew ever darker the higher they went, giving the impression of coldness. Even her countenance, which had seemed unemotional and matter-of-fact during their first meeting at the rocky outcropping below, appeared strained and dour. It was as if she were growing harsh and mean, more of a sense the men felt about her than the way she spoke—since she had not spoken once they had entered the ravine.

After several minutes, the horses began to grow uneasy, sensing, catching the scent of other beings watching. Soon enough, the soldiers all began to feel as if they were being watched. As they ascended further, the darkness of the narrowing ravine coupled with the clouds that began to engulf the higher elevations revealing an occasional glow from some nook or hidden cranny. There were other angelic beings observing the visitors—guarding the ravine, as it were.

Before long, the entire group came to a halt as Mercurial came to what appeared to be a dead end, the ravine ending abruptly at a tall and massive stone wall that rose hundreds of feet above them and disappearing into the clouds. Turning to face King Troyolin and his men, Mercurial nodded toward them as if to say, "Look behind you." As the king and his men turned to look behind them they saw that they were now being "escorted" by twelve other beings, similar in color to Mercurial—all blue and cold looking. Silently they gazed at the men with nonemotion, yet this conveyed a deep sense of foreboding to the men and their steeds. Once again, the pawing of hoofs and the murmuring of men could be heard. With great calm and no more than a whisper, the king simply said, "Do not be intimidated, mighty warriors of Bren. Remember: you are men of Bren." And the pawing and murmuring were replaced with quiet resolution and a return to a stalwart passion of purpose as to why they were there.

Turning back to face the rock, Mercurial placed her hand on a strange symbol that had been carved long ago, no doubt by strange dark magic. The shape was a five-point star with the image of a dragon etched in the center. As her fingers and palm touched the center of the star, the entire wall began to glow the same blue glow that emanated from Mercurial and the other beings in the ravine. Growing in intensity from light blue to deep, dark royal blue, the ground beneath them began to vibrate and resonate a low hum. At the same time, the wall began to shimmer and a slit began to open up from a point some fifteen feet above the floor of the ravine. As if a curtain were being pulled open to reveal a window, the slit went downward until it reached the ground where the king and his men were standing. The rocks began to be pulled back like drapery and a massive hallway lined with torches on either side began to appear before them.

Once the stone curtains had been pulled back fully, Mercurial began to move past them and into the hallway, beckoning the king and his men to follow. Passing through the hallway, the group proceeded to walk along the smooth marble floor of the hallway, but they all noticed right away the strange lack of sound as the hoofs met the stone. It was as if they were walking on granite so soft that no sound could be produced, yet the stone was as solid as solid could be. Without waiting for the uneasy response of his men and their mounts, King Troyolin simply whispered in the echoing hallway, "Remember who you are." Once again, peace filled the hearts of man and beast.

Once the entire group had passed into the hallway, the curtain of stone began to close behind them. After several minutes down this long hallway, they came to a massive cavern. Opening up before them like a grand cathedral of Bren, the entire chamber was adorned with grotesque statues of hideous creatures and beings unknown to men and many unknown to both Maison and Augurian. Made of pure gold and the size of men, the statues gave one an eerie feeling as if they were watching one's every move. The walls of the entire cavern were adorned with jewels of every shape and size. Diamonds measuring at least three feet in diameter. Rubies of even greater size. There were giant opals and carbuncles of garnet. Hanging from the ceiling and reaching down hundreds of feet along the sides of the cavern to just above the cavern floor were hundreds of the strangest looking stalactites, swirly and gnarled in shape and circumference. Just as many stalagmites strained up grotesquely from the sides of the cavernous floor. It was as if there was order to the arrangements—yet no order at all!

Walking through the statues and crystal formations was like walking through a dream or a nightmare. High King Troyolin continued to reassure his men and remind them of who they were, often times with a mere glance of knowing to the men behind him or a simple hand gesture that simply said, "Be strong. Be who you are."

By now, the twelve angelic creatures that had been following had now spread out to surround the king and his men. As Mercurial led them across the massive stone floor in silence, a circle of intense blue light now engulfed them as it shone from the beings. On the opposite side of the cavern room from the hallway they had just passed out of sat a large dais topped with a very large throne. Seated on that throne was none other than Tormentia herself. On her right side in a smaller seat, slightly less ornate than that of the sorceress, sat the miniscule Rubranna while seated on the opposite side was Dolus, now in the form of a man.

Approaching the throne, the king simply said, "Where is my son?"

"Well, well, no cordial greeting from one ruler to another? Where is the respect, King? Where is the common courtesy?" asked the snide Tormentia.

"I have no time for such meaningless drivel from one who is not so much a ruler but a tyrant. Where is my boy?" again demanded the king.

"Have you banished your seers as I have asked?" she went on.

"I am here, am I not?" responded the king.

"Yet you have not answered my question," came her reply.

Turning to Mercurial, Tormentia asked, "Has he met the requirements of our agreement?"

"Yes, milady. I, myself, heard him give the order of banishment and I, with my own eyes have seen them make their way back across the mighty Runland. Had I not done so I would not have led them here," said Mercurial.

"You have done well, Mercurial. Join your minions around the men of Bren," said Tormentia.

As the blue being took her place among the other angelic beings, Tormentia again addressed the king.

"As you have kept your word, I will keep mine. You shall now see your son." As she said those words, Tormentia turned to one of the angelic beings that appeared from seemingly nowhere—as if she had merely thought her into existence for her evil bidding—and said, "Bring the boy before my throne at once."

The being flew over the sorceress and disappeared behind the throne. After only a few seconds, the being once again appeared and seemed to be pushing one of the golden statues like the ones they had passed between as they came into the cavern. This statue was much smaller than the others and appeared to be human in shape and size, albeit somewhat smaller than the size of a grown man. This was the statue of a little boy. The being pushed the statue into position directly between Tormentia and Troyolin.

"Turn him around so his father can see him," demanded Tormentia.

As the being turned the statue around, the king was confronted with the image of little Leonolis, frozen in fear, looking longingly up toward the king as if to say all at once, "I am so sorry . . . I am so afraid . . . Papa, can you help me?"

"What is this?" asked the king incredulously. "I ask to see my son and you show me a statue? I demand that you honor our agreement! I would see my boy! Now!"

"And I have kept my word. This is your boy. I think you can now say the golden boy of the Kingdom of Bren truly is a golden boy!" said the sorceress as she erupted into laughter.

Leaping from his horse, the king ran to his son and embraced him as best he could. "Leonolis, can you hear me? If you can, know that I am here and that everything is going to be all right. I love you, Son."

Turning to Tormentia, the king simply said, "Release him—at once."

"I can only release him when you have crossed the river Runland. Once I am assured you are in your place, the boy will be free. But he will remain with me. How else can I be sure you will keep your end of our agreement?" asked Tormentia.

"This was not our agreement! You will release my son, now, or else . . ." said the king.

"Or else what?" demanded the sorceress.

"Or else you will feel the wrath of a father who is willing to die for his son!" shouted the king.

"That can be arranged!" With those words, the sorceress rose from her seat while Rubranna flew high above the king and his men to some place near the very center of the cavern ceiling, and Dolus again assumed the form of a lion, preparing to pounce at his queen's command. She then lifted her hands and began an incantation:

"Darkest night and days of old
Release the captive beings of gold
Let demons rise and ghouls now scream
Take flight at once—the captive free!"

All at once, the statues that had lined the massive room now began to writhe and squirm like a roiling mass of snakes trying to free themselves of their old skin. One by one, the stone shapes took the form of living breathing creatures of all manner and size and evil temperament. Demons began to run with frenzy around and around the king and his men. Ghouls began to scream and shriek, sending terror throughout the huntsmen and their horses. Werewolves and ogres. Miniature dragons and two-headed snakes. Witches and wailing spirits began to move

255

around the men of Bren in some weird dance of evil, being led in that circle by Mercurial and her twelve angelic minions.

As the dance moved from mere chaos to absolute mad frenzy, the sorceress shouted, "End them!"

All at once the circle began to close tighter and tighter upon the men. In that same moment, from somewhere high above, flashes of red lightning began to rain down upon the men, causing many to fall from their horses. Like some maniacal fiend, the lion Dolus began to dart in and out of the now-confused group of huntsmen and swipe at them with his sharp claws, wounding as many as he could. This only sent the already enraged demons and ghouls into a lathering frenzy as they began to smell blood. Foaming at the mouth, the hordes began to close ranks on the weakened, confused men.

While his men fought as valiantly and nobly as they could, King Troyolin turned to Justinian and shouted, "Watch over Leonolis, my friend of friends! I have an idea!"

As Justinian stood between the frozen boy and the sorceress, Troyolin turned his attention to the roiling mass of evil surrounding his men. Summoning the light of the Founders forged from the power of creation from before time began, the king began to wield his power to freeze objects and subdue them with the gift granted him by the Founders themselves. Suddenly, the werewolves and witches froze in midstrike. Demons and ghouls hovered in midair as foam drooled from their gaping maws. Even the blue angelic beings—Mercurial included—could not shake the mighty grip of the love-for-his-son-filled king. One by one, dragons and ogres and two-headed snakes stood motionless before the king, unable to break his magical power.

From high above, the red fairy saw what was happening and began to send bolt after bolt of lightning relentlessly toward the king, striking him again and again about the head and outstretched arms. Yet somehow the king did not seem to flinch or be swayed by the powerful blasts of the fairy. It was as if some greater force was at work in him than magic. Watching-Leonolis blurted out, "How my father loved me!"

The Voice interjected, "Now you know the truth of the power greater than any magic—the power of love—the power of the life laid down for the one it loves. Nothing is more powerful. Nothing is greater.

Not even the fear of death—not even death itself. It is not magic that spurs your father to greater feats of power. No. What you see is the power of love over the fiends of darkness. Love conquers all."

Once again, the action resumed as Troyolin continued to hold the evil horde at bay. Upon seeing the sudden turn of events, Tormentia began to unleash her power on the king. Joining Rubranna, she began to pummel the king with blast after blast of magical lightning, yet he did not release his grip on her minions.

"Men of Bren, rise up! Be the men of Bren you were born to be! Make haste with sword! Make quick work of arrow and spear! Dispatch the creatures of darkness that we may free my son . . . that we may preserve the good of Bren!" shouted the king.

At once his men shook off their fear and even those who had been wounded managed to take up weapons and begin to cut down the evil that stood frozen before them. Heads began to roll. Blood began to flow. One by one, the men of Bren began to put an end to the evil before them. Seeing this, Tormentia turned her attentions to the boy as she looked to Dolus. "Get the boy!"

Instantly the lion pounced on Justinian but Justinian had been ready for him. He actually had hoped he would make a move his way. As leaping lion met sword of Bren, the lion fell dead to the cavern floor and without wasting one moment of time, the good Justinian once again took his place between boy and sorceress.

"You fool!" she said to Justianian. "You are nothing to me!" Pointing her wand toward the faithful man, she sent him flying across the cavern floor and slamming into a very unforgiving stalactite. Falling motionless to the floor, the clink of Justinian's mighty sword could be heard throughout the expanse of the room. Still, the men of Bren continued taking out their passion for good upon the forces of evil until every last creature was either undone or sent screaming into the darkness.

While the men began to surround the king, Troyolin was now free to give his attention to Tormentia once again. Calmly yet very adamantly, the king simply said, "Release my son. Now."

"As you wish!" responded the sorceress to the stunned men.

Instantly the boy became flesh and blood again. Just as the king ran to his son, the boy began to rise into the air and fly toward Tormentia.

257

"He is free . . . but he is mine!" With that, the same misty cloud that had surrounded them at the Serpentine Steps surrounded the sorceress and the boy. As the roiling mist grew dark, it began to move away from the king and his men toward the area behind the throne.

"Quickly men! She tries to escape! Cut off her path!" shouted the king.

As the men ran around either side of the throne, her way of escape became obvious. A large, dark chasm leading directly into the heart of the mountain lay directly behind the throne. It appeared they were going to be too late, the cloud now moving quickly toward the opening.

Just as it appeared all hope was lost, a brilliant light burst from the chasm behind the throne, causing the cloud to vanish and the sorceress and boy to fall to the marble floor below! Appearing from this mighty blast was none other than Maison and Augurian! Their plan had worked!

Before Tormentia could reach the wand that had fallen from her hand, Augurian had secured it in his own. Speaking to the evil witch, he said, "Up with you, vile Tormentia! Men, bind her with these!"

Tossing a golden rope toward the men, they bound the hands of the sorceress who now appeared far less radiant and beautiful than she had appeared just moments before.

"This rope is imbued with magic from the Founders. She will not and cannot break its bond," said Augurian as he turned toward Leonolis.

"Go to your father, boy."

Without any hesitation whatsoever, the boy ran into his father's waiting arms.

Bursting into tears, the boy sobbed, "Father, I am sorry! Father forgive me! I was so wrong to have ever doubted your love for me. Please forgive me!"

"Forgiveness you have. My love you never lost. All is good, boy. All is good," said the grateful king.

Turning toward his men, he said, "Let us secure this cavern and rid it of any semblance of evil." Turning to his seers he said, "Maison. Augurian. How were you able to find us?"

"Well, sire, once we had passed over the Serpentine Steps we made haste in casting a spell of invisibility. We quickly made our way back to the rocky outcrop where we had last left you . . . but could find no way in. After a few moments of bewilderment, we realized that some magic kept our eyes from seeing the obvious, so we performed a bit of magic of our own. The opening to the ravine was made known to us. Quickly did we follow the stream to yet another dead end," said Augurian.

"Yes! Yes!" interjected the excited Maison. "Once there, we recognized the symbol of darkness—the dragon star—and knew this was not an ending but an entrance into the dark realm. We commanded the curtain to be opened and entered. Once inside, we quickly saw that you had everything under control, so we hastened to the only way of escape left to her and her minions. While still invisible we simply stole right past you all and sealed off the dark chasm behind us!"

"And the tormentress is subdued by the magic of the Founders. Though we cannot slay her, per the sayings of old, we can subdue her and keep her imprisoned once and for all!" chimed in Augurian.

All that had been chaos and turmoil but moments before was now replaced by utter joy and peace! The king and his son had been reunited and the realm had, once again, been delivered from the one who would overthrow it, and now she was finally subdued!

As the group prepared to transport their prisoner back to the confines of the royal dungeons, lightning pierced the peace and sent the king and the boy reeling backward to the floor! Rubranna! They had forgotten all about the sniveling little sneaky red demon!

Flying like a crazed bat out of "you know where," the little demonic fairy charged down from on high, her wand ablaze with the fury of her rage and lightning. Surprised by her sudden appearance, the seers had not been able to respond to the one bolt that had been directed at Tormentia. Finding its mark, the fierce red bolt of power struck the rope that bound the sorceress's hands and she vanished without so much as a puff of smoke!

Unable to make her own escape, the red fairy was met—unfortunately for her—by the fatal blow of a double bolt of lightning cast simultaneously from the wands of Maison and Augurian, turning her instantly into a tiny scattering of red ash to the floor below.

"It is done," said the king. "It is done, boy."

Without saying a word all the way home, the boy sat upon his mighty steed, Arolis, and never once took his eyes off of his father who led the way. Out of the cavern, back down the hallway, and coursing down through the ravine, the entourage followed the king and the boy. Through the woods until they could hear the mighty roar of the Banshee Rapids, they neared the Serpentine Steps just as the sun prepared to set.

"Can we make it, Augurian?" asked the king.

"Aye, sire. We have just enough time," said the seer.

Without any hesitation, the men and their horses followed the king and the boy across the Serpentine Steps. As the last man crossed, the bridge disappeared behind him. Had he looked back he would have received quite the shock. Had he stopped even for a moment, he would have met an even frostier greeting once he and horse had met the icy waters below!

Watching-Leonolis and the Voice followed in silence as they crossed the bridge. As the last man made his way onto solid ground, the king paused and turned around to face his son and his men. As he addressed his men—whether they would ever admit it or not—each shed a small tear or two in gratitude for all they had experienced that day and lived to tell about. They felt gratitude to live in such a land, gratitude to serve such a king. Glad to do it all over again—any day.

"Men . . . very good men . . . I can never repay you for the kind and valiant service you have given to me as a father and as your king today. Know this: I would do the same for any one of you. Indeed, let us see and understand that what we have experienced here today was, and is, for all of us. We are Bren. We are," began the king as the stern kingly demeanor of a look was betrayed by the twinkle of tears and righteous pride that glistened from his own eyes.

"This day will not soon be forgotten. The tales of valor will live on long after each of us is gone. But I tell you this: above all else we have proven the power of the Founders this day, that love—the laying down of life—is above all and conquers all, regardless of what we must endure to receive, believe, and experience it. Love is worth the risk love requires. Men—my friends and fellow Brenolinians—know this. I could speak the words of love to you and they would mean nothing had I not taken the action that love truly is. And know this: I have been shown love this day in the way you have chosen to lay down your lives . . . for me and mine. Men . . . I love you."

As the king's words wafted into the sound of the wind and mingled with the rage of the waters below, the king simply turned to his son and nodded. Little Leonolis understood. This had all been for him, yet this had all been for Bren. He felt at one with his father, and even though he was not officially a man (The Testolamorphia was still a few years off) he felt like one! As the king and the boy and the seers and the men made their way back toward Castle Aerie, watching-Leonolis and the Voice made their way back to the castle and the bedchamber of his dying father and the words he had left him with so long ago now.

Chapter Twenty-Five

THE KEY TO THE KINGDOM

Watching-Leonolis was silent as he looked once again upon the scene surrounding his dying father, the good king Troyolin. After a few moments, he simply whispered to the Voice, "Why are we here?"

"Dreams," responded the Voice.

"Dreams?" asked the king.

"Listen to your father," was all the Voice said.

Once again, watching-Leonolis watched and listened, and remembered as his younger self leaned down to better hear the raspy, weakened voice of Troyolin.

"Son, remember the dreams?" asked Troyolin.

"What dreams, Father? Your dreams for the realm? Your dreams for me? Of course I remember, Father—and I will carry on your dreams. You have my word. It is my honor to carry those dreams to even loftier heights for the realm and for the Founders," replied Leonolis.

"No . . . no . . . no. Those dreams are good and well, and I have no doubt you will continue to walk in them . . . as this is your destiny," said the king to his son. "Remember the dreams after the red fairy was slain? You were just a boy when they began. Remember Ideman?"

At those words, the heart of watching-Leonolis began to race. How could he have so easily forgotten about those glorious dreams from his childhood? His mind also began to recall with rapid pace all he had endured in the days and weeks and months and years following the incident with Rubranna and Ideman.

The memory of the little worm crawling into his ear had faded into the realm of distant memory soon after it had taken place. This had been part of the red fairy's scheme—to so delude the boy that he could not tell fantasy from reality, truth from deception. In the days following his deliverance from Tormentia, Rubranna, and Dolus, he had experienced a depth of love and acceptance from his father and from his family and, indeed, from the entire realm of Bren that he had not realized before that day. Yet, there was always the lingering doubt that this could have really been true.

You see, the worm—Ideman—had gone undetected, the king and his seers assuming the deception had ended with the demise of the red fairy and the lion, but Ideman was always there, whispering doubt into the mind of the boy. Rather than admit to his father his doubts, the boy discovered very quickly that if he could simply perform well on the surface—be the best at horsemanship, the best at scholastic endeavors, the best at mastering the weapons of Bren—then all would assume everything was fine. The love and acceptance and affirmation would continue, no questions asked. This had been a workable solution for the boy—mostly. It was not very workable whenever his performance happened to not measure up. It was during those times that he still felt like an utter failure and still battled thoughts as to whether his father truly loved him or not. In many ways he still felt captured.

The reality for the boy, Leonolis? He was still held captive in thought by the little worm, Ideman. Ideman continued to whisper his vile thoughts into the boy's mind for several years—especially right after moments of failure. "Your brother, Paulus, is a better archer. Your father loves him more than you. And your friend, Dreyden, always wins the equestrian events. Your father seems to love him more than you too. And even Maison thinks your younger brothers are more intelligent than you. You must try a little harder . . . work a little longer . . . be the best . . . or you will not find the love and acceptance you so crave."

At times, remembered watching-Leonolis, it felt as if he were losing his mind, so intense was the battle for his mind when he was a boy. He recalled running himself ragged physically to be the best. He remembered working harder than the other boys in tutelage under Maison to try and prove himself. He remembers the intense fire that burned in him to somehow earn his father's acceptance and approval as a boy that at times he felt he would be driven insane with the mental anguish he felt. His only solace had come in his dreams.

Dreams! Of course! Now his mind began to flood with the dreams of his childhood sleep. After a long day of mental anguish and battle in his mind, the boy Leonolis could not wait to get to sleep, because his dreams always led him to great adventure! Each night for several years, in fact, he dreamed the same adventure and the same dream and the same life. Even though the dream was the same night after night, the boy had never tired of dreaming it, because of the affect it had upon his life.

As he lay down in bed, his mind would be a-swirl with thinking about all his failures of that day. He never ever quite measured up so his last waking moments before drifting off to sleep always consisted of regrets—of what he could have done or should have done or didn't do that he might have done. Without fail, his last waking thought before sleep was how abjectly he had not lived up to his father's expectations that day. Of course, what he had not realized was that it was Ideman who whispered these things into his mind, but what Ideman had not counted on was the power of the Founders to speak to the royal line of Bren—even in their sleep!

With the first moment of sleep, the boy was instantly transported to another place and time. In fact, the place he lived in his dreams was not of the world of Bren! So surreal was this dreamland that the boy could not even give a name to it. Each night the boy found himself on board an amazing craft, much like a sailing ship of Bren yet fully enclosed—and traveling through the space above the world amidst the stars!

On this star-traveling craft the boy lived with his father who was the captain of the vessel. Called *Inceptum*, the boy had the run of the ship. Flying through the darkness of the realm above the earth, the boy was introduced to distant planets and stars and otherworldly scenes he had no words for! These dreams were always glorious in scope and grand in adventure. Each dream was always interrupted by the boy's eventual capture by some new and alien race from the realm of the darkness. It happened each and every night!

Just as these alien creatures were about to put the boy to death, somehow, someway, his father always materialized at just the right time. In his hand was the most amazing weapon that his father wielded with mastery upon the fiends. As if some type of magical wand yet much smaller and with a trigger mechanism like that of a crossbow, his father would pull the trigger and the most amazing beam of light would shoot forth from the weapon and completely disintegrate the beings that held the boy! It was at that precise moment each and every morning that the boy would wake from his sleep rescued!

With each new day the boy woke refreshed and hopeful and with a renewed strength to endure another day of performing his way through life for everyone's approval and acceptance. Even through the course of those long, hard days when Ideman whispered all those confusing lies into the boy's mind, Leonolis would hang on to the small thread of hope those wonderful dreams of rescue breathed into his heart and mind. Watching-Leonolis remembered.

"That was you wasn't it?" asked watching-Leonolis of the Voice. Before allowing the Voice to respond, he went on. "It was you who gave me those dreams! It had to be you! Those dreams kept me going . . . kept me sane . . . kept me alive! In the very midst of my captivity of my mind to the worm, you were there planting those dreams deep inside of me! You have been there all along!"

Without saying a word, the Voice took watching-Leonolis to the Chamber of the Seers—the place where Maison, Augurian, and the other seers of Bren conducted their sessions and spells of and for the realm. He saw himself as a twelve-year-old boy now, sitting on a stool in the middle of the room. Surrounding him were the twelve seers summoned by his father to perform the Spell of Casting—a special ceremony used to rid a person of evil spirits or spells or curses. As watching-Leonolis watched, he remembered.

"Leonolis," began Maison, "it has been foreseen by my own mind and confirmed by that of Augurian, that the lies you have been believing about yourself—that you are not loved, that you are not good enough, that you have no worth apart from your ability to perform—are completely unnatural and are being cast upon you by some agent of darkness. We have discerned a mind worm, Son."

"A mind worm?" asked the boy.

"Yes, Son. A mind worm. Do you recall ever having a dream or a moment when you conversed with a worm of any kind?" asked Maison. "Think, Son. There is no shame in admitting this."

Embarrassed, the boy instantly remembered the episode in his room with the red fairy and the worm. His reddened face and downcast eyes gave him away.

"Son, we cannot cast him out without your permission. You must confess the invasion and then ask us for the Spell of Casting. This will rid you of the vile creature. Do you wish to be free, boy?" asked the wise old tutor.

The boy sat ashamed and silent. Then Troyolin knelt beside his son. "My son, you are my life. When you hurt, I hurt. When you suffer, I suffer. My desire is for nothing but your best. There is no shame in admitting you allowed the worm access to your mind."

Burying his head in his father's shoulder, the boy cried out, "But I am so ashamed, Father! How could a son of Troyolin ever allow such a vile, shameful creature into his mind? I am not worthy to be called your son!"

"And just who do you think planted that lie in your mind, Son? Here is reality. I love you right where you are, but I love you enough to never leave you here. And Son, this is between you and me and these men who love you. I am going to tell you something few others know. When I was your age, I sat right where you are . . . and some of these same men did for me what we now hope to do for you."

"You had a mind worm, Father?" asked the boy.

"Yes, Son . . . I did."

The boy looked deep into his father's eyes, now, the shame having been dealt a deathblow by the confession of his father. Without any more hesitation the boy said, "When the red fairy came into my life she also introduced me to the worm, Ideman. She convinced me to allow him access to my ear. He crawled in, and I forgot he had ever existed . . . yet deep inside I somehow knew he was there. I just did not know what to do."

"What do you ask, boy?" replied Maison.

"I confess that a mind worm dwells in me and I ask you to rid him from my mind forever . . . this day!" proclaimed the now-confident boy.

At those words, the seers all began to hum an age-old Brenonlinian chant of freedom as Maison spoke the words of the Spell of Casting over the seated boy.

"From realms of dark this spirit came
From evil minds this seed
Hear now this one who speaks of shame
And of these words take heed!
From dark you came to dark you go
From hidden now to seen
Release your grip! Release your hold!
This mind is now set free!"

The boy's mind began to explode with pain as it was suddenly released from the chains and fetters of the worm. Just as it had hurt that night in his room when the worm had entered his ear, the boy's ear began to burst with pain as the worm tunneled its way out! Because the worm fought against the spell, the pain was made even more excruciating by the grip it tried to exert on the flesh of the boy. The magic of the spell was too much for the worm's feeble grip and he shot from the boy's left ear and right into the outstretched hand of Maison!

As the boy crumpled into the arms of his father, Maison spoke one last spell upon the worm.

"O, pitiful snake! O, wretched liar
Go back to the dark whence you came
And no more again to this realm to return
Submit now to purity's flame!"

Instantly, the worm burst into flame right there in the palm of Maison's hand! Before anyone could even complete a gasp of surprise, the little evil creature fell into a tiny heap of ash into the seer's hand! Without one more word, the good Maison walked over to the hearth and blew the ashes from his hand and into the fireplace to join the soot and refuse there.

Once again, watching-Leonolis and the Voice were back in the bedchamber of his dying father as he spoke these words to his son.

"Son, I go now from your side . . . but I will always be with you. Take the memories we made together and cherish them like precious treasure. And if you remember nothing else . . . if I could tell you only one thing, I would say . . ."

"What is it, Father? I listen," said Leonolis.

"Here are the keys to the kingdom. You have been given hidden treasures . . . that will be unlocked and opened to you as you live life according to the ways of the Founders."

"You are my treasure, Father. Life with you—knowing you—has been the greatest treasure any son could ask for," responded Leonolis.

"And you are mine, Son . . . but there is so much more," replied the dying king. "Remember the dreams of your boyhood? The star craft?"

"Yes, Father. Of course," responded his son.

"How were they used of the Founders?" asked the king.

"They filled me with hope and gave me strength to get through . . . another day," said the son as understanding began to flood his mind.

"My son, what you lost in innocence the Founders have seen to restore with great integrity. You found redemption and mercy and a deeper wisdom than you might have ever gained had you not gone through all you have experienced. Like a man who never appreciates the sweetness of rain unless he walks through the heat of the desert is he who does not see this truth: the Founders will waste nothing, if we will present them in honesty to Them. From wounds come healing. From pain comes comfort. From sorrow comes appreciation for life. From conflict comes peace. Do not see life as the darkenss would have you see. See life from the perspective of the Founders . . . who see from a higher plane than you or I."

"How do I do that, Father?" asked Leonolis.

"No . . . matter . . . how . . . mature you become . . . always . . . always . . . always present yourself to the Founders and the ways of Bren as a child," replied the now-weakening king.

"A child? What do you mean?" asked Leonolis.

"A child sees with eyes of wonder. A child sees with eyes of hope. A child sees what might be rather than allow their self to be shackled by what is. And the key to the kingdom . . .THE key . . . is . . ." said the king as his eyes closed and his voice trailed away into silence.

"Father! Father! The key to the kingdom is what?" asked the now crying Leonolis.

Summoning his last bit of strength, Troyolin whispered, "Power is not the key to the kingdom. Love is. Love is not a feeling, Son. Love is action. Love is laying down one's life for that—for those—it loves. From this comes all power . . . and . . . and . . ."

"Yes, Father?" asked the weeping Leonolis.

"I . . . love . . . you . . . Son. As I have loved you, love . . ." said Troyolin as he breathed his last breath.

As the Voice spoke, watching-Leonolis could feel himself rising into the air. "Sacrifice, Lee. Sacrifice. All along the way, love has paved your way. You have not gotten to where you are all by yourself. It has always been the Founders and others who have laid down their lives—for you. Remember that, Lee."

"Why are you calling me Lee?" asked the king as he flew through the air at an ever-increasing rate of speed.

All of a sudden, he heard the crack of thunder and began to feel the pelting of raindrops and small hailstones against his face and arms. Spinning and falling through the air, it was as if he were suddenly engulfed in a raging storm, flailing about like a rag doll as the wind tossed him to and fro! And then he saw the farm—several hundred feet below him. As he neared the ground, his speed began to slow and he found himself standing on the soaked ground and watched as the barn he had just been running for begin to rise into the air!

As the barn lifted high above his head, it began to spin around violently in a counter-clockwise manner. Almost mesmerized by the sheer power of the tornado he was now eyewitness to, he was shocked back into the reality of his very present terror as the barn was hurled into the ground and shattered and scattered into millions of pieces!

Then Lee remembered! His brother, Paul! Paul had taken the tractor out into the field to do his chores! Running in the direction he had last seen Paul go, Lee did not take time to look back and watch the storm blow away nor did he feel the sky began to clear and sunshine invade the darkness. All he could think of was getting to his brother and making sure he was all right.

In less than a minute, he was within shouting distance of the tractor and Paul, who did not seem fazed at all by the storm, so intent he was at performing his chores!

Running to catch the slow-moving tractor, He finally caught Paul's attention and yelled, "Are you all right?"

Turning off the tractor's engine so as to better hear his crazed brother, Paul yelled back, "What do you mean, am I all right?"

"The tornado!" screamed Lee. "Did you see the tornado?"

"What tornado?" asked Paul as they both turned to see a perfectly sunny day.

"The tornado that just ripped apart the barn!" said the frantically pointing Lee.

"Wow!" exclaimed Paul. "Is Grandma okay?"

"Grandma!" exclaimed Lee. In all the excitement of the storm (and that little adventure into Bren!), he had forgotten all about Grandma Jennings who lived in the mobile home right next to the barn!

Racing with all their might toward Grandma's house, they had to sidestep all the debris that the storm had left from the barn. Running up the steps to the little porch that spanned the front of the mobile home, they turned the handle of the door, but it was locked.

Banging on the door as loudly as he could, Lee began to cry out, "Grandma! Grandma! Are you okay? Grandma are you in there?"

Within just a few seconds, the boys could hear the doorknob jiggle as Grandma Jennings unlocked it. As she peered out, the boys immediately shouted, "Grandma, are you okay?"

Seeing the wreckage behind the boys, she stepped out onto the porch and surveyed the damage. All she could say was, "What have you boys done?"

This had not been the response the boys had expected! "We didn't do anything, Grandma! It was a tornado! I saw it!" said Lee.

"Well, I did hear quite a racket a few moments ago," she said, "but I thought it was your dad's bird dog dragging his chain against the house!"

After the boys settled down from their shock, and that shock was replaced with laughter at Grandma's response, they told that story for years and years. A neighbor had seen the twister, come to find out, but it had only been a small funnel that had dipped briefly from the clouds and only for a few seconds over the Jennings farm.

Lee—Leonolis—had lived a lifetime in only a few seconds time! Unlike his first adventure into Bren, this one never faded from his memory. The lessons he learned in the land of Bren would serve him well in the days to come. There's simply something about being the son of a king that sets the heart a little more free and makes life just a little more exciting to live. He would ponder the lessons learned and use the key to the kingdom often. Daily. As often as necessary. Maybe, just maybe, he would see Bren again. At least he could hope . . .

THE END

BONUS FEATURES

Dive deeper into the world of Bren with bonus materials only available at **www.thechroniclesofbren.com**:

- Listen to songs written and performed specifically for each book's journey. Unlike any series before, each book has a series of custom songs written and performed by the author as part of each book's story and journey. You won't want to miss these FREE songs that add so much to the story!
- Original sketches of each main character rendered by the author and available for you to connect deeper with the world of Bren.
- Updates about a new book series: The Bairn of Bren. This collection of stories features the grandchildren of King Leonolis and Queen Abila in daring adventures of their own! You won't want to miss this continuing series of adventures in the world of Bren.

GLOSSARY

Abutor—Offspring of Obscurum Nyoka; name means "blindness"

Abysstine—Capitol city of the region of Endoria; also called Dark City

Acerbia—Realm between darkness and light; located in the Mountains of Endor; it's people are the keepers of the realm between dark and light

Adage of Bren—"As a son or daughter of Bren thinks, so shall they be."

Almighty King of Creation—The Founder; God-figure

Annavan—Second-born of Leonolis and Abila; a daughter

Annum Serpentia—Year of the Dragon; a dragon appears every twenty-five years and gives birth to three offspring. This is one Brenolinian generation in time. A hunt for those three offspring takes place each 25th year

Arolis—Faithful black steed of Leonolis

Arucus—Eighth-born child of Leonolis and Abila; twin son

Ashland—King of Subdefero

Augurian—Oracle; seer; wise sage of the reign of Lairdon

Aquarain—Seventh-born child of Leonolis and Abila; a daughter

Banshee Rapids—Loud, dangerous rapids of the upper Runland

Barrelle—Wife of Dreyden

Beezlebird—A buzzard used as a messenger by the dark lord, Lucian

Belimond—Young boy Lucian used to trick Troyolin

Blood Moon Festival—Came about as a commemoration of a major Brenolinian victory over the marauders from Hemagenia—the Hemagens or People of the Blood, as they are known; Leonolis himself was the hero of this victory when he was only eighteen years old

Bren—The shortened, less formal name for Brenolin

Brenolin—The formal name of the land founded by King Bren

Brenolinian Battlecry—"This day we conquer! This day we overcome the Dark Lord! This day we live or die for the king!"

Brenolinian Saying—"May the strength of Bren be mine today."

Brestling—Town of the northern realm of Bren

Bria (Princess Bria)—Early royal heir almost captured; her near-capture was the catalyst behind creating the secret escape tunnels beneath Castle Aerie

Brumbycroc—A type of horse with the head and tail of a crocodile, found in the land of Subdefero

Caniday—King of the Wolfen

Canyons of Callay—Barren region between Brenolin and the Dark Lands

Carina—Crystalline boat of Scavengia; lead vessel

Carus—Firstborn son of Leonolis and Abila

Castle—Castle Aerie

Castle Jadon—Fortress of Abysstine; home of Lucian

Cavern of What-Might-Have-Been—a massively huge cavern with a ceiling hundreds of feet high. This cave is located directly to the east of Castle Jadon in one of the granite mountains; see also Needles of Regret

Ceremony of Homegoing—The name given to all funerals in Bren; national cultural belief is that those who are known to the Founder go "home" to Him at the time of their physical death

Center Isle—Solid ground in the center of Forbidden Swamp

Chiroptera—The bat-like people of the Mountains of Endoria

Chrissadan—Wife of Carus

Cleft of the Rock—Secret royal hiding place beneath Castle Aerie

Contemptia—Wicked queen of the frozen land of Hiemsland

Corellian—Royal commander of the King's Guard

Council Hill—Where the treaties unifying the many provinces of Brenolin were signed. This meeting place became the earliest known place where the leaders of the land met in council to discuss the welfare of the good people of Bren

Crooked Way—A secret passage through the Canyons of Callay into the Dark Lands; discovered by Leonolis

Crystal Cave—Cave from Castle Aerie where Phrygian Crystal is mined; where Leonolis and generations of boys of Bren learn swimming and water skills

Crystal Orb—Magical crystal used for conjuring up the deceitful images Lucian uses to trick his victims; the orb adorns the top of his riding staff

Dancing Meadow—A large, secluded opening in the Dark Forest where the local denizens meet for their moonlight festivals and dance the night away in graceful abandon on the first night of every full moon

Danwyn—Bodyguard for Leonolis

Day of Recrolution—Day of restoration; the end of time; when the Founders return to rule

Dark Lands—another name for the regions of Endoria

Decipere'—Offspring of Obscurum Nyoka; name means "deceiver"

Destrin—Second in Command of the King's Guard behind Corellian

Devotatis—Priests/Eunuchs of Scavengia; pilots of the crystal boats

Dolus—Man-eating lion of Bren; name means "treachery"

Dorimay—Princess of the mouse kingdom of Castle Jadon

Dreyden—Best friend of Prince Leonolis

Emissary King—A representative of Bren who serves an ally of Bren on that ally's soil; able to act on behalf of the high king

Evenhawk—King of the Hawken

Exaviance—Fifth-born child of Leonolis and Abila; a son

Falling Rocks—Lord of the Chiroptera

Faveo—Nineth-born child of Leonolis and Abila; twin son

Fire Skunk—so named for the rancid smell that made one's nose feel as if it were on fire!

Forbidden Swamp—Abandoned marshy area once used for Bren's supplies of peat moss; also known as Maudlin's Marsh

Forsten—Early great warrior of Bren who led the armies of Bren to victory against the Pestulents of Morbium

Forsythe—King of the mouse kingdom of Castle Jadon

Friend of Friends—The Brenolinian term for a man's best friend

Galennia—Maiden of the Hawken

Galensia—Sixth-born child of Leonolis and Abila; a daughter

Gloriana—Fourth-born child of Leonolis and Abila; a daughter

Gothgol—Wizard of the Heights; the White Wizard of Endoria

Graymon—Dreyden's horse

Great Contemptus, The—A time of severe winter for seven months on end due to all the women of Bren being frozen by the spell of Contemptia

Gregarian—High king of Bren, known for leading to victory over the armies of Nordegrun led by Nequam the Vile even though blinded. He was known for his great wisdom, insight, and unshakable joy

Hadian—King of the Terrebithians

Hangman's Rock—A place of execution from the early days of the kingdom.

Haventura—Third-born child of Leonolis and Abila; a daughter

Hawken—Hawk people of the Forest of Endoria; preservers of all that is good. They can transform themselves from their true hawk nature into a human form

Heath—Royal gardener; father of Dreyden

Hiemsland—Frozen land of the far north ruled by Queen Contemptia

Hollister—Friend of Augurian; of the Wolfen race

HommeDressage—Four additional years of constant training in the arts of military strategy and warfare for boys thirteen years of age and the horses they ride

Hyacinth—Queen of the mouse kingdom of Castle Jadon

Inceptum—Star craft in the dreams of Leonolis

Juji Fruit—A sweet, pithy apple-like fruit that grows in the treetops of the trees found in the higher elevations of the Great Forest; the main foodstuff of the Treesants

Justinian—Friend of friends to King Troyolin

Kangoala—Fierce hopping bears of Subdefero; they drop from trees onto humans and shred them with their fangs and claws

Kelsin—King of the Fairies

King Bren—First High King of Brenolin

King Lairdon—Father of Troyolin; grandfather of Leonolis

Larovia—peaceful kingdom lying north and west of Brenolin

Leonolis—Prince of the realm

Lucian—Dark lord of Endoria

Lupistad—King of the Werewolves

Maison the Wise—The tutor assigned to teach Prince Leonolis

Maudlin's Marsh—Abandoned marshy area once used for Bren's supplies of peat moss; also known as Forbidden Swamp

Melania—High queen of the realm

Mendax—Offspring of Obscurum Nyoka; name means "liar"

Menden Lake—Lake high in the mountains overlooking Abysstine

Mercurial—Angelic messenger of Tormentia

Merrywell—Second of Lord Dreyden

Messenger's Gate—A special passageway through the fortress wall where royal messengers could come and go during all hours of the day or night

Metamorph—A creature able to change his very appearance, moving freely between the animal world and the human

Mind Worm—A worm that is released into the mind of a person for the intention of controlling that person; of the dark realm

Miraculin—Fifth king of Brenolin; the miracle king; creator of the secret passages of Crystal Cave

Moonrysin—Trapper/hunter from the Forest of Endoria

Moralion—Son of Justinian; ruler of Abysstine after the reign of his father ended

Morbium—Land to the far east of Bren; infiltrated by the dark forces and violently opposed to all things Bren

Mostel—Leader of the Royal Guard of the mouse kingdom of Rodenthe

Mountains of Endoria—Northern boundary of Brenolin

Muriday—Prince of the mouse kingdom of Castle Jadon

Narrows—Narrow gorge near Treacherin

Needles of Regret—A crystalline formation rising up from the cavern floor of the Cavern of What-Might-Have-Been

Obscurum Nyoka—The mother dragon; name means "obscuring serpent"

Oriana—The first high queen

Ovulum—Nesting site of Obscurum Nyoka

Ovulus—The three-month period of the hatching of the three dragon eggs laid by Obscurum Nyoka

Pestulents—Inhabitants of the land of Morbium. These people take on the form of vermin in their habits, resembling a plague of insects when they attack

Phrygian Crystals—Crystals that emit a low-grade light and were thought to contain healing powers

Pinnacles of Bren—A rocky outcropping of granite that protrudes from the ocean floor forty-five miles south of Castle Aerie in the Sea of Aragon; a series of seven spires, the highest reaching to a height of seven hundred feet

Praemonitus—Seer from the realm of Acerbia; the Place of Gloom

Protected Place—Another name for Cleft of the Rock

Queensland—City in the southern area of the Forest of Endoria

Rania—Princess of the race of Fairies found in the Forest of Endoria

Recuperatio Somnium—The sleep of recovery

Reedincourt—Mouse; rescuer of Troyolin and Regalion

Regalion—Son of King Lairdon; brother of Troyolin; father of Lucian

Reginald the Bold—Commander of one of the dragon-hunting parties

Reuben of Old—The name given to the Sleeping Giant; the spirit of Bren

Rodenthe—Capital city of the mouse kingdom within Castle Jadon

Rubranna—The red fairy; evil demon of Tormentia

Runland—Main river of Brenolin

Sandovar—King of Larovia

Sea of Arabon—Southern boundary of Brenolin

Second—Military assistant; expert in military etiquette

Sacthian—A lord of the realm of Scavengia

Scavacine—The people of Scavengia, also known as seekers; portaying themselves as an advanced and enlightened race, their ultimate goal was to overtake a culture and utilize its resources without using force; they are part of Bren history known as The Blood Moon Uprising, which occurred in the fifth year of the reign of High King Leonolis

Scavengia—A land far to the south of Bren, across the Sea of Aragon

Senare Tempus Peragro—The healer who travels through time; Abila

Sleeping Giant—A hill whose outline looked like a giant sleeping man from a distance; see Reuben of Old

Sniffum—Turtle of Forbidden Swamp; brother of Snuffim

Snuffim—Turtle of Forbidden Swamp; brother of Sniffum

Solus Sidus—Kingdom to the south of Bren across the Sea of Arabon

Stephon—Commander of one of the dragon-hunting parties; also known as "The Doctor" to his men

Stirling—Royal messenger of the king

Subdefero—The kingdom far across the Sea of Arabon on the opposite side of the world

Subsidium—King and lord of the realm of Scavengia

Sylvan—King of the Treesant people

Terrebithians—Underground-dwelling race of earthen ogres

Teslin—Olden king of Bren; gift of seeing events before they occur

Testing of Blood—A duel of succession; feats of strength, agility, and logic meant to reveal royal lineage

Testolamorphia—The ceremony in which boys are welcomed into the fellowship of manhood at the turn of their thirteenth birthday.

Topherken—Husband of Annavan

Toralan—Mother of Lucian; also called Tormentia, sister of Gothgol; a sorceress who would become the White Witch

Tormentia—Mother of Lucian; also called Toralan, sister of Gothgol; a sorceress who would become the White Witch

Treacherin—City of the Forest of Endoria; also called the City of Thieves

Treesant—Tree dwelling, chameleon-like people who dwell in the treetops of certain regions of the Great Forest

Troglodytes—Ancient cave-dwelling creatures; they are able to breathe under water and on dry land; they have the ability to take on the form of those they touch and to cause those they touch to take on theirs

Troyolin—Father of Leonolis and high king

Valley of the Abyss—Valley in the Mountains of Endoria where Abysstine is located

Venere' Serpentia Trium—The hunt for the dragon's offspring every twenty-five years; the hunt for the three dragons

Ventus—Commander of one of the dragon-hunting parties; his name means "manly" because of his manly virtues

Warrior's Canyon—Assembly ground for amassing Brenolin's troops before battle; a natural amphitheater rising up from the banks of Runland and rising to the foundations of Castle Aerie

Werewolves—A wolf race different from the wolfen; evil in creation and bloodthirsty for human flesh; they follow Lucian

White Witch—Toralan; Tormentia; Mother of Lucian

Wolfen—Wolf people of the Forest of Endoria; fierce warriors of good magic

ADDITIONAL BOOKS BY DENNIS JERNIGAN &
INNOVO PUBLISHING

CHRONICLES OF BREN SERIES

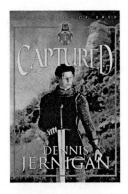

Captured (Book 1): What if your dreams became your reality? Young teen, Lee Jennings, bullied constantly by local boys, suddenly finds himself transported into a world of fantasy and adventure . . . and plunged into a whole new identity as the son of a king! How he traverses this new world and endures captivity at the hands of the realm's resident evil lord is also the journey of self-discovery that will one day serve Lee in his adult life. Full of fantastic beings and magical creatures from this new dimension and wrought with many twists and turns, Captured is just the beginning for Lee Jennings.

Sacrifice (Book 2): What if you learned about all of the sacrifices made—behind the scenes—that helped catapult you to the top? Lee Jennings, our protagonist from Captured, Book One in the Chronicles of Bren series, is now a teenager working on his family farm. While in the field, a strange tornado sucks him up and transports him into a world of fantasy and adventure, where he is king. Led by a benevolent creature called the Voice, Lee, now King Leonolis, discovers the sacrifices that so many have made so he could rule. It is a story of triumph and heartache as he realizes the costs that have been paid to allow him to rule.

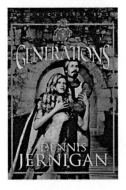

Generations (Book 3): Generations, Book Three in the Chronicles of Bren series, carries on the traditions of King Leonolis and Queen Abila as experienced through the lives of their nine children. If you enjoyed the wild adventures found in Captured and Sacrifice, you will thoroughly find your fill of adventure in Generations. Just as Leonolis did before them, his children grow up discovering their special gifts and talents while living out their very own wild adventures in the process. From magical spiders to Brumbycrocs, from alien beings to glass dragons, the saga of the children of Leonolis is the saga of nine very unique adventures found within the bounds of a single volume!

OTHER TITLES

How to Write a Book: Dennis Jernigan is a prolific writer with over two thousand songs, children's stories, fantasy novels, self-help books, and autobiographical works to his credit. In How To Write a Book, Dennis distills decades of writing and publishing experiences into ten simple steps for writing a book. This practical "how to" guide contains ten easy-to-read chapters and a treasure trove of creative, motivational, effective and easy-to-implement tips that Jernigan uses to guide the emerging and seasoned writer. How To Write a Book is a must read for every aspiring author as well as those who wish to become more creative and effective in their writing careers.

The Christmas Dream: The Christmas Dream is the story of a little boy who loves Christmas. He loves the festivities. He loves the decorations. He loves the wonder of Christmas. He loves everything about it. One night, he falls asleep and is transported into a realm where he meets God, and God teaches him about the true meaning of Christmas. Told as an adventure, Dennis Jernigan designed The Christmas Dream as a means of teaching his own son about the meaning of Christmas. This story can serve as a valuable tool in leading your child or grandchild to a saving faith in Jesus Christ. It also serves to remind the adult reader to not stray too far from the wonder of Christmas.

CPSIA information can be obtained
at www.ICGtesting.com
Printed in the USA
FSOW02n1629240916
25331FS